REMNANT

ENDORSEMENTS

Remnant is a fast-paced, hard-hitting sci-fi that echoes present day society. Reminiscent of the styles of Jerry B. Jenkins and Timothy Zahn, Daniel Peyton brings to life a world of science and faith by asking: how far would one go to erase God?

—Daphne Self
author of *Mississippi Nights* and *Alabama Days*

Remnant weaves an interesting, futuristic story from historic Old Testament threads.

—C.W. Briar
author of *Whispers from the Depths*

REMNANT

DANIEL PEYTON

Ambassador International
GREENVILLE, SOUTH CAROLINA & BELFAST, NORTHERN IRELAND

www.ambassador-international.com

Remnant

ISBN: 978-1-62020-984-4
eISBN: 978-1-62020-997-4

Cover Design and Page Layout by Hannah Nichols
eBook Conversion by Anna Riebe Raats
Edited by Katie Cruice Smith

AMBASSADOR INTERNATIONAL
Emerald House
411 University Ridge, Suite B14
Greenville, SC 29601, USA
www.ambassador-international.com

AMBASSADOR BOOKS
The Mount
2 Woodstock Link
Belfast, BT6 8DD, Northern Ireland, UK
www.ambassadormedia.co.uk

The colophon is a trademark of Ambassador, a Christian publishing company.

I would like to dedicate this book to all those people who helped me bring out this story I had been wanting to tell for years. First and foremost to Jesus Christ, for He inspired and helped me through this in amazing and profound ways. Without the amazing miracles along the way this book would have never found it's footing. To Julie Gwinn who helped me edit the original manuscript and gave me some of the most helpful advice about more than just editing. To L. Jagi Lamplighter Wright who stepped up when I was about ready to give up and helped me with the book in amazing ways. Finally, I thank my family who has been supportive of me in all of my writing endeavors.

AUTHOR'S NOTE

Dear Reader,

I would like to share with you why I wrote *Remnant* and what I want you to get from it. To begin, my goal was to write an epic science fiction story that would entertain. However, the real challenge came when I decided I wanted it to be Christian sci-fi. If you don't know what that is, you are not alone. Many Christians I know, either in person or online, love science fiction, but don't really have anything that speaks to their faith. I wanted to change that. I wanted to entertain that crowd, and more, with a story that was both science fiction and Christian.

Another element of this story is the faith. The Christianity in the story is not an afterthought, a sidestory, or just a hint. It is a vital part of the book. The main character is dealing with the risks of being a Christian in a time when all religion is outlawed, by penalty of imprisonment and worse. Harboring this secret, she allows herself to stay in the shadows while working for the organization that is ardently against religion. However, after a discovery is made and the facts of science starkly contrast the gospel, she goes on a journey to discover if she was truly wrong about there being a god. In this time, God begins a long, harrowing process to not only bring her back, but to expose the villainy of the world, save many souls, and ultimately begin to change the culture. The message of the cross is not a secondary theme of this story, it is the brunt of it. Faith is the truest, deepest, and most profound part of this journey.

Remnant is meant not only to entertain, but also to challenge the reader in his or her faith.

PROLOGUE

ANNA'S PALMS WERE SWEATING. HER heart raced so fast, she worried that it would jump out of her chest. Quickly, she hid around a corner of a building on campus and pressed her back up against the cold, rough bricks. Only now did she force herself to breathe, but it came out in a trembling whimper.

In her mind she repeated, *I'm just a short, blonde girl. Nothing special. They won't notice me. They can't notice me. Oh no, what if they find it?*

Anna clutched her bookbag to her side, tightly pinching it closed.

"Hey! You!"

Anna tensed up as she heard the yell of the security guard. A girl dashed into Anna's sight and was grabbed by a man in military garb.

"I swear I'm not one of them! Please, don't take me! Please, stop!" The girl screamed and struggled as she was unceremoniously dragged across the open quad, along with three others.

The brute of a soldier reared back and slapped her across the face, sprinkling the ground with blood from her nose. "Shut up!"

"We will not be silenced!" A new voice screamed; this time it was a young man. "The Word will live forever! Even if you kill all of the Remnants you find. God will find a way!"

Anna knew this voice well. She carefully looked around the corner and prayed she was mistaken. He was her best friend. She looked through the dark at the crowd and gasped. Yes, it was he. There, in the clutches of a well-armed man, was Gideon.

The word came out without her meaning to say it.

"No."

Gideon looked up and then quickly looked away, not wanting to in-criminate her. The soldier noticed this and scanned the crowd to see if he could spot any accomplices. Anna, who was now surrounded by a dozen con-fused and scared students, watched this in horror. They weren't part of the Underground, but that didn't make this scene any less frightening to them. The guard gave off a grunt and then dragged Gideon back to the military landing craft along with the other captured students.

As the shuttle lifted into the air, Anna realized how tightly she had held her bookbag. Her hand hurt; the impression of the weave was embedded into her palm. Finally realizing it was over, she leaned up against the wall and bawled like a child, letting out the fear and sorrow that had welled up inside her.

She was inconsolable. Several other students came over and tried to get her to stop crying, but she couldn't help herself.

"Stand back; let me through. Get to classes. I'll help her." A nicely dressed woman broke up the girls around Anna and then knelt down. "Anna, are you okay?"

Anna was finally able to speak through the tears, "It's just not right. He was my friend."

The professor pulled out a small handkerchief and wiped Anna's face. "It always hurts when you find out anyone is part of that Underground. Stupid fools. They should know that they will be discovered. Don't feel betrayed; he was never really your friend. Those types are here only to try and convert people to their backward ways and ideas."

Anna paused and then slowly nodded, while saying, "Sure."

The professor stood up as she said, "Good thing you're one of our bright-est students. Best Astro-Geologist major I've had the privilege of teaching in years. You would never have been brainwashed by them."

"Of course not," Anna said quietly.

"Okay, dry your eyes and dust yourself off. We have to get the class ready for the trip to the moon tomorrow. Being the teacher's assistant, you'll be leading the team on their mineral survey. I can't wait to see you in action again."

Anna didn't stand up just yet, "I'll be in class; just give me a moment."

"I understand." A buzzer sounded over the intercom. "Oops, I'm going to be late. Okay, see you in a few minutes." The professor left in a hurry.

Anna waited until she was alone in the quad again. Opening her bag, she shuffled several books out of the way and found the one on the bottom. If they knew she had this, she would be right next to Gideon, facing whatever terrible fate all the Remnants endured. Was it worth it?

CHΔPTER OΠE

Deep in a distant part of the alpha sector, a small, bright dot blasted out of hyperlight and entered the atmosphere of a large moon in orbit of a dark planet.

A pair of feline eyes peered from inside a thicket of trees. The skies were as blue as they had ever been, and the grass waved gently in the cool breezes. But this creature was more focused on the strange appearance of the object in the sky.

Through the calm and serene atmosphere of this lovely afternoon, a sonic boom exploded and was followed by the shrill sound of the braking rockets slowing down the probe's descent. The natural skies above were cut sharply by a straight-lined, unnatural cloud created by the entrance of one of the basic explorer probes. Its quick descent wasn't straight but purposefully curved, to lessen the impact.

Even so, the probe finally found the ground with a hard slam, skidding across the grass and creating a spray of soil as it plowed along, finally coming to a stop on the surface of this alien world. Smoke and steam poured out, almost as if it had not survived the crash.

A light beeped, and a panel burst off of the side. From inside, the opened compartment came an extension that planted itself into the ground and pushed the probe upright. Once it was straight, four legs shot out from its base and grounded the probe in the optimum position for analysis and communications with the explorer ships.

More panels opened—not like the first but more like doors being opened. Devices of all kinds came out and took readings from the area. Some took in the oxygen and tested it, while others absorbed any water in the air and ground for study. Finally, a camera poked out and conducted the visual scan of the planet's surface.

In the reflection of the camera's lens came a face. One eye was looking at the camera with scrutiny and fear; the eye wasn't human but more feline in shape. First, this creature sniffed at the smoke and steam. Then a timid and yet strong-looking, extremely hairy arm with a clawed hand reached up and touched the side of the device. The probe was incredibly hot from entry and burned the unsuspecting creature. The hand drew back quickly and was followed by a short roar and then low growling.

The camera and three other sensors were directed at the unknown observer for a moment, and then the device closed and sealed itself; only a small, protruding antennae came up and sent the signal that had been anticipated for two hundred years.

"Lifeforms confirmed."

* * *

FIVE MONTHS LATER

In a sector of space far from Earth, a small, unassuming spacecraft slowed from hyperlight speeds and moved using the sub-light engines. The basic Explore unit, number 313, had four engines, two that drove it in the hyperlight speeds and two that moved it in normal space. The normal space engines could reach speeds that were 0.1 percent below light speed, which allowed quick maneuvering inside solar systems. This craft was one of many currently in service to the Planetary Science Commission. Each worked the various exploration projects that kept the PSC going.

Anna walked through the doors into the cockpit where she took her seat at the command of this mission. Anna was the youngest full-ranked explorer in the PSC. She had graduated with a full degree in Astro-Geology from Central University, with a minor in archeological-anthropology. Her name was just Anna. No one on Earth had a last name, since no one had family. Being born in a breeding facility, handed over to the state, and raised in the school houses, everyone had only a single name. So, her name was merely Anna. Soon, if she kept working on her education, she could add Dr. Anna to it, but not yet.

Anna sat down next to the only other occupant on this spacecraft, Z. This faux person was a Z-550, a state-of-the-art multifunctional robot. Anna could handle the constant talkative nature of this robot, but she was tired of his vaudevillian sense of humor.

"Morning, Z. Enjoy the night shift?"

"Same as always." He flashed a handsome smile at her. "Sleep well?"

Anna kind of liked the 550 series. They were designed to look as human as possible, and this one was rather attractive, for a robot. The glowing joints on his body gave away his artificial nature, but otherwise, he looked just like another person. Of course, he had two million identical twins working across the known galaxy on other ships and around Earth.

She checked the sensor logs. "I sleep the exact same every night on this ship. I put on the mask, and the medication does the rest. So, yes, I slept well."

He navigated the ship toward their first target. "Well, back to the salt mines."

She bit. "The salt mines in the middle of outer space?"

"They don't make 'em like they used to."

She ignored that and asked, "Okay, what is our first target?"

"Y347-A, the largest moon of the nearest gas giant."

"All right, what did the probes say about this location's prospects?"

He faked a terrible accent as he said, "There be gold in them thar moons."

"Try that again, and lose the humor."

"Spoilsport," he muttered and then repeated the sensor report downloaded to his mainframe. "Sensors indicated satellite 829-A1 around the second gas giant might contain a generous supply of gold, platinum, and various other mineral resources of value."

She moaned and watched the lump of space rock come into view. "More gold! I'm tired of finding that junk."

"Hey, don't knock it. Gold is a primary metal in a lot of my own circuitry." He pretended to pout.

"Then again," she tapped her chin, "I might be able to use some to build a better brain for you. One that has a passable sense of humor."

"Oh, ha ha," he retorted sarcastically.

"Take us down through the atmosphere and activate the sampling arm." She got up and walked around to the station in the aft section of the compartment. From there, she would test the samples the ship had dug up.

Anna had known this particular Z unit since she graduated. He was assigned to her and hadn't left her side since. All Z units had the same emotional programs designed to make them seem as human as possible. They were all out-going, helpful, and friendly. While Anna could be a quiet person, Z always cheered her up. Some days, she forgot he was just a robot. Though she got tired of his humor, his friendliness had helped make her job easier. Traveling the stars with only a robot companion could be lonesome.

Six hours had passed in the geological survey of system Y347. The Explorer-class ship had examined twelve moons, discovered even more gold and other metals, and was now working on the first asteroid belt in the system.

Anna set the controls on the analyzer to sift out the compounds of the sample collected from a random asteroid. She then went back to her process of slowly beating her head against the bulkhead next to her while the computer did its work.

"So, get this—the turtle looks at his brother and says, 'I know she's just an army helmet; I still love her' HA!" Z was on hour six of his recently discovered archaic humor from watching too much ancient television.

Anna stopped beating her head against the wall and desperately asked, "Are you through yet?"

"Almost. I have a couple more great ones, but I'm gonna have to stand up to show them to you." He stood up from his seat and started the terrible acting routine. "Now, there's this guy who goes to his tailor . . ."

Beep.

The greatest sound in the galaxy just played, Anna thought as the communications board beeped loud enough to interrupt what was likely to be a terrible pun woven into an elaborate demonstration. Though it was only a signal telling them that an important newscast was being sent out, and they often just recorded those and watched them later, Anna rushed to the station like it was orders just for her from the president.

"Hey, that can wait; this is a really good joke," Z protested.

She pretended to be highly interested in this. "No, this might be important."

Z slumped right back down into his seat, defeated. "Fine."

Anna switched on the communications channel and hoped dearly it was truly important. "This is a special report from Global News One. Dr. Richard Skye has given us an exclusive interview about the launch of the new ship *PSC Sanger*. That report will . . ." Anna turned it down and sort of frowned at nothing in particular.

"Hey, they're interviewing your boss!"

Anna scoffed. "He's not my boss. He's the global leader of the organization I work for."

"Still pretty neato to see him on TV. From what I have been informed by other humans, he's quite the looker."

"Sure." Anna snickered at the old lingo. "He's got perfect features; the eugenics labs wouldn't have it any other way."

"What do you make of their new ship, the *Sanger*?" Z asked.

"What of it?"

"It's huge, the biggest ever built. And I heard it's armed to the teeth. It has the largest, most powerful weapon ever constructed on it. What do you suppose that's for?" He was elbowing her with a sly smile.

"I'm sure they have a logical, scientific reason. I really couldn't care less." Anna set the sampling unit to its cleanse-cycle so she could start a new batch later. "Why don't you watch and see if there's anything of real interest? I'm going to go back and eat some lunch."

"You don't have to go back and eat your nutrition bar by yourself. I don't care if you get crumbs on the consoles."

Anna swiveled out of her chair and shook her head. "No, a little alone time is nice every day. Just keep piloting around these asteroids, get the samples, and watch the interview. I'll be back in a bit."

She got up and left the cockpit, heading for the small compartment in the back where they had recreational space. It wasn't much of an area—just a couch with a small table and the treadmill, so she could jog.

Z knew what she was doing. He'd discovered her dirty little secret only a couple days into their first voyage together. But he respected her enough to keep it to himself. She knew it, but still felt it was better to not talk about it or to have him around when she did it. Besides, if she got too relaxed doing it in front of others, she might forget herself and get caught one of these days, and that would ruin her career. Heck, they might even throw her in prison with the others.

$$\ast \quad \ast \quad \ast$$

Anna shut her book and held it against her chest. She closed her eyes and remained quiet for a long time. With a robot like Z, quiet was an uncommon commodity on this little ship. She enjoyed every minute of silence she could get.

Just then, the door opened to the recreation room, and in walked Z. Anna quickly hid her book under the cushion nearest her and tensed up like the police had just stepped into the room.

"You know you do that every time I come in on you. You don't have to," Z stated very plainly.

Anna relaxed and looked back at the bulging cushion. "It's habit by now. Every time I pick up that book to read it, there is a fear that swells in my stomach that someone will report me."

"You know I'll never report you. And you know that I know all about your shameful secret."

Anna sighed. "You know the consequences of being discovered with a Bible."

Z laughed and pulled over the only loose chair in the room. "So, I've been meaning to ask you—where did you find that book? I mean, a print book is rare, but a Bible . . . Those were all destroyed after the laws were passed."

"Not all of them." Anna pulled out the ancient book from under the cushion. It was a large, leather-bound, printed Bible with unevenly sized pages and larger-than-usual letters. "Back when I was going to school, I met a young man who was very nice but struggling with his Astro-mineral survey tests. I helped him out, and we got to know each other. His name was Gideon. I asked him why he picked the name Gideon, and he said that it was from the Bible. I was shocked that he even mentioned that book. In time, he told me that he was part of the Underground; he was one of the Remnants."

"Wow. A Remnant at the University. I thought they screened the students pretty hard."

"They do." She stated rather crassly, remembering her screening. "Anyway. I liked him, so I didn't turn him in. But I had to know why he would believe in all that ancient mumbo-jumbo. He told me about his faith and his beliefs, and it made a lot of sense. I wanted to know more. His group worked out of a secret base in Antarctica, where they handprinted these Bibles for the Remnants to read and use. He gave me one, and I hid it, but didn't read it."

"Wait, I thought that base was destroyed in some accident?"

Anna slowly nodded. "One day, I was working, and a team of top-level security came and dragged Gideon and five others out. I was so scared they'd find me and take me with them. But I wasn't discovered. A month later, we learned about the destruction of the base, and the news reported that a science lab in Antarctica had been lost in a freak accident. Gideon died, having never hurt anyone. I don't know what came over me, but I had to know what he died for. What was so important that he would risk his life? I started reading, and I couldn't stop. There are so many truths, so much history, so much . . . reality in this book, that it just sang to me. I thought that as a scientist, it would be a laugh; it would be stupid; it would be everything I was always told it was. Yet, it wasn't. I . . . " She looked up at the robot. "I guess it really doesn't make sense to you, does it?"

"Not really. It's just a book."

Anna set the book down and smiled. "It's so much more. But I suppose you'll never understand. This God—the God of this book—is about unconditional love, forgiveness, sacrifice. But, most important of all, He's about love."

Z laughed. "And that is the one emotion that the programmers have yet to figure out how to give us robots. Love is a confusing and rather foolish idea— at least while I'm unable to fully process it." Z cocked his head and asked, "One last question, and this is a doozy. Why did you stay in the Explorer program after you decided to follow this book? The whole program is designed to prove religions wrong."

"I know the mission. I've known about this mission since my earliest days at the school house. When I first joined, I was eager to be part of it. But I was never worried about the whole proving religions wrong thing; I was fascinated by rocks. After my decision to be a follower of Christ, I stayed because I'm still a fan of rocks. I don't consider myself a betrayer of my faith, only doing what I love. Seeing God's work on every lump of space rock we come across helps me forget the ulterior motive of the PSC. Besides, it's a good job."

Z shrugged and agreed with a little smile. "True. And knowing what Earth is like, leaving isn't a bad idea." He cocked his head. "One more thing. I have never fully understood the rationale that finding aliens would disprove any god? Can't these all-powerful gods make aliens?"

Anna laughed as she replied, "Several reasons. First, our Bible does not say that God created life anywhere else. It teaches that humans are the greatest of His creation. This kinda precludes aliens in our faith. Also, if we do find aliens, it would be near impossible that they would be at the same stage of evolution as us. They would either be above us or below us. So, the logic goes that if we do find aliens, we can prove evolution by witnessing a different stage of it through them."

"Oh. Still doesn't make sense that you would put so much faith in this. All humans are bred in special breeding hospitals, then taken and raised from infants up to adults in the school system. How anyone could break the constant anti-religion teachings given through this is beyond me. But there's a lot about humans I don't understand." Z stopped and thought for a second. "Okay, so, I know that every time we are back on Earth, you avoid any sexual contact with anyone. Is this because of your faith stuff?

Anna nodded at first and then shook her head. "Yes and no. It is true that because of the teachings in this book, I have a different moral standard than most other people on Earth. But I have other reasons to not want to be a part of that element in our society."

Z stuck one eyebrow up and stated the obvious, "That really sets you apart, you know. People even notice it. I mean, everyone has sex. It's part of life. You see it in almost all the public areas. The pleasurers are out and about daily. Why would you avoid this? From what I understand, it is enjoyable."

"Not for me. After I left the State School House I was put in, I started col-lege right away. My first day, I was raped. It was horrible. I had never been so scared. It was my first encounter with a man, and I was terrified. I reported it, and they told me that it was no big deal. Since everyone is sterilized anyway, they considered it just a minor problem. They gave me some meds for my bruises and told me to get used to it."

Z squinted as he thought. "But . . . everyone is sterile. It really isn't a big issue. Unless he gave you an STD . . . "

"It's just wrong. Besides, not everyone is sterile."

"Wait . . . don't tell me you're not sterilized. But . . . " He looked away as his computer accessed files. "I show that you've been cleared as sterilized."

Anna was silent for a moment. "Don't worry about it. Trust your records."

Z ignored this and only smiled. "Fine. Whatever. You can live your life how you see fit. As for this robot, I've got a ship to pilot." He got up to leave.

"One question for you. Why?" Anna asked.

Z frowned at her. "Why what?"

She slid the Bible back under the cushion, just in case someone else hap-pened to step onto their ship. "Why have you not reported me all this time? You've known for some time. Now that we are discussing this, I would like to know why."

Z looked back. "I really don't know. They never programmed me to be a tattletale, just a helper. I know you do a good job, and you will listen to my jokes; so, I guess I don't want to have to break in a new geologist." He was kidding her now.

Anna snickered at him. "Fine. Just remember that you promised to keep my secret, even when they plug you in for your yearly check-up."

"Yup. Don't know squat about love, but loyalty I understand."

"What did you need?" Anna finally asked.

"Oh, yeah, why I came in here in the first place." He could be distracted for a robot. "I got a warning today, and I have to update my software. I'll be offline for a bit. My memories about all this illegal stuff will be sealed. Don't worry."

"You really are a good friend."

He gave her a sneaky grin. "Nope. Just keeping those secrets with me in case I gotta blackmail you later. Have fun." With that, he left the rec deck and went to plug in for the update.

Anna laughed at the foolishness of her traveling companion. He was probably the best friend she had in the universe, which put her prospects for husbands extremely low.

With a defeated sigh, she put her hand on the cushion next to her and thought. What would life be like if she didn't have to hide this part of her? What if she could find another who believed? What if she was the last one in the whole universe?

*   *   *

The *Darwin 1 Space Station* bustled with media and dignitaries. Most of Earth had turned out or tuned in to watch the launch of the largest ship in history. The monolithic *Darwin 1 Space Station* had one hundred and fifty levels, a large docking arm that could hold over fifty ships, and fully self-sufficient solar power system.

The *PSC Sanger* was docked and ready for launch. The *Sanger* was a long ship with dozens of levels and every type of known sensor system attached to the outer hull. An impressive array of basic weapon platforms attached to the ship was all overshadowed by the massive, one-of-a-kind main weapon.

The bridge was an awe-inspiring command center designed to manage all the various scientific operations. Right now, most of the stations were vacant, while the crowds of reporters packed in to speak with Dr. Skye.

"And, as I said before, this ship's purposes are many. The primary mission of the PSC is paramount, of course, to locate alien life. But this ship was expensive and difficult to construct. If and when we do make the breakthrough in discovering a form of alien life, the mission will change. Space exploration will begin a whole new chapter, and this ship will not be obsolete," Dr. Skye said.

A reporter stuck a small, handheld recorder in his face and grilled, "Critics are still concerned about the weapons on this ship. My viewers would like . . ."

"Enough questions; it's almost time to leave." Dr. Skye held a hand up to the young reporter who was trying to get the answers the PSC didn't want to give. The charismatic leader of the science community took his place at the captain's seat. "All right, it's time to get under way. Ladies and gentlemen of Earth, the *PSC Sanger* is ready to depart. Helm, release the docking tethers and take us out at standard sublight speed."

The reporters all applauded, and the young woman at the navigation controls punched in the commands. The station's docking ring released, and the largest ship ever constructed left the station to begin its historic journey.

Dr. Skye smiled as he asked, "I don't suppose you would mind spending one day with us to see what we do?" He knew full well that not one reporter had ever been allowed on an exploration trip. It was a unique opportunity. Responding to all the eager smiles and quick head nods, the doctor gave the order, "Helm, take us to hyperlight."

"Sir, what is our course?"

Dr. Skye paused, as if to consider this. "Communications. Open all channels. Let's see if there is a location we need to visit."

"At once, sir." The young man at the com station activated his system, and there was a strange alarm sounding. "Oh my . . . no . . . It can't be. Checking the source . . . checking again . . ."

"What is the problem?" Dr. Skye angrily barked.

The young man stood up, his eyes wide, his smile even wider. He was trembling all over. "Sir . . . it . . . it's happened."

✶   ✶   ✶

It had been two days since they first started the mineral survey of the Y347 system, and Anna was getting bored finding, sorting, and testing so much gold.

This morning, she didn't go for a jog. She wanted to spend the time in deep thought and speaking with the only other non-robot person she had to speak to on this mission. Sitting on her bed with crossed legs, she looked around the tiny compartment that she called home. Her cabin was a small room, hardly tall enough for her to stand up straight. Along one wall was a bed attached; it could slide in, so she would have more room. For what? Sitting on the floor, perhaps? There was also a sink and mirror for her personal use. She had two doors in the cabin—the main door that led out into the rec deck and a smaller door that let her into what the PSC jokingly called the bathroom. Looking around this "living space," Anna realized how much she must really love her work because it certainly wasn't for the perks.

Truly, the work made her life worth living. Earth was such a dismal place, for the most part, but out here, she could find and see the most amazing things. Crystals the size of starships; rock formations that held every color of the rainbow. Once, they had come across what appeared to be a rather spherical asteroid, only to slice it open with the ship's laser and discover the largest known geode. That one had put her name in the museum that it was now housed in. Nothing she had found had radically altered the scientific community or made much of a difference to the rest of mankind. But it didn't matter; she couldn't help but love what she did.

That was exactly what she was thanking God for at this very moment: giving her the love and desire to do this job. She couldn't imagine doing anything else and having as much appreciation for it.

Lifting her head, she paused to think about everything. Praying seemed to lift her spirits in ways she didn't understand. She felt stronger, better, wiser after she had prayed. If only she could tell others and give them the same feeling of strength and hope she felt every day. The world was in such need of this saving message. It hurt her on the inside.

Anna picked up a picture from her days at the University. It was a special item—a physical photograph, which was rare to find. The group with her in the picture were the students she had called a family back then. Most of them were taken by the Religion Hunters. Of those in the picture, Anna was the only one who escaped being captured.

She touched the face of Gideon, standing next to her in the photo. "I wish you were here. I need a real friend who understands faith." Gideon was her best friend for three years. He had the most brilliant mind for computers. He had even rigged the system to show that she had been sterilized like everyone else.

Anna missed having friends like them. After watching so many of the other Christians be taken, she distanced herself from most people and confided only in her one friend, Z. She had no coworkers around her; and when she was back home, she stuck to herself. The lifestyle of most people on Earth was so far departed from the morals she lived by, having friends was hard unless they were also Christian.

Suddenly, the door to her room opened, and there stood Z with a shocked look on his robot face. "Anna! You need to come up here."

She quickly got out of bed and grabbed her uniform jacket. "What is it?"

"The news is blasting through all the comm channels. It's unbelievable!"

"What?" She was getting worried that something horrible had happened: the *Sanger* had crashed on Earth and killed thousands? Dr. Skye was assassinated? Something just as awful?

Z was almost happy, but it was restrained by worry. "They've done it. They've found alien life."

Anna froze from the inside out. She slowly looked into his eyes and said, "No, it cannot be."

"Come, see for yourself."

CHAPTER TWO

"THIS IS LINDA WITH WORLD News. No sooner did the *PSC Sanger* begin its historic mission to search for life on alien worlds than the first indications of life appear. A probe that was launched two years ago for initial investigations landed on a moon in the 201 alpha sector of space. The moon already exhibited more evidence for life than any other location explored so far. The probe's first telemetry indicated a habitable biosphere that supported plant life, as well as water in every natural form. Then, at 0900 hours earth time, the probe detected living creatures and set itself on the automated calling signal. *Explorer 117* first landed on the moon and signaled the *PSC Sanger*, which arrived and began the official research. We are about to start the live feed from the surface of this moon, which is being dubbed New Eden." The newswoman smiled brightly and waited while the screen changed to show the forested surface of a planet.

President Richard Skye smiled brighter than the newswoman. "Yesterday morning, we arrived at New Eden to investigate what we presumed was a faulty signal sent by the probe. What we discovered was far from a faulty message. Our teams set out to check all the data. We discovered this moon does indeed exhibit all the requirements for developing life. Primarily, it has a thriving ecosystem, supported by a well-balanced weather pattern. After a short search, we first discovered insect life, as well as small avian and fish life. Then, early this morning, one of our scientists captured this image." He looked over to a person standing near him, and the screen changed to show an image. It was a human-like figure but covered in a thick fur. The face was feline, and there was a lot of hair around the head.

Dr. Skye's proud, smiling face returned to the screen. "That was the first encounter with a species of subhuman-like creatures. We have observed them several more times. Savage and potentially dangerous, we are taking precautions about approaching them. But based on observation alone, I am willing to theorize we are witnessing a species that is what could be called a missing link. A race of beings that are on their way through the evolutionary lines to being fully upright, homo sapien-like creatures. I can say for certain that on this day, the twenty-first of July, 2522, the skeptics have been silenced. Evolution is victorious." The team of reporters called out questions.

The screen returned to the newsroom. "You've heard it here first, ladies and gentlemen; the Explorer Program has finally achieved its goal. As Dr. Richard Skye announced moments ago, with incontrovertible proof: 'Evolution is victorious.' We will go back to the field to listen to some questions and . . . "

Anna shut off the monitor. There was a dark silence in her eyes as she continued to stare at the screen. Z watched carefully to see if she were still breathing. She was, but it was shallow, shaky; and she was on the verge of crying.

"Anna, are you going to be all right?" Z asked.

"I don't know. I . . . I just don't know."

"How about we do more mineral surveys? Check for precious gems on that moon we passed the other day? You always like finding sapphires and rubies. We might even find emeralds. Wouldn't that be fun?"

Anna gulped and watched her own eyes in the reflection of the monitor that had just shattered her universe.

"Come on. Scream, yell, cry, do something. I can't stand watching you just sit there!"

"Just keep working. I'm . . . I'm gonna go to bed." Anna drug herself up and scuffed her feet across the deck as she headed for her room.

Z wished he had never brought her in here, spared her a few days longer before she found out. It was just so amazing, he couldn't stop himself. He piloted the ship around and went back to check for precious stones on some of the volcanic moons. It might help her mood if he found her some special gems.

*   *   *

Anna stayed in bed for two days. She tried to read her Bible, but it almost hurt. More than once, she attempted to pray, but her words felt empty. If she prayed for answers about God being real, it was like admitting she no longer believed. Yet, anything else felt wrong to say.

Finally, after sixteen hours of staring at a metal ceiling, listening to the sample arm digging on whatever rock they were currently hovering over, she decided to reach out. Getting onto her knees beside her bed, she buried her face in the thin mattress and sobbed one more time. She fully believed that the Holy Spirit would pray when she had no words for the pain she felt. Her desire was to hear some kind of answer, some kind of truth to counter what has just happened. The only words she spoke were, "Lord, if I am all that is left, use me to make this right." Again, she felt and heard nothing.

A thought came into her mind. She had trusted and believed in God for years now, and yet truly had not seen Him. These aliens were real—at least that is what the news said. With determination, she had made her mind up about what she was going to do next.

Z locked the sample arm back into place and was about to store this last dig into the pod for Anna to analyze later. The door of Anna's room opened, and she stepped out in the most disheveled state he had ever seen her in.

"Anna? Are you okay?"

"I have to see this for myself." Her voice whispered, soft but determined.

"What?"

Anna walked over to the controls and sat down. "I have to go to this moon place and see these creatures for myself."

"Wait. We have our orders, mineral survey and all. Remember?"

"I don't care. This is more important than that." Now, she worked the controls, taking charge of the ship.

"Anna! Anna, you aren't a pilot. You barely know how to fly this bucket. That's one of the many reasons you need me around . . . remember?" Z was startled by her sudden grab for control.

"I can fly; it's been a while, but I took basic space piloting at the University. I can leave you behind with some equipment. You can keep studying that moon until I come back. That way, you won't betray your orders."

Z punched in a special command, and the control station went dark.

"DON'T DO THIS TO ME! I HAVE TO SEE THIS! I . . . " Before she could utter another complaint or argument, the ship took off at top speed and then slipped into hyperlight.

Z smiled at her. "I know. I don't know what love is, but I know what friendship is. This means a lot to you, and you do need some closure. Those rocks will wait on us. They ain't go'n anywhere. If we get into trouble, I will tell them that my computer crashed, and I flew us way off-course. After all, you are terrible behind the wheel. No one will believe you stole the ship."

Anna leaned over and hugged him around the neck. "You're a good friend—for a robot that is."

Z feigned a terrible gangster accent as he replied, "Babe, you and me, we're in this together, see. Bonnie and Clyde, Rose and Morey . . . "

She finished his thought. "Abbot and Costello?"

"Right. Now sit down and shut up, or I put you on ice . . . whatever that means."

Anna left him to pilot, while she took some time to figure this all out. She had never failed to find an answer in the Scriptures before; surely something would stand out to her now. Something would make sense. This couldn't be the end of all she had believed in.

✳   ✳   ✳

A harsh sniffing cut through the low din of the forest. The grass and twigs crunched with each cautious step taken toward whatever smelled so good. A very light brown, furry woman with more cat than human facial features lifted her nose slightly to sniff the air. Each time she paused to sniff, her course altered slightly.

Then she came upon it. There, hanging from a low branch on a tree, was a hunk of red meat, bloody and raw. Just as she put her hand out to grab it, she stopped and looked at the rope tethering it to the branch. It ran up the tree and then back down and connected to some kind of trap device. If she were to just grab and yank the meat to her, she would be caught in something. Picking up a branch, she reached out and poked the rope, listening with her tall ears. She heard a creaking sound and realized something metallic was attached. With a swift slice, she hit the rope and triggered the trap, but she was far enough away to not be caught by the net that lifted up from the ground. A metal pulley system yanked up hard to suspend the catch—had there been anything inside the net.

Triumphant over the trap, she reached into the baggy net and retrieved the now-free meat. It was a cut of something she had never smelled before, a meat not native to her home. She sniffed it and bent to lick it, but felt a strange sensation on her upper arm. Something poked her and hurt at first, then a warm sensation was followed by an awful numbness.

Before she could determine what was wrong or run away, the world went blurry, and she fell into a hard, deep sleep.

Two men in PSC uniforms came out of the brush and looked down at the woman on the ground. One knelt low and pulled the dart from her arm. "Good thing this stuff works fast. Have you seen the way they can run?"

The other checked his gun to be certain it was still loaded. "I know. Get her up. We need to get back to the ship. I don't want to run into any more of these creatures."

The first man looked at her with the exuberance of a scientist. "She was smarter than I expected. I wasn't sure if these . . . people . . . were at the tools stage yet or not. It's going to expand all we know about pre-human life forms when we get to study them."

"Sure. Just get her up; we're going to be late."

"Late? Late for what?" The man stuck the used dart down into a pocket and pulled her up as best as he could without hurting her, or him.

"Dr. Skye wanted to see the specimens immediately."

"Well . . . " he grunted as he put her over his shoulder to carry her. "It's a good thing these creatures are on the petite side. I wouldn't be able to carry someone much larger."

"It's a good thing that the serum is still working. Get moving. If she wakes before we get back, this could get ugly."

"All right, all right, sheesh. Who stuck a hornet up your nose?"

Dr. Skye's face hurt. He had been smiling and talking non-stop for what felt like a week. It was nice to have all these reporters present for this historic occasion, but it was also very tiring. Finally, after dismissing the last man from the room, Richard was able to step into his office aboard the *Sanger* and get a moment of peace and quiet.

The private office for the president of the PSC was plush. The room had a few accents of color here and there, but for the most part, was a sterile snow white. The back wall was a large bay window that looked out with the best view of any spot from this ship. Near the window sat an enormous desk with different monitors and devices for the president to use in his daily work. The room had a sunken floor in the middle, where a semi-circular couch was inlaid for comfort. The left side of the room's walls were all screens and controls for the president to keep his thumb on everyone's operations. Unassuming white panels made up the right side of the room, each one hiding a different door. Press a button, and you open up to the private washroom. Another button opened up a holographic generator that created whatever the president needed, such as a woman or man to help him relax.

Richard looked at a gold plate embedded in the wall—"Office of Dr. Richard Skye." That name—it was glorious. He was the only known human with a full name, outside of those living in Jerusalem. Everyone was born and raised in the state school houses, never knowing their parents. No one had a family name, just the name they chose. He liked Richard as a boy. It sounded regal. But it was when he was given this job that he gave himself the right to a second name. Why have a single name like all the other humans? He wanted to call himself Sky, which was the direction people used to look when praying to a god. But that might've been a bit too obvious. So, he added a single letter and made it his own. The name, Richard Skye, would always mean knowledge to the rest of humankind.

A woman's voice brought his hopes of privacy to a crashing halt. "Looks like this is working out better than we had expected."

Richard quickly looked around and found a woman seated on the long, white couch. She was tall, slender, and had a perfectly crafted face, though her age defied the expensive cosmetic procedures she'd had done to keep her looks. "Oh, I didn't realize you were on board, Jessie."

"Don't sound so pleased." Putting down her own glass of white wine, she patted her tight hair bun to see that it was still in its proper place. "I just arrived, and I wanted to see you. I suspected the media would be all over the place, but I didn't expect to see them crawling all over this ship like an infestation."

Richard pressed a button on the white surface of the wall. The whole panel slid up to reveal a fully stocked mini-bar. He went for the brandy. "It worked out just fine. They were here for the launch and were on board for the discovery. What are you doing here?" He poured a rather healthy portion of brandy for himself and then walked around the upper level of the office toward the window. Jessie stood up and followed him to the window overlooking the moon. About two dozen other ships were flying around the moon, some leaving the system while more came in.

"And miss all this? You couldn't pay me enough to not be here. This discovery is going to be the bolstering my armies need to finish the job. By this time next month, there won't be a single religious nut left on earth."

"What about Jerusalem? They're harboring the last known settlement of religion, and they still refuse to be part of the World Corps. Do you expect them to just shut up and obey, now that we have the proof we need?"

Jessie smiled, her tight face reflecting right back at her in the glass window. "I know we'll still struggle against that particular location, but they're going to lose a lot of supporters in the next few weeks. People will come to their senses and turn away from those ridiculous old notions. With a little . . . encouragement, I suspect their own people will turn on them and oust what meager government they have left. The last city-state left on Earth that hasn't bowed to the wishes of the World Corps will finally fall in line."

"You speak as though it is already assured that they will fall," Richard said.

"It is only a matter of time, Richard. Their citizens will betray them for us. Their government will bow to our whims, and once they are members of the World Corps, I will descend upon them and eradicate every last vestige of religion left. It will be a bloody, beautiful victory for us."

Richard, surprised by the level of coldness in her words, began to smile. "It'll be nice to have them gone. The influence of the PSC will grow rapidly now that we hold all the cards."

She reached over and stroked his chin with a red, silk-gloved hand. "Think about it. Dr. Richard Skye, president of Earth. Has a nice ring to it, doesn't it?"

"And what will you do once the religious Underground has finally been crushed? You've worked your entire life to destroy them. Though, you once did beautiful design work for clothing, even had a few dresses featured at the Paris Fashion Week."

Jessie stepped away from the window and brushed her hand across his desk. "My old hobby isn't even part of my life anymore. No, I have other ideas. The PSC will need leadership, with you responsible for the Earth and all. I suppose my managerial skills could be put to use."

"You're not even a scientist."

She sat down in his seat, enjoying the sensation of control. "What does it matter? When's the last time you did any actual science work?"

"True," Dr. Skye admitted. "Though I believe my talents as a scientist will prove especially useful over the next few weeks. This mission—no, this event—is exactly what I was designed for. Every president of the PSC has been prepared for this day, and now that it's here, I'm glad to put my science to work."

"Don't get in too deep. Remember what this is all about. Can't have you getting lost in science playland. We also have other important things to take care of." She touched a button, and a screen lying down on the desk lifted up and turned on with the PSC logo blazing across it.

Richard leaned over and looked at her from the side. "I am first and foremost a scientist. Dedicated to the advancement of the human race."

She corrected him, "So long as your science doesn't contradict what the PSC has already confirmed."

"Of course."

Just then the screen she had activated changed color and started beeping. Jessie reached to answer it, but Richard stopped her. "It's not your office, yet."

"Yet," she repeated and then got out of the seat.

He sat down and then answered the com, "Yes?"

"Sir, we have an incoming ship."

He rolled his eyes and stated, "There are many ships coming and going; why bother me about one more?"

"The ship is an Explorer-class vessel, and it's requesting clearance to land."

He looked up at Jessie and frowned. "The orders were that no exploration craft is to land without my personal permission. Relay the orders to them about exploration of this system right now."

"I did. Their Z-bot explained that they are mineral surveyors and are here to survey the system."

Richard scoffed and started to answer. "Tell them not to . . . "

"Wait!" Jessie stopped him.

"Hold on a moment," he ordered and then closed his end of the intercom system. "What?"

He noticed the devilish smile on her face. "Let them land and survey."

"But, there's no need to do a mineral survey. And we cannot have them uncovering . . . "

"They're just mineral surveyors, not biological explorers. They don't know anything about researching the people down there."

Dr. Skye wasn't getting it. "But they could get killed. You know how dangerous those creatures are."

"Precisely. So far, we can only relay 'observations' about the primitive nature of these cat things. If we reveal just how dangerous they are by showing the bloodied body of a surveyor and the broken remains of their robot, the people of Earth will understand just exactly what we are dealing with. They will know that these creatures are as dangerous and as violent as we've said. No one will want to come and land on this planet and potentially wreck everything."

Richard pondered this for a moment. "I suppose. And it's just a mineral surveyor and his robot. We can replace them tomorrow."

Jessie nodded slowly. "Now you're catching on. Let them land. And make sure they're alone. Don't let any others from this ship go near them, to hear the screams for help. Give them a day or two, and then hold a press conference about the poor missing surveyor. You will send in a team to extract them, only to find the bodies. On the way, you can bag a few of these creatures, so we have bodies to put on display back home. We'll tell them we caught the responsible primitives near their bodies. Heck, we can claim to have found the remains in the stomach contents. How gloriously gruesome that will be."

Richard began to see the brilliant complexity of her plan. "Yes. That would be perfect. We need to show real, physical evidence, but we cannot bring any back alive if those back on Earth aren't completely convinced these things are dangerous primitives."

"Precisely. We need to show how primitive and unevolved they are. To make our case. Perhaps we can bring one back who is . . . shall we say 'prepared' for display." She was getting a little overly excited about this wonderful plan. "After the death of the unimportant PSC scientist, no one will want to get near the primitive but will be fascinated to see it in a cage."

Richard held up a hand to quiet her down and then activated the intercom for the worker waiting on the other end. "Tell the surveyor they can land. Send them to these coordinates. Tell our scientists down there to keep their distance. We wouldn't want to interrupt their work, and they don't need to be stepping on our toes."

The voice that responded sounded unsure but was smart enough not to question. "Understood." With a short beep, the com closed, and the plan went into action.

"Where are those coordinates?" Jessie asked.

"Near where my personal scientists have been dropping off the creatures we've already picked up and changed."

Jessie frowned. "But the new scientists have captured the altered specimens."

"Not all of them. There is at least one more down there."

"Perfect."

Richard stood back up and walked over to the window with Jessie. "This is a dawning of a new age of man."

"Yes, an age that will be controlled entirely by man."

*   *   *

"This is your pilot speaking," Z spoke through the intercom with a phony, fuzzy sound to his voice. "We're on approach for our destination. It's sunny with a slight chance of meteor showers later this afternoon. The current time is 3:45 pm. Thank you for flying Z airlines, where our motto is 'don't step outside until we land, or the cold vacuum of space will kill you.'"

Anna came out from the back of the ship, her eyes red. Her whole appearance was tousled. The depression was practically tangible. She sniffed once more and then asked, "How long till we land?"

"I have to get clearance first, but if we get it, we should be setting down in about ten minutes."

Anna seemed to be lost, unable to gather her thoughts. "I . . . I will go get ready for a ground mission. Might as well do some soil samples and rock studies while we're down there."

"Hey, if this is going to be too hard, we can turn around and go back."

"No. I have to see this."

Z couldn't understand, but he didn't need to. "All right. I'll tell them we're here for a survey. Technically that won't be a lie, but . . . Would you look at that!"

Anna quickly looked, and her eyes bugged out. The *PSC Sanger* was near the moon. They had seen it under construction the last time they were on Earth, but they hadn't seen it in operation yet. Dozens of smaller craft buzzed around it.

Anna's jaw dropped in awe. "I've never seen anything like this. They're like bugs attracted to a light."

"Well, this is pretty big news. The PSC has pulled out all of the stops to research this place."

Anna leaned over to get a better view. "Look, the Spacation tour ships are already here. Since when do they change their routes?" She could see several medium-sized ships that were luxury cruise liners.

"I guess everyone wants a piece of this pie. I doubt the PSC is going to let any tourist down on the planet just yet. I mean, come on, they haven't even trapped one of those cat things yet. At least that was the last report I received."

"Just get us through this mess. I'm going to get ready." She left the cockpit for her cabin.

Z maneuvered the ship through the swarm of other ships around the moon. He was approaching the *Sanger*, whom he would contact for clearance to land. The last thing he wanted was for that mothership to turn her massive laser turrets on them for landing without permission. The closer he got, the bigger that mother ship looked.

"Wow, now I know what a mosquito feels like when he's approaching a really fat guy," Z muttered to himself and then punched up the call signal.

Almost instantly, someone responded, "This is the *Sanger*; what do you require?"

"Uh, *Sanger* this is *Explorer Craft Delta 313*, requesting permission to land on the moon for a mineral survey."

The conversation continued as the man on the other end of the comm channel said he had to get clearance from his superiors.

Anna dressed in her field gear for exploration. The uniform was dark green with several pockets for her instruments and sample containers. It was a jumpsuit design that felt like a body stocking. She was used to working inside the ship or in the vacuum of space in a full body suit. It had been a while since Anna actually did field work in a breathable environment. So far, the

PSC explorer program had only come across two other worlds with remotely habitable environments. Though neither supported any form of life other than some oxygen-producing moss.

Once Anna had herself ready, she packed a bag. She put in a few of her instruments and a couple sample containers. A large handful of the nutrition bars was packed into the inside pocket, since it wasn't clear yet if anything down there was edible for human consumption. Then she stopped and looked at the large book sitting on her bed.

Taking the Bible into her hands, she wiped the cover off. It was wet from where she had been crying against it for the past hour. Somehow, it felt different in her hands right now, heavier than usual. She wasn't sure why. Should she bring it? Why? Then again, if this was going to be the experience that would determine the rest of her faith life, then she ought to have this book with her. Heck, if she realized it was a fool's book, she could bury it on this planet and leave it to fade away with her last vestige of hope. With that idea in her mind, she stuffed the Bible deep into the bottom of the bag. Even though she was questioning everything she believed in, the idea of someone catching her with this was still dangerous.

With the bag slung over a shoulder, she stepped back into the cabin and closed the door. "Well, are we cleared or not?"

"I don't know. I sent the request, told them what we are doing, and they're just making us wait."

She sat down in the co-pilot's seat. "They're very busy right now. I doubt we will get a quick response. It could be . . . "

"*Sanger* to *Explorer Delta 313*, you are cleared for landing. We are downloading the coordinates into your nav computer. You have full clearance for a mineral survey in sectors six through nine; do not stray from that area unless permission is granted. *Sanger* out."

Both were highly surprised at this response. Anna looked at Z with a confused expression. "Wow! That was fast. Normally the red tape around anything the PSC is up to is sixty meters thick. I would've thought this, being what it is, would be three times as bad."

Z checked the landing instructions and punched in the commands. "As I always say, don't look a gift horse in the mouth, especially one that cost three billion credits. Taking us down."

The small craft flew out of the throng of spacecraft swarming around the mothership and headed for the dark side of this moon.

Anna watched the moon with a cold, hard feeling in her chest. She didn't want to be here. She hated this place so much right now, it hurt. But she knew there was a reason for her to see this for herself. Something had to make sense about this. She had come up with a few dozen ideas about how to explain this away or justify it within her own logic, but they all seemed flimsy. Worse, they all meant denying part of the Bible. Watching the atmosphere pass by as they sunk deeper into the moon, heading for a landing, she noticed the heaviness in her chest was heading for her stomach, and her throat was as tight as it could be. It was not unlike the last time she was at a funeral for a dear friend. She had to walk up to that casket to see him there and know he was gone, yet every ounce of her being didn't want to take the last step.

He liked that it was quiet in the dark. The practiced footsteps of a careful hunter could avoid any noise if he wanted, and he certainly wanted to avoid detection right now. So many strange people had been coming around, and they didn't look too friendly. He had already seen them capture three others of his kind, and he didn't want to be the next.

The others were too scared to go and learn more about these abductors, but he wasn't. He had to find answers. So, he went out on his own, looking and waiting for the next lights in the sky to fall down.

Since they took the last female, there had been fewer falling lights. It seemed as though his search was in vain. He had traveled for days looking for these furless, tailless abductors.

Stopping in a clearing overlooking a lush valley divided by a clear water river, he peered into the sky. The night skies had changed so much these past few days. The stars moved around. Some were larger than others. Some were fast, while others seemed to move randomly.

Then it happened. One of those moving stars got bigger and bigger and approached the planet's surface. They were coming back. His heart raced, and his insides were quivering, but he was determined. So, he watched with a keen eye to see where this star fell and would follow it until he came upon the furless ones.

✶ ✶ ✶

Z locked the controls and turned off the main drive systems, so the radiation that normally was released upon shutdown didn't kill anyone who got close. Once he had secured the Explorer, he turned around and looked at the pale woman.

"Are you ready for this?"

She nodded and stood up with a stoic attitude. "As I'll ever be."

Z forced a smile and picked up his sensor equipment. "I will be right there with you. This is an amazing time to learn and discover."

"Sure. Right. Let's move." She didn't want to look on the bright side; she was not ready to find the silver lining just yet. Without indulging any more of his pleasantries, she pressed the open switch and stepped out onto the ship's short, metal stairs.

It was dark, as dark as any night on Earth. It was as though she had stepped out onto a grassy field in the middle of Kentucky, not an alien world, filled with undiscovered lifeforms. She didn't expect to see all the grass and trees; it didn't feel alien enough to her. She wanted it to be like one of those ancient science fiction novels, where every last detail was so alien that human life couldn't possibly be supported.

Yet, it wasn't anything like that. The grass was cool and slightly damp. The trees rustled in the gentle breezes, and the bugs sang their songs on the night air. It was rather pleasant. Amazingly, it smelled just like an early summer evening.

Anna just stood there, staring at the shadowy night landscape, transfixed on what was around her. Z had already begun to take his sensor readings, absorbing all the data he could for this trip.

"Anna, what's wrong? I thought you would be looking for the nearest alien to introduce yourself to," Z asked.

She slung the bag over her shoulder, shrugged off her surprise, and marched on. "That's not exactly what I plan on doing. I just need to see this place and its people. Right now, I need to get a few soil samples and do some rock surveys."

"But you said you were coming to see these people?"

"I am. But if we leave without any sort of report to file, they'll suspect we were here to sightsee, and the last thing I need right now is to lose my job. I've already lost so much. Come on." She looked up at the starry sky. "How long till the sun comes up?"

Z checked the data he had been able to get from what the PSC had already released. "Looks like sunrise will be in four hours. Wow, this moon rotates every fourteen hours. Day and night go quickly for these people."

Anna sourly retorted, "That would be normal for them."

"I guess." Z shook his robot head and continued getting his data readings. "Hey, look at this. This moon is perfect. It is exactly seven percent the size of Earth; the gravitational pull on the planet it orbits does not hinder its axial rotation; and the radiation emitted from the . . . " his voice trailed off as they moved further and further into the thick of trees nearest the ship.

CHAPTER THREE

DAWN APPROACHED, BUT IT WAS still pretty dark. He had to hurry if he wanted to learn about the falling star and its inhabitants before it became daylight. He had seen it fall and followed it all the way here.

There it was. It was so alien, so unusual that it *had* to be the fallen star, or so he thought to himself. It was shiny on the surface, but where was the light it produced up in the sky? He slunk across the ground, prowling with all the natural talent that came from his feline nature. If these strange stars stole people, then he would need to be extra cautious not to be caught by it and stolen as well. He noticed it hadn't made a sound. Was it dead?

He reached up and held his furry, clawed hand near the surface, not touching it yet. He knew that one of his kin had been burned badly by the surface of the first fallen star, and he didn't want to suffer the same way. It seemed cool. Slowly, he pushed his hand down until it touched the metallic skin of this thing. It was cold metal. What could it be?

As careful as a new cub taking his first steps, he placed his ear up against the surface to listen to it. It made no noise. It wasn't alive. It wasn't hot. What was it? He walked down the side of the thing until he found something intriguing—windows. What he thought were the eyes of this beast were actually windows to the inside of it. Those furless ones did not ride this thing down; they were carried on the inside. Looking in confirmed this theory, for there was a living space within the star.

For a moment, he checked to see if any of the lost kin were inside this thing, but it appeared empty. He sniffed the surface and detected an odd odor. It smelled familiar. Like smelling a new person, but not one of his own kind. Could they be like him? Could they have scents and odors just like his people? There was one scent; someone was here, and it was a female. Perhaps they weren't as alien as he thought.

He sniffed from the door to the ground and discovered this person had left the star and was moving away from it. She was heading into the forest. For a moment, he felt the ground and cocked his head. There were indentions in the ground that looked like footfalls. But they weren't anything like he had ever seen. No toes, very flat, uniform in size and shape. These creatures had the weirdest feet. And they must have four feet, since he smelled only one person, but there were two sets of tracks. Perhaps his conclusion that they weren't all dissimilar was premature; a four-legged being was truly nothing like his kin.

He quietly followed his nose and the footprints into the forest just as the sun was rising in the west.

✳   ✳   ✳

Anna sat down on a fallen tree and rested one leg on top of the other, so she could pull off her boot. "This forest is lovely, but it's also muddy."

Z, who continued to scan the area with his sensors, answered, "Complains the geologist."

"Hey, I like rocks, not mud. If that mud contains some interesting rocks, then great. But I'd rather be looking at it through a microscope and not on the bottom of my feet." She ripped a small twig off the tree trunk she sat on and chipped the mud from her shoes. "Anything more to report?" She had listened to him go on and on about this planet for the past five hours.

"Well, for one thing, this place has an extremely similar climate to parts of Earth. And these plants are so similar to Earth's vegetation that it could easily be transplanted without many issues. But tests would have to be made to prove this. My sensor readings are just preliminary."

Anna yanked her boot back over her socked foot. "Though I'm still not entirely pleased about all of this, I must admit that this place is lovely. The flowers, the trees, the skies even, very beautiful. At one time, I would have appreciated God's work in the beauty of nature."

"Hey, you haven't disproven your theories about your Deity yet. We haven't even seen one of those creatures."

"Look who's telling me to hold out on hope. You're a robot; you cannot even fathom the notion of a god of any kind."

Z put a sympathetic hand on her shoulder. "It's important to you; that's all I need to know."

"Man, if only you were a real human, you'd make one heck of a husband."

"Maybe we can find a fairy godmother to turn me into a real boy. Or is that the wishing star? I forget." Now he was teasing her.

"If we do, I'll ask the star to make your nose grow every time you crack a bad joke."

"Bad joke! I've never told a bad joke in all my active life. I am full of comedy gold!"

"You're full of something all right."

Z took offense to that. "Oh yeah, well, how about this one? Two drunks are walking through Central Park and . . . " He was shushed by a finger to her lips. "Oh no, you don't; you asked."

"Shut up!" Anna was looking away with a bit of a squint in her eyes, and her left ear poked out to listen.

They stayed like this for a moment, Z oblivious to what she was waiting on.

"What is it?" Z finally ventured to ask.

"Nothing, I guess. I thought I heard the sound of someone walking toward us."

Z turned his sensors back on and scanned again. "You had better get at least one sample to examine—just in case we come across any other scientists. They shouldn't see us only admiring the scenery."

"Sure, hand me the sub-surface geoscanner. I need to make a map of this area's geological image before I decide where to pick out a sample."

"Just pick up a rock, and stick it in a sample container."

Anna marched over to retrieve the scanner herself. "If I'm gonna do this, I'm gonna do it right. I'm a professional and should act like it. While you're scanning the area, set your sensors to look for any seismological activity. We should make a fault line map in case they haven't gotten to that yet."

"Aye aye, captain."

Anna scanned this part of the terrain. "Don't call me captain."

Jessie and Richard rode the lift from the command level over to the examination area. When people saw them, they went the other direction. While Richard was a nice-looking, charming man, Jessie was a startling and cold woman that put fear into others just by the look on her face.

They walked out onto the deck and continued toward their destination. The corridors of this massive ship were wide and very stark. Everything was a shade of white or gray, with lights illuminating panels and doorways.

There was already a throng of reporters waiting for them at the observation level of the laboratories. There was a big story that was unfolding. When one caught sight of the two dignitaries, the frenzy started.

"Dr. Skye, Dr. Skye, is it true? Was one of these creatures captured?"

With that excited question and the recording device shoved into the smiling man's face, the rest of the eager reporters followed suit and rushed up to the president.

"Please, hold the questions until I have had a chance to examine the situation myself."

"Are you going to keep Earth in the dark about this until a later date?"

Richard cleared his throat, irritated by that question. "When I have confirmed this discovery and decided which method of display would be the safest for you and for the creature, it will be presented. Rest assured, I do not intend on keeping anyone in the dark. This is a delicate situation and must be handled with care. Now, if you will excuse me." He backed away from the reporters and flashed his palm at the sensor on the door for it to open.

The reporters shot a few more questions his way, but all they got was the back of his head. More than one asked Jessie something, but she ignored them completely.

Once the door closed and they were alone in the tiny access room, Jessie asked Richard, "How can you stand all that attention? I would keep them in the dark as long as possible, build the suspense, and then let them have it at a later date. Don't let them pull you around. You hold the strings."

Richard smiled, happy to see her so bloodthirsty. It suited her. "This whole situation is going according to a plan concocted by men two hundred years ago. Trust me, they will get the information exactly on cue. Now, why don't we inspect the others before we have a look at that specimen?" He stood in front of a wall that seemed as ordinary as any other. Placing his hands on two areas, he waited for a moment while the hidden scanner checked him in.

"Welcome, Dr. Skye," the computer announced, and the wall opened up to reveal a hidden laboratory.

Richard walked in with Jessie behind him. Immediately, the wall nearest them on the inside of this room opened up, and a laser protruded out, pointing right at her. "This is a restricted area; please leave. You have five seconds, or you will be terminated."

Richard casually announced, "Administrator Jessie is with me, computer; allow access for the duration of her visit."

Instantly, the laser returned to its slot, and the wall panel closed up.

Jessie, who had been holding her chest and looking scared, gulped down her heart and then got mad. "Why didn't you warn me?"

He snickered. "Forgot."

Yeah, right. He had enjoyed every moment of that.

Now that nothing was pointing dangerous weapons at her, Jessie had a chance to see what was going on in this room. There were a dozen beds attached to the walls, each containing a single occupant, a male or female cat person from the moon below. Two doctors were examining these patients and checking the readings on the computer monitors above their beds.

Jessie walked a little closer to Richard as they passed bed after bed. These creatures looked dangerous. They had claws, fangs, and muscles. She was worried that if one woke up, he might look for dinner; and she was a prime target.

"Richard, what is all this?"

"You should know all about this." He stopped and took up a tablet with the information reading across it. "This is exactly what we have been planning all along. We've already sent down a batch of them, and the regular scientists have picked up a few."

Jessie leaned over to look at the man lying in the bed. "I guess I never imagined how it would look. They are so . . . different."

"Isn't that the point? They are unique-looking, aren't they?"

Jessie asked, "Can they wake? Are they fully sedated?"

"They are completely sedated. They won't wake up until we're ready to wake them."

More relaxed now, she walked around the bed to get a better look. This creature had a figure not unlike a human, with ten fingers, ten toes, regular legs and arms—even the muscles were all the same, well, almost all the same. His body was covered in a thick fur that was brindle with more dark than light colors. His head was surrounded by a mane of hair that was as glorious as any lion's back on Earth. The mane was darker than the rest of him. The mane grew down his shoulders and over the top of his chest and back.

His face was extremely feline, with a puffy upper lip that had whiskers on it and fangs protruding from the upper plate down over his lower lip. He had a dark nose that glistened with moisture. His ears were higher up on his head than a human's and sticking out from the mane, which showed that they were larger and rounder than a human's.

Oddly, this person was naked, except for a necklace of strange rock beads.

Last was his tail, which was longer than his legs, thick, and had a tuft of fur at the end that was colored like his mane.

Jessie pointed at the man in the bed and asked, "Are they all this short?"

Richard shrugged. "Not all of them; this one is about average. Some are taller than him; some are shorter."

"What about clothing? Why is he naked?"

"He's primitive, remember? Clothing is a few evolutionary mutations down the road." He waited while one of the doctors pushed a hover cart over with an impressive array of medications on it. "Now I get to see them in action." He was handed a vial of red medicine that looked almost like it was glowing.

Jessie's face stretched into a grin. "Is that the stuff that will make our friend perform for the media?"

"Of course. I've been assured it works properly; in fact, a few of my scientists have barely avoided being mauled on the planet. Now I get to see it work firsthand." He plugged the vial into an injector and walked toward the other end of the laboratory.

Jessie wasn't far behind, still nervous in this room of beings she feared, yet also admired.

They entered another lab, this one much smaller and a lot less secure. On a bed was the female trapped yesterday. The doctor working on her was doing a physical examination. She was just like the male in the other room, only with the obvious female attributes. She was also just as naked but covered enough by her thick fur to be almost decent.

"Oh, good morning, Dr. Skye, it is a pleasure to see you." The doctor was reverent of his superior.

Richard hardly gave the man a smile and then asked, "So, what have you discovered about their biology?"

The doctor eagerly picked up his tablet with the notes on it. "This creature is highly fascinating. Very human in a lot of ways, but not human in others. I only wish we had a dead specimen that I could examine, to learn more about their biology."

Richard feigned interest. "Well, that wouldn't be proper. We must respect them and not kill them until they start killing us."

"True. But, after seeing what these people have as weapons, I don't doubt they could do a great deal of harm." He pulled up her hand and pressed her finger to push out the claw. "See, this claw is very similar to a feline claw on Earth, sharp and hooked. Get that stuck in your skin, and you'll wish you had a nail trimmer." He laughed nervously and then let go of her hand, letting it thump back down.

Then he pressed up on her face to show her teeth. "See these fangs, obviously used to tear and rip at meat. They might fight with their claws, but they kill with their teeth. That is, I suspect they do, having not observed any of their habits firsthand."

Richard stopped what was likely to be a long talk. "Fascinating, truly. And I am sure in time, we will learn a great deal about these creatures. Right now, I'm on a tight schedule. Why don't you go and prepare the containment unit, so we can wake her and let the press have a look."

The short, older, overly-excited doctor quickly obliged for the famous Dr. Skye. It was a pleasure to help the man in charge of PSC.

Once the bothersome doctor was out of the way, Richard pressed the syringe into the woman's neck and emptied the vial into her blood, all the while keeping a close eye on the door, just in case his eager friend was quicker than expected. Finally, the vial was empty, and his work was done. He shoved the whole device into the wall disposal unit, and it was sent off to be destroyed and recycled into other items.

Jessie hid behind Richard, terrified of this female on the bed now that the medication had been fully injected. "Are you sure this is going to work?"

"Have faith . . . Ha! Look who I'm talking to about having faith. Trust in me, Jessie; this is going to put on quite the show. Now, here comes our friend."

The eager doctor came back in with a happy smile. "The room is ready." He snapped his fingers, and two assistants came quickly from the enclosure area. "Take her, and lay her in the spot. I'll administer the medicine to wake her."

"Yes, sir." The boys lifted the gurney with the female creature and carried her into the next room.

The doctor happily conversed with Dr. Skye. "It's wonderful that we had space to create the enclosure here on the ship. This room was perfect."

"Yes," said Dr. Skye, "Coincidence and luck are two of the greatest tools of mine. Now, I am going to go address the media. I suggest you give her the wake-up shot and get out of there. We cannot be certain how violent she will be."

"Yes, sir. Right away, sir." He rushed back into the room.

As Richard and Jessie left, she whispered to him, "It could've been fun letting her tear that little man apart. The media would've had a field day. And he was getting on my nerves."

"Now, now, Jessie. If we let that happen, then the media would've focused on the wrong thing all day. We have this planned down to a nanosecond. Besides, he's a good doctor—excitable, but good. Now, let's go speak with our adoring public."

CHAPTER FOUR

Z HELD UP HIS SCANNER and changed its programming to snap a photo. He didn't take just one; he took about two hundred, standing there staring at a strange bird.

Anna rattled another rock sample around in her container and looked at the results from the automated mineral analyzer.

"Hey, come look at this one. This bird is amazing." Z held very still while he spoke, so not to startle his new find.

"Look, you've been mesmerized by about ten different bugs, birds, and other random creatures for an hour so far. I'm not going to pop up and run to your side each time you discover something new."

Z grunted while holding still. "Look, I know that you're all mopey about this whole thing, but try to show some interest. This is a fascinating place."

Anna took in a deep breath and then let it out slowly. She attempted to muster the same enthusiasm as her robot companion and joined him for whatever he had found this time. To her pleasant surprise, it wasn't just another gross bug crawling down a twig. Perched on a branch not too far away from them was a strange-looking bird.

Its size and wing shape were that of a bird in the falcon family. Its tail was made up of very long feathers that curled up just slightly at the tip. Its head was not a falcon, but a parrot in type, especially with the large, hooked beak. What was the most astonishing feature of this bird was not its physical shape or large size, but that it was brilliant pink—a pink that seemed almost unnatural. At this time, it was knocking on a tree trunk with its beak, seeming to search for something.

"Do you suppose it can talk like other parrots on Earth?"

"Don't know," Z answered. "There's not enough information to determine that this is like a parrot at all. Heck, this might be a serious bird of prey."

"Hey, look, it's flying toward that next tree." Anna walked quietly along the natural path, following the bird to see where it went. Maybe they could see a nest or another one like it.

The large pink bird came to a tree. The tree was tall, thin, and had a small tuft of wide leaves at the top. It almost appeared cartoonish, comical in shape. From the tips of the branches hanging down were long vines that stopped halfway down the tall trunk. Each one had a bunch of what looked like flowers at a distance. Z focused the lens of his camera in the scanner and got a closer look. Those bright pink things weren't little flowers at all, but berries. The parrot thing clung to the side of the bunch and then hung upside down to start picking the berries. It ate them heartily. Then it plucked a bunch off and flew away.

Anna was intrigued. "I wonder if that's how it gets that lovely pink color. Like flamingos back on Earth. What they eat provides the color for their bodies."

Z was following the bird with his camera as best he could and was just about to answer her hypothesis, when he heard a strange sound. "Did you hear that?"

She looked around and then down toward the distant forest floor. They were high up on a ridge, and the floor of this forest was deep below them, hidden by shadows from the canopy above.

"No. I heard nothing."

Z smiled. "I didn't hear anything. The motion sensors in my eyes picked up anomalous movement in the trees below. My programming mistook that for a sound. I'm gonna have to get that looked at."

"What kind of movement?"

Z lowered the scanner and then used his own eyes as a scanner, checking the motion sensors. "I don't know, but it's bigger than any bird or bug we've seen so far."

Before either could answer, something made a great leap into the air right where the pink bird was flying and caught it. The thing landed and held the now-dead bird in his mouth. Anna gasped and then covered her mouth, Z scanning like crazy. It was one of the cat people they had come to see. It was a male with light brown fur and red hands. He had been hunting and eating recently, and this was just another one of his meals. Like a hungry lion, he tore into the poor, dead bird and ripped its flesh apart, scattering lovely pink feathers all over his face and the ground.

Anna was in shock. She didn't want to watch this act of carnage, but she couldn't tear her eyes away from the beast. She had traveled a long way to see one of these people, and it wasn't a pretty sight.

"Do you think they eat those birds as their primary nutrition?" Z quietly pondered.

Anna was so stunned, she couldn't answer. Though it was a gruesome sight, all she could think about was how human-like this person was. His body, his arms, even the way he used his hands, all made her think of a primal human. Every story, every theory she was introduced to about primitive humans was playing out right in front of her. He wasn't ape; he was cat, but the results were the same. A pre-human lifeform that was in the middle stages of evolution. The longer she stayed here without seeing one, the more distant it had become in her mind. All of that now suddenly changed.

"Anna? You okay?"

She surprised herself with the rather sharp yelp she made when she opened her mouth. The terror in her at the shock of the moment escaped her lips.

Suddenly, the creature down below looked in their direction. Z was extremely quick and shoved Anna down as he fell lower to avoid detection. Anna was scared to death, uncontrollably shaking and making small noises. "Anna, Anna, get ahold of yourself. Please. This is no time to fall apart," Z whispered.

Carefully, Z slipped a small gun out of a compartment in his side. It was an emergency weapon placed in all Z-550 robots, a sonic stunner. Non-lethal but it would stop a charging rhino in its tracks. He hoped that these people were just as easily stunned.

Z slowly let her go. "Anna, I'm going to scan with my motion sensors to see if he's still there and coming toward us. Stay down, and try to stay quiet." With that, he let her go and then turned his head around one hundred eighty degrees. It was quieter than moving his body. To his great relief, he didn't see anything, not even where the creature had been moments ago. "Okay, we're clear."

Anna wiped some tears out of her eyes. "I'm sorry, Z, I didn't realize how it would be. I didn't know how weak I was."

Z did not replace the sonic stunner; he was not going to until they were safely inside their Explorer. "Hey, it's all right to fall apart now and then. It can really make you feel better." He purposefully caused his left arm to fall off his body and plop on the ground; then he comically looked as pleased as a man after a good cup of coffee. "Ahhh."

Anna actually laughed at that, perhaps the first time in a long time she had laughed at one of Z's terrible jokes.

He picked up his left arm and plugged it back in the socket. "See."

"Sure."

Z looked up at the sky to figure the time here on this moon. "I think we'd better find a place to set up camp for the night. We've been at this for ten hours, and I know that you're tired. My batteries are worn out and need a recharge."

"Camp? With those things running around? I don't know. I wanted to see one, but I didn't want to become its dinner."

"I can handle the ten-hour walk back to the ship from here, but I don't know if you want to. Besides, I'll be awake all night with my gun ready. You'll be safe, m'lady; your valiant knight in polymer armor is ready for some good fisticuffs should the need arise."

She snickered at his terrible try at an old English accent. "All right. There was a clearing a little ways back that should be a good place to set up camp."

These two people were interesting. Weird, but interesting. The female's scent was getting stronger and stronger as the day went on. But that strange man had no scent—at least not any which made sense.

He was equally startled when one of his own attacked that bird and then screamed at them. Why attack the bird? The fish in the river were much easier to catch. He wouldn't track the bird-eater down to ask, because his self-appointed job was to keep an eye on the strangers.

The flicker of the firelight danced throughout the makeshift camp they had set up. Anna reclined on the ground propped up against a large log that Z had dragged over for them to sit on. From where she lay, she could look out over the landscape that surrounded them. This clearing was up on the side of a hill, which gave a beautiful view of the forests of this moon world. The deep valleys were lush and filled with all sorts of life. Nature sang all around them with the rush of waters tripping and falling across the stones in the river that cut the valley, the birds singing as the sun set, and the bugs taking over the chorus when the night sky reigned.

The air was cool. In fact, it was getting downright cold, and this was supposedly the summer season. This moon had a cool climate, explaining why the people evolved to have such thick fur.

There was that word. It broke her moment of peace with doubt and anger. Evolve. How could she allow herself to believe that notion? For six hundred years, there hadn't been a decent shred of evidence supporting the theory of evolution, and now she had come face to face with the real deal. With a species that not only perfectly fit all the ideas and beliefs of the evolutionists but was on another world. The wonder, the amazement, the true awe that she should be experiencing being here as a scientist was tarnished by her depression.

It seemed illogical anymore, but she turned to the one place she could always look that helped her during her times of depression. For years, she had dealt with depression that would cripple her. When she talked with counselors about it, they told her she was being foolish. The reasons behind it weren't logical, according to modern society. When she came upon the Scriptures and God, her depression was eased, and she felt comforted. Now she needed that comfort more than ever. But her faith was so shaken, how could she find it? She had to try.

The book was heavy and old. Somehow, it felt older right now. Flipping back and forth through the pages, she wondered where she should turn. Each place she looked was about man talking with God, or God talking with man. It was hard to read without her unanswered questions screaming in her ears. Where could she turn to find what she needed to find? Then it dawned on her—flipping to almost the first page, she looked upon the first words of the Bible. From there, she read through the Creation story over and over, pondering it, wondering how to fit it into the new universe that had opened up for mankind. In only six days, God made everything? Okay, but on which day did He create the people on this other world? If He made them when He made Adam and Eve, why were these people so primitive? Were humans like this a long time ago? No, Adam wasn't a beast who hunted with claws and ate like a wild animal. Not according to the Scriptures.

She lowered her head and quietly asked, "God, if You're real, please help me. What is the answer here? What am I missing? If You made man in Your image, whose image did You make these people in? Please, Lord, answer me, please." She was trembling now, ready to start crying again. The effect of reading the Word of God was working the opposite of what she wanted. Comfort was disintegrating into confusion.

"Anna?"

She wiped the one tear out of her eye and then looked up, closing the Bible on her thumb. "Yeah, what is it?"

"You okay?" Z asked.

"I'll be fine. What did you need?"

Z held up his computer pad. "I just received a broadcast from Earth, via the ship in orbit right now."

"So?"

"They've captured one of these people and put them on display for the reporters. It's amazing. But . . . uh . . . maybe you shouldn't worry about seeing it."

Anna took one look down at the cover of the book in her lap and then looked at Z. "Let me see it."

"You sure?"

"Yes. I'm going to have to face this sooner or later. I've already seen them once; this won't be as scary."

Z let out a sigh and then reluctantly sat down next to her with the pad held up to watch.

On the screen stood Dr. Richard Skye, Administrator Jessie quietly behind him. He stood in front of a large, clear, glass wall with about two dozen reporters waiting to ask questions.

"As I said before, this specimen is the first and only captured member of their race. We have created the most approximate environment we could, so she would be less traumatized by the experience. Once we have compiled a few test results and observations, she will be released back on the moon to go on with her normal life."

"Dr. Skye! Will she speak to us at all?" one reporter called out, even though Richard had already said something about not asking questions until the floor was opened.

"Nothing we have seen thus far has shown that these creatures speak any kind of language. It is assumed that they have not developed linguistic communications as of yet in their evolutionary process." With that answer, the reporters all started blurting out questions. Holding up hands in defense, Richard stopped them. "Please, please, people, the questions can come later. Right now, I would like you to see this creature alive and well within her own environment—or, at least, the best version we could recreate."

Dr. Skye stepped aside, and an aide quickly moved his podium out of the way. The reporters swarmed the window, and all looked in for the audience back home to see. The woman in the cage walked around the area with great confusion. She was stumbling a bit and obviously woozy from having just been awoken. Her breaths were cutting quicker and quicker through her fangs as she became more agitated for no apparent reason. She growled, and her tail twitched faster and faster. She clawed at a tree and then another and started screaming with a cat-like yell that made the reporters jump. Shaking her head and running around, she was demonstrating that the anxiety was building fast. Her hands were constantly on her head as though she were brushing something away that wouldn't leave.

Richard quietly spoke. "Now we will introduce fresh meat into the environment." He was eager for this particular demonstration.

A rather small goat was lowered into the room, until it was about two feet off the ground. The straps under it let loose, and it plopped down. It was on another side of the room, which gave the tether operator time to retract the line. The goat was confused but otherwise content to just investigate the ground for something to eat.

The female alien wasn't so complacent. Her nose started sniffing, and she went right into a prowling posture. She crept around the enclosure for a few moments, until she came upon the innocent sacrifice. In a quick and efficient strike, she attacked the goat, sinking her fangs into its neck. Blood gushed out, and it screamed for only a moment until it hung limp from her mouth. Then she tore into it with the ferocity of any lion. It was a gruesome scene that made the gathered reporters, and even Richard, wince. Only Jessie seemed rather unscathed by the whole experience.

"As you can see," Richard quietly spoke, "they are truly primitive. Efficient hunters and deadly killers, these are the reasons why I have not allowed any sort of tourism to start coming to this planet. We have not had any incidents yet, but the possibility remains that these creatures wouldn't think twice about attacking us."

The reporters backed away from the window, not wanting to keep watching the nasty scene of this thing gnawing out the edible parts of that goat's body. Unfortunately, one of the reporters lost his grip on his recorder, and it banged against the window. The female inside looked up and saw them gathered to stare at her. She roared louder and deeper than seemed possible and then jumped from tree trunk to trunk until she got a good launch at the window and struck it with her whole body. She had intended on getting to them but did not realize that there was an invisible wall between her and her prey. She bounced off and fell back down to the artificial dirt floor. Getting to her feet quickly, she made for another strike, but a dart flew out from somewhere else. She crashed into the dirt under the power of the tranquilizer. The window they had been looking through was now stained with the blood of that goat.

Richard bristled with happiness on the inside at how well that turned out. It worked better than he planned.

* * *

"Turn it off. I've seen enough." Anna looked away from the little screen.

Z flicked the image off and then put the tablet away. "I guess we can assume that they are all this dangerous. I think I'll double up on my watch. I can set one eye over there and . . ." He noticed that Anna was sort of scrunched up, holding her large Bible against her chest. "What's the matter?"

"I guess I was hoping we were wrong. That these things were some kind of animal like a panther or lion or something. That the idea of them being humanoid was just a misconception."

"But we saw one earlier."

"I know. I know. I guess all I have left is lying to myself." She slowly released her hold on the Bible and looked at it with a critical eye. "I have to admit, it's over."

"It's over?"

"After all these years, centuries—heck, millennia—nothing has been discovered that completely discredits the Holy Bible. Historians have found more truth than fiction in the Word of God. Until now. Everything is just a farce."

"There are some theories that might apply. At one time, there were followers of this Bible that believed that evolution was God-inspired and driven. Couldn't that be an explanation?"

Anna snickered. "Sure, I've thought about that, too. But it just doesn't add up. Read the book. It says that God created man and spoke to him, walked with him. That wasn't an ape-like creature; it was a man. It says that bad things like death, thorns, and illness didn't exist until after man fell and left the Garden. Evolution is filled with billions of years of dead things. Until now, I could accept that the science was wrong, that what we perceived as millions of years was just theory, supposition, and unprovable ideas. But this throws it all out of balance. One cannot stand, while the other is provable."

Z shrugged. "I guess. It's up to you what you believe. I'm just a robot. Faith is not computable, so I don't fully comprehend your situation. I just wish you didn't feel so bad."

"I'm thankful that you've been so nice about all this. And I do understand that you were trying to help, but I have to face facts. It's over. The whole thing is OVER!" She let out the anger that had been trying to get out. With a good throw, she lobbed the Bible away from her, never wanting to see it again.

Z plucked out one of his eyes and placed it on a part of the log to keep a look out on that half of the camp, and he placed himself on the other side to keep watch here. His visual processors managed the dual input with ease.

Anna, feeling worse than she had in years, lay down on the ground in front of the fire and tried to get some rest. It was very unlikely that she would sleep tonight, but she would try. Tomorrow, she would leave this place and go back to work. All she had left in this life was her work. She wanted a husband; that was illegal. She wanted children, also illegal. She wanted a saving God and hope for a better tomorrow; that was now impossible. The only thing left in her life that brought any happiness to her was her geology, and that was exactly what she would focus on for the rest of her meaningless life.

The large book tumbled down the side of the steep hill and landed with its cover splayed open, the pages bent against the ground. It was only half a foot away from washing away in the river. A single caterpillar-like bug started to investigate this new item, tasting the corner of one page.

Just then, a furry hand brushed the bug away and cautiously picked up the book. With the care of holding a newborn infant, he examined this object. What could this be? Why did she throw it away? He expected it to be something precious the way she held it close to her like a child. Now she tossed it aside as trash. Did it hurt her?

More confused than ever, he remained in the shadows to keep a critical eye on these strangers. He was still baffled that only one had a scent. He just about screamed when he watched the male pull out one of his own eyes and set it on the log. It didn't hurt the tall one. What sort of monsters were these things?

✴   ✴   ✴

It was a long, hard night. Anna had a dry sleep; her mind was so active and the pain in her chest so deep, she couldn't seem to stay asleep long enough to count. When she did sleep, she had horrible nightmares of being torn apart by wild animals. The dark images she had witnessed yesterday were traumatizing. She couldn't wait for a few weeks of flying around lifeless rocks in space. She could even take a few sessions of Z's incessant bad jokes. Anything to get her mind off of her troubles. Yet, she would have to sleep sometime, and that was what she feared the most. That time to herself, that time to ponder all the questions she thought had been answered in her life.

She lay against the hard, dirty ground and watched the log next to her. Her body was scrunched up, and her face half buried into her arms. Though she hadn't slept much, she really didn't feel like getting up. Every time she considered moving, the question, "What's the point?" ran through her mind. Did life even matter any longer? What if she just died on this stupid planet? Maybe she could let one of those beasts have her, a fitting end for the last believer of God. Killed by the very creatures that defiled thousands of years of faith.

"Anna, you awake yet?" Z asked.

She mustered a pathetic sound from her mouth that came out almost intelligible. "What time is it?"

"It's 1332 hours Greenwich on Earth; here, I would wager that it's mid-morning."

Anna sat up, which allowed her to feel every ache and pain from sleeping on the ground all night. "Oh, I'm gonna regret this for two days."

Z held his little gun in his hand as he moved around. On the other side of Anna, sitting on the log, his eye turned and looked inward. He leaned back, "Whoa! That's a sight—Anna in stereo." He got up and fake stumbled across the camp to get his eye. He pushed it back into his head and then blinked a few times, which reset his visual programming.

Anna sneered. "That's just gross."

"Hey, having detachable parts is a joy. You're just envious."

"Envy, well there's another thing I can experience or feel now without guilt," she muttered to herself.

Z stuck his weapon back into his side and helped gather what little they had out. He pulled out a nutrition bar from her bag and handed it to her. "Eat, and get ready. We'll head back to the ship from here. I've calculated the best route."

Anna unwrapped the basic nutrition bar and bit a large bite out of the substance that she swore was just pressed cardboard with a little added flavor. "I was kinda hoping that we would've found some unique, tasty fruits or vegetables to eat here. I would kill for a banana right now."

"I have picked up a few items that my sensors consider edible. But since this is the first alien world we've even encountered, I would think it would be unwise to just up and eat anything without full tests first. It might contain some chemical that humans haven't ingested before and would prove lethal."

Anna laughed at something and then bit off another bite.

Z frowned. "Fine, laugh."

"What?" Why he was suddenly insulted made no sense.

"I give you my treasure trove of great one-liners, stand-up routines, and limericks, and you barely crack a smile. I tell you something logical and scientific, and you laugh. I thought I understood humor."

Anna forced down the last dry bite and answered. "It wasn't you. It was me. I was just thinking of how perfect this place is. The name that the atheis—we scientists—have given this is New Eden, and it sort of fits. It's a garden with amazing, natural, unspoiled beauty. Save the roaming, deadly, half-human beasts, it's a paradise. The idea that a piece of fruit would kill me is sort of poetic, when you think about it."

"I don't see the humor in that. But I guess it does make sense. So, you wanna look for an apple?" He was teasing her.

She got up and stuffed the wrapper into her pocket, then brushed off her hands. "Not really. Let's just get moving. I want to take a few pictures on our walk back. This place may have killed my faith; but it is extremely beautiful, and I doubt I'll be coming back for a long time. They'll probably limit all travel here to top-level scientific teams for a long time."

Z picked up the fully packed bag and slung it over his shoulder. He handed her a special scanner. "I thought you might, so I set this one up for the best landscape pictures. I also put a special one-button setting in it for close-up shots of flowers. You seemed interested in some of these large orchids."

Anna was impressed. She grinned when she took the device from him. "Thanks. That was very kind of you."

"You seem so down and upset. I'm just trying to help."

Anna tried it out and took a picture of the view from the hillside out over the valley. "This is great. You know something Z, if you were only real, I might just consider you good husband material."

"I don't know about that. I still don't understand the whole love concept. But I did download some old videos about old-fashioned courtship."

Anna slowly turned her head, giving him a cold look. She knew he was about to pull some kind of joke on her. "What do you mean?"

He started counting comically on his fingers, "Well, first, I'm supposed to nervously ask you out. Then, second, I'm supposed to adorn myself with loads of cologne and a dead flower . . . oh, and slick my hair back with some kind of oil. Then, third, I show up and embarrass you as much as possible in front of parents, which you don't have. So, we can skip that part."

"You can skip all of this."

"No, I did a lot of research. Fourth, I'm supposed to take you to dinner. Steak is great, but we'll have to go with nutrition bars."

"Shut up," she muttered at him.

"Wait, here's the best part. We get to watch a movie while I put my arms all over you and we smooch."

Anna frowned as she asked, "What is 'smooch'?"

Z had a big smile as he answered, "Oh, it's an old word for kissing. And I know I can do that." He puckered his lips up and made kissing noises. "Come on, give us a kiss."

Anna pinched his lips together and glared at him. "Make one more kissing sound, and I'll rip your lips off and throw them in the river."

From around the pinched lips, he said, "Spoilsport."

Anna let go and held up one of her scanners. "Come on. We've got work to do, and this isn't helping."

"But you didn't even ask which movie I wanted us to watch. I have a whole list of great . . ." His voice trailed off as he kept talking about this phony date he had planned.

MOMENTS BEFORE

He was lying across a tree branch, asleep with the Bible firmly held to his body. He had tried his best to stay awake all night but had exhausted himself keeping up with the two beings and staying out of sight. Only one leg and his tail were dangling from the tree as his snoring came between his fangs.

Suddenly, a nearby bird screeched loudly and woke him up. He was not prepared for the shock and fell right out of the tree and hit the ground. He stood up and yawned big with a lot of teeth showing. Smacking the taste of dryness out of his mouth, he looked around the camp to see that he had let them get out of his sight.

Fortunately, with the way those two were bickering back and forth right now, he caught up to them quickly.

* * *

Anna stopped again to get a snapshot of a tall peak with snow on it. It had the most amazing clouds encircling the summit with deep blue skies behind it. They were traveling down a natural path in the forest and were surrounded by vegetation with the hill to one side. Once in a while, there was an opening with a marvelous view, which she took advantage of.

"There, got it. I don't know who I'll ever show these to, but I'm glad to get the pictures."

Z couldn't stop looking behind them. "Do you hear something?"

"If you aren't sure with your robotic hearing, I'm certainly not able to help. I think you're just jumpy after watching that attack last night."

"You could be right. My motion sensors aren't picking anything up."

Anna walked on down the path and rounded a curve to stop and get a snapshot of an orchid-like flower growing in the crotch of two thick tree branches. The flower was huge and bright orange with a sprinkling of white in the center. "Hey, Z, do you recall the history lessons on the terraforming projects two hundred years ago?"

"I never went to school; after I was first constructed, they downloaded all the information I would need into my mainframe. From there, it has been what I can watch or download myself. So, yes, I know, but not from a class."

"Anyway, doesn't this place remind you of some of those theories?"

Z looked around critically. "Kind of. Though the idea behind the terra-forming projects were to create the perfect habitable planets. Large areas for construction next to the best man-made gardens and forests for produce and beauty." He stated what was written in the encyclopedia in his brain.

"True. This place doesn't really have many areas for development that wouldn't require work to clear. Terraforming would make it so that clearing was naturally done to begin with. Still, this place is so balanced, so lovely. The river is in just the right place; the mountains, the forests, even the paths are all just right. If this place weren't crawling with dangerous primitives, it would be a wonderful location for vacations."

Z nodded in agreement. "I have to admit this place is very pristine. More than I had come to expect from a natural environment."

Anna stepped out from the path on some vines and leaves. "Now, this is impressive." She pointed the camera at a huge rose-type flower that was about two feet across. The vines around it were covered in thorns as big as steak knives.

"Anna, be careful. My sensors indicate that area isn't safe."

"Don't worry. I'm light enough. I . . . " She felt the ground giving out from under her as the vines shifted and cracked. "Maybe I . . . should . . . " She was reaching out for Z's hand when the vines under her finally gave way, and she fell part-way down the hill. The top of her jumpsuit tore, and she was suspended by the thorn's grasp and by Z.

"Hold onto something. I can't keep you like this." Z tried to get more of her torn clothes in his hands, but each second came with further ripping sounds.

Anna had tears in her eyes from the thorn that had gnashed right into her ribs and left one heck of a cut. "I . . . can't get anything; these vines are . . . YAAAAAAAA!" Her clothes ripped, and she fell down the hill and out of his sight.

"Anna!" Z called out, with his hand now holding a large part of her bloody clothes. All the way down, he heard her screaming and the sounds of the vegetation crushing against her weight. His motion sensors and temperature gauge followed her quite a ways down until she met the bottom. She wasn't moving, and that scared him. He didn't understand love, but he knew fear all too well.

"Calculating, calculating, calculating," he robotically muttered as his systems analyzed every possible way he could make it down by jumping or sliding. All potential ideas were dismissed as too dangerous; he could be highly damaged, and that would do neither of them much good.

Next, he pulled out his sensor device he had used yesterday to map and scan the terrain. He would use this to find the quickest way to her and then take it.

✳   ✳   ✳

"You've made my job a lot easier, you know that?" Jessie stood by the window of Richard's office, observing the fleets of ships coming and going.

"And what is it I've done to make your job so easy now? You're in charge of looking after the state school houses so that the children grow up according to design."

Calling the locations school houses was a bit of a misnomer. The state bred the children through selective breeding programs; and from the time the child could walk until they graduated the program, they were kept in these special locations where they were taught everything they needed to know, trained for whatever task they were bred best for. And then they were ultimately released into the school or job of their choice, according to all their upbringing by the state. There hadn't been a real parent-child relationship on Earth for three hundred years.

Jessie bit her lower lip while she smiled, anticipating all the wonderful jobs she would get to do when she returned to Earth. "You know perfectly well what I'm talking about. My other job. Seeking out and destroying the last vestiges of religion on Earth."

"Oh, right." The media cleverly disguised the methods by stating that those found still practicing the banned religions were re-educated in a prison near the North Pole. In truth, Jessie took perverse pleasure in sticking those who were still out there in the cold, unforgiving climate of the North and waiting until they died. That prison was just an icebox filling with the bodies of pathetic hold-outs. The Nation States probably wouldn't be happy to know that the government had sanctioned a cold genocide of religious groups. This was why part of her work was secret. As long as she helped rid the world of religious zealots, the states didn't ask questions.

Jessie strolled back toward Richard's desk and picked up a glass of wine she had helped herself to from his private stock. "Did you hear? They tore down that old cathedral in Paris this morning."

"Oh, really? I thought that would be argued about for at least a few more years before something was done." Richard was trying to pay attention, but he had a stack of paperwork that needed his attention.

Jessie mused at the thought of the Notre Dame cathedral being demolished. "Nope. Unlike what the protestors tried to say, some were actually part of the Underground. But when the good news of the primitives here spread, their faith was broken, their spirits dashed against the rocks, and their enthusiasm crushed and left to die in the sun." She was enjoying this all too much.

"Why are you going back so soon then? It seems like your work is done. Religion is defeated; we've won."

Jessie gulped the last drink of wine and set the glass down with a bit of anger. "There is still the Jerusalem problem."

"Jerusalem? Don't tell me that they're still holding out? After all we've done, all the proof we have."

"Yes. They're still in denial. And it'll be my responsibility to make sure they fall in line."

Richard pushed the stack of papers aside. "And what do you propose for a solution? They're not part of the World Corps. They don't owe us any allegiance, and they certainly don't like you."

Jessie glared out the window into the blackness of space, considering how nice it would be to just drop a few sub-nuclear bombs on that stupid city and flatten the whole place. "While we have been bringing the glad tidings of evolution to the universe, the World Corps passed a few resolutions to nip the Jerusalem problem right in the bud. After we finish setting everything in motion, the only thing to stand between us and taking that old waste of sand out of the picture will be their forcefield defense system."

"Well, good luck with that. I don't know much that can penetrate that field they use to defend the city. As for me, I still have a lot of work to do up here. We have to maintain this place for as long as the news wants to keep breaking in with new stories."

Jessie smiled brightly as she watched her ship dock with the mighty *PSC Sanger*. "Keep up the good work. Every new news story that comes through this ship only helps my work all the more. If we can convince enough of those under the field of Jerusalem to abandon their beliefs, we won't have to attack. They'll just walk away."

Dr. Skye looked up at her. "Jessie. I do love your passion for hunting down the Underground and your dedication to destroying Jerusalem. I have always wondered, where did that passion come from? I don't think I've met anyone with your level of . . . shall we say . . . zeal in hatred toward religion."

She took in a slow breath and gave off a devilish smile. "Power. It has taken this world centuries to finally remove any idea of invisible beings controlling destiny. When we did, people began to look at the government for answers. We are everything. I help control the birth and education of the population; I have great power. It is gratifying, glorious. Then I see that hideous city, smugly thumbing its nose at the world government." Her whole demeanor became bitter. "It galls me to think that they are allowed to even exist. I find immeasurable pleasure each time I commit a new religious nut to prison. To finally remove that city and have the entire world free of any safe place for religion, that will be true ecstasy."

"I see," Dr. Skye said. "It will be a glorious day when we get to reduce that place to ashes."

Just as she anticipated, the intercom activated. "Docking station to Jessie, your ship is ready to depart."

"Thank you. Tell the navigator I'll be there soon."

"Yes, ma'am," the intercom clicked off.

Jessie headed for the door. "Richard, do you want me to send you one of my meds? They'll help reduce all the stress. A little fun can go a long way to reenergizing you."

"Thanks, but no. I left all my pleasure drugs back on Earth for this mission. I can't be distracted by anything."

"Suit yourself. The stuff I have is taken from the streets. It's a better high than the over-the-counter stuff."

Richard rolled his eyes. She was a rather dirty lady when it came to pleasure. He just waved a hand in her general direction. "Have a nice trip home."

"I plan on it. Goodbye." She got a few steps toward the door and stopped quickly. "Did you put her on my ship?"

"Her?" He had to think about that, then nodded. "Oh, right. Yes, she was put in the storage as an unlabeled item under PSC protection."

"Good. Now, goodbye." With that, she left his enormous office and headed for her personal starship. It wouldn't be too long of a trip home, just enough time for a good night of relaxation.

*　*　*

Z had given up on finding a way to get to Anna without some help. He tracked all the different paths he could find, but each one led him to impassable locations. The only places he could find to continue went right through the river, and he wasn't wearing the right legs for that. It would do her little good if his mechanisms stopped working properly, and he was carried away by the currents. Or worse, he sunk and couldn't get out of the water.

Understanding all of this, he trekked back to the Explorer. He was able to make it back in double time, since he was faster than her and wasn't being forced to walk at her pace. Unfortunately, it still cost him four hours of travel one way.

"Where are they?!" Z dug through a packed closet near the storage bay. He threw out hands, feet, a few fingers, a couple different hair replacements, and more than one box that contained spare processors for his various functions.

"AH-HA!" he proclaimed in victory and pulled out a pair of legs that were strapped together.

He sat down on the bench and detached his current legs and tossed them aside, then he worked on attaching the waterproof legs. They weren't as good in hot climates or lifting heavier objects, but they were perfect for swimming and hiking. Why he hadn't changed to these legs to begin with, he wasn't sure. Then again, he assumed this mission would be quick.

Once he had adjusted the legs to operate properly, he stood up to get his bearings. They felt wobbly, not quite as stable as his others, but still good. He jogged in place for a second, and his system reset all the operations for the new appendages.

Just then, he had a great thought. There was one more alteration that made perfect sense. He took off his left arm and threw it aside. Then he rummaged through the pile of spare parts. "I know I have one. I'm not allowed to leave without it." He shifted enough parts to build another one of him, save another head. The head was the most expensive part of any Z series robot. Finally, he picked up a new left arm and stuck it in place. He held it there for a second, while the automated attachment system worked its magic. In his brain, the processors changed to match the different uses this arm had over the other.

After he was sure his new left arm was properly affixed to all the systems, he moved it around. He pointed his hand, and two of his fingers lifted up to reveal strange devices sticking out. He looked in the five different compartments to make sure they were all filled properly and then flexed the artificial muscles to see that the system was online. Everything checked out.

"Okay, now for the bag." He grabbed up the travel bag he had carried back here and took out the mineral survey stuff and replaced it with a new set of clothes for Anna and some more food bars, as well as a few trinkets that would help. He was certain she would want to change her clothes after they tore like that.

"One more thing," he muttered to himself before leaving. He reached over and activated the emergency distress signal. He spoke into the recorder, "This is the Z-550 assigned to *Explorer 313* on the moon's surface. Anna has had an accident, and I will be searching for her. Assistance is requested. Please send search parties as soon as possible." With that recorded, he set the system to repeat until deactivated, and then he left in as much of a hurry as a robot could muster.

Anna couldn't feel her body; her mind was all that seemed to work. What happened? Why was she unable to do anything? Did something terrible happen to her? Was she dead? Wait, she fell. From what?

Everything was fuzzy; her memories were oddly distant. What was sniffing her?

Anna had a warm feeling inside her as she thought about the dog she had when she was in school. Was she still in school? Was her dog waking her up for his breakfast? He was always good at that. He would sniff her with that cold, wet nose and whimper at her until she got out of bed and made his breakfast. But . . . he died. He had been gone a long time. But that sounded like his sniffing. Why was she so cold? Where was her blanket? Did Rex take it off of her again? *Give it back! It's cold.*

There it came again, a harsh sniffing sound. Something was definitely sniffing her. *I'll get up and make your breakfast; just stop sniffing!* She wanted to say this, but she couldn't even open her eyes or move her body. Oh, her body—it was tingling and feeling oddly heavy. The feeling in her was slowly coming back.

There was a cliff. She fell down a cliff. Or was it just a hill? *Z . . . where are you?* The last memory she had was Z holding onto her. He got her clothing, and it tore. It was soaked in blood—her blood.

Who is sniffing me? She thought and finally was able to force her eyes open and moan.

Oh my word! she thought to herself. *I feel awful.* Her eyes were open, but they were just as foggy as her head felt. All she could manage to see was a milky white light and some indiscernible shapes. She couldn't tell who, but there was definitely a shadow leaning over her.

"Who . . . who is there?" she mumbled out.

The sound of hurried footsteps and then the harsh rustle of leaves immediately followed her question. Whatever had been standing over her, and apparently sniffing her, had run away.

Everything came back quicker. The tingling that started as just a few pin points had turned into a dazzling array of pricks across her skin. Those small pins spread and felt like large sores.

With her eyes clearing up better, she looked to see the forest around her and the damaged remains of the plants she destroyed on her descent down that steep cliff. There were bits and pieces of foliage all over, as well as a lot of red from her own blood that had spread across her open skin. Looking down her body, she realized she had lost most of her top when it tore off in Z's hand. The only thing left covering her was her bra and the tattered pants. Fortunately, the belt around the middle of the explorer jumpsuit had kept enough material around her midsection to keep her decent, though it really didn't matter on this moon.

Anna shoved against the ground to push herself over to lay on her back. That hurt. After a moment to gather her breath from that little venture, she pushed herself to be sitting up a little to see how bad the damage was.

She had gashes across a lot of her body and a lot of blood to show. But it didn't feel like she had broken any bones. She wiggled her toes and then her fingers and was satisfied that the damage wasn't too severe. Her head hurt, and that worried her; she could have suffered a bad concussion and wasn't sure what to do about that.

"I better try to get up and move. I have to find Z," she said to herself and started to push up. A stabbing shot of pain at the base of her spine took her breath away for a moment. She had hurt her lower back, but she wasn't sure how. It would be foolish to move too much right now; she was stuck.

"Z! Are you still up there? Z?" She looked around but didn't see or hear anything from her robot. She was aware he was programmed to do everything in his power to keep her safe and protected, so he would find her. But would she be alive by the time he did?

"What is this?" She saw large leaves stuck to her leg; at first glance, she had dismissed them as just more plant matter that she had accumulated during her tumbling down. But now that she looked at it, it was stuck on smoothly and sort of tied with other vines. Someone had done this to her. Maybe it wasn't just her imagination. There had been someone standing beside her a moment ago. But who? Were they sniffing her? Why?

If the shadowed person wasn't her imagination, then the sound of them leaving in a rush was also not just her imagination. Someone had been there, ran, and was probably still hiding in the brush nearby. Anna weakly picked up the biggest rock she could handle right now and then demanded, "Come out, whoever you are." No one came.

"I'm warning you. I have a Z-bot nearby, and he will protect me. Don't try anything. Just show yourself!" She was scared to death but knew a bluff was better than acting worried. She had no idea where Z had gone, and she knew perfectly well her one little rock was not likely going to do much damage.

Still nothing.

Anna's paranoia softened into reasoning and logic. Someone had helped her. This thing on her leg wasn't hurting her; it was like a bandage. Maybe she shouldn't be so angry. Perhaps a diplomatic attitude was in order. Setting down the rock, she gulped, and then smiled. "Look, I don't care if you aren't supposed to be here. I know that the PSC has said that anyone caught trespassing will be executed. I won't turn you in. In fact, I might be in the position to protect you. Just come out; I promise not to hurt you."

This time, she heard the distinct sound of brush crunching as someone slowly stepped through the thick greenery. She was prepared for another human to step out, someone who was here without permission. There had been a few eco-protestors who had already started petitions to force the PSC to leave this world and not disturb its natural populations. If one had come, they would certainly not want to be found.

Two clawed hands gently pushed aside the branches, and a figure slowly emerged from the shadows. He was one of those people, one of the cat creatures. He was short, probably half a foot shorter than her even. His body was a light brown, not unlike a lion on earth. His mane was even the same darker brown of a lion's mane, and his tail had the same tuft.

Anna gasped and quickly put her hand back on the rock in sheer terror at the sight of the wild beast. He flinched and paused in his motions. It was then she saw it. He wasn't like the others she had seen. He was wearing pants, made of some kind of rough, woven plant fiber, and he had a vest of some kind of leather material. Around his neck was a string of beads strung on a line of woven cord. This wasn't a wild, untamed beast; he was civilized—at least enough to wear clothing.

She had a hard time shaking the fear, the images still lingering of the bloody feedings she had witnessed in the forest and through the newscast. But the look on his face wasn't that of a ferocious monster; it was more a scared cat. He was actually kind of cute.

"You . . . you . . . did this?" she pointed at her leg.

He frowned and then followed her pointing finger. He did not understand her words but understood the reference. With a seemingly kind look in his eyes, she could sense he agreed.

"Thank you." This came out slowly, as though the speed of her words would make them translate.

He carefully approached her, taking gentle steps across the ground. She could see his feet and was a little surprised that they looked very human-like. Five toes per foot—basic human-style construction—but covered in that same thick fur with very sharp claws growing out of each toe. She could see that the bottom of his foot wasn't fur-covered but was rough skin.

His eyes reminded her of a kitten that was investigating a new person, curious to a fault and afraid. This was somewhat endearing. After he walked a few more steps closer and was not afraid of being stoned by this woman, he slunk down and came next to her, with his eyes about an inch from her body, his nose sniffing her. That was the sensation she felt when she woke up; he was sniffing her. For some reason, he was focused on her side, where the thick thorns of that alien rose vine had raked across her skin.

"What are you looking at?" She gulped, wondering if the smell of blood was tempting him.

He looked up into her eyes with those golden eyes of his and put his hand against her skin where the scrapes were bleeding still. The roughness of his palm was like sandpaper and made her jolt slightly. He quickly took his hand off of her, scared that he had hurt her.

"What . . . what are you doing?" she asked, realizing that he had little concept of her language.

He looked at her side and then at her eyes. His mouth opened to say something but stopped. It was likely he realized he was unable to speak her language. Then he saw her arm covering her chest. She had covered herself without even thinking about it. Perhaps it was because she was cold, or it could be that she felt naked sitting here in just a bra.

"*Ghoka,*" he said to her and pointed at her arm.

"*Ghoka*? What does that mean?"

He put his hand back on her, near the wound but not on it. He looked at her and said, "*Ghoka.*"

"I don't know what you mean."

He stood up and then pulled off the loose vest he had on and held it out to her. "*Ghoka.*" He held his arms up against himself to act as though he were cold.

"I don't understand. If you are asking if I'm cold, then the answer is yes."

He leaned over and wrapped his vest around her bare shoulders. He pointed at her wound and then back into the forest to indicate something that she did not understand. Without another attempt at communication, he left her in a hurry.

She pulled the vest around her, happy for a little warmth. This was so very confusing to her, but in a good way. He wasn't what she expected. Then again, nothing about this place was what she expected. If she survived this, then she would have something extremely groundbreaking to bring back to the PSC. These people were not as primitive as believed—at least some of them weren't.

All the same, she really wished Z was here. She had no idea what to expect from this person. He could still be dangerous. Unfortunately, she was unable to do much to protect herself based on her condition right now.

✳   ✳   ✳

Two searchers from the *Sanger* scanned the mountain path with a special tracking device. It picked up the trail of displaced plants and dirt that gave them a walking path to follow. They could trace Anna and Z's footsteps and hopefully find them. At least, they hoped it was the right footsteps; they could be trailing one of those cat things.

"You don't know how to use that thing; let me see it." The botanist grabbed at the tablet-shaped tracker.

The shorter biologist held it out of his reach. "Not likely. The last time you tried to help me, you wiped the memory on three of my dioscopes."

"That was three months ago. I've gotten better with these gadgets. Besides, what do *you* know about tracking?"

The short man held the device over the ground. It was a rectangular, flat scanner with a clear, see-through screen. Holding it over the ground, it overlaid a highlighted footprint path to follow as they continued on their way. "I don't know squat about tracking, and neither do you. But this device sort of takes care of all that stuff."

The taller botanist folded his arms in annoyance and walked behind his companion. "I just want to get this over with. This place gives me the creeps."

"Why should it? You like plants, and the plants here are amazing."

"Sure," the tall man sarcastically replied. "They are lovely plants, and I'm so very glad to be so near them. However, it is what could be hiding behind every tree and bush that scares me. Did you see what that creature did to the goat they put in her cage?"

"Don't worry."

"Don't worry! All I have to do is think about the way she sunk her fangs into its neck and watched it bleed to death as it hung limply from her jaw. How would you like to have your neck in her mouth? Huh!"

"Listen, I'm one of the biologists on this project, and I know we haven't seen that they are built to take down and eat a person."

"And what makes you so certain? Have you put a person in her cage to see if she attacks?"

The biologist altered the scope on the device slightly and then continued scanning the ground and walking, "Look, her jaw isn't wide enough to do that to your neck. Besides, we haven't come across any animals large enough to compare to a human. They didn't evolve to kill people."

"I hope you're right. I also hope you aren't using that stupid tracker wrong."

"Wrong? How can I possibly be using it wrong?" The short man got frustrated with his cowardly companion, whom he was stuck with for this mission.

"What if we are following the wrong tracks? I know we haven't found anything yet to solidly confirm they would attack and eat us, but I don't want to be the test animal for that study."

The short man continued scanning and following the footsteps. "Don't fret. This thing estimates that the footprints we are following were made by feet with shoes attached. So far, we haven't seen any shoes on these things. Heck, we haven't seen any clothes at all. Besides, you have nothing to worry about, even if we do come across any of these things."

"What do you mean?"

The short man snickered. "You're too skinny. They'd take one look at you and dismiss you as a random twig. They do like meat, you know."

"Ha ha, very funny. Crack jokes while we are risking our lives for some lost geologist. Why was a geologist sent down here, anyway? I thought we were focusing all our efforts on the primitives?"

"I don't know, but . . . hey, I think I found something. The tracks change right here." The short man showed that the tracks did indeed change; they were all over the place and scrambled, not in any sort of path. "I think they stopped here. Maybe . . . what is it?" He felt the sleeve of his shirt being tugged on.

The tall man had gone white and was pointing at something dangling from an outstretched branch. He wheezed out, "It . . . it . . . it's blood."

The short man gulped and walked over to the scrap of fabric that he recognized all too well. It was a piece of outdoor uniform, the standard for any PSC scientist in the field. It was only the upper half of a standard jumpsuit, torn to shreds, and covered in streaks of blood. He, too, became a new shade of pale, which was saying something for a man who spent most of his life inside. "Do you think it's hers?"

"Only one way to find out." The tall man took the scanner from his friend and pointed at the fabric with expectation. His hand was shaking so hard that the scanner told him twice to hold still.

"Oh, right."

The reason that the teams were made up of botanists and biologists was to maximize their skills for search and rescue. The botanist was to help, since he would have a better knowledge of plants and the land, which might help in searching. But the biologist was there to inspect any physical remains to determine if they found their target.

Getting an inconclusive reading on the blood source, he changed systems. He produced a small, tube-like device and held up the blunt end against the blood-soaked part of the fabric. Then he pressed a button and waited a moment until it showed him the data.

"Well?"

With another gulp, the short man nodded. "It's human all right. I will have to check with the database to confirm that it was the person in question, but my data shows that this person was female and in her early twenties."

"Sounds like a match to me. Now, what do you say about your hypothesis?"

"I say, let's get out of here."

For once, the short man did not argue with his tall companion. He grabbed the scrap of clothing and ran as fast as his feet could carry him. The whole time, he fought back the horrific images being conjured by his imagination. The idea of being torn to shreds by one of those things was enough to turn anyone into a marathon sprinter, even a laboratory jockey.

* * *

Z placed the strap around his neck and held up the bag so that it wouldn't get wet. He waded out into the river and crossed it. At one point, the only thing showing were a pair of hands holding a bag above the currents. It was a good thing that he didn't require oxygen and now his whole body was waterproof.

This wasn't the first crossing he had to make in his search for Anna, and it wouldn't be his last.

"Anna, I will not give up," he confirmed to himself as he got back onto the dry land.

Z had known this woman since she first joined the PSC as a full-fledged geologist. It wasn't uncommon for the PSC to keep a pair together; the Z-550 series were designed to adapt and grow in friendship with whom they were assigned. Some weren't given that luxury and spent their entire working life as a dull, unattached robot servant on one of the ships or back on Earth. But the lucky ones developed their own personalities and connections with their assigned scientists.

One of the attributes that develop over time for the Z-bots was loyalty. Z would not give up on her until his batteries rusted right out of his body. And considering they were dio-plastic, that wasn't going to happen anytime soon.

* * *

After a short trek down the hill, he found the place where all the medicine plants grew. His people called them cold leaves, since the juice inside them always felt cold to the touch. The plants grew on the side of rocky walls. The leaves were all different sizes, ranging from just an inch across to three feet. The larger leaves were past any use. The juice inside them would seep out as they got older. The tiny leaves hadn't developed enough juice to be of any use. It was the mid-sized variety that he would pluck. Pushing aside the larger leaves, he searched for just the right ones.

The whole time, he had a happy smile on his feline face. He liked this strange person. She was pretty and seemingly nice. He wanted to get to know her, to learn her language so to talk to her. If she wasn't the evil demon that the others thought these star creatures were, then she might help him. He would take her back to the others, and they could find out what had happened to their stolen kin.

Right now, she needed help. Her fall was bad. It worried him that she could be hurt worse than just the cuts he was mending. His home was too far away to go get help from one of the healers. Quickly plucking the ripe leaves he found, he hurried back. He didn't want to leave her alone for too long right now. He was concerned that the other members of his kind who had gone insane might find her and hurt her.

Anna held the vest around her as close to her as she could get. It was cold here with hardly any clothing on. The sun was setting, and soon it would get even colder. She thought about trying to make a fire, but she didn't know the first thing about old-fashioned camping. How does one start a fire without a portable laser starter? How did they do it three hundred years ago?

She tried to get her mind away from the cold. Looking down at the vest, she was amused by the workmanship. It was a rough piece of clothing compared to modern human design, but it was rather clever for a people without technology. The seams were sewn together with a very even stitch, and the leather itself was tanned and colored very nicely.

If these people were as primitive as the PSC was telling the media, then this wouldn't be possible. She could be all over the news in a very short time if she brought this guy back with her to show him off. He wasn't the devilish killer everyone assumed. She might even be rewarded, given a special place in the PSC.

Before she thrusted him into the spotlight, she would need to earn some trust. Learn more about him and let him know that humans weren't as dangerous as they probably seemed.

All this thinking didn't help. She was still cold, and the sun was almost set. It would get cold tonight, and she hoped that this cat man knew how to build a fire, or where to find warm shelter.

Just then, there was a rustling of the bushes near her. She was still worried about being found by one of these people with a taste for fresh meat, so she armed herself with a rock. She hoped that Z would step out. She knew that he could make a fire with his laser igniter attachment.

The cat man appeared from inside the brush, holding several large leaves and looking a little scared at the way she was holding the stone.

"Oh, it's you. Sorry." She dropped the stone on the ground.

He smiled at her, which was terribly cute on his muzzle face. He came over to her and knelt down to the ground at her side. He held up the leaves for her to see, as though she would recognize them immediately.

"Oh, are these food?" She wasn't sure what he was showing her.

He pointed at her leg, and she looked down to see that these were the same leaves that were tied to her leg. "Oh, they're bandages. You want to bandage my side."

Having no idea what she said, he only smiled. Setting one of the two leaves down, he held the other in his hand. She could see they were from a succulent plant but were shaped a lot like a large grape leaf. It surprised her when he held out his free hand and extended his claws; her surprise was flavored with a touch of fear at the sight of the sharp points on each finger. He gently used the claws to rake across the surface of the leaf, creating five oozing cuts. Without warning, he put the leaf on her side and pressed it in. That hurt and was as cold as ice being poured on her already cold skin, but then the cooling sensation soothed the stinging feeling of the wound. This cold feeling wasn't just because the leaf was chilly; it was also from the fact that there was some kind of natural menthol in this plant's juice. It was then that she realized why her leg felt a lot cooler than the rest of her.

Anna was amused. She now knew for sure that this man wasn't as primitive as the PSC advertised. This kind of medicinal knowledge was impressive. For a moment, she was watching his body, thinking about his biology and how similar he was. At least under the fur. His muscles were in all the same places; his proportions were very similar; the way he used his hands, the way he scrunched up his face as he focused seemed very human to her. Then she looked at the tail behind him that was slightly moving here and there as he worked. From this vantage point, she had a pretty good view of his mane and tall ears. The feline side of him was certainly present as well.

There was a little snicker that she couldn't keep in as she watched him work. He had a pretty good figure, and his muscles would certainly be attractive on a human. She wasn't romantically interested in him, but it did amuse her to think about the situation. It was like one of those ancient Earth books about romance. The damsel in distress under the care of the ruggedly handsome savage man. He even had the big hair. Why did all the men in the old days have long, flowing hair?

He stopped and leaned back to look at his work. With a smile, he indicated he was satisfied that the stickiness of the leaves' own juices would hold them in place. He patted the leaf softly and smiled at her to show he was happy with his own work.

Anna reached down with a hand and felt the leaf herself. It was smooth on the surface with tiny little needles growing out of parts of it. It was a type of alien cacti, one that apparently grew in forests, since there weren't any arid lands on this moon. It felt good against her skin, the cooling sensation replaced the stinging of the scrapes.

She returned his smile with her own and even a nod. "Thanks." Looking into his feline face, she sighed and said, "I wish we could talk. You're being so nice to me, I would really like to thank you and ask a few questions. My people are so curious about you and your kind."

He just smiled and cocked his head in confusion at her words.

Anna looked around, not sure what to say or do. It was going to be awkward just sitting here and waiting on Z, while this cat person stared at her. What if he had romantic thoughts about her? It could get extremely awkward. Wait, no, she wasn't going to think like that. He seemed nice and kind, not the rapist type. She had to find a way to communicate. But how? Then she had an idea.

"Anna," she pointed at herself.

He got very curious and followed her pointing fingers with his face until he was only inches away from her chest, staring at her skin. He seemed to be looking for something. He looked up into her face, almost as close as he was to her chest and gave her a raised eyebrow. "Nana?"

She shook her head and pushed him back. "Anna." She pointed at herself again. Then she pointed at him and he only frowned in extreme curiosity.

He pointed at her. "Anna?"

With a happy face and nod, she answered him, "Anna." Then pointed at him again.

"Anna?" Clearly, he wasn't sure what she meant.

She cleared her throat and pointed at her. "Anna, Anna."

He seemed to catch on. He pointed at her and said, "Anna." Then he pointed at him, "J'kla."

Now she pointed at him as well, "Jakla?"

With a quick shake of his head, he corrected her, "J'kla."

"J'kla." She said this slowly to make sure she pronounced it right.

He nodded quickly and excitedly pointed at her and said, "Anna," and then back at him, "J'kla."

"Okay, is that your name, your species, or the word for man?" she asked herself.

"J'kla," was his response.

"Fine. Whatever that means, it refers to you, and that's good enough. Now . . . uh . . . what else? How do you teach an alien English? How do I learn his language?" She looked at his smiling face. He seemed to be waiting for more conversation. "Oh, my. Uh . . . " She pointed at the night sky. "Stars."

He looked up and sort of scanned the heavens with his eyes. "*Neja,*" which was the word for sky.

"Kneejah? What does that mean?"

J'kla looked back at her with those same curious-as-a-kitten eyes.

"I'm not the person for this job. I wish Z were here." She groaned and held her face. "That is, if he is still in one piece."

For a long few moments, she considered how to start finding a common language between them. Could she learn words for little things and build up to something—like his word for rock, leaf, sky? But how could she be certain? How would she even start?

While she pondered the possibilities, she had started writing out words in the dirt on the ground. It wasn't to teach him, just a way that she thought. This caught his interest; in fact, he was utterly fascinated by it. She had written out the word APPLE, as she had been thinking about starting with basic words, and she was also getting pretty hungry. J'kla scratched into the dirt with his foreclaw the same word, though it was very sloppy compared to hers.

"That's very good." She was sounding like a child instructor at one of the schools.

J'kla was overly excited; he pointed at the letters and then said, "*Chi ola noka!*"

"Sure."

He pointed at the letters and repeated himself, "*Chi, chi?*"

"What is it? Do you know these things? Have you seen these letters before?"

He stood up and rushed away to where he had been hiding when she first came around from her fall. In moments, he returned with a book in his hands. Anna was fascinated; she hadn't seen any other bound books outside of her Bible. Then she realized what he was holding. J'kla quickly set the book down. It was her Bible.

"What are you doing with this? I threw it away." Then it started to make sense—how he got this, how he found her so quickly. "You've been following me."

"Chi noka?" He opened it and pointed at the letters on the pages. He had it upside down, but he couldn't possibly know that.

She softly flipped it back over and looked at the words he was pointing at. "You want to know what these mean?"

"Chi noka?"

Anna let out a hard sigh and closed the book. "You want to learn about letters. Wow, I don't know." All it took was one look in those kitten-like eyes begging her for more, and she couldn't say no.

"Fine. I guess I have time right now. First . . . can you build a fire?"

"Chi?" he cocked his head at her.

"Fire, fire." She rubbed her hands together and held them out like she was warming them, and then made fire sounds with her mouth. "Hot, warm, fire."

He frowned and rubbed his own hands together like her. As he held them out, he realized what she was saying. "Fire." He repeated her own words.

"Yes, fire. Wow, you are a fast learner. Maybe this will be easier than I thought."

He was excited to learn a new word and kept rubbing his hands together and then holding them out, "Fire, fire."

She shivered and then did the same thing with her hands, only this time said the word as a request. "Fire?" After that, she pointed out toward the trees.

"Kimli." He held out his hands to show her to stay here. Like she was going to move right now. Then he got up and slunk into the trees. It was amazing how little sound he produced as he moved.

Anna picked up the Bible and opened it. For a brief moment, she considered the miracle that this book had come back to her. Then she reminded herself that she had abandoned the notion of miracles. "Oh well, at least I can teach him to read with this. There are some amusing stories in it."

✳ ✳ ✳

A small, luxurious spacecraft dropped out of hyperlight speed near Earth's moon. This ship was only four decks with large wings designed for atmospheric flight. It was a standard craft given to important officials in the World Corps government.

"Ma'am, we are entering Earthspace. Please prepare for departure at your convenience," the Z-bot at the helm announced over the intercom.

Jessie lay in her large, plush bed with a satisfied smile painted across her surgically modified face. "Thank you. Land near the capital. I have business to take care of there."

"Understood. Command level out." The intercom beeped off.

Having applied all the makeup and perfume she needed, Jessie got up to find the perfect dress for today. She opened a panel on the wall, revealing a nice selection of her most official looking outfits, all perfectly balanced to strike a strong pose while in court. Moving aside the dresses, she found an old memory frame. It was a picture frame that held dozens of moving pictures. This one displayed runway models walking in gorgeous gowns.

One of the Z-550s working on the ship came into the room with her itinerary. He set down the computer tablet and looked at the pictures she was currently watching. "What's that?"

Jessie smiled as she picked up the frame. "Oh, just something from my past."

The Z-bot cocked his head as he looked at it. "You were a model?"

Jessie carried the frame with her back to where she could sit down. "No. I designed dresses."

"Really? I didn't know that."

"Yes." She actually smiled when a particular dress walked by, a blue outfit that she was extremely proud of. "It was a hobby at first. Something to pass the time after college before I started working for the government. But I excelled at it . . . just like everything else in my life."

The Z-bot let out a laugh, "Fashion design? That's so different than being a high-ranking government administrator."

"Not really. Fashion isn't just about picking out pretty fabric; it's a head game. You have opponents who are trying to thwart you; you have people you have to step on; and occasionally, you have to take someone down who is getting in your way."

"Sounds like you were really into it."

"Yes. I don't do anything half way. I took some designs to a studio, and they let me work there for a while. Then I got my break, and one of my designs was showcased at a fashion show in New York. I saw the opportunity and played all the right cards to get the right attention. Soon, I was designing dresses to be shown at Paris Fashion Week."

"Really! Why give all that up to work for the government? Sounds like you were big time."

Jessie's nostalgic smile faded. "I didn't own the studio; I worked for it. I would never have the kind of clout and money I wanted. Oh, I had power within my own circles, but not enough. However, my break came. I got a job as an adjunct to the administrator over education. It was a good job; I just had to give up my designing career ambitions."

"Was it a hard choice?"

"At first, yes, it was. But then something happened. Right before I got the job offer, a new girl arrived in the studio from Japan. She was good. Her designs were already turning heads and shifting the accolades away from me."

"So, they had a star designer even after you left. Good for them?" The Z-bot could hear the venom in her tone and was curious.

Jessie gave off a smug sneer. "I wasn't going to leave as a has-been. That little girl didn't deserve my place. So, right before I left, I got into the studio after hours, destroyed all of my final designs and framed her. I had name, clout, and beautiful designs; she was a nobody, and no one listened to her defense. She was ruined, crushed, absolutely run out of the business."

The Z-bot quietly said, "That seems a bit . . . harsh."

Jessie set the frame down and calmly stood up. "Do you know what I learned then and still carry with me today? When you have power, never let it go. Crush any who would dare to challenge it."

"I guess so. My job isn't about power, just service." He picked up the tablet and handed it to her. "Your itinerary."

"Thank you. Oh, good, I'll have time after lunch for a quick meeting with the Canadian representative. He isn't being as cooperative as I like, needs to be convinced on a few things." She continued talking, mostly to herself, as she left for her day of court manipulation and politics.

The sun rose in the distance as Anna was woken up by the nudging of her new friend. She had hoped Z would find her last night, but that didn't happen. The first feeling she had before she even opened her eyes was the pain in her stomach and her muscles. The soreness of the fall she experienced was really setting in, and she didn't have any medicine to help. This herb J'kla had put on her was helping, and her skin didn't sting. But her muscles were screaming things at her that weren't nice.

She opened her eyes and smiled. Beside her knelt the friendly face of a man she was getting to know through a painstakingly-slow process. He looked into her eyes with that anticipation of a new puppy. She kind of liked the little tips of his fangs protruding from the sides of his mouth when he smiled. When she first saw his fangs, she couldn't stop thinking about the way the woman in the newscast tore apart that goat. Now, it only made her think of his smile, for that was when these fangs showed the best.

"Good morning. You're certainly up early."

"Kunja?" he held up a softball-sized fruit. It was red-skinned and looked a lot like a pomegranate from Earth.

Anna pushed herself up and moved her head around, feeling every kink and hard rock she slept on last night. "Oh, is that for me?"

He nodded and then clumsily said, "Yes."

Anna was happy. Though he truly did not understand what she had just asked, he knew the feeling and knew the right word. They had spent the better part of last evening learning. She got him started with the alphabet and simple words. He caught on quickly and was as thirsty for knowledge as any bright student. She reached up and took the fruit from him. "What is this?"

"Yes," he said again, which was a bit funny to her.

Anna turned the fruit over in her hands and wondered if it was safe. Z had never figured out if anything was safe to eat. But she was starving, and her body wouldn't heal very fast if she didn't eat something. So, the test would be done right now.

"I wonder what it tastes like?" she muttered to herself as she felt the leathery skin of this heavy fruit. Was it sour? Was it sweet? Did it taste like steak? She had no clue, but she was willing to try. So, she lifted it up and started to take a big bite.

"NO." The other word he was good at now. He stopped her quickly and pushed her hands down, so she wasn't holding it so close to her face.

J'kla picked up his own strange fruit and took hold of a small bit of the skin that was flayed out on the top, most likely where the stem nourished it. Pulling down, he peeled it much like a banana. Inside was a ball-shaped purple fruit that smelled sweet. With that same grin, he held it out. *"Kunja,* yes."

Anna carefully peeled hers and held the ball of inner fruit, with the splayed skin in her hand, like a plate. Touching the fruit, it now felt a great deal like a banana and smelled like a cross between a banana and a strawberry. "Wow. This does smell good. I hope it tastes the same."

J'kla took a big bite and smiled as he ate, to encourage her to do the same. She did and was very pleased by the taste. It was marvelous, if not a little awkward to eat. "This is good."

"Good! Good!" He was happy to say the words he had learned.

While they ate, he sat down on the ground cross-legged and scratched into the dirt a letter *A*.

With a mouth full of food, he said, "Ah," then scratched a *B* and said, "Beh."

Anna smiled. She was as happy as she had ever been. She never thought this kind of happiness could be with her after her faith had been crushed, especially when that happiness was being brought to her by the very being who unwittingly crushed her faith. But it was exciting to watch him learn, to know he was friendly, and to accept his kindness and return that kindness.

It also made her very excited at the thought of bringing him to the *Sanger* and showing him off, even if he learned only a few more words and some of the writing. That was a big jump from the idea of the primitives that the PSC had assumed were down here.

"Okay, now, I'll show you how to write your name. This is a *J*." She continued with his lessons as best as she could think to teach him.

*   *   *

With a sharp click of her heels against the ancient stone ground, Jessie walked across the square in the middle of the government buildings. This was the one place on Earth that had not been torn down when the religious disbandment act was passed. The Vatican, just like all other religious property, came under the control of the World Corps. Instead of tearing it down, it was remodeled to be the head of the government. Just like the United Nations of Earth's past, this government was that of representation. All the former countries, now called states, each had several representatives here to cast their vote and discuss matters of the day.

Of course, almost all the religious artifacts that once littered this pristine property had been removed and destroyed. Many of the artistic works, as well as ancient manuscripts and holy items to the Catholic Church, were burned right in the middle of the former St. Peter's Square. A few of the statues and paintings were left only at the permission of the World Corps. Often, these items were used not to teach about history but to mock and belittle the foolish religions of the past and their devotion to the idiotic marble and stone gods. Many of the nude statues were not destroyed but displayed alongside the nude statues from the ancient Greco/Roman era in the pleasure parks. Sort of a form of inspiration for the visitors. Certainly not the intention of the artists, but the World Corps cared little about that fact. Private art collectors did not purchase any of the ancient religious art. They feared being accused of supporting the Underground by merely owning the art.

Jessie couldn't help but notice the large group of children being escorted through the plaza by their instructor. This group belonged to one of the state school houses here in Europe. The students were the perfect model of their year of breeding. The boys all had blond hair, and the girls all had red hair. The hair, eye, and skin tones were all genetically manipulated in the womb of the breeders.

Turning from her path toward the main building, Jessie stepped aside to meet this class and their teacher. She could hear the teacher explaining the functions of the World Corps and was pleased that these children were being introduced to the political system that would guide their lives.

"Good morning, children of the future." Jessie said that every time she spoke to the schools as the head of the education system for the World Corps.

The teacher bowed her head to her superior. "Class, this is Administrator Jessie of the Corps. She is in charge of the education and rearing program."

The class, in an almost eerie unison tone, greeted her, "Good morning, administrator."

Jessie stopped and stood before them, enjoying seeing the grand work of the breeding program. "Good morning, class. I hope you are finding this tour to be highly informative."

"Oh, yes, they are learning quite a bit today," the instructor replied.

"Good, very good. That is the important function of our system, the perfect allowance of information to everyone."

Just then, one of the girls stuck her hand up and waited.

The instructor asked, "Linda, what is it? We will have a bathroom break in five minutes."

"No, instructor, Greta, I wanted to know about those cats."

"Cats?" The instructor was not prepared for this.

The child spoke directly to Jessie, "Administrator, I saw you standing with Mr. Skye when they showed us that cat lady. Is that real?"

Jessie's smile grew so much, her teeth were showing. "Oh, yes, they are most certainly real. I have seen them myself. They are primitive and dangerous, but perfect proof of the facts of evolution."

A boy piped in. "How are they primitive?"

"Oh, they are so backward, they don't wear clothing. They don't speak. They hunt with their teeth and claws. But they will one day evolve into people like you and me."

The first girl spoke up again. "The news man said that they are so behind us that they have moms and dads. Is that true?"

Jessie knelt down a bit to get closer to the children. "We haven't seen that yet in our study. But we know that they cannot be evolved enough to have the perfect breeding programs like we have. They probably just procreate like our backward ancestors, without forethought or logic. Then, like our ignorant predecessors, they probably raise their children one at a time in homes."

"Why would anyone live like that?" a boy asked.

Jessie shook her head. "I don't know. It took us eons to get past the foolish notions of families and individual child-raising. Now, you get to grow up with a lot of friends and a lot of guidance. You don't want for anything and are provided a perfect education. It is a great system that prevents foolish ideas like religion and faith to cloud judgment and logic."

"Can I see one?" the little girl eagerly asked with a big smile.

The instructor quickly answered, "No, sweetie, they are a long way away on another planet. Tomorrow, I will talk to you about planets and distance in space."

Jessie stood up and corrected the woman. "Don't be so certain about that." She addressed the children. "If you behave and listen carefully on this tour, you might just get the opportunity to see one of these primitives in person."

The kids all became very happy with that notion, but they retained the excitement for fear of spoiling the opportunity.

Just then, the clock on the capital building chimed a quarter to the hour. "Looks like I have to get back to my work. Have a good day, children, and remember, what is your school motto?" She held a hand to her ear to listen to them recite.

In perfect unison, they all said, "Obedience brings knowledge."

With that statement of their dedication to the system, Jessie marched onward toward the capital. She worried that her crew from the ship had not brought her surprise in yet, but she had little time to fret about the details. She had to speak with the counsel if she wanted to keep pushing her policies forward.

CHAPTER FIVE

AN OLDER MAN STOOD IN the middle of the large forum where the delegates met. He was on a platform, standing before a podium. The platform hovered a few feet from the ground. It was designed to lift up higher when someone was overseeing court sessions. Right now, this speaker was just relaying information before the session came to order. The delegates sat in the cylindrical room with their name and state of origin on a plaque before them.

"The martial law decree in the old Canadian state has ended as the crime rate and the opposition has been brought into line. Martial law was declared in the state of the Philippines due to the outbreaks of drug-induced violence that are currently being quelled as quickly as WCS forces can respond. Prison Administrator Arnold is still on location in Antarctica, where the five new prisons are being constructed to relieve the overcrowding across the planetary prison system. The murder rate in—" He was interrupted by the head judge.

The judge, the head of the court sessions, banged his enormous gavel and got everyone's attention. "Session will begin immediately. Thank you, Administrator Dolph. Your report was enlightening. I am sure we will keep all our eyes on every security situation as it arises in our own states."

The old man stepped down from the platform and made his way over to the seat that was assigned to him. On the bottom row of the house was a selection of seats designated for the administrators of each cabinet department. Dolph was the administrator of the media relations for the counsel, and so he had a seat awaiting him. Near him was an empty seat that was assigned to

Jessie, but Jessie hardly bothered herself with court sessions unless it would benefit her causes. Otherwise, she found them terribly boring. Today, though, she had an important matter to discuss with the World Corps leadership.

The head judge waited while all the delegates took their seats and quieted down. He pressed a button and a holographic screen appeared in front of him to show a list of names and times. "First on the agenda for this day is Administrator of Education Jessie. Please step forward."

The room looked at her seat and found it empty. A few murmurs could be heard here and there; no one was sure where she was. Then, as if on cue, here she came. The clicking of her high heels echoed inside the court, and this announced the arrival of the most self-important member of the administrator counsel.

Jessie entered the court wearing a black pantsuit that glinted slight hints of crimson red. Her top had a long train down the back that gave the impression of half a dress. Her dark hair was neatly put up on her head, and her face was perfectly made up to give her a strict, severe look. She stepped up to the platform and struck a very commanding pose before the gathering. She did not betray her strong appearance with any of the irritation within her at not seeing what she had brought to show the people.

"Administrator Jessie, you have the floor." The head judge banged his gavel once to relinquish control of the room to her for the time she was allowed.

With that tight-as-leather smile, she looked around the room. "Ladies and gentlemen, I am not here to discuss education progress or any of the breeding programs. The breeding and education system is functioning perfectly at this time. I am here representing my special job that I was assigned."

This drew a few mutterings and confused looks. Not everyone was fully aware of her role in the seeking and execution of the religious Underground. "For one hundred years, we have enjoyed the peace and tranquility that has come from the Religious Disbandment Act. But, unfortunately, the ignorant few who remained loyal to their religions posed a threat to our peace.

They formed an Underground and were determined to undermine all our progress. They sought to convert new followers and attempted to reestablish so-called religious freedom. More than one member of this very court has been discredited and lost his or her status for supporting acts that are clearly attempts to remove the solid writing of the Disbandment Act. Ten years ago, I was approached by then Head Judge William. He ordered that I use my resources and skill to search out and squash this Underground once and for all. He and I both knew that this Underground was unfairly targeting our minors in attempts to corrupt their education, so it was logical to use my department against them. I am here to report that my work has been a monumental success."

"Success? This Underground religious movement is still around; we are still being asked to devote resources to finding them," the representative of the state of Spain interrupted.

Jessie took a moment to glare down this man, then continued. "Yes, the fight continues. But with the discovery of the alien species, the Underground has lost steam. This morning, we were approached by six separate cells who surrendered to us willingly. And yesterday, demolition of the old cathedral in Paris was started when the protestors laid down their signs and walked away. The last days of this sorry, backward belief system are at hand."

"That is all well and perhaps true, but, what did you need from us today?" The representative from the state of India asked.

Jessie was quiet for a moment, building up the tension so that everyone was sure to be listening. Then she spoke. "I want the go-ahead for Operation Dome Breach."

This stirred the room considerably. Some were against this; others were for it; more than one person was already standing to leave in protest.

The woman representative from the state of Brazil said, "My state and many others are unaware of the details. The media has spoken a little about this, but we don't know what to believe."

The representative from Sweden asked, "Please explain the details, Madam Administrator."

Jessie grinned. She always liked talking about this. "With the support of the World Corps military, we will go in and finally take down the Iron Dome force-field that defends the old city of Jerusalem. We will remove their leadership and free their people from the tyranny of the religion that controls their lives."

"I don't believe I understand. It has never been the policy of the World Corps to conquer, only invite. Every nation that has joined us has done so willingly," the woman representative of Iceland frankly stated.

"I understand the reluctance. But one of the vital goals of the Corps is to bring about a new age of enlightenment. No more dependence on foolish, imaginary ideas—only real science. That city happens to be a pitiful reminder of the backward world we came from. While it stands, we will not have the utopia that we deserve."

"This isn't enough, Madam Administrator," the Head Judge stated. "By the laws of the Corps, the only way a nation can be forcibly added to us is if the citizens are calling out for help against their leadership. Other than that, our hands are tied by the very laws we wrote."

Jessie sighed in irritation; this gathering was always obstinate. "Can't you hear them? They are calling to us every day. We just ignore their pleas for help."

"I am afraid you're hearing what you want to hear and not the truth." The deep, older voice of Jessie's arch annoyance in this courtroom approached.

She watched a man dressed in proper Jewish attire come out from another hallway toward the center of the room. He had a long, white beard and a pair of thin glasses on his nose. He bore a special sash that displayed his place of origin, Jerusalem, and the Messianic symbol of the fish and menorah combined with the Star of David in the middle. He was the single ambassador to the World Corps, since there was only one nation who was not a member.

His duty had been to represent Jerusalem, and he had done this magnificently for nearly twenty years.

Jessie smiled politically at her enemy. "Ambassador Elijah, I did not think you had been called back to Rome so soon."

The wise, old man, who had absolutely no fear of her, strolled right up to the platform. He spoke primarily to her. "Your Planetary Science Commission has declared God dead. You have stepped up the destruction of religious property and the lives of those involved with the remnant of God's followers, and you make a special trip back to Earth to speak with the Corps. Nothing short of an act of God would've kept me from being right here."

Jessie addressed the head judge. "Your Honor, would you please ask the ambassador to take his seat until I'm through."

Elijah spoke before the head judge could say anything. "By the laws of the Corps, when anyone is speaking accusations about a non-Corps nation, then the representation of the accused may speak in response. Administrator Jessie of the Corps has not only claimed that the people of Jerusalem are crying for help but has suggested a military attack. I would say my place is right here to speak for my people."

Even the head judge was grinding his teeth. "Rules are rules. Madam Jessie, you must address his concerns until such a time as this bench deems the arguments finished."

"Thank you." Elijah bowed his head to the judge.

Jessie was fuming but maintained a powerful posture. She addressed her adversary. "Are not the people of your city calling out to the Corps for help?"

"What would make you think that? We have peace; we have freedom; we want for nothing."

"You have enforced control under foolish religious rules dictated by imaginary beings to nomadic herders five thousand years ago. Surely, no one can be satisfied with such an oppressive system."

Elijah strolled around the platform. "You keep your people at an arm's length at all times. They are born according to your rules and live according to your rules. How is that any different?"

Now she thought she had him trapped. "Then, if you believe this to be the way of things, why fight us? Why resist joining? If you like rules to live by, ours are working perfectly."

He stopped and gave her a sideways glance. "Perfectly? The crime rate is so bad that martial law is declared on a daily basis in one state or another. Rape is a custom so common that some of the outlying districts of your states have stopped punishing the rapists unless the act results in death, and only if that death was deemed harmful to society. Drug use is so out of control that your morgues cannot keep up with the demand."

"Crime has always been around," Jessie stated. "And besides, with the sterilization protocols, rape really isn't an issue, other than a minor inconvenience."

"That is, unless you are murdered during the act," Elijah interrupted her rebuttal.

She snarled at him, "Yes, of course. But we have taken great steps to help alleviate the situation. We breed special people who are out there to help satisfy the itch that causes the problem to begin with; and when both are willing, then nothing is wrong. So, eventually, we will eliminate this crime altogether."

"Oh, yes, state-funded prostitution is a wonderful solution to the problem." Elijah's response dripped in sarcasm.

Jessie turned the table on him. "At least, we have the sterilization protocols to solve the ultimate issue with rape. In Jerusalem, when an unwanted baby is born, you are forced to take care of yet another hungry mouth. Not only that, its genes are questionable, and that baby will likely grow up to be the criminal of tomorrow. Our breeders are specially selected to avoid such unevolved humans being thrust into the gene pool."

Elijah erupted in argument. "At least, our babies are allowed to grow up. The forced abortions are appalling, especially the post-terms."

She got closer to him. "Mistakes must be corrected if humanity is to progress."

"You call this crime-infested, murder-centered, godless wasteland progress?" He was practically nose to nose with her now.

"You filthy . . . " A tirade of racial slurs was about to come pouring out of Jessie's mouth, but the head judge had heard enough.

"Order! Get back to a proper discussion, or I will sit both of you down."

Elijah stepped back from Jessie and gathered his thoughts. He looked around the room to address the rest of the representatives and other administrators. "Aside from the lies that the anti-religion committee has been spreading, the people inside the dome over Jerusalem are not calling for help or begging to be released. One important fact has been utterly ignored—anyone can leave if they wish. We hold no one against their will. We force no one to do anything unless it violates God's absolutes. And freedom of choice is actually a gift of God. We are allowed to choose Him or not. It is our will, our love, our faith that we choose to follow the one true God of the universe. No one is forced."

Jessie asked, "Then can we send in teams to investigate your claims? Can we come in and establish a school, so that we can give your people the options you claim they are free to choose?"

Elijah answered, "We have offered to allow a single house to be established as an embassy for the World Corps, with one appointed ambassador and his staff. But you continually turn that down."

"That isn't an answer, Ambassador," said Jessie. "If you're as open-minded as you claim, let us bring a school in."

Elijah addressed the gathered people again, to make his point clear. "We aren't as backward or foolish as your propaganda purports. We watched as you developed this World Corps. It wasn't as easy a transition as you teach your students about. Nations resisted the notion at first, but you slowly built your base up through these so-called schools. Instead of sending in ambassadors or other representation to make a connection, you convince nation after nation to establish a few schools within their lands. These schools would bring a full and free education to the children. The schools were amazing, filled with every new piece of technology, teachers that were highly trained, and buildings that were years ahead of most schools on the planet. There was just one catch: the schools were houses to keep the children. They weren't allowed to go home."

Jessie knew where he was going; she knew exactly what happened back then. "The nations of the Earth were suffering overpopulation and economic issues. Housing, feeding, and educating the children alleviated a lot of problems."

"In all these years, we have never actually seen proof of over-population, the single loudest battle cry of those enforcing this international school system. But slowly, nations bought the notion and allowed the schools in. Soon, their children no longer knew of mom or dad. They only knew of the leadership they were to follow. A generation down the line, the perfectly brainwashed children graduate and then cannot seem to understand why they aren't falling in line with the idea of the Corps. Education was replaced with regurgitated propaganda; loyalty replaced faith; and the birth of this glorious Corps is the result of these schools. No, Madam Administrator, we won't allow you to take our children and turn them into tools of our destruction. They are in God's hands, not yours."

Jessie addressed the council as a whole now, feeling that she had a perfect opportunity with the speech he just made. "You see, ladies and gentlemen, he admits to the fact that the children of Israel do not receive education, but religion. They are held back from understanding the way the universe works to favor their misplaced faith in imaginary beings. We eliminated religion a century ago . . . "

"And what progress has been made?" Elijah interrupted her, a talent of his.

Jessie let out a hard sigh, controlling the urge to punch him right in the big nose. "As I was saying . . . "

"No, answer my question. Your actual job is overseeing the education system of this glorious Corps. What progress has been made in the past century?"

"I'm sure I don't understand what you are talking about."

He smiled and strolled around her. "Look back and examine what you have done for the past one hundred years. Up until the forced removal of religion and establishment of the Science Commission as the state religion, the progress in all the sciences was moving along. Space flight, advanced robotics, advanced computer programming, and even laser sensor systems. The medical field alone was running along with great speed. Then this body focused all their attention on destroying religion; and for one hundred years, all you have done is search for solid ways to discredit the idea of a Creator. You have wasted time, effort, and, frankly, people in a war against something you proclaim isn't even real. Why would anyone trust an education from a system that purposefully stalls itself to fight a battle against something you don't even believe in?"

"We have improved robotics, advanced the computer systems, built better ships . . ."

He interrupted her again. "All minor improvements on existing products. True scientific advancement is dead. Look at the terraforming programs. They were on the verge of massive breakthroughs—breakthroughs only made possible by new discoveries and advancement. Now terraforming is just a history lesson. After the *Terra 5* went missing, you shut it all down for no logical reason. But then again, the way you continually rewrite history means that your students probably don't even know this."

Jessie was silent for a while, considering how to answer him. The room was focused on him; and in the time it took her to ponder her response, she was sure to get all the attention back on her, which was her goal. She even checked a message on her watch, a message that made her smile. Finally, she broke the tension. "Breakthroughs? I'll answer your challenge. The very breakthrough that we've been seeking has come. Our scientists have discovered alien life that is in the early stages of evolution. Primitives of another world that not only prove the facts of evolution but preclude the ludicrous notions of your all-powerful Deity. A Deity Who supposedly only created humans." She was pleased with the expressions on the faces of most of the people in the room. Satisfaction and confirmation of their own version of faith by what she just said. This statement would certainly put him in his place and crush his little dreams.

Elijah stopped and shook his head. "I am fascinated by your so-called discovery, Madam Administrator, but I need proof."

The representative from the state of England stood up from his seat and yelled out, "Proof? Don't you watch the news, or does your stupid God keep you from watching broadcasts? How ignorant can you be?" More than one person applauded this juvenile outburst.

The head judge banged his gavel again. "Order!"

Elijah smiled. "How many times in history have the anti-religious sciences been proven liars in attempts to disprove or discredit God? No one will deny that the respected scientists have rewritten numbers, altered pictures, and ultimately lied. I, for one, will not forget that the early followers of Darwinism fabricated many things to 'prove' their science. What about the Haeckel diagrams that were discredited almost instantly but continually taught for over a hundred years."

Jessie asked, "So, what are you saying? That the recordings and broadcasts aren't true? That we fabricated all this?"

Elijah nodded. "I am not going to abandon the notion."

The room burst out in more people muttering about him or asking their neighbor a question about this man's sanity. Jessie stopped them before the head judge had the chance. She held up her hands. "If it is proof you want, then I will be more than happy to oblige. Bring her in!" she called to someone in the hall.

Two men carefully wheeled in a large, rectangular box. It was covered in a thick cloth and was about twice the height of anyone in the room. Every few moments, a thumping sound came from inside the box.

"What is this?" the head judge asked, not happy that she didn't clear this with him yet.

Jessie walked over to the box and took hold of one of the corners of the cloth. "My friend here wishes proof. Then it is proof he shall have. I give you . . . the primitive." She yanked hard, and the cloth fell free from the box.

Inside was the same woman from the broadcast. She was still crazed and scared but appeared groggy, probably from the tranquilizers they pumped into her for the long trip. She looked around at all the people staring at her, then saw the woman beside the cage. For some reason, she went into a rage and screamed like a wild cat. She flailed against the side of the clear, plastic container, digging deep gouges into its surface. It seemed that most of her anger was directed toward Jessie, but most were too startled to notice this.

"Down!" Jessie pressed a button on a small control panel, and the floor flashed as a jolt of electricity zapped the poor woman. She yelped and jumped to get away from what had just hurt her. For a few moments, she tried to crawl up the slick plastic wall to get away from the biting ground but realized that was hopeless.

Jessie smiled victoriously at Elijah. "There's your proof."

The representatives and administrators started asking all sorts of questions, eager to learn more about this creature.

The woman inside the box was scared out of her mind. Her eyes darted back and forth in fear of all the loud, strange-looking creatures. Every so often, she would let out a hiss to show her disdain, and she continually shook and appeared agitated.

Elijah sat down and absorbed what he was looking at. He truly had convinced himself that this couldn't be true, that the PSC was at it again in fabricating information to support their claims and theories. Yet standing before him was living proof of what they claimed. Outside of being the ambassador, he was a highly trained surgeon with many years of medical history behind him. He knew what he was looking at was more real than just a make-up job on a human. He would dearly love to examine her to see for himself the truth beneath the fur. But he realized that the World Corps would never release her to the custody of Jerusalem.

Jessie stood before Elijah. "So, are you going to go and talk to your God anymore? If you do, ask Him if He misplaced some of His creation."

Elijah looked up at the woman in the box. The people now surrounding her were all taking pictures and gawking like this was some zoo exhibit. He closed his eyes and shook his head. "Jessie, I know there is something you are not telling us. Something about this just doesn't feel right."

"The only thing that isn't right around here is your faith, your blind stupidity leading you to ignore science. You have invisible gods and ancient books. I have a physical, living, breathing reality standing right there. Open your book; find me an answer; and I might listen."

"I will open my Bible, and I will find you an answer. It just . . . might take some time." His whole demeanor had crumbled. His strength was gone, and his brashness turned to sorrow. Unlike Anna, he hadn't abandoned his faith just yet, but he was starting to question it.

"Good." Jessie looked back at the terrified woman and all the people. A man tapped the glass, and the cat woman flew into a rage, roaring like a lion and attacking the glass with her claws. The gathered people all took a sudden step back, even though they were not in harm's way. Jessie scoffed and marched right back over and hit the same switch, only this time, she triggered it three times. The first one stopped the outburst. The second put the female on her knees. The third just made her scream. None of these responses seemed to move Jessie in the least.

Elijah slowly stood up and walked toward the case. The gathered crowd became hushed at the sight of these two meeting. Elijah paused for a moment and looked at the creature inside and then walked on. For a brief moment, their eyes met, and he saw something that broke his heart. Tears rolled down her eyes and soaked her fur. Somehow, he knew that these weren't just the tears of physical pain, but a deeper emotion. There was a real soul in that creature, the breath of life. But who breathed it into her?

CHAPTER SIX

Z FOUGHT AGAINST THE FOLIAGE as he ascended a steep incline. His mapping system had determined this was the best path to get back to where Anna fell. It didn't seem like a real path, but he was making it. It worried him that it had already been a full cycle of a day here. That wasn't a full day on Earth, but still too long for her to be injured and alone.

"She's a resilient and bold explorer. She can handle herself." He tried to raise his own confidence, but it wasn't helping.

He stepped on a mass of vines and nearly put his foot into a hole. Unfortunately, as he jerked back out of the hole, he slid and fell partly down this ridge. He landed on his butt and said something that hadn't been in common lingo for a long time, and for good reason. Dusting his rear off, he got back to his feet.

Taking a moment away from his onward march, he paused to look out from where he had stopped. He was climbing the side of a set of hills that surrounded a forested valley. It was beautiful, with all sorts of flowers blooming. He could hear the birds singing in the trees and the river rushing over stones. If this place wasn't infested with dangerous creatures, it truly would be the most idyllic destination.

Then his mechanical ears picked up something rather odd. A very familiar sound of engines turning on. Looking off in the distance, he saw his ship lifting up from the ground.

"Good grief, what's going on?" He pressed a switch on his wrist communicator. "Explorer computer, respond."

"Computer online," it announced.

"Deactivate autopilot!"

"Autopilot has not been enabled."

Z was stunned. "Who is piloting the ship?"

"*Explorer 313* is currently under the control of two pilots from a docking ship in orbit. Estimated time of arrival is ten minutes."

"I don't care when you are going to arrive. Stop the ascent; recall the ship."

"Communication has been terminated with the mothership. Access to this ship's systems has been denied. Have a nice day." The system shut him off.

"Have a nice . . . why, you pile of rusty bolts!" He was furious. His ship was leaving them behind. There must be some kind of malfunction. Surely, the *Sanger* wasn't retrieving the ship, while he and Anna are still here on the planet's surface.

Grumbling to himself in more of those old words that were not fit for social gatherings, Z continued on his way. He would send for a ship once he found Anna, and then he would have a nice, long discussion with that ship's motherboard.

⋆   ⋆   ⋆

Dr. Skye sat back and beamed in pride as he watched the broadcast.

"This was the scene earlier today at the World Corps headquarters. One of the feline beings from New Eden was put on display by Administrator Jessie." The news image focused on the crowd gathered around the caged woman. "Just before the display was revealed, a heated debate on the floor between Administrator Jessie and the ambassador from Jerusalem was underway. Sources say the ambassador was demonstrating the lack of scientific understanding that seems customary for the people under the dome. But he was silenced, and the debate was stopped as soon as the feline primitive was revealed." The view returned to the newsroom. "The office of the ambassador was contacted for comments and questions, but their response has remained 'no comment' for the time being. We turn to the chief political analyst . . . "

The sound muted on its own as a small button appeared on the bottom of his screen. Richard knew exactly who was calling and tapped the button. Instantly, Jessie's happy face filled his screen.

"Have you heard?" she asked immediately.

"I was just watching the news. You did a perfect job. I don't think you have executed a plan with such efficiency in all the years you have worked in the anti-religion corps."

"I know. But it has only just started. If we are to keep this momentum going, we need more. I was thinking that we might bring more of them to earth, show them all over the place. Turn this into a circus. Keep 'em doped and watch them dance for us. People will come in droves to see the cats, and they will beg for more. All notions of religion will dry up and blow away as we put on the perfect show. It will be brilliant, wonderful, absolutely devastating." She was nearly foaming at the mouth.

"That is an idea—a good idea—but it will take time. Besides, we need to keep other problems from arising."

"What sort of problems?"

Dr. Skye held up a tablet. "I have over fifteen thousand messages this morning from all sorts of groups asking to visit New Eden. I have tourism companies, schools, individuals, some protesters, and at least three hundred politicians."

"You know we can't allow that." Jessie's frothy excitement toned down.

"I know. I believe I have the answer. In one breaking story, we will stem this tide before it arrives *and* keep this story fresh in the daily news." He stopped and smiled at the brilliance of this.

Jessie grinned. "Oh, don't keep me waiting, you naughty boy."

Dr. Skye held up the blood-stained cloth that had been Anna's top. "Your plan worked. Our little geologist met her demise down on the planet."

"Oh, that's wonderful. But we need to be certain that it was an attack and not some accident."

He flopped the dirty rags on his desk. "A body wasn't recovered. Even if she just injured herself, one of our friends got to her, I'm sure."

The politician side of Jessie came out. "They will ask for proof. There are still some idiots around here that want to try and shut us up, so they can keep harping on about their God or goddess or whatever. They could even claim that we had her murdered or are faking the evidence. That Jewish pig spent most of his time saying that this whole discovery is fake. If I didn't have that female . . . "

Dr. Skye leaned over and looked closely at his screen. "You are forgetting one thing. The Planetary Science Commission has worked for decades to get control. What we say is true. We don't have to prove ourselves anymore. We cornered the market in truth. When anyone challenges an official PSC statement, the media opens polls about that person's sanity, not about their validity. Trust me, if I say it, then it becomes truth. Besides, if they want to run tests, they can. We didn't shoot her ourselves; we merely let nature take its course."

"You are a powerful man, Richard. Sometimes, you amaze me."

He laughed. "It's a gift. Now, get your people ready. The PSC will have terrible news to announce soon, and I'm sure you will have a few questions to answer."

"I'm very ready. After all this, it won't take much to convince the Corps to finally launch the attack and crack that annoying dome." Another sound beeped in her office. "Oh, I have a meeting with the head of the breeding program. Gotta go. Good luck with your announcement. And remember, lots of tears, lots of remorse. Show a little sorrow, and let them eat it up." With that, her screen darkened, and the news returned to his monitor. By now, they were talking about the weather over Australia. He flicked it completely off and sat back, enjoying his reflection. He was a really handsome man.

*   *   *

J'kla sat cross-legged on the ground near the edge of the cliff. Behind him lay Anna, sleeping. He had the Bible in his lap as he carefully looked at the letters to see how quickly he could remember them. He was determined to learn how to talk to her as soon as possible.

Letting out a big, feline yawn, he blinked with weariness in his eyes. He looked up at the stars to relax for a bit. He always enjoyed watching the stars; they were beautiful and serene. But the moment he looked up, he was reminded of who this person behind him really was. While the stars had not changed their places in all the history of his people, now some moved all over the place. One star was going from left to right, another right to left. A few moved, and then stopped, and then moved again. There was a new, large star that moved oddly, yet more slowly than the others. A sick worry rumbled in his belly as he watched the dance of this strange star. What could it mean? Why were they affecting his people so much? Would he go insane as well?

His attention was grabbed at a particularly harsh snore from Anna. Looking back at her, a half-smile came to his face. She seemed like such a gentle person.

"They can't all be evil beings who live on these strange stars. Anna is a nice person," he confirmed to himself.

Looking back down at the book in his lap, he tried to start working again but kept nodding off. Finally admitting defeat, he set the book down and stretched out his arms. He needed sleep, but first he would go through his routine. First, he looked around to see if anything dangerous was close. Then he closed his eyes, and his ears stood up a little taller as he used them to listen for any danger. If any of his own kind who were driven mad by the stars were near, he wouldn't sleep. But he heard no screams. There weren't even any heavy footsteps.

With a feeling of security, he curled up and allowed himself to sleep.

✶   ✶   ✶

Anna laughed and wrote out the word in the dirt: "G-O-D."

J'kla cocked his head, looking at the letters. They were some of the few he had learned, and it was a word on the first page of that book he was interested in. He sounded it out as best he could: "JEE-OH-DEE."

She snickered. "No, no."

"No?" He frowned. That was a word he knew.

"You don't say the G like . . . jee. It sounds like 'guh,' a short 'guh'."

He tried, "GUH!"

"No, shorter G'uh"

J'kla wrapped his lips around that. "Guh . . . g'uh." Finally, it was sounding right.

"Yes!" This really excited her.

Her happiness was infectious to him, and he smiled brightly. "Yes, yes!" Then he tried again, "G'ah OH DEE."

Anna laughed again, "This is going to take time. I don't know how I'm going to explain that you are learning Bible verses when you speak to the news people for the first time. I hope they're more interested in your ability to speak rather than what you are saying."

"*Chi?*" he asked.

She had learned from him that this word was the general question meaning "what," but it could also be used for any basic inquisitive moment.

"Nothing. Now . . . oh, I'm getting a little tired. This is taking a lot out of me. I wish I had some regular instructions to use, or at least Z. He could probably teach you a lot better than me." She realized she shouldn't have thought about Z; it only made her sad.

J'kla noticed her change in emotion. "Chi rhala?"

She forced a smile. "I'm okay. Just thinking about someone who is probably dead . . . well, not dead, just in pieces." She saw that curious look on his face, completely oblivious to what she was saying. Patting his hand, she said, "Don't worry. I'm okay."

Even though she had some fruit, she really hadn't eaten much, and she was still recovering from her ordeal. "You." He pointed at her and then down, meaning she was to wait on him for something.

"I'm not going anywhere," she said, while sitting back and relaxing a bit more to let him know what she meant.

"Good," he said with a big feline smile and then hurried off into the foliage again.

✳   ✳   ✳

Not too far from her, Z was climbing the steep hill. He was using the sturdy roots and vines to assist his ascent, but it was still a hard climb. His readings didn't show a quicker way. "I sure hope you're all right. This would be tragic if I find you dead," he muttered to himself. Then he shook his head. "No, I'm not going to think that way." He yanked on another root and then swung his arm up and grabbed a long vine.

After a little while, he pulled out his tablet and checked the map he had created for this. It was a composite of the information he had gathered on their first trip and his own data gathered from this second venture. The computer compiled an approximate map with some liberties taken about unknown areas. To his great surprise and happiness, he should be nearing the natural landing where Anna had stopped falling.

"Well, this is it." He held up the tablet and changed it to sensor mode. He checked the temperature readings and created a heat map. To his great relief, he detected one person sitting on the ground exactly where she had fallen. The heat signature matched a human's, and the height was just right. It had to be her. And since there was heat, she was still alive.

Tucking his tablet away, he continued the ascent that would bring him to her.

*   *   *

J'kla prowled through the thick foliage covering this part of the forest. He had retrieved what he wanted and was on his way back to his new friend. Even if these strange, furless creatures were taking his people away and doing strange things to them, this one was nice. She wasn't mean. In fact, he found her kind of cute.

After a brief excursion through the trees, he stopped, and his ears perked up. He heard someone else coming his direction. He was worried it was one of his own, driven mad by the star people who had been stealing them. When he made his way through the forest, he moved just like everyone else of his kind, with the natural stealth they were accustomed to. But the mad ones made a lot of noise. If one of those crazed people came upon her, they would kill her and try to kill him. He would not allow this.

Getting as low as he could in the foliage, he prepared his very best attack-pounce posture. He was trained by the best of his village and could handle a fight with ease, even against the insane ones.

Anna looked down at the open Bible and considered the first page that she had been pulling words from to show J'kla. It seemed odd to think about this first passage. It talked about Creation and the way God formed the heavens and the earth and everything on it. It said nothing about creatures on other planets.

When she first heard the news of these things, she tried to convince herself that this could be read two ways. It didn't say God created any people elsewhere, but it didn't say He didn't either. It was a gray area open for interpretation. But she couldn't settle her faith on the notion of ambiguity in the Scriptures. It was either right, or it was wrong. God—the God she once believed in—didn't leave anything out that was important. And this was pretty important.

Closing the book, she gazed out over the rather lovely view across the valley. The sun was already lowering toward the horizon, and very soon, it would be evening.

The way J'kla was so naïve and childlike was enviable. She longed for that attitude, that innocence. He didn't know that his very existence was challenging her beliefs. It wasn't his fault that everything she believed had been torn apart the very moment she first set eyes on one of his kind. He had no idea that she enjoyed watching him from behind and seeing those well-toned muscles.

"Oh, good heavens, where did that come from? No, he's cute and has a nice body, but we aren't even the same species." She was talking to herself.

It wasn't that she was uncontrollably attracted to him. He did have a nice body and was being very kind to her, which she told herself made him more attractive. She liked looking, and that was it. But she confirmed in her own mind that it would be wiser to avoid staring at his body; in any case, it might make him uncomfortable. Besides, if Z ever found out, she wouldn't hear the end of the jokes. He would tease her mercilessly. That is, if Z was still operating and not gone.

Just then, there was a rustling in the bushes. This time, it was on the other side from where J'kla normally left. Besides the direction, J'kla was a much more silent mover in this area. She picked up her stone again and prepared to defend herself.

At that moment, Z stepped through the brush and smiled at the sight of her. He was pulling off small leaves and just about to say something when a furry blur blasted by and headbutted the robot right in the chest. J'kla landed a pretty good attack on Z, but miscalculated the strength of a man mostly made of metal. Z didn't budge. J'kla flew backward and landed on the ground, splayed out and groaning.

"J'KLA!" Anna called out to her unfortunate hero.

Z had dropped the bag and already pulled out his stun gun from his compartment. He went to shoot the attacker, sure that he arrived just in time to save her.

"NO! Don't shoot J'kla!" Anna cried.

Z, still holding his weapon out, asked, "Jclaw? You know this cat?"

Anna tried to move, but it still hurt too badly. "Yes. He's been taking care of me. He's not like the others."

Z watched carefully as J'kla slowly came around. "He's wearing clothes? And . . . what is that you have on?" He saw the leather vest she still wore around her shoulders.

"Yes, he wears clothes, and this is his vest. I was cold, and he let me wear it. Now, put your gun away."

"I . . . I'm confused." Z finally put his gun back into the slot.

Anna sighed and smiled as she saw what was in J'kla's hand. "Awe, he was bringing me another fruit." She pointed at the injured cat. "Help him up. See if he's okay."

Z leaned over and took J'kla's shoulder. "Uh, are you okay?"

J'kla came around and looked up at the strange face of the robot. His eyes widened, and he hissed hard. Then he scrambled to his feet and ran to the side of Anna. J'kla protectively knelt beside her, his fangs and claws both at the ready.

"J'kla, J'kla." Anna took his arm. "Please stop."

J'kla was too focused on protecting her to listen.

She put her hand on his chest and pushed him back. "Stop!"

Finally, he relaxed a little but did not take his eyes off of the strange man.

"Look, I don't think . . . " Z started to say something but was stopped by Anna holding up her hand to him.

She spoke to J'kla, "J'kla, he's good."

J'kla frowned and said, "Good?"

"Yes, good. He's friend."

J'kla searched his thoughts for a moment, trying to recall that word. He could say it, but did not remember what it meant. "Fend?"

"No . . . friend." She corrected him and then directed his face to look at hers. She pointed at her and then him. "Friend."

"Friend?" He thought about that and then recalled its meaning. "Friend, friend."

She then pointed at herself and then to Z. "Friend."

J'kla pointed at Z with a lot of disbelief. "Friend?"

"Yes. Friend. Good friend." She hated sounding like Tarzan, but it was all she could do when trying to converse with J'kla.

J'kla looked back at Z with an intense stare. As cautiously as any cat, he slunk closer to Z and then slowly stood up to look at the man. J'kla was chest-high to the tall robot, but that didn't diminish his fierce attitude. For a moment, he sniffed Z's chest and then stared intently at the glowing connection socket of his arm. The ferocious protector became the curious cat pretty quickly.

Z was flabbergasted. He watched the feline man sniff him all over. "He . . . he can talk?"

Anna was amused by how personal J'kla was getting with his sniffing. His curiosity was insatiable, which is probably why he was such a quick learner. "Not much, but he's picking up a few words. If I were a better instructor, he probably would have a lot more to say by now."

Z realized his inspection was over, and the cat was searching for the fruit he dropped. Z grabbed the bag he carried and came over to Anna. "Are you injured? How bad did you fall? Did he hurt you?" He held out his newly-replaced arm and started scanning her.

Anna was relieved to see that Z had attached his medical arm. "I think I broke something in my lower back; it hurts like the dickens. But other than that, I've been doing okay. J'kla has been helping. He has been very gentle with me."

Z looked at the leaves attached to her skin. "What is this? Some of his medicine?" He peeled off the leaf, only to realize it was attached by some goo.

Anna winced at the ripping feeling of the partially dried sticky juices being pulled across her skin. "Yeah, he put them on where I was cut and scratched. It felt pretty good."

"I can tell you that he did a fine job. This substance is full of natural anti-bodies and some type of menthol. My scans don't show any of the expected infections from exposure for this long. I'm very impressed." Suddenly, Z's hand was slapped away from Anna. J'kla was scowling at Z as he slowly reapplied the leaf to her skin and patted it back down.

Anna was holding in the laughter, but not well. "Don't mind him. He's proud of his work."

Z stepped around her so that he would be on the other side from this pushy cat. "Okay. About your back. My scans don't show any broken bones; you fared better than I expected."

"But it hurts to move. I can barely sit up."

Z held up his hand and let the mechanisms inside do the work he required. "You didn't break anything, but you bruised your tailbone, strained some muscles; and there is swelling around your sciatic nerve, which is probably what's hurting the worst right now. I'll give you a shot of a steroid to reduce the swelling and then a strong dose of pain medicine that'll help. By tomorrow, you won't know you hurt anything." As he talked, he unscrewed his forefinger on his hand to reveal the syringe that was prepared with the proper medications.

J'kla set the fruit right on Anna's lap and immediately crawled right over her to get a close look at the hand that was just disfigured. The cat was curious, and at the same time protecting her from being unscrewed in the same manner by this odd man. J'kla's eyes were about an inch away from Z's hand, and his nose sniffed quickly.

Z pushed on J'kla to get him off of her. "It's okay. I NO HURT." Now he was talking like Tarzan.

Anna snickered at that. "Talking like an idiot doesn't translate."

Z went to give her the injection into her hip, and suddenly, there was J'kla's hand again pushing Z's arm away, still protecting her. Z huffed at this predicament. "Anna, could you tell your boyfriend that I'm not going to hurt you."

"J'kla . . ." She tried to get his attention, but the missing finger was still all he could stare at while he was leaning over her. She tried again. "J'kla!" This time she grabbed his tail and pulled him back.

He growled at that but did sit back down where he had been a moment ago. He was frowning at both of them.

Anna put a gentle hand on his chest and then smiled. "Okay."

He shook his head. "Okay." Which was his way of saying not okay.

She smiled again and said, "Okay good."

J'kla nodded. "Okay." The tone was that of relenting.

"Z, give me the shot."

Z was annoyed that he had to wait on this silly exchange before he could help her, but he finally got to give her the medication to make her better. He carefully pulled down on the ripped clothing and got to her hip to press the hypospray into her skin. Anna felt it go in. It hurt, but she just smiled and let J'kla hold her hand while she leaned over in the awkward position.

"Okay, done," Z said as he reattached his finger.

"Okay!" J'kla happily replied.

Z laughed. "He doesn't know many words, but he likes to say them."

Anna sat back into her normal position and sighed with a big smile. "I'm glad to see you. I was worried something happened to you."

Z stood back up and picked up the bag. "Funny, I was worried something happened to you. I was scared to death that one of these cat people had found you . . . " He looked at J'kla. "Well . . . one of the dangerous ones, at least. I was surprised to find that my sensors showed no other life forms his size anywhere. He is the only cat within my sensor range, which is considerable."

"Where are they?" Anna looked around.

"You'll have to ask him. I'm glad they aren't around. They're dangerous."

"They aren't what we think—at least, he isn't. And I bet there are more of them out there. Just imagine what this will mean to the PSC!"

Z rifled through the bag. "I don't know. He might just be more evolved than the others. Sort of the next phase or something. The others we've seen are nowhere near his sophistication."

Anna looked over at J'kla, who was cocking his head as he continued to examine Z from a distance, not sure about this odd-smelling person. "I don't know about that. By all logic, evolution doesn't work one person at a time. It's supposedly about whole species changing over time. If he's like this, then there have to be more."

"What? Don't tell me you want to go and find them?" Z muttered as he found what he was looking for. He pulled out one of the nutrition bars and brought it over to her.

Anna took the bar and started unwrapping it. This caught J'kla's attention immediately. "I just want to bring him back to the ship and let them see him for themselves. They'll look for the others. Heck, with how well he has learned, they might even be able to talk to him and get to know him. They aren't the animals we believed." She was about to take a bite when she saw that deep curiosity in J'kla's face. He was staring at the nutrition bar intensely. She held it out. "Wanna see it?"

He took the bar from her and sniffed it. *"Chi?"*

Anna put her fingers to her mouth like she was eating and then said, "Food."

"Foooood," he slowly stated, not sure exactly what that meant.

She tried again by pretending to eat. "Food. Yum."

He smiled as he started to get it. "Foood." He took a bite. Then his whole face scrunched up, and he spit it out.

"Ugh!" Which apparently was a universal response to bad taste. He held it up and curiously said, "Food?"

"Yes. It takes some getting used to, but there's a lot of good stuff in that little bar." She knew he didn't understand, but talking to him like this would help him understand how to speak.

He shook his head and picked up the fruit again and held it out to her. "Food."

She took the fruit and then got the bar from his hand as well. "I'll take both. Thanks."

He furrowed his brow and muttered, *"Glotha?"* his word for "wood," which he assumed that bar was made of.

Z scanned the fruit with his medical hand. "What is that?"

Anna took a big bite from the bar and then started to peel the fruit. "It's a banana-like thing they have here. It's pretty good."

He processed the readings in his mind and then shrugged. "It reads much like any fruit from Earth; no toxins detected. We should bring one back to the ship to let them take a look at it. I'm sure they would love to see this. You're lucky it didn't kill you when you first ate it. You don't have a built-in sensor system."

"I'm an explorer; taking risks is part of the game."

"You're a geologist, not a space jumper," Z sarcastically replied. "Taking risks is stupid."

"Fine, but this risk worked out." She looked at the bag, which J'kla was secretly looking into behind Z's back. "Did you happen to bring me something to wear? I like this vest and all, but as soon as I stand up, these pants are going to come off; and I don't think I want to ask J'kla for his pants next."

"Oh, yeah, I did bring . . . hey, get out of there." Z found the cat pawing through the stuff he packed in the bag.

J'kla was holding up a small power generator and flashlight. He accidentally hit the switch and beamed a bright light into his eyes. He dropped the device right back into the bag as he swung his hands in front of his face to get the light out. *"Kneejah!"* he called out as he attempted to pull the star from his eyes. After a few blinks, the spots were gone.

Z rolled his eyes and pulled out the fresh jumpsuit he had packed for Anna. "Serves you right. Don't put your hands where they don't belong."

"Hey, be nice. He's just a curious person. I guess the feline in him really comes out with that curiosity." She held out her hand for the jumpsuit that Z was handing over.

Z kept his eyes on J'kla. "Let's just hope some of the other feline tendencies don't come out. They do like their meat."

Anna's attempt at standing was unsuccessful. She groaned in pain and tried again as she spoke with Z. "Look, he's been very nice. I don't think he's going to get hungry and decide I look tasty."

"Sure. Whatever you say. As for me, I'll keep my stunner charged and ready, just in case he or one of his friends gets too hungry for their own good." He helped her stand up.

Finally on her feet for the first time since the fall, she had to hold onto the pants to keep them from falling off. "At least, we know they won't find any meat on you."

J'kla excitedly came over to her and smiled. He was happy that she was standing. "Good," he said as it was the only word that seemed right that he knew.

"Here, you can have this back." She took the vest off and held it out for him.

J'kla took the vest, but he was getting a pretty good look at her chest with only the bra on. Though he did not show any excitement in his face for what he was looking at, Anna noticed that his tail was a little happier than usual. He was male all right. "I'm going to change now," she said to him, but he didn't get it.

She turned around and slowly pulled the pants down. J'kla got the message then and quickly turned around as well.

"Hey, if you want . . ." Z was about to offer for her to use one of the quick body cleaning cloths, when J'kla grabbed him and made him turn around. Z looked at the cat, and J'kla was frowning and shaking his head. "Look, I'm a robot. It doesn't matter to me if she takes her clothes off." He turned again to give the wet cloth to Anna, but J'kla stopped him and then pointed at his own eyes and then pointed away from where Anna was changing. Z admitted defeat and waited alongside the cat. "I'll say this for your discovery: he's modest."

Anna pulled on the jumpsuit. "Courtesy is a dead art on Earth. It's kind of nice to see it here."

With a final zipping sound, she was done. "Okay, you can turn around."

"Okay," J'kla said and then turned back around. He smiled and nodded at her. "Good." He liked that she looked more comfortable now in complete clothing.

"I think I'll take the opportunity to . . . wow that hurt." She tried to step away for a moment, but she was still in a lot of pain. It didn't hurt so much standing still, but moving was a challenge. "Hey, Z, when's that medicine going to start working?"

"It should be working in about half an hour, but you will feel tired sooner than that."

"Will it do any damage if I move too much?"

"Not really. It'll still hurt like heck, but you should be able to move."

She gingerly stepped away as fast as she could. "Good. I'm going to take care of some personal business. Why don't you get out your tablet and find some of that old stuff you like to watch?"

Z asked, "How the heck did you hold it for fourteen hours?"

"I didn't. J'kla helped me up once to go into the bushes over here. I thought I'd pass out, it hurt so much to move, but it was unavoidable. Now . . . I gotta go." She gingerly stepped into the bushes out of sight of them.

Z pulled out the larger tablet in the bag and activated the ancient television programming he watched while he piloted the ship. J'kla was sneaking into the bag again to pry, but Z stopped him by zipping it closed before he could get to it. "Pets not allowed," Z comically stated.

J'kla sneered at him and then walked away. This man was no fun. Worse yet, he might be Anna's mate, and that annoyed J'kla.

After a few moments, Anna carefully walked out of the bushes. "I'm not waiting that long ever again." She tried to sit back down, but it hurt too much on her own. "Ow, please help." With her hand held out, she found J'kla's hand holding hers as she made her way down. He was really a nice guy, so unlike a lot of the men on Earth. Since no one looked for true romance anymore, human men acted a lot more primitive than this man. If anything, she should bring him back, so he could teach people a thing or two about courtesy and compassion.

"Did you get your programs loaded?" she asked with a bit of a sigh of relief now that she was all the way down.

Z nodded. "Sure. I got them. Did you want to watch something?" He had never had her offer to watch any of his programs.

"No, I'm getting sleepy really fast. I was wondering . . . " She yawned really big, which made J'kla yawn and show off all his impressive teeth. "I was wondering if there were any of the ancient children's programs that teach the alphabet and stuff like that."

"Sure, lots."

"Do you have them on there?" She was closing her eyes, the weight of the tiredness pressing down hard.

"Yup. When I loaded the old programming that was in the archives, it put everything on the memory. I've got hours and hours of the public programming from the twentieth and twenty-first centuries."

"Show them to J'kla. Maybe they'll help." She nodded off and then woke back up. "Show them to him. Let him watch." She wasn't sure if she had already said this.

Z kindly picked up the tattered rags of her discarded jumpsuit and rolled them up into a pillow. He tucked it under her head and helped her lay all the way down. "Go to sleep. I'll help your friend out."

CHAPTER SEVEN

ELIJAH HAD THE SAME ROUTINE every time he was outside his embassy, either coming or going. His escort, a security guard from the court, walked so close to him that the two would occasionally bump into the other. This guard was supposedly there for his protection, but Elijah knew the real reason they had a guard stick so close to him. They were afraid Elijah would try and proselytize. Worse, he might even try to stir up members of the Underground to rise up against the state. He had no such intentions as that would be highly counterproductive to his real work in keeping the voice of Jerusalem alive in this court. But the more ungodly a society, the more paranoid they become.

The strange pair crossed the large square and headed for the embassy just outside of the old Vatican City. A group of school children passed them, which caused Elijah to shake his head in sadness. They were indoctrinated at such a young age, they had very little chance to think on their own, believe what they wanted, know that there was more out there than what this system provided. But he couldn't say anything.

Though his mind was troubled, he normally maintained a happy expression and gait. It was the practice of any politician to not betray his true feelings when facing the public. Today, his mood was noticeably gloomier. To get his mind off of what he had just witnessed in the courtroom, he struck up a conversation with today's charge.

"So, you're certainly the silent one. Are you not a talker?"

The guard continued walking with the ambassador. "I really don't have anything to say to the likes of you. I'll do my job, and that's all."

"Oh, I see." Elijah heard the disdain in his voice. The seed of hatred was planted firmly in this man's soul and was blossoming perfectly.

Elijah walked along and remained quiet for a bit as they passed more of the ancient architecture. With a kind smile, he made a second attempt at friendly conversation. "You know, Paul was once chained to a Roman soldier all the time. He never let it dampen his enthusiasm for God or writing. Don't you think it's kind of funny that you're sort of chained to me to keep an eye on me, and here I am . . . "

"Shut up," the guard blurted out.

Elijah had a stunned look on his face; none of the guards had been this brash with him. "Look, I'm not trying to convert you or anything. Just passing the time with some conversation."

"Your whole stupid religion is dead; that thing in the courtroom proves that. I don't see why they even allow you to speak anymore or offer you the right to protection. You people make me sick. You're blind and ignorant, and you act like you're better than us." This guard was certainly letting it all out.

Elijah took a moment to answer that diatribe. A man who studies God's Word knows that a rash answer isn't the best way to defend the faith. He gathered his thoughts and replied as he would to anyone who made such accusations. "You know, it *is* amusing how often I hear someone tell me that we are the ones acting like we are better than others. The truth of the matter is that we know more than anyone how broken we are. That we aren't good, but we are forgiven. I know I'm a sinner, and my God has forgiven me because I admitted how low I am and how great He is. If anyone acts like they are better than others, it is a society that fights to proclaim that they are better than God and can find all the answers on their own. Arrogance, my friend—that is an enemy that must be defeated . . . "

The guard surprised and slightly frightened the old man. "I brought the voice terminator with me, if you don't shut up. You know that talking about your God and your backward religion is forbidden. One more word, and I'll put it on you. Is that clear?"

Elijah closed his mouth and nodded. When he first became the representative for his people, he had to wear that inane device around his neck every time he left the embassy. It muted him, so he couldn't talk; they were that frightened of his words. In his mind, he realized it was "pearls before swine" trying to get through this man's thick head. So, he would oblige and not wear that horrid collar.

With that, they marched on toward the only embassy left. Elijah stepped inside the embassy, and the guards at the door activated the security system.

Inside here, he was safe from any such threats of silencing him. Everyone inside was from Jerusalem. They were not allowed outside the compound, but no one cared. It wasn't a pretty world out there—at least not for a people who knew what sin was.

"Elijah! Elijah!" A woman came rushing to him.

He smiled as he sat down and rested his knees and feet. "Esther, my dear. Why are you yelling at me?"

His secretary and daughter-in-law ran to him with a panicked look on her face. "Is it true? Did they bring one of those . . . things back here?"

"Yes. I saw her myself. She was on display on the floor of the main room."

More people had come in to listen to him. Esther asked, "What does this mean?"

"I don't know. I have to communicate with the prime minister and let him discuss it with everyone back home."

Another of his aides stepped up, her face white and her breathing shallow. "It can't be. This . . . this . . . I just don't know what to think anymore."

Elijah kindly took her hand and addressed everyone. "Look, we serve Yahweh first, and His Word has never failed us. Don't panic, and don't abandon hope. There are answers He will send to us. Have faith. Now, go and prepare dinner, please."

"Yes, at once." The staff slowly left to go about their daily duties. Only Esther stayed behind.

She stepped up to her father-in-law. "Elijah, this is going to be devastating back home."

His congenial attitude melted. "I looked at that primitive woman and thought for a single moment that it could all be true. No God, no Creator, nothing to pin faith and hope on. It really scared me that I could go there. I have dedicated my life to serving Yeshua, and yet I could suffer a moment of broken faith. What will this mean to those back home whose faith isn't strong?"

"Did this really hurt your faith? How did you get it back?" She wanted to know, so she, too, could find the same strength.

"I passed that woman in the cage and looked at her. I wanted to see her for myself, up close. It was only a brief moment, but I looked into her eyes." He paused, deep in thought for a moment. "There was a pain and fear in her eyes. She was aggressive, angry, yelling, scratching—everything you'd expect from a caged wild animal—but in those eyes, I saw a person in pain."

"What are you saying?"

He shook his head, "I don't really know. I felt God showing me something in that moment, something very important, but I don't know what it was exactly." Taking a deep breath, he let it out slowly to gather himself. "All I do know is Administrator Jessie is up to something. There is a great deal more to this than she is letting on. Her plans are what we should be worried about, not this creature. Our duty is first to the defense and continued freedom of Jerusalem."

LATER THAT EVENING

Elijah sipped some tea and calmly waited for the interview to begin. The media wanted to ask him some questions about today's surprise in the courtroom. He knew it was likely to be a fiasco. The media always fought hard to discredit anyone who spoke against this government or its state religion. He liked using that term—state religion. They got so frustrated when he said that. It usually helped stop their long-winded arguments against whatever he said and started them off in the wrong direction. It derailed the conversation when they had it so perfectly planned out. And just what was the state religion of a state that recognized no religion? Atheism, of course. Faith in that system was no different than anything they fought against.

"Sir, the prime minister is on the main channel. He wishes to speak with you."

Elijah looked at the antique clock ticking away on the wall. "I have a few minutes; put him through."

The television screen flipped off and changed to the view of the inside of the prime minister's office in Jerusalem. The older man on the screen smiled and nodded his head. "Shalom, Elijah, my old friend."

"Shalom, Jacob. Have you seen the news?"

Prime Minister Jacob shook his head in sadness. "I have, but I haven't let it out to our media just yet."

"You cannot keep this from everyone. Our theories were mistaken. Those things do exist."

Jacob leaned in a little close to his screen. "Elijah, you're a doctor. Is it possible that this is all made up? That creature they have on display is just an actor or something?"

"I would have to do a full examination to be certain, and you know they wouldn't allow that. But from afar, I cannot see anything to say that this isn't real. That woman is a living, breathing creature, who is not human. We must face the facts, Jacob. They may have found the answer they were looking for."

The prime minister sat back, and his whole body sunk a little. "What am I going to do?"

"It gets worse," Elijah admitted. "Jessie is calling for an attack on the dome."

"IS SHE MAD?" Jacob came right at the screen. "The Corps attacking us? What right do they have? Whether or not this thing is real, they have no reason to launch an attack."

Elijah held up his hands in surrender. "I know. I will do everything in my power to keep the peace."

"I'm sorry, my old friend. This has just been a terribly stressful time for me. Tell me, what are their reasons for calling for an attack?"

"Jessie has spun quite the story about our people being in need of freedom from our captive regime. She hopes to convince the Corps that our people are asking for help."

Jacob sighed hard as he prepared to tell Elijah what he called about. "She may have what she wants soon."

"What?"

"The people, our people, are beginning to question their faith. The younger people are talking about leaving and finding answers elsewhere." Jacob's tone grew soft as he spoke.

"Haven't you told them what it's really like out here? This utopia is a pit of sin and hedonism. They won't be able to have children. They won't be able to get married. And they won't be able to worship. If they ever decide to go back, it's . . . it's . . . "

"I know. We try to make that clear. But with this news coming through every day, confirming the anti-religious beliefs over ours, the youth are starting to question everything. This may be the end, if we don't find something to stop it."

Elijah nodded in agreement. "I do have a plan."

"What sort of plan?"

"Go into space." Elijah smiled. "We send a team of our best doctors and scientists out there to this planet or moon or whatever it is. See this for ourselves. We cannot let all the answers and information flow only from the PSC. That organization has been the root of many of our problems."

"What do you hope to accomplish?" Jacob leaned in, knowing this man was one of the smartest and most clever men he knew.

"We have to find out what is really going on. There are things they aren't telling us. And not just about this primitive thing. The PSC has been a power-hungry organization for two centuries, and now they have a battleship that has no rival. They have control of this situation without anyone to check them, and they have a strong voice in the capital leading the charge against both religion and science. This little venture to their discovery will not only give us a chance to check it out for ourselves, but it will buy time for me to really find out what is going on."

"But, Elijah, we don't even have any spacecraft anymore."

"Then we will use one of theirs." Elijah was very confident about this.

"You think they would allow it?"

"If they are so confident in their discovery, then they would welcome this joint mission. In fact, I will make the request on the floor of the court. If they turn us down, we will have the evidence to say that they are hiding something. If they don't, then we will get what we want."

Jacob laughed. "You are clever, I grant you that."

"That's why I got this job. Now . . . wait, my assistant is trying to get my attention." Elijah looked over to the young woman waving wildly at him. "What is it?"

"Change to the news." She was frantic about this.

"Turn on your news channel. Something is apparently happening." Elijah changed the view back to what he was looking at before. In fact, he had just noticed the time, and he should have been called up for the interview three minutes ago.

The screen filled with a dual picture; one side was the newscaster, the other was that of Dr. Skye holding up some odd scraps of cloth. Both people looked terribly scared and sad.

"So, Dr. Skye, was there any other evidence of struggling or fighting? Did she provoke this attack in any way?"

Dr. Skye, playing the best sad face he could muster, shook his head. "My sources tell me that this young lady was a gentle person dedicated to her science. She was the only geologist allowed down on the planet, and all she brought with her was her equipment to do her mineral studies . . . excuse me." A hand off camera handed him a cloth to wipe his eyes.

"I am sorry for your loss, Doctor. Do you believe it was a painless death?"

Dr. Skye shook his head and swallowed the crying down a little. "I'm afraid that our evidence shows that these primitives fight and hunt much like large cats on earth. Any person caught by one and eaten probably suffered horribly."

"Were there no procedures in place to protect her?"

"We assumed that her Z-550 was strong enough to fend off any attacks, but we haven't even found remains of the robot," Dr. Skye said.

The newscaster was noticeably stunned. "A Z-550 was destroyed . . . by one of these primitives? But the Z-bots are a great deal stronger than a human. How is this possible?"

"We don't know. Our studies of the woman we captured did not indicate that kind of strength, but perhaps the males are much stronger. Either way, it would be highly unwise to have anyone down there that could be in danger. This is why . . . as of this day, the Planetary Science Commission is recalling all staff from the moon's surface and evacuating the area. We are also instituting a ban on travel to this moon." The PSC did not have the authority to just banish travel to this moon, but they often made decrees without getting full approval. The Corps had never stopped them before.

The newsman repeated, "Ladies and gentlemen, you heard it here first: travel of any nature to the moon New Eden has been banned until further notice. We have the head engineer of the *Sanger* on next to talk to us about the . . . " Elijah muted the screen.

"Esther, have we heard anything from the news about the interview?"

She came in and was shaking her head. "They just called and canceled. Apparently, this is more important than your rebuttal to the situation today in the court."

"I see. Put the prime minister back on."

She left his office, and the screen before him changed back to Jacob.

Jacob had the most defeated look on his face. "It just keeps getting worse and worse."

"And a little suspicious."

Jacob frowned at that. "Suspicious?"

"Yes. Something about this just doesn't seem right. Everything is working out too good for them. How convenient that they get all the answers they need and then have the perfect accident occur that incurs a ban on traveling to that place. But, then again . . . " He sighed hard. "Perhaps I'm just getting paranoid living out here for all these years."

"Stay paranoid, my old friend. Right now, it might be the means to finding the answers you need. I have a hard choice to make."

"What is that?"

Jacob smiled. "I have to decide if I let this spread all over our news or keep a secret until later."

"Don't keep it a secret," Elijah said. "Our people have the Divine right to make their own choices. Even if we don't like what they choose. The worse thing that could happen is if the information leaked out, and it looked like we were trying to just cover it up and ignore it. Then we would have a bigger problem than what is already sitting in our laps."

Jacob kept smiling. "Elijah, my old friend, you aren't paranoid; you are wise. Shalom." He switched the signal off.

"Shalom," Elijah quietly answered in the dark room.

CHAPTER EIGHT

ANNA WOKE, FEELING THE HEAVINESS from medicated sleep. The pain was nearly gone; Z's medication had worked. At least, the pain she had been feeling was gone. A whole new pain was aching across her that told the story of how she just spent twelve hours on a hard ground.

She could hear snoring and knew that it wasn't Z. He didn't sleep. Looking over, she saw J'kla passed out with the computer tablet partly in his hand while it laid across his chest. She hadn't seen this cat sleep yet, and it was kind of cute. With his mouth slung open, she could see those long fangs of his. They were terribly deadly looking, so sharp and long. But the ferocious appearance was destroyed by the ragged snoring and twitching of his tail now and then. She hated to admit it, but it sort of reminded her of her pet dog back on Earth.

"Z?" She found him sitting with his back to her on the other side of the way. He probably had been keeping them safe while J'kla watched the videos. Perhaps he didn't hear her. "Z?" she said again. He still remained silent. She spoke a little louder, "Z."

"I am sorry, but this Z-550 is currently in standby mode while its power reserves recharge. If you would like to leave a message, he will be glad to get back to you as soon as his power cells are fully operational. Beep." Yes, the old joker actually said *beep*. He probably pushed himself too hard getting to her and drained his power reserves. Fortunately, a short time with his solar cells collecting energy, and he would be good as new.

She pushed herself up, so she was able to see better. It was remarkable how refreshed she felt. The pain was gone, and she could stretch out her arms without feeling like her back was about to crumble behind her.

As quietly as she could muster, she slowly unzipped the top half of her suit. She had put this loose fit jumpsuit right over the leaves that J'kla had attached. Anna didn't want to wake the sleeping cat. He looked like he was really out of it. She finally had the top unzipped enough to pull out the arm on the side where the leaves were. With the leaves and her upper half exposed, she started to pull them off.

"OW!" She instinctively yelped as she felt the glue-like substance trying to take the top layer of skin off. With a slap of her hand, she covered her mouth and looked around to see if she had woken J'kla. He stopped snoring for a moment, smacked his muzzle a few times, and then continued his snoozing. Lowering her hand, she thought to herself, *He's a sound sleeper.* Then she gingerly tugged at the corners of the leaf to test it. It really stung as it pulled on her skin. The ones on her legs would hurt just as bad to pull off.

"I'm gonna need some water. That should help," she whispered to herself.

"Here, I brought some bottles." Z scared Anna as he was now standing next to her holding a bottle of fresh water.

"Z!" She whispered loudly and then put her hand on her mouth and looked back. Satisfied that J'kla wasn't roused by that either, she harshly whispered at her old friend, "You scared me."

He whispered back, "Sorry. What do you need the water for?"

"I want to get these leaves off; I don't think I need them any longer. But this sticky stuff has dried hard and is trying to take my skin with it."

Z reached over and tested the leaf for himself. "Wow, it's really stuck. Water should do the trick. Then I can administer a coat of synth-skin. That will keep it from getting infected and won't hurt."

"Sounds like a plan. But I don't want to use the bottled water; we might need that to drink. When we get back to the ship, I can use the wash basin to take care of this."

"The ship's gone," Z frankly stated. "It lifted off about the same time as most of the rest of the ships left. I don't know why, and it refused to respond to my orders to come back."

"The ship's gone? My ship! That was my home! And now we're stuck?"

"For now, yes. But I'm sure that when we get a clear signal out to them, they will send our ship back. For some reason, the signal here is weak, or blocked, or something. I can't get through to anyone. But a little elevation should fix this problem. I wonder if these cats have any coat hangers?"

"What do you propose?" Anna asked.

"We need to move. Find a place with a better signal," Z said.

Anna looked back over at the sleeping cat. "Just as well. I wanted to get some more information about him and his people before we took him back to the ship."

"You still think it's a good idea to bring him back?"

"Sure, what's the problem?"

Z pulled over the bag and got out a nutrition bar for her. "It's just, the only experiences with his people the PSC have shown so far are all dangerous and bloody. They could see him and overreact badly. I would hate for us to not get the chance to explain ourselves before they throw him in a dungeon, lab . . . or something."

Anna carefully opened the bar and took a bite. "I thought about that. But you and I can keep him safe until we explain. Besides, by his clothing alone, they should stop before they jump to conclusions."

"What's your plan once we get past the potential crisis?"

"I'll show them he's smart, sophisticated in his own way, and able to learn."

"Very true." Z gave off a half-smile toward J'kla. "You should've seen him last night. After he realized that the people on that screen weren't really there, he started watching with an appetite for learning. He watched for seven hours or more. My auto-recharge system initiated about four hours ago, and he was still at it. I could hear him repeating words, singing the songs—mind you, he's a terrible singer—and even writing in the dirt the words he learned."

Anna was even more impressed than she expected. "What exactly did you show him?"

"Deep in the old archives are some ancient programs designed for toddlers. It teaches letters, numbers, and basic words."

"Toddlers? Don't you think that's kind of too young?" She took another big bite, wishing this was one of those fruits.

"Hey, they speak very slowly, expect the viewer to be developing the ability to communicate, and give time for a response without rushing anything. It worked. After he watched two programs about five times in a row, he started watching an old puppet show for children a little older that also taught words and letters. He was switching back and forth for hours."

"He enjoyed it?" she asked.

Z shrugged. "I guess. He was smiling and all. I can't say if he was just excited to be learning a new language or if the colors and happy pictures were catching his eye."

Anna thought about this. "Truly, I have no idea how old he is. For his people, he might be a child."

"I have no idea." Z brushed some leaves off of Anna's side. "He's a good learner; that's all I know."

Anna carefully removed the tablet from J'kla's tender grasp. The cat scratched his chest where it had been and then rolled to his side and kept sleeping. He was really exhausted. She walked back over while she shut it off. "I wonder how much he retained."

"I don't know, but I do know that he'll keep learning as long as we help. He has a real appetite for knowledge."

"Why do you suppose he is so concerned about learning our language?"

Z grinned that sneaky grin of his. "Maybe he thinks you're cute. From what I learned in the old television programs, men have done some pretty strange stuff to impress a girl."

"Whatever." She brushed that off quickly. "Still, can you imagine what it would do to the whole primitive image, if he stands there and talks to people? Even in broken, bad English, he would blow the lid right off of their theories about this species. What are you smiling at?" She noticed Z was still grinning.

"Just you. A few days ago, you were moping around, acting like the universe had come to an end. Now you are eager, excited, maybe even giddy."

"I'm still working through a lot of mixed feelings about what's going on. There is a giant hole in my heart, and it made me feel so lonely. I guess meeting J'kla helped, a little. At least, the monsters that destroyed my faith aren't all bloodthirsty demons. He's nice, honorable, clever, and genuine."

"You do like him." Z gasped in faux surprise.

Anna punched him in the arm. "Stop it. Yes, I like him, as a friend. He is a nice guy. But he isn't even the right species to be that kind of friend, anyway. I decided that I would not treat him like an animal. He is as much a human being—well, a being like a human—as I am."

"So, when did you make this profound decision to give him the honorary title of human?"

"When he offered me his vest. I saw a person there—not a cat or beast or alien—just another person. I know he's not human, but I'll respect and treat him like a person. When we go back to the *Sanger* to let them see him, I'll make it clear that he's to be treated like any other person visiting the ship."

Z could see this meant a lot to her. They both knew that everyone from the people back on Earth to the scientists in orbit above all acted like they had just discovered a new animal. "Okay, I will respect your choice. He's a person. You know, there won't be a news source around that won't want a statement from him."

"I hope so. He needs to show them that he is the amazing person that we know he is. They'll look at his people in a completely different light."

Z had to ask. "I wonder something. Why are some of his kind the primitive, vicious creatures?"

"I don't know. I guess that will be one of the things we will try to uncover while we study and learn from him. Now, did you happen to pack any instant coffee tablets in that bag?"

"No, I . . . " He was interrupted by the loud sound of a lion roar.

Both Anna and Z jumped into defensive postures, only to find J'kla sitting up and stretching. As he stretched, he yawned and let out another roar-like sound. He then proceeded to scratch himself and get up. He looked over to Anna and Z and smiled with a disheveled look on his face.

Anna laughed and said, "See, the same groggy expression any person gives when they first wake up."

"I haven't heard too many persons who roar when they get up in the morning."

"You should've heard my roommate back in college," Anna retorted.

J'kla scratched his head through the billowing mane, which was scrunched all over with terrible bedhead. He searched the ground for something.

"J'kla," Anna called out and held up the tablet, correctly assuming he was looking for that.

With a smile, he came over. "Thank you," he said very clearly.

Anna was impressed. "You're welcome."

J'kla pondered something for a moment and strained in his thoughts until he finally broke into a big smile and said, "Good night."

Anna was shocked. "That was good. But incorrect."

J'kla could see her shaking her head at his words, so he tried again. "Good . . . good . . . good morning!" He remembered it.

Anna answered him, "Good morning."

"Good morning! Good morning!" He was very happy to get it right.

Z zipped up the bag he was going to be carrying, "See? Told you he was a quick learner."

Anna stretched out her back. J'kla followed and was very amazed. He touched her back, "Good?"

She nodded. "Good."

"Happy!" he said and clapped his hands. This made him look about five years old, but that was on par for the programming he had watched intensely.

"Very happy," she said and stiffly rolled her shoulders.

Z got the backpack strapped around him and then asked, "So, what now?"

Anna knew what J'kla would most likely want, and she could use some as well. "Food."

"Chi?" J'kla knew that word, but couldn't remember what it meant.

She tapped her lips in the sign that had come to mean food between them. She sort of hated using sign language with him, but that should pass as he learned more words.

"Food, food!" He joyfully understood, then pointed in another direction indicating where he was going to take them.

"I guess breakfast awaits." Anna walked with J'kla, who carefully moved the thick foliage out of the way for her. Z was not far behind, having to move the foliage for himself.

Anna stepped carefully through the thick forest with J'kla as her guide. She wasn't sure what was beyond each patch of trees, but he walked with certainty. After her painful fall, she was glad to be with someone who knew where he was going. At times, when the ground was slick with wet leaves or a large root was protruding from the surface, J'kla would hold out his hand and help her along.

She liked holding his hand. It felt so different than a human hand, so rough on the palm, and yet the fur was soft on the backside. What she hardly admitted to herself was that she liked feeling his strength as he held her hand. He was a gallant and kind person.

Hilarious, universe, just hilarious, she sarcastically thought as she held that firm hand and stepped over a pile of slimy looking leaves. She had prayed for years to find a man who was this kind and honest with her, a man whom she could marry . . . or at least connect with like a husband. The two men in her life that had actually accomplished this were a robot and an alien. One could not feel love and was more like a father to her. The other was an alien. Besides, even if she did attempt to foster that kind of relationship with J'kla, he was probably too young and would rather have a woman with a tail and fur.

J'kla paused at a natural barrier of vines growing down from the taller trees. He smiled at her with a lot of eagerness. Using his hand to guide her, he positioned her right up near the foliage.

Z stopped abruptly, having nearly run right into J'kla. "What's going on? Are we stopping right here?"

"He wants to show me something." Anna caught on quick.

J'kla let go of her hand and then used both of his to pull the vines aside. Before Anna lay a large, lush valley. A river broke the valley in the middle with soft grasses on either side. In the distance was a line of rather tall hills or short mountains. Trees of all kinds sprang up as far as the eye could see, low trees with heavy orbs hanging from the branches on some. Others had tall flowers and leaves that hung almost like Spanish moss. Along the ground grew plants that had three or four tall stalks shooting straight up, each one covered in blossoms that appeared much like morning glories, only clustered together.

Tiny birds flew around the tall columns of flowers, plucking flowers off here and there and then eating the whole flower. The birds were brightly colored and flew much like hummingbirds, only they were about five times as big as a hummingbird.

J'kla gasped in happy surprise and pointed off in the distance. Anna followed his direction and saw a small herd of animals grazing. They were horse-like creatures with dark brown fur and flowing manes and tails. On their heads were racks of antlers. The antlers were surprisingly similar in appearance as the branches of the trees bearing the heavy fruit. These things were about the size of small donkeys.

"Z, are you getting all of this?"

Z rotated his head slowly, absorbing everything he could. "My visual databanks are taking as much of this in as they can hold, but I doubt I will do this justice."

J'kla pointed down. There was a steep slope that met the grassy plain. "Go," he said.

Anna looked down with a worried frown. "Uh, right now I don't trust slopes. That's pretty far down."

J'kla took her hand and then slowly got down, so he could climb while trying to help her. "Go . . . go," he kept saying.

Z held up his hand. "No go." This drew a furious frown from J'kla. "Hey. She just about killed herself in a fall. I ain't gonna watch her fall again."

J'kla begrudgingly let go of her hand and then looked right at Anna. "Go." He put his hands on the side and slid down using the vines to help him from freefalling.

Anna watched him go. "Wow. He's done that before. I guess he was going down here to get those fruits. But I don't know if I should . . . " She knelt down, but found Z's hand on her.

"No. I got this." He shifted the bag so his back was free and then got Anna up on his back, her arms around his neck, her legs around his waist, his left arm holding her as much as he could. He turned and then slid down the side of the cliff much as J'kla had.

Once they got to the ground, Z returned Anna to her feet, and she found a smiling J'kla waiting. "All good."

"Good." J'kla clapped his hands.

"Thank you, Z," Z sarcastically said.

"Oh, don't be so whiny. You know I appreciate you."

J'kla waved his hand at her to follow him. "Go, Anna, Go."

Anna looked up from J'kla and found herself even more impressed by her surroundings. The world was so beautiful, it took her breath away.

J'kla walked out into the grass toward one of the fruit trees. He paused and looked back to see that Anna was a bit overwhelmed. Coming back to her, he took her hand and led her beside him. The terrain wasn't full of obstacles, but he still held her hand all the same. She was likely to walk right into a tree with the awestruck look on her face.

J'kla paused to show her a pillar of the flowers. "White," he pointed at them.

Anna was impressed. "You know colors?"

"Colors," he eagerly stated and then pointed at the grass. "Green." Then to the sky, "Blue." Then to another flower, "Yellow." He was so happy right now that it was contagious, though he called a pink flower yellow. It was still impressive.

Anna clapped her hands. It felt odd to be this happy to hear something delineate the basic colors, but it was impressing her to no end. "I'm very proud of you."

He took her hand again and walked her quickly through the fields of flowers and short trees. "Fruit," J'kla said as he stopped them near one of the fruit-bearing trees.

Anna let go of his hand and approached the tree. The large fruits were those that she liked so much. "Amazing. This tree is so small, and yet it produces these huge fruits. I would think it would be more tropical, or bigger, or something." She reached up to pick one that was not bringing the branch down so hard.

J'kla stopped her and shook his head, "No." He pointed to one that was darker in skin color and was bending the branch nearly to the breaking point. Taking up the fruit in his hands, he lifted it up slightly and then took hold of the small stem holding the fruit to the branch. With a pinching motion, he plucked the stem from the fruit and let the branch snap back up. With a big smile on his face, he presented her the fruit.

"Oh, I see. Thank you." She took the fruit.

J'kla took the fruit back from her and held it up to Z. This time meaning for him to take it.

"Uh . . . thank you. I don't eat, but I guess I'll take it."

J'kla pointed at their bag and then reached over and picked another fruit.

Anna got it. "Oh, he wants us to collect a few."

With that little epiphany, the trio gathered a few of the large fruits and stuffed them into the bag for Z to carry. Z was strong enough to carry five hundred times this weight, but he complained all the same about being the pack mule on this safari.

After a short walk, they arrived at the destination J'kla had intended them to reach. They were on the banks of the large, gently moving river that bisected the valley. The babbling waters were soothing to hear as they tumbled over the smooth river stones.

J'kla held out his hands and authoritatively exclaimed. "Stop."

Anna obeyed with a smile and waited for what he was going to do next. He showed her the ledge of grass at the edge of the sandy soil of the banks of the river. She was to sit down and rest there. She didn't mind at all and sat on the thick grass. J'kla proceeded to walk out toward the water and looked in for a moment.

Z, who was standing behind her, leaned over and quietly asked, "What do you suppose he's up to?"

"I don't know, but I bet he's going in the water for something. Maybe he's looking for a way for us to cross."

Z snickered. "That'll be amusing—a cat in water."

"He's not a cat; he's . . . "

"Yah, I know, a person." Z's eyes widened, and he smiled. "A person getting undressed."

"What . . . oh my." Anna watched as J'kla took off his vest and then undid the belt around his pants. In a moment, he slipped them off and was only in a roughly wrapped bit of undergarment. He did not remove his underwear but seemed to be prepping himself for his dip in the water.

Z asked, "Do you think he missed his early morning bath? I have some soap in the sanitation kit."

"Something tells me he's going after something." She couldn't take her eyes off of him, partly out of surprise, and partly out of the admiration of his rather handsome figure. His tail particularly fascinated her.

Z comically added, "Imagine how much shampoo he would use."

J'kla held his arms up and sloshed out into the water. He made it to the middle of the river where he was chest-high in the flowing water. Frozen in place, his arms were held up like he was about to grab something, and his eyes were fixed on the water. In a burst of motion, J'kla launched himself in and then came back up, slinging a large arc of liquid off his mane as he threw his head back.

In each hand, he held a nice, large fish. In victory, he held them up and smiled at Anna.

"Oh, he's fishing!" Anna stated. "That's impressive."

"True, and he didn't use his mouth either," Z jokingly jabbed.

Anna scoffed at that. "He's not an animal; he's . . ."

"Yes, yes, a person. I get it. And I'm a failed comedian."

"Since the day you were activated." Now she took a jab at Z.

J'kla made his way back out of the water, soaking wet but smiling. His mane was flattened against him, and his body was dripping wet. When he reached the shore, he stopped and shook hard, sending a rather amusing spray of water all over the place. The shaking went from his head to his shoulders, down his body, and finally with a flick of his hips to cause his tail to shake hard. It was potentially the most feline thing that Anna had ever seen him do.

Z whispered, "That person sure knows how to shake out the water."

"Oh, shut up."

J'kla, having removed as much water as he could, quickly came to her to show her the fish he had caught. They were large and looked a great deal like salmon, only without the pink coloring. Where a salmon would be pink, they were shades of blue. The happy cat smiled and said, "Food."

"I think he wants you to cook them," Z said as he held in the laughter. Anna's attempts at cooking had been few and rather disastrous. To ask her to clean and cook freshly caught fish was something Z was going to record for later viewings.

Anna watched as the two fish were set on the ground near her. "Uh, thanks. Sure, we can cook them."

J'kla pointed a sharp claw at Z, then pointed at the ground. "Hot" was all he said.

"Hot?"

"I think he wants you to build a fire."

"I'm not under his authority. Besides, we don't need to eat those fish; we have all the nutrition bars we could want." Z was a practiced complainer.

Anna jabbed Z with her elbow. "Don't insult him. Besides, fish might taste better than those bars."

"Fine." Z stood all the way up and looked around for any loose wood on the ground. The whole time, he was indignantly muttering to himself, "That person sure has a grasp of command and knows what he wants. He wants fish, like any good cat—person—then he's gonna get fish. I have to make fire. What am I, a caveman? Z make hot. Hot good . . . " His voice trailed off as he got further and further away, his arms filling with twigs and branches.

Anna just broke out with a good, honest laugh. She had been so sad when she arrived that it ached. Then she added terror to that after watching the wild antics of the other cat people. Nothing seemed good in the universe any longer. She was ready to die. Now she couldn't stop laughing. There was a sense of peace watching J'kla fish and listening to Z be his usual stubborn self.

The happy emotions bubbled right to the surface at this moment and came out as a deep, satisfying laugh.

In a short matter of time, Z had collected a healthy supply of old wood and some dry grasses. He built up a very nice little fire and sat with Anna while a short pile of fish was being collected. J'kla had skewered three of the fish and staked them near enough the fire to cook them. He was out getting a couple more while these two watched the roasting dinner. It had been a long time since Anna had ever seen any real cooking being done, and Z hadn't ever witnessed it in person, only on his old shows he watched.

"What are you doing?" Anna asked as Z stared off into space, which meant his processors were working on something.

Without blinking or moving anything but his lips, he answered, "I'm testing a sample of the river water. I didn't stop to test it before, when I was searching for you. I needed my processors all working on finding you. Now, I want to see what's in it."

"What for? We have enough bottled water to drink."

"You want to get those leaves off your skin or not?"

Anna scratched at the leaves on her side, through the cloth. "Absolutely. They're beginning to feel like I have old honey stuck to my skin. Every time I move much on that side, it pulls hard. I wonder how they stand using this stuff. With all the fur, it probably hurts like heck to remove them."

Z finished processing and now looked at her. "Amazing. This water is almost pure. There aren't any toxins, dangerous bacteria, or medically dangerous anomalies. You could drink this stuff."

"Good. Then get some, and we'll wash this stuff off of me."

Z got up and walked over to the edge of the river. He stopped to look at the determined fisherman standing in the middle of the light rapids. J'kla was so focused on watching for potential catches that he didn't notice the robot at the shore swallowing a lot of water into his mouth. Z used his internal storage system to absorb an amount of water. It could be used when he was asked to do missions on uninhabitable planets where he would need a ready supply of coolant for his systems.

Z came back and unscrewed his right hand. His left arm was the medical assist arm, and its components did not detach so easily. By taking off his hand he had an opening to use the tube that allowed the coolant to flow out. Anna unzipped her top and peeled it back so he could work. Z carefully went to work dribbling water on the edges and meticulously pulling back the moistened substance of the leaves. After a few moments of work, he had the whole leaf off and only a layer of the goo was left, which would wash off pretty easily. He started on the next leaf down on the same wound.

"Wow, this looks worse than my sensors were reading. But this stuff has certainly helped. It's healing really well," Z commented as he worked.

Anna leaned back and tried not to giggle as he tickled her side. "This place is amazing. The fruit is perfect. The trees are beautiful, and the medicinal herbs are impressive. Just look at that sky. It's so blue, it makes me want to lie back and watch the clouds roll by."

Z peeled the leaf off fully and tossed it aside. He carefully pulled up her pant leg and washed away the other leaves. "I was thinking about that. Everything here is very perfect. It reminds me of Dr. Jefferson's theories."

Anna had to think about that. "Dr. Jefferson? Dr. Jefferson? Man, that name sounds familiar."

"He was the scientist who first came up with the methods for terraforming. He wanted to construct perfect worlds out of uninhabitable lumps of space rock. He theorized the notion that if planetoids had the same gravitational pull as Earth, or very close, that they could be made into habitable places like Earth. He created the two domes that are on Mars."

"But those domes never worked out. They're not habitable."

"True. But his theories were never fully tested. About two hundred years ago, the first PSC counsel abolished all work toward the terraforming projects."

"So, what makes you think of him?"

Z carefully pulled the leaf off her leg. "This place is so balanced, so perfect. Everything a person would need is available. So far, I haven't detected any natural dangerous bacteria, venomous insect life, or viral agents native to this environment that pose a threat to human life. The climate is balanced; the water is clean; the air is pure. Other than a few thorny plants, this place is almost perfect. There is only one element of this whole moon that would defy it being the perfect representation of Jefferson's theories."

"The cats," she stated, knowing exactly what he was going to say.

"Yes. They pose a significant threat to human life. Such an element would never be allowed on a created habitat."

Anna was intrigued. "True. To me, I'm thinking about the work of Sarah Toblin in the late twenty-second century. She believed that we would find planets and worlds that were pristine and harmless. She presumed that all dangerous elements in nature were evolved into being because of human involvement. Without humans, nature would be more balanced and perfect. This place seems to fit that as well, outside of there being a human-like race here."

Z pulled off the last leaf and then washed the gunk off. "I guess we'll just have to leave that kind of research up to the PSC. Dr. Toblin's theories could be proven by this moon, as well as work on the terraforming projects might get a boost and be started again." He sat back. "How does that feel?"

She brushed her hand down her damp, but clean, skin. "Oh, much better."

"Good. I'll apply some synth-skin . . . "

Just then, a rather loud roar and yelp could be heard.

Both Anna and Z looked up to see a grimace of pain on the face of J'kla who was coming out of the river with two more fish. He lost one fish as he hopped around holding a bleeding foot.

"Go help him," Anna ordered as she zipped up her jumpsuit.

Z grabbed his hand and quickly screwed it back on while he ran to get to J'kla. He gave J'kla support to hop back over to the campfire.

J'kla tossed the fish he had managed to save into a pile and then grabbed his leg. He whimpered and rocked a little.

"Hold still," Z commanded as he tried to get a look at the injury.

"J'kla! Stop." Anna got his attention.

J'kla held still, and Z finally got a grip on the foot. "Oh, dear. Looks pretty nasty." With a slow pull, Z extracted a sharp bit of wood that was about six inches long, half of it bloody from entering J'kla's foot. When Z pulled it out, J'kla made a rather harsh but short roar and then whimpered some more.

"This is going to help," Z slowly explained.

"Help?" J'kla repeated, that being the only word he understood.

"Yes. Help. Now, hold still." Z still fought the fidgeting of the man with the injured foot.

Anna averted her eyes as J'kla was still only in his underwear, and he was soaking wet. She was being modest while also trying to be kind. The fact he was soaking wet made him look really funny. Add to that the pitiful look on his face, and she was about to burst out laughing again. Which would be terribly insensitive to the situation.

Z injected a medication to the foot that caused the healing process to move at an exponential rate. Then he sprayed a layer of synth-skin over the wound. Unfortunately, the skin on his foot was rough and not nearly as smooth as a human's. "Drat," Z muttered.

"What's wrong?" Anna asked.

"I can't contain the bleeding with the synth-skin spray. The healing medicine will work better if I can stop the bleeding."

"I have an idea." Anna reached into the bag and pulled out the tattered remains of her last jumpsuit. Tearing along one side, she ripped a long strip off and held it out. "Tie it up with this."

Z took the strip, sprayed it with a disinfectant, and then tied it around the foot. "Hardly twenty-sixth century medicine, but it should work." He smiled at J'kla. "There, all better."

"Good?" J'kla asked.

"Uh, just one more thing." Z unscrewed his index finger on his right hand and pushed it into J'kla's leg. He extracted a small amount of blood. Then with a wave of his hand, he scanned the leg and then smiled. "Good. Your wound should be fully mended in two hours—unless your biology rejects the medication. Then we'll have to amputate."

"Z! Don't scare him."

Z didn't answer her but spoke only to the confused cat. "She thinks you understood me; she's silly."

"Good?" J'kla asked, horribly befuddled by Z's conversation.

"Yes, good."

"Thenk yoo," J'kla clumsily stated.

"You are most welcome. Now, put on some pants, and eat your lunch."

"Yes. Pants would be nice," Anna added while she continued to avert her eyes.

J'kla just sat there, confused as to what they both were saying to him.

Z rolled his eyes and then rattled the hem of his own pants with his hand. "Pants, pants." J'kla looked down and then smiled. "Pants." He had learned a new word.

Z pointed toward the folded-up pile of his clothes. "Pants."

"Oh." J'kla stood, then fell back down with a grimace of agony on his face.

"Come on. Let me help." Z got the cat up and then helped him put on his pants. Both were having new experiences today.

∗   ∗   ∗

J'kla's foot was sore, but he was thankful they had helped him. He pulled a chunk of meat off of the cooked fish-on-a-stick stuck in the ground next to him. While he ate, he finished a word game Z had called up for him on this strange object that showed pictures of new and amazing things.

He had decided when he was more able to talk to them, he would bring them back to his village and show everyone that the furless ones weren't as mean as they thought—at least, not all of them. He knew the elders would get upset quickly at the sight of the furless ones and probably demand punishment for all the missing people. But he would defend them from being taken away, so he could explain what was happening. Somehow, he was sure that this Anna and her strange-smelling friend were not responsible for the missing people and the deaths. She was too nice. And attractive. He liked her figure, the sound of her voice, her pretty eyes . . . and she was a nice person. Outside of those few reasons, he didn't find her attractive enough to pursue any romance. Besides, she was probably linked to that strange-smelling man.

"House!" he proclaimed with a mouthful of fish and tapped the screen with his finger to choose the right word.

The game finished, and he got an eighty percent score, his highest so far. He couldn't tell his score; numbers bigger than ten were still hard for him to get right. The game was dancing and happy for him, so he knew he did well. With a big smile, he looked up at the pair sitting on the other side of the dwindling fire. They had looked up at his outburst and were smiling back.

J'kla noticed Anna was picking at the fish with a funny look on her face. What if they didn't have fish on the star where they lived? No, he saw fish in the cartoons and in the word games. They knew what they were and even had a word for them. She probably just didn't like it. He wanted to make her happy. Oh, how to ask this? He knew so few words, but he would try.

"Anna?"

She gulped down a tiny bite of fish and forced a smile. "Yes?"

"Fish . . . uh . . . no good?" was all he could come up with.

"Fish good," she lied.

He didn't accept that but knew she wanted to make him feel good. She liked the kunja fruit, and there was plenty of that right now. At least, she could eat that if she really didn't like the fish. And that would certainly keep her from eating that awful wood stuff her man friend brought.

J'kla switched on the tablet again and changed the screen to show a young kids' program he had seen a dozen times already. It sang the alphabet to him slowly and made the various sounds of all these letters he needed to learn. It was boring, but he was so close to remembering all of this. Maybe he'd just listen to the song once through and then ask Anna the question he wanted to ask all day.

*   *   *

"Do you think he ever gets tired of listening to that song over and over?" Z asked as he poked the fire.

Anna watched J'kla as he sat there with the most childlike expression on his face. His tail was even tapping to the rhythm of the song. "Don't know. But he's making progress. He's all the way up to T the last time I heard him try it on his own."

"I know; I think I heard a few birds weeping while he sang his little song."

"So, he's no opera singer," Anna retorted.

"That he certainly is not."

Anna carefully peeled another bit of the fish flesh off and tried to eat it. "This is by far the bitterest meat I've ever eaten. Are you sure it's all right for me?"

"For the hundredth time, yes. In fact, it's more densely packed with good proteins and oils than any fish on Earth. It's almost as good as a nutrition bar."

"I don't want to insult him. He worked all day catching and cooking these fish for us. If I can eat it, I will. It'll just be . . . an adventure."

"Sure, call it what you will, but my sensors also indicate that it's as bitter as chewing on aspirin."

"Just about." She gulped down the next piece and resisted shuddering. "Speaking of sensors, did you take a blood sample from him earlier?"

"And a bone scan," Z added nonchalantly.

"Why?"

"You wanted to know his age. I think I can determine it through a little medical investigation. And it wouldn't hurt to know more about these people."

"I never asked you to get his age. I just postulated that he's probably a teen—at least in his people's years."

Z watched J'kla get up and dust the wet sand from his rear end. "Sure, keep telling yourself that."

"What does that mean?"

Before Z could crack any jokes, there stood J'kla next to them. He was smiling big for Anna.

"Sit?" he asked pointing next to her.

She nodded. "Please."

He crossed his feet at the ankles and then sank down to the ground in a quick motion. "Read?"

Anna smiled at him. She couldn't help but smile at that curious face of his. "Read? Read what?"

"Uh . . . book."

"Z, do you have any good books downloaded to that tablet?"

Z, who was walking away at this time to scan the area with his motion sensors, answered, "Sure. I have the complete library they send for long missions. All the classics and a few modern books."

"I guess a classic will work. How about *Beauty and the Beast*?" she joked. J'kla didn't get it.

"Big book," he said and pointed at her bag.

"Big book? What . . . oh, you mean . . . you want me to read from that?"

J'kla leaned over her, nearly crawling across her, and pulled out the Bible from the duffle bag. He held it up to her and gave her the eyes she couldn't resist. "Please," he asked.

"All right. If you insist. You won't understand it." She took up the Bible and opened it to the first pages. J'kla got extremely close, looking intently at the words on the page. "In the beginning, God . . ." He stopped her and took her free hand and put it on the page. She knew he wanted her to point to the words as she read them. She started again, reading as slowly as possible.

"In . . . the . . . beginning . . . God . . . created . . . " She read and read while J'kla was mesmerized by the story.

J'kla barely understood what she was saying, but it was more than Anna believed he knew. He liked listening to her read. It helped him hear how the words were supposed to sound.

CHAPTER NINE

JESSIE SAT AT HER DESK in the capital. She had about two dozen tablets scattered across the desk, along with all the paperwork she had to finish. Her plans were complicated and required her name on so many documents, she was tired of writing it.

"Computer, security channel seven. Authorization PSC Alpha 2."

"Channel accessed." This was a channel that not even the World Corps knew about. It was her way to speak with Dr. Skye privately.

The screen filled with his face and a big smile. "I see that you're busy," said Dr. Skye.

"Sure. I've had to answer about a thousand questions and contact two hundred people in the past hour alone. Busy isn't the word for it."

"Is anyone suspicious of what you're doing?"

Jessie stopped mid-motion as she had picked up another tablet to sign. "With seven different world media outlets wanting every ounce of breaking news they can get their grubby little hands on, I'm swimming in the sea of suspicions. They have made every wild speculation imaginable. The most prevalent is that I'm leaving due to health issues. Some claim I got injured on New Eden by that woman I brought back. And one states that I'm the first official ambassador to Jerusalem, to help them transition as the last member of the World Corps."

Richard laughed at that last one. "Wow. They really haven't anything better to do than guess."

"As long as they don't find the truth behind all of this, they can assume anything they want. They can believe I'm the transition ambassador. After all, my job will soon be solely to rid this planet of the blight of Jerusalem."

"So," Richard asked, "did you name someone to take over the position of education administrator?"

Jessie quickly signed her name with the stylus and then set it in the "out" box. "Does it really matter? By the time all of our plans come together, the entire administrator board will be gone."

"I don't know. A few might be retained. There are some good people working on that board."

Jessie rolled her eyes at the thought of the idiots she'd had to work with. "No. If we want complete control, we will need to place only members of the PSC in those positions. I have a hand-picked list ready to go—pending your approval, of course."

Richard was aware that Jessie would rather be the top dog here, but she knew that when the time came to replace this government, it would be him in charge, not her. He gave her a political smile. "Of course. How long do you think it will be until we can set them up for the vote?"

"Soon. I have a few more details to establish. When the time comes, they'll be begging to hand the military control over to the PSC. And by the time they realize what has happened, it will be far too late."

"Good. Now I have to do an interview with the Chinese news service. It's been a while since I spoke any Mandarin." Dr. Skye cleared his throat.

"Zhù nǐ hǎo-yùn," Jessie comically retorted and then cut the channel.

She picked up a tablet and read over the information. It was another request form from one of the state school houses. She still had to take care of some of these details until the transition happened. Though she was ready to dump this government as soon as possible, the functions needed to continue. This world was well-balanced. It just needed better leadership—her leadership. She was willing to let Richard take the top title, but she was well aware of who would really control everything. All she had to do was convince this stupid gathering of representatives and their administrator pawns to focus on the enemy, Jerusalem. That shouldn't be hard; in fact, it would be a great joy for her. Seizing control of the government was her objective, but her pleasure would be in destroying Jerusalem.

$$* \quad * \quad *$$

Three days had passed, and the trio were on their way through the valley toward the mountain chain in the distance. J'kla had been a wonderful guide, stopping to show them every minor detail. Z found it monotonous, but Anna was more and more thrilled each day. When they would stop to eat and rest, she would take out the Bible and read to J'kla. In just two days, he started reading a few words to her—of course, with a lot of help.

Right now, J'kla filled some of the empty water bottles with more water while Z and Anna picked up the stuff from their campsite. Anna didn't know where J'kla was leading them. She would keep following him, which gave them time to learn more about him and his people. Z expressed his concern about their aimless wandering more than once, but Anna did not believe it was aimless. Z used their hiking to look for a better signal, so contact with the *Sanger* would be clear.

"Good morning, my . . . uh . . . name J'kla." J'kla practiced his sentences while he bottled up the water.

Anna was thoroughly amused by this and extremely impressed. "He certainly loves to learn."

Z watched the cat work at the river. "Yes. It is impressive, and a little strange. I've never known anyone who can pick up languages like that."

Anna asked, "Has your examination finished processing his data? How old is he?"

Z closed his eyes and processed this. "Not yet. Without any existing data on his species, I'm having a hard time evaluating the samples. All I can tell you right now is that he is extremely healthy, and his genetics don't have any of the signs of potential medical problems . . . at least none that humans could get. It might take a little longer for the data to come back with an answer. His biological readings are close enough to human that the process is going quicker than I expected."

"Let me know what you find."

"Sure." Z stuffed some rock samples Anna had collected back into the bag. "Hey, it's been almost five days Earth time since we arrived. Don't you think it's about time we call the *Sanger* and go back? J'kla is all talk now; he's sure to impress them."

"I don't know," Anna hesitated.

"Look. I know you're having a lot of fun with this guy, and I respect that. But we need to get back sometime."

Anna relented. "All right. Give them a call. Let them know where we are. Tell them . . . to take their time in coming to get us."

"Sure."

"What doing?" J'kla came up with four bottles of water in his arms.

Z took them from him and put them into the bag. "Thanks."

"You am welcome."

Anna answered J'kla's broken question. "I was just thinking about jogging, while Z is going to . . . do some things." She didn't want to alert J'kla right now.

"Jogging?" He had yet to hear this word.

Anna thought about that. How do you explain jogging to someone who has never heard the term before, without using other terms he is unlikely to know? "Running."

"Running?" He thought. "Run?"

"Yes. For fun and health."

J'kla smiled. "I run."

"Thought you might," Z muttered.

Anna shot Z a glare and then asked J'kla, "Foot good?"

J'kla lifted his leg and happily showed him his foot. "Good." The medical attention of Z worked wonders for the big cat.

"Okay. Then, let's go. Show me a good path."

"Good path." J'kla responded and then pointed into the woods.

Anna jogged in place for a second, and J'kla mimicked her. Both dashed off into the trees for a lively jog in the crisp air.

J'kla and Anna jogged along a path for a while. It wasn't a worn path where others had spent much time running before, but it was clear and flat enough to follow without much struggle. Anna was steady in her pace, keeping a good rhythm going. J'kla sprinted a little, fell back a little, and ran ahead at times. He didn't quite understand the basic philosophy behind jogging, but he enjoyed himself. When he would run ahead of her, she couldn't stop looking at his tail. It was a fascination to her. The way it moved to keep his balance in check, how it wasn't just flopping around but was really a part of him. She looked at his face so much that she often forgot he even had this tail.

They ran through a natural grove of fruit trees that were growing what looked like small apples. Then they ran along the side of the river that was faster moving and deeper than where they had made camp. After that, the terrain inclined a bit and turned upward toward some hills leading to the mountain ridge in the distance. The path got bumpier and more twisted as they moved along. Soon, the trees got closer together, and more varied in type and height.

Anna stopped and held her knees to catch her breath. "J'kla, stop. Please," she puffed heavily, dripping in sweat.

J'kla had run ahead a little and now made it back to her. He was panting. Anna looked at him with astonishment. He was really panting, not as quickly as a dog, but through his mouth and with his tongue hanging out a little. His eyes were lit up with excitement, and he was smiling through the pant.

"Do you exercise?" She knew he had to with those muscles.

He gave her a funny look. "Exsize?"

"Work out . . . body build . . . oh what would make sense?" She considered what words he might have learned from those kid programs. "Get healthy?"

"Healthy? Eat good food," J'kla said, repeating the words from one of the educational programs he watched.

Anna walked over and pointed at his defined arm. "How do you do that?" He looked at his arm. She flexed up like she was posing for a bodybuilding competition. "Build muscles?"

He held up his arms in the same motion and happily flexed his muscles. Then he got it, what she was saying. Looking around for a moment, he found what he was looking for, a sturdy, low-hanging branch. He jumped up and caught it with his hands, then bent his legs at the knees and lifted himself up so his chin would go over the branch. He pumped up and down a few times and then dangled from the tree with the goofiest grin. "Exsize?"

She was impressed and amused. He was really good at that; obviously, he had done this before. "Ex-er-size," she stated slowly.

He dropped down to the ground again. "Ex . . . er . . . size . . . Exercise."

"Yes, good." She ran her forearm over her sweating brow. "Other exercise?"

He nodded quickly, dropped to the ground, and executed a perfect pushup. Then showed off by doing one with only one hand.

It was interesting to Anna that these people had developed the same forms of basic exercise as humans had used for centuries. Some things were truly universal, like J'kla's desire to show off his body to her. She had spent a lot of energy trying to avoid admiring his muscles and right now was especially hard with the way he was showing off. He was certainly male—human or cat kind—they show off at the drop of a hat.

J'kla got back up and looked at the surrounding trees. He smiled big and pointed ahead of them. "Come," he said and then ran ahead.

Anna started off, this time running along to catch up, not her normal jogging. "Hey, wait, don't lose me. I don't know my way around."

J'kla led them to a darker part of the forest where the trees were covered in thick moss, bugs, and flowering vines everywhere. He had stopped to examine the flower buds on the vines.

Anna caught up to him and was out of breath again. She wasn't used to this kind of thicker humid air; she normally jogged in the perfectly moderated air system of the ship. "Wow, I gotta work back up to running on a planet. You know, I used to jog around the university back on Earth, and I didn't have this much trouble."

"Come. See flower," he pulled up the vine to show a large bud that looked like a morning glory all closed up for the day, only five inches long.

"Yes. It's very pretty. What does it look like open?"

He didn't understand. "Cloth flower," he carefully stated.

"Cloth flower?"

"Yes. Uh . . . this one." He searched down the vine and found one that was the same closed bud, only very fat. He plucked it off and then squeezed it to make it pop open. Inside was a colored mass of cotton-like substance. The cotton was the same color as the flower petals, a light pink.

"Wow. I see why you call it cloth flower. Do you use this stuff?"

J'kla took the cotton and expertly pulled it out. He handed the fluff to her. "Grains." He said this as he pointed to the little seeds mixed into the fluff. It was the only word he could think of that would explain what he was showing her.

"Oh, just like cotton back on Earth. Do you eat these?"

"No eat. Trash." He took the fluff and then used his own claws to pull through the fluff, and it strung out with a few of the seeds getting caught in his claws. "Make cloth."

"Oh, I see. You use this exactly like cotton. Wow. Very nice."

He reached down and pinched up a small section of his pants. "Cloth."

It was then she realized that his pants were woven out of this flower fluff. They had been dyed dark brown to match the vest. This was a legitimate industry. She felt the strung-out part of the fluff; it was rougher than she expected. "Did you make this cloth?"

"No." He tossed aside the fluff and then pointed at himself. "Artist."

"Artist?"

He nodded, and then said, "Mommy, Daddy, J'kla, artist."

"Oh, your family, they are artisans."

J'kla didn't understand what she said. He thought she might not get it, so he wanted to show her. He took her hand and sat her down beside the tree. Reaching up, he took one of the vines and pulled on it. It came off in a long strand, with some snapping and ripping noises as it broke free. When he had enough, he bit into the vine to cut it.

With the focus and skill of a craftsman, he worked down the vine and plucked off the leaves. Each leaf he pulled off came with a string of the vine behind it, stripping off the rougher, tattered surface as he worked. Each time he came to a flower, he would carefully pick it off and then rub it between his fingers until it opened up for him. Setting aside the nicer flowers, he worked until the whole vine was completely stripped.

Once done with that, he tied the vine with a select pattern of loops. He made a perfectly even crochet chain out of the vine using only his thumb claw and his fingers to work the chain. Occasionally, he wound one of the stems of the flowers into the chain as he worked.

Anna watched with rapt attention. This was amazing workmanship that hasn't been done on Earth for centuries. It would take time, but she didn't care. She did take the chance to ask him something she wanted to know. "What are your people called?"

"Huh?" he grunted as he focused on looping the vine.

She pointed at herself. "I'm human?"

"No. Anna," he corrected her.

She laughed. "No. My name is Anna, but I'm a human. What are you?"

He stopped and cocked his head at her. What was she saying to him? Was her name human?

"Anna?"

"How do I ask this? Oh, I have an idea. Plant." She pointed at the vine. "Cloth flower is a plant." She knew he had learned basic identification on one of those kiddy programs. "Dog named Fido, Cat named Whiskers." Now she turned it back around to her. "Human named Anna."

"Oh," he understood. "*B'reann* named J'kla."

"*B'reann?*" She hadn't heard this before.

He gave her a short nod and then gestured all around him, "Home *B'rea*, J'kla *B'reann*." With that, he continued working on his masterpiece.

Anna looked around and smiled. "So, this moon is called *B'rea*. Short, sweet. I like it." She then asked a question she had been thinking about for days now. "J'kla, where are the rest of your people?"

He continued working as he answered, "They on B'rea."

She giggled. "I know that. But where are they now? I haven't seen any since I met you."

He stopped working for a second and gave this some thought. "They . . . uh . . . home. No here, far away."

"Oh. I see." She realized that this was a conversation for when he could understand her better and elaborate with more words than he currently knew.

"For Anna." He held up the now short crochet chain with the intertwined flowers.

"What is it?" she was happy to accept but had no idea what this was.

He took her hand and held it out, indicating that she should hold it up for him. He then wrapped it around her wrist and tied it with the two tails left at each end of the work. It had three flowers on it and fit her nicely. He had done this before, probably as part of the family business. She was impressed and a bit enchanted. "Thank you. It's pretty."

J'kla grinned with modesty and nodded. "Anna pretty."

Anna blushed. This was the most charming thing anyone had ever done for her. "Thank you. J'kla handsome." She spoke like him as though that would make it understandable.

J'kla merely smiled at her, those little fang points showing out from under his muzzle. He was cute, in a kitten you just brought home sort of way. If he were just the right age—and species—he might make a good husband. *Good heavens! One little bracelet, and you're ready to marry him. Get your head on straight,* she thought to herself. She was caught up in the romance of the moment.

"Good grief, look at the time. We've got to get back. Z will start looking for me again." She and J'kla got up.

They had a ways to go to get back, and neither were running as fast as they had to get here. The short day of this moon was already growing late.

Z watched, with folded arms and a tapping foot. He had been done with the packing for hours, and they were just off playing around. "I'll give them ten more minutes; then I'm going in to see if they got into trouble," he said to himself. Just then, the foliage in the distance moved, and there they came, walking side by side in not too big a hurry to get to him. Z saw they had stopped walking, and then J'kla waved at him to come over to them. "Where that cat gets off ordering me around, I'll never know." It wasn't that Z disliked J'kla. He just wasn't as enamored as Anna. Besides, Z hadn't completely set aside the notion that this creature had the potential to be dangerous. What if he suddenly turned on them?

"What are you two up to?" Z asked as he approached the happy joggers.

Anna smiled and showed him her new bracelet. "J'kla was showing me his talents."

"Did he make that?"

"Yup. Apparently, he and his family are artisans. He just cut down a vine and used his fingers to whip this together in a short time."

Z was truly impressed. The tension was balanced. The design was basic but good, and the weaving of the flowers into it was rather masterful for someone just using his hands. For the first time since Z had met this creature, he realized he could be totally civilized.

While Z looked at the bracelet and Anna admired the flower blossoms on it, a grumbling could be heard. J'kla smiled sheepishly and held his stomach. "Food time," he said.

Anna chuckled. "Yeah, I'm hungry, too."

Z pulled out a nutrition bar and held it out to J'kla. "It's easier to eat than that fish you put in my bag, stinking up my stuff."

J'kla snarled at the bar. "Wood."

"Wood?" Z looked at Anna, hoping for interpretation.

"He thinks the bars are made of wood. I think he might be partly correct."

"Fine, you guys can eat more of that smelly fish."

Anna started back toward their last camping spot, so they could sit and eat something. About that time, another rumbling echoed throughout this valley. Dark clouds were coming overhead, and curtains of rain could be seen in the distance. It was very obvious where this storm was heading.

"J'kla, where can we go for cover?" Anna asked.

J'kla frowned at her with a furrowed brow. He did not understand her.

She pointed at the rain and shook her head to indicate she didn't want to be in the rain.

He got it and smiled at her. "Come. Trees." He took her hand and led her in an entirely new direction.

CHAPTER TEN

"GROWING SUPPORT FOR THE VOTE has people discussing the potential across all borders. If a vote is called, then it will be the first election of its kind in well over a hundred years," the newscaster said to the audience as the screen displayed the face of Dr. Skye smiling the day the *Sanger* launched. "With the recent discovery of the alien primitives, public support of the science commission is at an all-time high. Approval ratings of the PSC are higher than any of the council members or the head judge. More than one prominent citizen has called for Dr. Richard Skye to be put up for election to be the first global president in history. Our reporter on the streets of Boston this afternoon spoke to a few people about the situation."

The image changed to a woman walking down the ancient roads of the old city of Boston. She stopped a passerby who was willing to give his opinion. "Sir, what are your thoughts on the current call for election?"

"I don't know; ya know, it's like this. Those reps are all talk and debate. They got nothin' going on but politics and more politics. No one of 'em has much power. We need someone who can, y'know, really be in power. Someone with a final say."

The reporter asked, "So, who would you support for global president?"

"I don't know. That science commission, they got da answers. They ain't ever been wrong. They just killed like millions of years of religion with those cat things. That's real intelligence. I s'pose I'd support that Dr. Skye. He's smart and all. With politics, it's all about who gets the last word; but with science, y'know, it's about the facts."

"So, you would vote for Dr. Skye. Any others come to mind?"

"Nope. Nobody really good for the job."

The image changed to a woman who was interviewed just moments later. "Ma'am, who would have your vote for global president if an election were called?"

"Oh, I don't know. I guess I'd have to hear the candidates speak about what they believed in."

The reporter quickly asked, "Some are calling for Dr. Richard Skye to run for president. Would he have your vote?"

The woman giggled. "Oh, he's handsome. But I don't know much about him. Though he did discover those cat people. They say he's moved science forward better than any scientist in history. So, I guess if we're gonna have a president, a smart one would be best."

The image returned to the news desk. "And there you have it. The people have spoken. Only two other people have thrown their hat in the potential ring in the event of an election. Dr. Mikado of the Global Revenue Service and Administrator Sandra of the Department of Energy. The potential candidate with the most support seems to be Dr. Skye, but he is reluctant to accept even a nomination.

"Next, we turn to the bittersweet end of a long and successful career. Administrator Jessie over education has stepped down. She will be the first administrator to actually step down in fifty years. We have been unsuccessful in reaching her office for any interviews at this time, but they assure us that her work isn't finished with the PSC. Administrator Jessie has been the voice of the PSC in the World Corps for many years and intends on continuing that role. When asked to comment as to what she will be doing with the PSC now that she isn't representing the education system, she declined to comment, other than to say big things are coming."

Jessie shut off her screen and sat back to smile at the brilliance of her plans. It was so easy manipulating everyone. She needed the people to be reverent of the PSC if her plans were to work out, and listening to them speak so highly of Skye was practically euphoric. They thought he would make a good president, which would keep them talking and admiring him, while she worked her machinations behind the scenes. By the time she was done, they wouldn't know what happened to their government or elections, but they wouldn't care. They would be so happy thinking that they got what they wanted, while the whole time, their desires were being directed and orchestrated into her master plan.

✳ ✳ ✳

Anna groaned and opened her eyes with a few blinks. It was becoming easier to sleep on the hard ground, but her body still ached in all the same places when she got up. It had been five days since they left the spot where she fell, and she still longed for a soft bed. Her first sight was the green canopy of leaves from those tall palm-like trees they had been walking through for three days. Though she discovered that these trees produce a waxy textured fruit that tasted kind of like coconut but grew in bunches of small berries. She would eat it together with the fish, and it actually tasted good.

As Anna quietly thought about the sweet coconut berries, she suddenly found Z taking a large step over her. He was heading for J'kla. The cat slept on the ground in much the same position as he had every night. And just like every morning, laying on his chest was the computer tablet. He worked and worked on learning English until he couldn't keep his eyes open. It was paying off; he had actually begun to read the Bible to Anna with her helping him, instead of just listening to her read. Last night, he started asking questions—like what is a king and could she explain the commandments.

"Morning, Z." Anna sat up and stretched.

Z, back in his original seat, worked on the tablet. "Morning. You two certainly stayed up late last night."

"He wanted to keep reading." Anna gave off a big yawn, then continued, "We are going through First and Second Kings. There are a lot of stories, and he asks a lot of questions. I have to admit that he's amazing. He's speaking in sentences and understanding us in less than a week's worth of study. Either his people are all unmatched geniuses, or he is some kind of kid savant."

"Oh, he's not a kid," Z said.

"Wait . . . what? Did you figure out his true age?"

"Not really." Z shifted through several different programs working on the tablet while speaking. "I can tell you that he is around 20 to 21 in human years."

"What makes you think that?"

Z stopped for a second and looked back at J'kla as he processed his data. "My analysis of his blood and bones indicates that he ages at a rate that is exactly like a human. And with that information, using his bone scan, I can determine that he is approximately twenty to twenty-one."

"Are you sure?"

"Well, I guess the calculation could be off by two or three years, but that is unlikely. My systems might not be the same level as a true medical drone, but this kind of stuff is not that hard to figure out with some processing time."

Anna was shocked. She had set it in her mind that J'kla was a kid, a teenager, or maybe even younger. Being like a cat, he could grow much faster than a human and be only four or five years old. Somehow, this was unexpected. He was her age. She noticed the way Z worked on the computer tablet. "What are you doing?"

"I was just looking to see if our friends up there have been trying to contact us at all. I've been checking every day, and they haven't even once sent us a message."

"Really?" Anna came and looked over his shoulder at the screen. "Are we getting a clear signal?"

Z pointed to the signal indicator. "I show we have contact strength. But I haven't tested it. Something about this moon might be giving us a false reading. I'll try picking up a newscast." He switched on the news channel and checked the list of old broadcasts. "Yeah, I got some . . . wait . . . what on earth?" He was shocked and quickly accessed a news story.

"What? You just find out they canceled your favorite show?"

"This isn't funny. Look." Z held up the tablet and showed her the headline of the story that was coming through.

GEOLOGIST ANNA OF THE PSC KILLED ON NEW EDEN.

"They think I'm dead?"

"That would explain a lot. Check out the broadcast." They both watched the reporter talk to Dr. Skye and what Dr. Skye said. Then he showed the bloody remains of her uniform.

Anna was stunned, though a touch amused. "Hey, he was crying over me. That's sweet."

"Sweet? He thinks you're dead!"

"Shhh. Don't wake up J'kla," she whispered.

Z repeated in a whispered tone, "He thinks you're dead."

"Well, they're obviously wrong. But that does explain why they took our ship, and why we haven't heard anything from them."

"I think we should correct this for them. Let them know we're down here."

"Right. Wow, won't that be something. Not only will I be coming back from the dead, but I'll be bringing back one of these 'primitives,' who will hold a conversation with the media."

Z accessed the communication channel to send the full signal. "Hope you're ready for the media firestorm."

"I'm willing to endure it, so long as we get the truth out there about these people. I bet I'll get some kind of science award for this. I'll be all over the news." She thoughtfully looked at the clouds rolling by. "You know what I'm going to ask for?"

"A bigger space helmet for your head?" Z muttered.

She elbowed him and then continued. "I'm going to ask to stay here on New Eden to be the ambassador or official researcher or whatever they want. We'll need some kind of liaison between our two peoples."

"Won't hurt that you'll get to be with J'kla," he added.

"And what's that supposed to mean?" She knew exactly what he was inferring, and she didn't like to hear it. She had NO romantic interest in that cat. They were just friends. At least, that is what she kept telling herself.

"Huh?" He was frowning at something on his screen.

"Huh? What's huh?" She knelt down to look closer at his computer.

"I'm trying to send our signal, but it's not opening the communication channel for us. It's like we aren't allowed. I hope they didn't close out your codes, now that they think you're dead."

"Oh, crud," Anna retorted. "You're probably right."

"Well, that's just stupid." Now he was angry with the device.

"What?"

"Mine aren't working either. I mean, you're dead, but I'm left to wander this glorified litterbox for the rest of my unnatural life?"

Anna frowned at him. "Somehow I think you just insulted me, but I don't know how."

Z stood up and held the tablet up, looking for a clear shaft of sunlight for the quarter inch square solar panel on the top of the device. "Maybe the lower power is making the signal not work properly."

"I hope you're right. I doubt these people have much of an intergalactic communication device."

Z smiled as he walked around with the tablet. "Oh, don't worry, you'll still get your Nobel Prize in cat training. I promise."

"Smart aleck." She pulled out half of one of those sweet fruits she had left and took a good bite.

"J'kla is really out of it. He hasn't budged since I got up. You took the tablet from him, and he didn't even roll over like usual."

Z angrily punched in his code again. "Oh, he was up all night, long after you went to bed."

"What was he doing? More games and lessons?"

"Just a few before he fell asleep. Actually, he spent most of the night reading. He picked up your Bible and started reading and reading it. He kept going back to the tablet to check words. He even asked me a question or two."

Anna was amazed and a little bewildered. "How long did he stay up?"

"For three hours after you went to sleep. He's an avid reader but a slow one."

"I guess he's just hungry for knowledge."

"Are you going to tell him?" Z asked rather nonchalantly.

"Tell him what?"

Z moved around with the tablet held out looking for the best light shaft. "That you don't believe any of that stuff anymore. I mean the way you two talk, it sounds like you are giving him quite the lessons on how to be a good Christian."

"It might sound that way, but I'm just telling him a story. From his perspective, it's just a myth or fable. It would be no different than letting him read Cinderella or Aesop's Fables. He probably doesn't even realize that humans used to think of that stuff as real."

Z lowered the tablet for a moment. "Funny, he looked at some of the books on here a few days ago and kept going back to the Bible. I do happen to have Cinderella and Aesop on here, you know."

"He just likes a physical book."

"Okay. But, if you're going to let him get caught up in the reading, you might tell him how you feel, just to be on the safe side." Z finished putting in his commands and then set off the signal again. This time, it let out a shrill sound that they could hear. Anna threw her hands up to her ears, while Z held the tablet away from him for a second. When it calmed down, he stopped the transmission. "Ouch, that frequency isn't right."

Anna shook her head, the ringing still buzzing in both ears. "Wow. That was . . . Oh, you're up." She found J'kla up and ready to pounce. He was in a defensive posture, claws out, teeth bearing, and crouched down. Since he used his vest as a pillow last night, his well-toned chest was flexed up for any combat he could be ready for. When he saw the smiling face of Anna, his tension relaxed, and he started to smile, too.

"What scream?" He brushed his hands over his ears, still hearing a ringing as well.

Z waved a hand while he kept working. "Sorry, my fault. Don't worry."

"Good morning, J'kla."

"Good morning, Anna." This was the usual greeting every morning; it was nearly ritual.

"Would you like some fruit? There's half a piece left."

J'kla nodded. "Thank you, yes." Since he was learning English from children's programming, he was being taught politeness without realizing it. Anna was happy about that. It would make a good impression on the reporters.

"Here you go—not too fresh but still tasty." She handed him half of one of the large banana-like fruits. The other half of what she had just eaten. For some reason, she liked that he was almost the same height as her. However, she wasn't certain why this made her smile.

He accepted it and then took a big bite. "Anna. What milk and honey?"

"Huh?"

"Book say lands flow with milk and honey where God promises. What milk and honey?"

Though she was used to fielding all his cultural questions, they were getting harder and harder to describe. She had never had to describe what milk or honey was to someone. "Well . . . let's see . . . Uh. Milk and honey are food on Earth. Honey is sweet and is made by bugs." She felt dumb saying that; it sounded awful.

J'kla smiled and nodded. "We have sweet stuff made by a bug. Very important."

"It is on Earth, too."

He took a bite of fruit and asked with a mouthful, "What milk?"

"Milk . . . wow . . . okay. Uh, let's see. Milk comes from females. It's made in . . . their . . . " She was pointing at her chest.

J'kla stared at her chest with a mix of confusion and a touch of admiration.

"Oh, dear. I don't know how to explain it without . . . "

Z interrupted to help with the confusion. He came over with the tablet prepped to help. He showed J'kla a cow. "See those. Do your people get stuff from animals like this?" He touched the screen, and the image changed to a pair of hands squeezing the udders to get milk.

J'kla excitedly nodded. "Yes, yes. We get from M'kan. We also get meat and skin." He flapped his vest, which he had put back on.

"That white stuff is what we call milk," Z said.

J'kla smiled big. "B'reann people like milk."

Z went back to where he had been working on the communication channel, though he muttered humorously, "Go figure, the cats—persons—like milk." J'kla didn't get it. Anna was about ready to unscrew his head.

"Want jog?"

"Hey, Z, you gonna be busy here for a while?"

"Sure. I'm going to get through to them if I have to hack the network."

She smiled at the happy cat. "We can jog."

Anna and J'kla jogged through the forest. After a rather short trip, they finally reached the edge of the forest and were back out into the open. Only this time, they were near a ridge of the mountains that had seemed so distant days ago.

Anna was about to keep jogging along a different path, when J'kla stopped her and pointed up. "Up mountain."

"Climb up there?" She panted out, having to catch her breath.

He nodded and took her hand to direct her. It was easier to take her by the hand than to try and tell her where to go.

J'kla found a narrow path that zigzagged up the side of the mountains toward a natural pass in the cliffs. For the first time, Anna was going to see what was on the other side of these mountains. She wasn't even sure that the science teams had come this far.

After what seemed like an hour of climbing, Anna slipped and had to grab a nearby spindly tree to keep from falling.

J'kla grabbed her by the arm and pulled her in closer. "No fall," he commanded.

She laughed and nodded. "Understood."

"Come. No far." He took her hand, a little tighter this time. By his sure footing, it was apparent he knew this climb well.

The path widened as they approached the pass. Soon, they were walking on a flat area between two mountains. Anna still held J'kla's hand as they approached the other side. He stopped her and then positioned her for the best view.

Before her lay deep, dense forests spread as far as the eye could see. Large bodies of water dotted the landscape with rivers spread out like veins. Even more mountains were in the far distance, and they were taller and sharper than these, as evidenced by the snowcaps.

Her breath taken by this view, she couldn't help but notice that part of the forest was on fire. At least, there was smoke. Before she could warn him of this, she noticed that near the smoking area was what appeared to be farmed pastures, for the trees and fields were neatly organized in lines.

Some pastures were fenced in with those large deer-like creatures grazing on the fine green carpets. It finally dawned on her what this place was. "Is this your home?"

"Home, yes," he nodded, then pointed at another part of the trees. "My village."

"Does this have a name?"

He thought and thought about that, translating his own language into hers. After pondering the right words, he smiled and answered, "Land of tall trees."

"Descriptive, but it hardly does it justice." She looked at the vast spread of land between where his village was and the farming was being done. This wasn't a small area. It was large. "J'kla, why haven't we seen more of your people? Where are they?" She approached this question again, hoping he could explain better now that he was slightly more versed in her language.

"B'reann all home. I leave, learn about star people. Elders no happy. I sneak."

"Your people are not allowed to leave? Why?"

He mulled over her words and then answered, "People allowed to leave and go across all lands. But, uh . . . day . . . no . . . week . . . no . . . year . . . no . . . "

"Month?" She gave him the only word he hadn't used yet.

"Yes, month. Two month . . . uh . . . before now . . . stars come. My people change."

"People change?"

"Uh . . . We no understand. Some B'reann disappear, return angry, then die. Leader make everyone no go. Must stay home until stars be normal."

"What do you mean 'angry, then die'?"

His attitude depressed quickly as he answered, "Not understand. Friend act strange, angry, no clothes. Then he run away. We find; he dead. Others do same."

"That doesn't make sense to me either. I wonder . . . wait . . . the primitives."

"Primtive?" He didn't know that word at all.

She shook her head and then thought aloud for her own benefit. "The primitives aren't primitives at all. This explains a lot. If your people are being affected by something in the atmosphere—some kind of celestial anomaly in the space around this moon or something in the habitat that has changed—then it would make sense why you aren't like them. They aren't primitive, just out of their minds. Oh, the PSC will want to hear about this. We might even be able to help. Oh, this is wonderful."

J'kla was befuddled by her attitude. Not only did her words make little sense, she seemed happy that he just told her that one of his friends had died. "Dead no wonderful!"

She laughed and patted his arm. "Sorry. I know, and I am very sorry you lost a friend to this strange event. But we might be able to stop it. Do you understand?"

He thought and then slowly nodded. "You want help?"

"Yes, we certainly will help. We are a good people."

Now he smiled. "I understand." He pointed at the path they had just ascended. "Want go back for Z?"

"Not yet. This is so beautiful, and my feet are killing me after that climb. How about we just sit and relax for a minute or two?" She got down to the ground and sat up against a large rock.

J'kla was perfectly fine to sit with her. "We sit."

"Oh, J'kla, you don't know how nice this place is." She looked out over his homelands. "I've been in space too long. Looking at dead rocks and the black void of space is boring as heck. This kind of view, this kind of place, is rare."

"It land flowing with milk and honey."

She laughed. "It is sort of a promised land. It is so serene and peaceful. Everything you could want, moderate climate, and a sweet people."

"Thank you."

"Are all your people as nice and kind as you?"

"Some are meaner; some are nicer. We just people."

"Good answer." She was relaxed and comfortable and rather enjoying looking at him right now. There was this urge in her that had been building for days, practically since she first met him. Now she was going to ask him. "Do you like your head scratched?"

"What scratched?"

She started to rub her own head and tried to explain. But no matter how she considered explaining it, it always sounded too personal. "Uh . . . oh, never mind."

He had watched her motions, and a smile was growing on his face. "We do that."

"Do what?"

He scooted closer to her and took her hand. "We like this." He put her hand on the side of his head near his ear and ran her hand around the ear and part of his head. Then he forced a purr out to show that he would like this.

This was so enticing that she put both hands on his head, one on each ear, and started to rub away. "Wow, your fur . . . hair . . . mane is softer than I thought it would be. Your ears are so . . . furry." She could feel his head moving with her hands, making a circling motion. He was sighing every few seconds, and that purr had started and was rumbling like an old engine.

In a surprise move, he took the sides of her head and rubbed as well. He got closer as he did this. He didn't tell her, but this was the first step of courting for a B'reann. He finally asked what he had wanted to ask since he learned the right words for it. "Is Z husband?"

"Husband?" she stopped rubbing his head, humorously shocked by that question. "No. He's just a friend."

J'kla smiled and used his gentle grip on her head to pull her in closer. "Good."

Anna returned to rubbing his head and enjoying it. He softly put his forehead on hers, and they stayed like that, both petting the other. It was the most intimate she had ever been with a man. At least, willingly. Was this just friendly petting, or was it more? She had no idea. He seemed content to just keep doing this.

"WHOA! Sorry, didn't mean to interrupt." Z came up the hill at that time, the bag slung over his back and the tablet in his hands.

Anna and J'kla quickly let go. J'kla was still purring.

Anna felt caught, though it truly wasn't a compromising position. "Z, what are you doing up here? Did you get worried about us?"

Z snickered at that. "Nope. I'm not all that worried about your safety while you are with Tarzan here. I just needed to find a higher place to send the signal. I'm still having trouble getting a clear signal through."

"Tar . . . tar . . . sand?" J'kla was lost.

"Tarzan, and . . . never mind." Anna didn't feel like confusing him more.

"Hey, look, I got a signal. It's weak, but I got one." Z worked quickly with the limited amount of signal he had finally found.

Anna looked over his shoulder at the screen. "Why is the signal so weak? This thing has the same quadrasyncratic amplifier as all other communications devices. We got the newscasts down on the forest floor."

"I don't know. My best guess is when they recalled the scientists and ships, they cut off the comlink with the surface. Whatever is happening, I've got something now. Just . . . let me . . . what is going on?" He was becoming frustrated again. "I have a clear signal, and yet they aren't answering. I don't get it."

"I help?" J'kla asked.

"Not unless you have a processed, gold-lined filament antenna built for hyper communication." Z was so frustrated that he purposefully answered with a completely incomprehensible statement to the poor native.

Anna patted J'kla on the shoulder. "Don't worry. You can't help with this." She asked Z, "Okay, is there anything I can do?"

"Just set up camp."

"Camp? Here?"

"Yup. I finally have something to work with up here, and I don't want to lose it. So, for tonight we are sleeping on the mountain. Well, you are; my batteries are fully charged."

"Must be nice," Anna retorted while pulling out the stuff from the bag.

J'kla smiled and started down the hill. "I get fire."

Z watched him leave and then returned to the tablet. "Oh, and if you two want to keep necking, you can have fun. I won't gawk or anything."

"We weren't necking."

"What was that you were doing then?" He was teasing her.

"I . . . it . . . we . . . I don't know. It was probably just a friendly thing they do. He liked it; that's all."

"You seemed to be having a pretty good time yourself."

Anna pulled out the food. "Just get the communication signal working." She didn't want to talk about this any longer.

CHΛPTER ELEVEN

FOR A COMMUNICATION OFFICER, IT couldn't be more boring to just sit here and wait for the random signal to come from Earth. Even on the luxurious *PSC Sanger*, Henry hoped for more ships to come. Then he would have a lot more work to do; but now that the moon was off-limits for most of the universe, it was . . . dull.

"Hey, you wanna play chess?" Someone woke Henry as he nearly nodded off.

Henry answered, his face smooshed up against his palm as he leaned on the communication panel. "We play chess at lunch. We play chess at dinner. We play chess in our quarters. I'm sick of chess."

The officer on the small screen near him smiled wickedly. "That's because you always lose."

"Sure. I'm a communications officer trained in all this sophisticated technology. You were specially bred for creative engineering. You have the brain built for chess; I don't. And you like to hold it over me by playing game after game."

"But you're improving," his friend and roommate answered.

"Yes, I lost in more turns last game."

"That's something. Come on, one quick computer game. I'm so bored, it hurts."

Henry smiled and laid his head back, swiveling back and forth in his chair. "You need to learn to sleep with your eyes open. Works for me."

"That's easy for you to say. You work in a single room with only you and a bunch of computers around you. I have five other scientists working around me, all with higher rank. I take one nap, and I can kiss this cushy job goodbye."

"But you aren't afraid they're going to catch you playing chess on the job?"

"Nope." His friend answered confidently. "The moment they see it, I tell them I'm testing the logic protocols in the system."

"Don't they wonder why you're beating a computer?"

"They don't look close enough. Now, I'll even let you start this time."

Henry swiveled in his chair all the way around once. "No means no."

"Okay, here's the deal. I didn't want to play this card now, but I'm so bored I gotta do something. I bought some pleasure chips."

Henry's swiveling suddenly stopped. His attention was thoroughly grasped. "Pleasure chips! How did you afford those?!"

"Just got lucky and got a deal on them. Look, they're both good for one dose of the drug of our choice. They've got all kinds of the best hallucinogenic pills down in the pleasure deck."

Henry was eager. "So, what's the deal? You and I both go and choose . . . "

"Wait, hold it. These are mine. If you want to *win* one, play me for it. If you make it past twenty turns, I'll share one with you. If you beat me, you can have one all to yourself."

"Man, you really are bored. If I had some chips, I wouldn't be worried about chess."

"Are you in or not?"

Henry switched off one of the redundant monitors and accessed the chess game. It came up on a screen near his friend as well. "Okay, but I get to go first. Pawn to . . . "

"INCOMING COMMUNICATION." The computer interrupted their important game.

Henry gritted his teeth. "What now?" He pushed on the console and moved his chair across the room to the monitor that had been activated. Each monitor was connected to a different receiver on the ship.

"Who is it?" his friend called out from the monitor where they had just been talking.

"Oh, probably another call for Mr. High-and-Mighty upstairs. About the only communication I have to deal with anymore is setting up his interviews."

The engineer was looking around on his monitor, trying to see Henry across the room. "Well, Dr. Skye is an important person. I would hate to waste my life being on one interview after another, always having to be on, ya know."

"I would love his money," Henry retorted. "Wait . . . this isn't from Earth. This is too local. It looks like a signal from a processor tablet."

"A processor tablet is contacting the *Sanger*? That's like an ant knocking on your door. How'd they get through? Who is it?"

"This doesn't make any sense. It looks like it's coming from the planet's surface."

"But no one's down there. This has got to be some kind of mistake. One of your systems is acting up. Hey, I could come up there and fix it for you. Then we can play our game face to face."

Henry was a little insulted. "I can fix these systems myself. I may not have many talents around here, but I know communication systems better than anyone. Even you. Okay, I'll check the signal origin with another receiver antenna. Cross-checking with the data strength analyzer . . . wait . . . this isn't showing any problems. This signal is real."

"Who in their right mind would be down there right now?"

"I don't know, but they're in for a world of trouble. That moon's off-limits." Henry changed to a security station that wasn't often accessed. "I'm going to get to the bottom of this. If some joker decided to go there and get some pictures for the news or something and then got into trouble, he's gonna wish one of those cat things ate him."

"What are you doing?"

"I'm running the signal through the code identifier. I want to know if they . . ." Suddenly, the screen went black. "What the . . . Not now! I'm gonna . . ."

"SECURITY ALERT ALPHA STATUS. REPORTING," the computer announced, and then the screen came back on with no information on it. In fact, there was nothing on any screen to show that anyone had contacted the ship at all.

"Henry! Henry! What's going on?"

"I don't know. I just ran the security clearance number on the signals origin, and suddenly the system shut me out and sent the information somewhere else." He accessed all his programs. "This is amazing! Whatever that was just wiped all records of that communication from the logs. It's as if that didn't happen. I can't even re-access the signal; that code I found is completely blocked."

"Did you see who it was?"

Henry shook his head slowly. "No. Whoever they are, they are in deep trouble. They're on some kind of big-time security list. How about we get back to our game and forget we ever saw any of that?"

"Sounds good. Where were we?"

Henry looked at the virtual chess board. "I was about to kick your butt. Pawn to E-4."

*　*　*

"Everything is going according to plan. They have no idea what is happening. Support for the PSC is through the roof, while confidence in the counsel diminishes." Jessie spoke to Dr. Skye through their private comlink.

Dr. Skye sat at his desk, happy as he could be. "I must admit I was worried people might see through this, or at least question it. But stacking the discovery right on top of the call-to-arms against Jerusalem was inspired."

"Thank you. You might be the most brilliant scientist ever bred, but I know politics better than anyone. I have the courts and media outlets all tied around my little finger. The moment anyone begins to question our call to strike Israel, I merely get someone to shift the subject back to the marvelous discovery, and that's all it takes."

"Tell me, how do you answer the questions on Jerusalem? I am sure that your little games of intrigue and diversions aren't keeping every question quiet."

"I tell them that the citizens of Jerusalem are calling out for help. I tell them the truth: we need to liberate that pathetic city from its religion and bring it into our utopia of intelligence."

Dr. Skye leaned in toward the screen. "Are they calling out?"

"Of course not. That infuriating city is actually keeping its word. People are leaving in droves who have abandoned their former life in that religion-based culture. No one is stopping them. No one is persecuting them." She sneered like a two-year-old child not getting her way.

"So, how are you going to answer any critics who ask for proof of your claims?"

Jessie slammed her fist on the desk. "I'll smash them. I won't let them ask the question. If they dare to question me, then they will learn quickly who holds all the power." The mere thought of her precious media turning on her was almost too much. "We need a common enemy, someone who we can turn all the attention onto if we are going to get the military under our control. There are few enemies left when the world government has unified all borders. The small splinter cells of anti-world corps idiots aren't enough to call for full military control. We need someone with power, someone with teeth whom we can target. That's Jerusalem."

"It won't hurt that you will finally get to decimate that city," Dr. Skye casually added.

Jessie sat back and smiled with elation at the thought. "Yes. That is a very delicious bonus."

"Why do you hate them so much? Don't get me wrong. I've enjoyed watching your enthusiasm for wiping out religion. It just seems your dislike of that one city is stronger than anything else. Why?"

"I don't know. There's just something about that place that grinds on my nerves. They hold to everything we are against. They believe in their mixed-up morals, created by some imaginary Deity. Children are brainwashed at an early age to not want to learn or grow but just bow down and worship air . . . or a statue, or whatever it is they worship. It's an outdated piece of garbage that I intend to clean off the face of the earth."

"You know, with all the talk of elections and the amount of support I'm getting from all over the world, we might change our plan."

Jessie was dismayed. "What?"

"Oh, we won't have to overthrow the government if I'm elected president of the Corps. We can just step into power legitimately and . . . "

"AFTER ALL I'VE DONE . . . " Jessie was infuriated. She was about to tell him exactly where he could stick this plan of his when she noticed that snarky look on his face. She laughed. "Oh, you little tease. How dare you scare me like that?"

Dr. Skye flashed that famous flirty grin. "Just having fun."

"Whew, for a second there, I thought we were going to have trouble. I mean, if you take the job as president, we'll be stuck with all those bureaucrats arguing every piece of minutia. We would never get to do anything, and I wouldn't get to take out Jerusalem. The vote would spend years in debates and arguments. I would probably have to argue with that idiot Elijah over and over and over. I couldn't take it."

"Speaking of the vote, when are you going to introduce it on the floor?"

Jessie held up a tablet. "It's ready to go. The counsel is almost primed enough. I have every news outlet spilling a different version of the same story about Jerusalem calling for help. When the first rep asks what can be done, I will be there with this proposal. They won't know what hit them."

"Aren't you worried they might question giving the Planetary Science Commission control of the global military?"

Jessie sat back, perfectly satisfied with the ingenuity of her plans. "No, they will beg for us. They know that nothing the military has can crack the Iron Dome forcefield. Well, short of using the type 40 nuclear launcher, but that would wipe out half the planet; and even I wouldn't do that just to get Jerusalem. The weapon systems on the *Sanger* are strong enough to irradiate an entire planet surface but precise enough to take down the forcefield in a single shot, without harming the surrounding area. It might take some explaining to get it through a few of those thick skulls, but they will realize the brilliance of the team up."

"I still don't see why they would let us take the lead? Wouldn't they want to put one of their generals in command?"

Jessie sighed hard and rolled her eyes. "*Try* to keep up. It's all about you. The world is begging for an election, and there is only one candidate they are calling for: YOU. While the world is rejoicing at the notion, the counsel is quaking in their boots. They don't want a president. That would dilute their power. When I convince them to strike Jerusalem, I will persuade them to give you the control of the operation. A military position. I'll let them believe that giving you this seemingly unimportant title and power will keep you from wanting anything else. They will feel they have averted the presidential election."

Dr. Skye finished the thought. "Instead, while they are trying to keep the power in their own hands, they will be giving me all the military power without realizing it."

Jessie nodded. "By the time they see their little political empire is about to fall, they will be begging you to put them in whatever court you are willing to establish. You will have ultimate control. Jerusalem will burn, and the world will be everything we have desired."

"Two hundred years of planning will come to fruition." Dr. Skye was finally seeing the intricate brilliance in all of this.

Jessie grinned as a snake about to feast. "I think that when we destroy Jerusalem, I will invite Elijah to watch. He can . . . "

The computer station near Dr. Skye changed from the normal readout to solid black with a warning symbol blinking on the surface.

Jessie asked, since she couldn't see, "What's going on?"

Dr. Skye turned to the monitor. "I think we have a minor problem. Let me check . . . yes, just as I thought." He called up the information.

"Come on. I don't need anything else to raise my blood pressure right now."

"It seems that I was right. The Z-550 that worked with the geologist who died is still active. It is contacting the ship." He called up the information on the screen. "Oh, no."

"Oh, no . . . oh, no . . . blood pressure, remember? What's 'oh no'?"

"The robot sent a short message on a repeating loop. It says: 'We are fine, please retrieve.'"

"We! We! Who are we?" Jessie didn't like even the slightest glitch in their plan.

"I don't know for sure, but, considering that all the other scientists and robots were accounted for, it is likely that that geologist didn't die."

"That's just great." Jessie threw her hands in the air. "We can't have any interruptions in our plans. Just leave them on the planet. They can't possibly survive down there much longer."

Dr. Skye thought about this for a moment. "I have another idea."

"What would that be?"

"When you call for the vote to pass military control over to the PSC, it is sure to make headlines. It will probably cause quite the stir. I imagine that not everyone will like the idea."

"So? Where are you going with this?" Jessie wasn't used to him being the political one.

His grin was particularly vicious. "What if we have a breaking story to put out there, one that will warm hearts and make people like the PSC even more?"

"Like the rescue of a woman given up for dead?" Jessie finally saw where he was going with this.

"Precisely. We could send down a shuttle to pick them up. And then give them a few days to relax and recover in the lap of luxury here. Then, at the right moment, the media will be alerted."

"Oh, you're good. I think some of my cleverness is rubbing off."

"Perhaps."

Jessie's exuberance faded quickly. "What if she knows something that we don't want the world to find out? What if she's uncovered any of our little secrets?"

"We kill her." Dr. Skye said this as casually as if he were ordering a glass of water.

Jessie tapped her chin. "She's good as dead as far as the world is concerned. Just make sure you make it an accident. We can't have any investigations right now."

"Don't worry. I'll think of something perfectly reasonable. For now, I have a scientist to rescue, and you have a court to manipulate," Dr. Skye said.

"Goodbye, Mr. President," she teased him and then turned her monitor off.

CHAPTER TWELVE

THE NIGHT SKY WAS ESPECIALLY clear on top of this mountain. Anna had forgotten how beautiful the stars could look from the surface of a planet.

It didn't help in the least she was snuggled up against J'kla. They had no blankets, and it was rather chilly up on this mountain. They did have a nice fire in front of them, but they still cuddled together. Z sat at a distance to keep watch for any predators.

Usually by now, J'kla would be asking to read with Anna or to play word games on the computer device, but while Anna gazed wistfully at the stars, J'kla gazed into the fire in dismay.

"J'kla, is everything all right?"

He smiled, the flicker of the fire dancing in his eyes. "I good." It didn't sound too convincing.

"We can play a word game or read some. You could tell me a story of your people."

He shook his head and then started to say something. After he opened his mouth, he closed it and lost himself as he watched the flames. Something weighed heavily on his mind, and he couldn't seem to shake it.

Anna thought she knew what it was. "J'kla, I'm sorry if I came on too strong earlier. I didn't mean to. I really like you, but if you don't like me like that, then . . . Oh, this probably doesn't make any sense to you."

"I understand. I like you, too. It me that . . . uh . . . come on strong." He wasn't sure what this meant, only a general idea, but it worked.

Anna laid her head over onto his mane-covered shoulder. "Look, we can be good friends and just see where it goes."

"Good friends," he said and smiled at her. Slowly, he returned to staring and pondering something.

Anna had thought if she sorted out their relationship, then he would feel better, but he was still just as lost in the flames. He was normally such an eager, happy, fun person. Seeing him so mellow was hard. She wanted to help him if she could. "Look. I know there's something wrong. What is it? You have helped me a lot; let me help you."

J'kla sighed again and waited a moment. She could tell he was considering how to say what he wanted to say. More than once he glanced over at the Bible. "Anna . . ."

"What?"

"Anna, can Jesus love me?"

This caught her off-guard. "What?"

J'kla looked at the fire, not wanting to look at her right now. "I know what sin is now. I know I sin. I read God forgive sin through Son. Son love world; God love world. I don't want to . . . uh . . . what word . . . stop living . . ."

"Die."

"Die. Yes, die. I don't want die sinner."

Anna was not prepared for this. She had never helped anyone convert back when she did believe. Now she was trying to unbelieve, and here was a person asking the big questions. "Well, J'kla. According to the Bible, Jesus always loves you. He loves you because . . . well . . . He is love. He wants us to follow Him and believe in Him and accept that He paid the price for our sins. The fact that He died for sins committed by bad people shows that He is all about mercy, grace, and love."

"But, B'reann not in world of Jesus. B'reann not have Savior. I want Jesus; I want believe."

"Oh, my. Uh. You see . . ."

J'kla became very worried. "You believe, right?"

"I did . . . once. Things just came up that . . . altered my beliefs."

"I'll say," Z added from a distance.

Anna answered, "Not now."

J'kla asked, "What wrong? You sin too much? Jesus no forgive you?"

Anna didn't want to look him in the eye and tell him it was his people who destroyed her faith. He was so innocent in so many ways. She couldn't tell him this. A lump formed in her throat looking into those quivering eyes and sorrowful brow. "I don't know anymore."

With a worried look, J'kla got up and retrieved the Bible. He sat it between their laps and opened it. He was really good at finding passages, which amazed Anna every time. He turned to Romans 6:23.

"I read that gift is free. You no earn it. You get it." This was emphatic.

Anna smiled; she was surprised. "J'kla, we hadn't even finished the Old Testament. Why are you reading this?"

He flipped to the back of the book, where a list of verses were written out by hand, by the man who first gave her this book. "I look these."

"Oh, my. I had completely forgotten those."

J'kla thought she meant she had forgotten the verses. "Oh, no forget. They important. See." He carefully turned to Romans 8:1. "See, you know Jesus, you no condemnn . . . cond . . ." He couldn't say the word.

"Condemned. How do you know that word?"

J'kla pointed at Z. "He told me."

Z defended himself. "Hey, he asked for definitions. I didn't know I was converting the cat . . . person." He spoke with his back still to them.

"Well . . . let's see what you've learned." Anna was more entertained than concerned. She wanted to see what else J'kla had read for himself. She still questioned her faith, but she wouldn't burst his bubble right here. He was so happy, it was contagious to listen to him. Besides, he had been so gloomy a moment ago, it was nice to see him smile.

For the rest of the evening, they went from page to page looking at all the verses he had read for himself. He had questions, and she answered them. Though she worried this house of cards was growing, she couldn't help but give him the answers. Something in her just liked telling him and couldn't hold back.

✷   ✷   ✷

Anna woke up with the sun glinting in her eye. Sitting up, she stretched her arms and tried to work out a few kinks from sleeping on the ground. She really looked forward to a real bed soon. Even though she wanted to see J'kla's village or at least meet more of the B'reann, she was also hoping Z's efforts with the signal worked. A hot bath and a soft bed would be really nice about now.

She looked over and saw J'kla had fallen asleep with the Bible laying on his chest. He was a voracious reader. Sometimes, she forgot he taught himself to read only recently. His spoken English was extremely rough, but he grasped the written word better than some people she knew back on Earth. A part of her really wanted to bring him back to Earth to show him one of the remaining libraries. He would probably pass out at the sight of all that reading material.

Anna scooted closer to J'kla and looked down at his sleeping face. He was a sound sleeper, which might be in part because he stayed up late reading. Even through his ragged snore, he was cute. She was reminded that at one time she prayed for a man to come into her life who would want to be with her, a man who would love God and her and be honorable. In this feline man, she has found what she prayed for, and yet she had resisted the idea of love every time.

Why did she have feelings for him? She asked herself this last night for a while before drifting off. Was it just a curiosity? He was very different and unique. Was it his mind? Though he had a primitive grasp of English, he was actually very smart and talented. Was it his body? Yes, even though she had stuffed those feelings as deep in her as she could possibly muster, she liked looking at those muscles. She wanted to grab him by his shaggy mane and run her hands all over that fur, feeling every line and curve. However, she kept any rather lusty feelings in her locked away tightly.

Truly, it was a deeper struggle than she wanted to admit. She fought within herself to answer some deep questions. Looking around, she found Z wasn't sitting in his usual place. He probably went to get some water. Reaching over as carefully as possible, she slid the Bible off of J'kla's chest. This caused the big cat to turn over in his sleep and scrunch up his body a little. Looking into the open book, she considered the outrageous notion God really did exist. If He had answered her prayer for a man, she wanted to be certain.

"God, if You are there, please let me know this. I cannot reach him with certainty. If I ask him if he really cares for me, he may not understand and agree without fully comprehending what I mean. I need to hear it from him in a way I cannot miss." Realizing this was the first time she had prayed since she landed on this moon, she knew it was pointless and silly to be addressing a God she no longer believed in. "Oh, this is just stupid." She closed the book and quietly put it back into the bag.

"What's stupid?" Z whispered as he came up the little hill.

Anna got up quietly and walked over to him. "Nothing. Where have you been?"

"I went to get some water and to see if I could find any of those fruits you guys like so much. You are out of them, you know."

Anna was honestly surprised. "Thanks. Normally you just push those nutrition bars when we ask for the fruit."

"Hey, I can be a nice guy, when I want to."

Anna looked around. "So . . . where's the fruit?"

"Oh, I didn't find any. But I did look—still counts . . . right?"

"I guess. Maybe J'kla will know where something is nearby. I'm starving." She started back to the sleeping cat. "I'll get him up; it's about time . . . "

Z stopped her. "Wait, I want to show you something real quick. Let the cat-person sleep."

"What is it?"

"It's something I found." He walked her down the hill a little and brought her to a tree, which had a loud buzzing sound. More than once, Anna had to dodge from being struck in the path of a bee.

"Bees? You brought me to look at bees?"

Z nodded and got closer than her to the natural hive. "Take a look at this. I was looking for food and thought this honey might be a good source of nutrition. I wanted to test it and see if it was edible for you and J'kla when I found something very interesting." He held up his hand where a bee had landed on him. "The honey and these bees are identical to those found on Earth."

Anna stepped closer, but not too close. She couldn't tell much, hardly ever having looked at bees before. "Are you sure? They could be very similar."

"No. Everything about them is identical. I took one that had been killed on the ground and got to look at it internally. There is nothing about these honey bees that is different than those on Earth. Just about the only alien thing I found was the nectar and pollen used is obviously from alien plants."

"I guess they evolved the same here as on Earth."

Z shook his hand to get the bees that had gathered on him to leave. "It is possible. But calculating the variables which go into the idea of evolution is hard enough; to have two different species of insect evolve the exact same way on two different planets is incalculable."

Anna smiled and patted him on the shoulder. "Well, then when we get back and after I show off J'kla for the media, you can show off your discovery as well. Maybe we'll both win awards."

"Sure, a Z-550 winning an award," Z scoffed.

They came back to camp just as J'kla was waking up. He smiled with a groggy face and his mane askew. "Good morning, Anna."

"Good morning, J'kla."

"Good morning, Z," Z cheerfully added.

"Did you sleep well?" Anna asked J'kla.

J'kla almost answered when his eyes widened and he pointed upward. "Star fall!"

"Falling stars? But it's daytime; you can't see those now."

"No, look, it's a shuttle." Z excitedly pointed up into the sky.

Anna saw one of the shuttles from the *Sanger* was coming down. "Wonderful! I hope they're coming for us."

Z turned on the tablet quickly and accessed the communication logs. "Yes, listen."

"*Shuttle A17* coming in for a landing in Zone 22. Z-550 of the *Explorer Craft 313,* please adjust your direction to meet landed shuttle in zone twenty-two. *Shuttle A17* coming in for a landing in zone twenty-two . . . " It repeated itself over and over, the voice on the other side exactly like Z's.

"Looks like we've been sprung." Z nearly hopped around with excitement.

Anna was all smiles, but J'kla was petrified. "J'kla, don't worry. They are our friends."

He quickly shook his head. "No friend. Steal people. Come for B'reann."

"Steal people? Oh, you mean the lady they took. They didn't know what she was. They treated her well, I'm sure. They will help us. They will find a way to heal those people who were acting strangely."

J'kla was still scared. "You no go. Come to village with J'kla. I protect."

"I promise to come to your village and meet your friends and family. But I want to introduce you to my friends and family first. They won't hurt you, I promise."

J'kla huffed a few times in disgust, then finally said, "I go with Anna. I no like. But I go. They no hurt Anna, while I there. I promise."

"They won't hurt me. Now, come." Anna held out her hand for him to follow.

The trio trekked quickly through the forest to get to the landing zone. Anna was pleased the shuttle landed on the opposite side of the mountains from the B'reann area. It would do little good to scare them when she wanted to make friends.

"Why did you call it a falling star?" Anna asked as she climbed over a large root.

"New stars move in sky. Some fall. Then climb back." J'kla explained it as best as he could.

"I guess it might look like stars coming down," Anna mused. "The ships in orbit reflect light and look like stars above, and when they come down, they would kinda look like falling stars for a bit. So, I guess that makes sense."

Z shoved over a large tree, which had fallen in the path and then held his hand out. "Our chariot awaits."

In a clearing near where they had camped only a few nights ago, a standard shuttle of the PSC was standing by with its back door open.

"All aboard," Z called out as he stood next to the open door.

Anna got to the door and stepped up on it. "I can't wait to get back; this is going to be amazing."

J'kla was still unsure. He approached but didn't step onto the lowered door just yet. Z was trying to get him to come by continually waving his hand toward the inside like an usher.

"Come on. Don't act like a housecat at the back door; just go inside."

"Z, what did I say about the cat references?" Anna scolded her Z-bot.

J'kla got a little closer and just as he was about to step aboard, he was startled by something he had not expected to see. A duplicate Z angrily approaching.

The shuttles pilot came out with his stun gun ready. "Primitive life form detected."

Anna jumped to the rescue and stopped the Z-550 from stunning poor J'kla. "No! He's with us."

"With you? My orders did not include any more retrievals."

"More?" Z caught that word quickly.

Anna was too worried about the stun gun to catch exactly what this robot had said. "He is my guest. Do not harm him or stun him."

"I understand. But this must be reported to Dr. Skye as soon as we arrive."

"I will accept the responsibility for this," Anna stated. "Now, put the gun away."

The pilot Z replaced his gun into the side compartment and then waited while J'kla slowly approached the ramp.

Through all that, J'kla remained there. He felt the urge to bolt at the first sign of danger, but his desire to protect Anna outweighed his sense of self-preservation. Constantly, he stared at this new person with the same face as the other strange-smelling man. Could they be brothers? Finally sensing the tensions ease, J'kla took Anna's hand and made his way up the ramp and onto this craft of theirs.

Inside, Anna seated him in a chair and then sat right next to him. The whole time, she hardly ever let go of his hand. She could feel his hand quivering, yet he never showed fear on his face. He remained strong, and that was rather impressive.

After the door closed, J'kla's nerves were tested once again. This whole thing lifted off the ground and flew toward the sky with great speed. His face remained a stone fortress of determination, but there was a very slight whimper that came out when the first bout of acceleration hit, and he just about lost his composure.

✳   ✳   ✳

The clouds passed by; soon he could see the amazing curvature of his world. The land and water below looked like a delicate painting viewed from afar. Then the heavens themselves parted, and they flew into the endless void of stars.

"J'kla, look." Anna pointed toward a window near her.

He peered out into the vast nothingness and saw the universe like no other B'reann had ever seen before. His world—a mere drop of life in orbit around a dark planet made of storms. The sun, the center of the B'reann universe, glided slowly across the horizon as the brightest orb, but not the only one. The heavens were filled with these lights. Distant points all reflecting the same glory.

In this moment of exploration, Anna could see in J'kla's eyes that which had been lost in humans for far too long. Wonder. His breath was taken away by everything around him; a joy filled him, mixed with awe and a touch of dire terror. The twinkle of the distant star danced inside his eyes, and he could not tear himself away from watching the galaxy around him shrink his understanding of life itself. When he finally found the words to speak, he whispered, "And God created the heavens."

Anna held his hand a little tighter and gazed out into the endless wonder of space and answered.

"Yes, yes, He did."

Then it came into view—the massive mothership of the PSC. The shuttle headed directly for the hangar bay of the aft section of the ship. J'kla's hand gripped Anna's so tightly, he accidentally forced his own claws to come out. They pinched her skin but did not break through. This was still painful enough that she let go. "Ow."

He realized what he had done and quickly retracted them and said, "Sorry."

"It's okay. I would be scared, too. But try to relax a little. I'll stay with you the whole time, and you will not have any trouble. They're going to love you."

The shuttle flew into the bay. It was a large room with a honeycomb to one side filled with these shuttles.

"Please declare your arrival." The intercom system announced.

While J'kla searched for the source of this new voice, the Z pilot answered, "*Shuttle A17* arrival as scheduled. Request decontamination scan."

"Please repeat. Did you request a decontamination scan?"

"Yes. I have one unexpected guest on arrival. He is a primitive, and I require a decontamination scan before I can dock."

"Scan commencing. You will be notified when you have clearance to disembark."

"Thank you. *Shuttle A17* out."

Just then, the interior of the shuttle glowed a slight blue hue from the emitter outside the craft.

J'kla got really nervous. "What that? What that?"

Anna held him down as he struggled against the seat restraint. "Don't worry. Calm down. They're just making sure you aren't bringing anything dangerous."

"I no danger. I scared," he finally admitted.

Anna reached over and rubbed the side of his head; his tense muscles slightly relaxed, and he sank a few inches down into his seat. "Calm down. This will be over soon, and we will be seeing a lot of people who will want to ask questions. I will be there, and it will be fine. I promise."

J'kla purred for a second and let himself decompress into her hand, giving in to this and putting his trust in her words.

The blue light stopped, and the little side door of the shuttle opened up near the pilot. He stood up and robotically left the ship.

Z muttered, "That was rude. He should wait for you at least." It was customary for the Z-bots to show deference to the human when entering or leaving a ship like this. "Whatever. Let's just . . . " Just then the door shut, and the locking mechanism could be heard. Z got up and hurried to the front. "What is going on?"

Anna stopped rubbing J'kla's head and got up. "Is there a problem?"

Z looked out the front window to see everyone in the bay quickly leaving. "I don't know. I hope we haven't brought some kind of dangerous alien virus with us or something."

"I don't think so. Your medical scans should've shown something . . . right?"

"I didn't test for alien pathogens. Wait . . . A team is coming. Hey, it's Dr. Skye. Wow, a personal greeting from the big shot."

Anna felt better. This was probably a publicity thing. Dr. Skye wanted to be here when she got back; after all, he had declared her dead. If there had been some kind of dangerous virus detected, the head of the PSC certainly wouldn't be hanging around to pick it up.

She helped J'kla out of his seat restraints and brought him to the back door, which is where the team of people was just now arriving. The lock on the aft door buzzed, and then the door slowly lowered down.

Anna straightened out her outfit and then sort of straightened out J'kla's vest for him. "Okay. Just relax, and let me do the talking. If they ask you questions, I will help. Okay?"

"Okay."

The door was down, and there stood Dr. Skye with a big smile and two other scientists. There were no media people with him at this time, which surprised Anna greatly.

"You must be the famous Geologist Anna," Dr. Skye greeted her with a handshake.

She did her best to remain cool in the presence of such a famous person. Shaking his hand, she nodded. "Yes. And, as you can see, I am certainly not dead." Well, that blew it for the whole acting cool idea.

Dr. Skye looked over at J'kla and quietly examined the poor, shaking, young man. "So, you brought one of them back with you. Weren't you scared to bring him without any sort of supervision in the shuttle? He could be dangerous." He was leading her on with these questions.

Anna happily announced, "I believe you are mistaken, sir. I have spent some time with my friend here. His name is J'kla. His people are the B'reann, and they are not the dangerous primitives we have come to expect. He is quite intelligent. He can read. He speaks some English, and he is a master craftsman." She held up her arm to show the bracelet.

She had expected some confusion, or excitement, or something on that level. Instead, there was a cold moment of consideration from the leader of the Planetary Science Commission. After a long pause, he smiled in a way that was a little more terrifying than comforting. "Come. Let's have the doctors take a look at you two."

The two doctors at his sides approached and directed Anna and J'kla toward the exit of this strangely empty area.

Z walked behind and couldn't help noticing both doctors had small hyposyringes aimed at Anna and J'kla. Something was up.

* * *

Anna watched with a growing confusion and concern as they walked down the long corridors of the *Sanger*. She had expected more people to be manning the ship, but instead she found robots sparsely scattered around doing the simple tasks of ship maintenance. There were some Z-500s and Z-550s, as well as a few special Z types designed for security. The only people so far she had seen on this ship that weren't robotic were Dr. Skye and his two assistants.

Why were they so quiet? Why didn't Dr. Skye have a million questions? He had thought she was dead only a few days ago. Now, she had come back perfectly healthy, and he was as silent as if this were her funeral dirge.

Z was even more curious and concerned than Anna. He was afraid to say anything in front of the others, but he wasn't going into this without being on his guard. His duty in life was to protect Anna at all cost. If something was happening that could put her life in danger, he would die to protect her. But besides the programming, they were friends. Most scientists weren't as friendly with their assigned robots as Z and Anna. She let him develop his own personality, interests, sense of humor. He wasn't going to let that friendship down.

They turned a corner and entered a rather small area, where Dr. Skye had stopped. Z paused just before entering the area and grabbed the shoulder of another Z-bot. He pulled him aside.

"I have a few questions." He spoke quietly, so as not to alert anyone.

✶   ✶   ✶

Dr. Skye led them toward the medical bay but stopped at a seemingly blank wall. He opened a secret panel and put in a code. After a few confirmations, a door appeared, and they were led into a separate medical bay with empty beds and very little staff.

"This is Doctor Skye with guests. Do not activate laser defense system," he announced nonchalantly.

"Dr. Skye, what is going on?" Anna finally asked.

He looked around. "Where is your Z-550?"

Anna quickly looked behind her, expecting him to be on her heels. "Z?"

Dr. Skye didn't wait. "Z-550 come in NOW!"

Z hurried into the room with a puzzled look on his face. "Sir?"

"Good. Seal the door," Dr. Skye commanded one of his fellow doctors. The man went over and pressed the button, and the door shut.

Anna got angry. "Dr. Skye, what is going on? I demand answers!"

"I would love to give them to you, but you know too much already." He walked over to a cart prepared with vials of the same liquid that he had injected into the woman.

"What do I know? I can't possibly know more than you about this moon, other than these primitives aren't what they appear to you."

Dr. Skye tested a syringe he had just prepared and then started another. "Exactly. They aren't. They are much more advanced. I'm sure you discovered a great deal about them that would be of incredible interest to a lot of people on Earth. Unfortunately, there is an image that must be maintained if certain things are to go according to plan."

"Plan? What plan?"

Dr. Skye filled the second syringe. "Oh, just a little something my predecessors concocted to help our cause. Trust me, it is better that the people of Earth don't know your friend here can speak anything other than grunts."

"I am J'kla. I scared." J'kla thought that if he said something, this scary man might realize he could speak, and things would get better.

Dr. Skye grinned. "Oh, you did a good job teaching him. That is almost passable. Too bad we can't put him on display back on Earth."

Anna was infuriated. "Listen to me. I will see to it that the truth about who and what he is gets out. You can't fight the truth."

"My dear girl, since the inception of the Planetary Science Commission, truth has become exactly what we design it to be. The people of Earth will believe and trust whatever we say. It is the best way, really. Look at what they did before they had real scientists to direct their thinking. They created imaginary gods, studied horoscopes, chanted to spirits for rain. Now we let pure, undiluted science provide the answers they sought."

"UNDILUTED! But you are lying to them!" Anna had to be restrained by one of the doctors nearest her.

"My foolish child, truth is in the eye of the beholder, and it is the job of the PSC to paint the picture. Please, don't hate me for this. My goal is nothing more than the betterment of mankind. This person and his people will be the means to achieve that goal."

"But they are so far behind us?" Anna asked. "What could we possibly learn from them?"

This stopped Dr. Skye for a moment. He was truly surprised. "Oh, so you don't know the whole truth yet. Pity. You might have seen the absolute brilliance of this plan had you discovered it. But, unfortunately, I cannot let you live long enough to learn it for yourself." He pointed to one of the security Z-bots. "Put the primitive on that bed."

The nearest Z grabbed J'kla by the arms and held him. J'kla fought against it, but it was ten times his strength. The bot dragged J'kla over to a bed and then lifted him on it and held him down while another bot attached the restraints.

"Z! STOP THIS!" Anna yelled.

Z, who was extremely confused, began to say something.

"Z-550, override command authorization 001100, Skye," Dr. Skye announced without an ounce of concern in his voice.

Z stopped mid-motion and froze in place.

"What did you do to him?" Anna was beginning to cry as she struggled against the man holding her arms.

Dr. Skye examined J'kla and ordered one of the Z bots, "Take his vest off."

"Z! Do something!"

Dr. Skye hardly even seemed to care as he said, "It isn't common knowledge, but three people have an override command authorization for all Z-bots, and I am one of them. At this time, your pet robot is under my command. And seeing as I don't need any witnesses or someone with knowledge of the planet down below . . . " He looked directly at the paused robot. "Z-550, wipe your memory and reset to starting condition."

"Understood," Z answered, and then he fell over as his programming completely wiped his memory records and then reset to the condition his computer was in on the day he was first activated.

Anna cried out and sobbed uncontrollably. In a sense, Dr. Skye had just killed her Z. All his memories, all his emotions, all his life was destroyed in a nanosecond of computing time.

"Z! Please don't do this! Don't listen to him!"

"There's no point, girl. He's as good as a computer chip right now. Don't worry, I'll put him to use on this ship. A Z-550 is a welcome tool. Now, your other friend . . . I'm afraid he won't fair as well." With that, he plunged one of the prepared syringes into J'kla.

"What are you doing?!" Anna tried to break the grip of the doctor holding her, but she couldn't.

"I'm giving your friend here a little medicine. It's a nasty concoction I created a while back that reacts rather harshly on the primitives' minds. It is a soup of hormones, toxins, and a couple narcotics that will cause him to go a little crazy. The basic amount, you see, is enough to drive one of these creatures wild for about two weeks. But we have found that with each individual's biology, it has a chance of not killing them but wearing off over time. Our most recent subject proved that, and this is why she was not sent back to the surface."

Anna realized he was talking about that woman in the video. "What did you do to her?"

"Don't worry. She has a very nice job at the Museum of Natural History on Earth."

"You put her in a zoo?"

"Not at all. She required several more minor doses for demonstration purposes. Even with her natural resistance, she couldn't take all that, and she died. But she is on display as a lovely exhibit," he said without a care in the universe for admitting to murder.

"You monster!"

"Scientist, not monster," he quaintly corrected her. "And to be sure that your friend here does not live to utter another word to anyone, he gets a special double dose of the medication. I wonder what the side effects will be? The madness should be most entertaining. I hate that we will miss the show." He picked up the second syringe.

"What?! NO!!!" Anna watched as he shoved the second dose of this horrible drug into J'kla's body.

J'kla was already shaking and losing consciousness as the first dose took effect. He fought and kicked his legs, breaking through the nearly unbreakable restraint straps. Two more guard Z-bots had to hold him down.

Anna sank to the ground, unable to think. Both of these wonderful friends were virtually dead now. Z was gone, and J'kla had only a matter of time before this stuff took him from her.

In a move which surprised even her, she felt the hand of the man holding her slip, and she took the opportunity to attack Dr. Skye. She was angrier now than any other time in her life. She didn't care if someone killed her. She jumped up and raced toward him. Just before she reached him, one of the guard drones shot her with its standard stun gun.

Hitting the floor, she looked up through a haze at the face of her new enemy. He was grinning at her in complete victory. Her world was torn apart, and he couldn't care less.

Dr. Skye ordered the two subjects carried into the shuttle for their return visit. Anna was out cold from the stun gun and would remain unconscious for a bit with the help of a minor sleeping drug Skye had given her. J'kla bore a headband mechanism that induced a coma-like state until it was removed.

"Where should I deposit them, sir?" the Z pilot asked.

Dr. Skye looked at a topographical map of the moon's surface. "Put them down here. None of the observation decks on the ship are currently examining this area. We can't risk anyone even *seeing* her until she is finally dead."

"Understood."

"Make sure they are together when you drop them off. He will kill anything living near him until he dies from the blood poisoning."

"As you wish."

"Now, go. When you return, you are to return to your charge station and wipe your memory of this day."

The Z-bot boarded the shuttle and left for his secret mission. Dr. Skye almost felt guilty about all of this. Almost.

*   *   *

Jessie sat at her desk in her new office near the counsel. She was ready for the next move, but couldn't execute it without the proper conditions.

In front of her were three monitors. One had several windows open, displaying the various news stations' hourly reports. Another monitor kept an eye on the counsel, where the proceedings were happening every day.

The third screen was fed by a secret camera. It was on a tower near the city of Jerusalem. Jessie had it placed a long time ago, so she could keep a watchful eye on this despicable city. It annoyed her to no end that she had never been able to get a spy inside who could place observation equipment under the dome. From this vantage, she could see the perfect hemisphere of the energy barrier protecting the ancient city. This Iron Dome, as the Jews dubbed it, was one of the most sophisticated pieces of engineering ever constructed. It was impervious to all standard weapons. The PSC had yet to develop anything which could disrupt it, and hardly any sensors got through to get a good look on the inside. Only the heat sensors showed anything, which wasn't all that much to work with.

Right now, Jessie needed Jerusalem to do something to provoke an attack. So far, they had actually done what they said. The media under the dome were reporting everything without bias, so the people inside were fully aware of the discovery of the moon and the primitives. As such, people inside were leaving. No one was stopping them. Just like Elijah had promised, the people were free to choose to stay or leave. Not one who had left had said anything about persecution or something that would give her a reason to call for an attack. It was like they purposefully followed their agreements just to annoy her.

"You will slip up. I know it," she whispered to herself.

An assistant peeked around the corner. "Administrator Jessie. We have the numbers back on the recent poll."

"And?"

Her young assistant reluctantly stated, "The trending topics aren't about the primitives any longer. They have fallen to second place behind the singer Vicki."

"That drunken pop star?!" Jessie blurted.

Her assistant nearly hit the floor when her boss exploded. "Yes. She . . . uh . . . came out with a new album and . . . uh . . . it's . . . a hot topic."

Jessie let her fury pass as she considered the positive spin on this. "Fine. It's at least a distraction. Anything else?"

"Not at this time, ma'am."

"All right, go tell the chef to make lunch. I'm hungry."

"At once." Her assistant bolted.

Jessie tapped the desk harder, wishing her brilliant political mind could figure out how to push the next step. Nothing was coming. She was forced to do that which she hated most—wait.

"Computer, run the heat sensor analysis," she asked, and the monitor of Jerusalem changed from the live feed of the force field dome to a much more detailed map of the interior of the buildings and people. The image was in shades of blues and reds indicating temperatures. "All right, scan," she ordered.

The image focused in closer to the city and then began a slow movement to the side. She could see families walking down the street, people talking, hover cars passing by, animals playing with children. "Wait, stop. Go back." She watched as the image swung back a bit, and she could see a pair of very bright dots that were much too large to be people, and they were shaped oddly. "Analyze heat signatures in grid twenty-seven B."

The computer quickly responded. "Heat signature corresponds to only one known source. Type ninety laser cannons."

"Do they normally emit this kind of heat?"

"Only when active. Power signature indicates energy cells are in the process of charging."

"Scan the passage through the force field."

The computer analyzed the information for a moment and then answered. "The force field is at full capacity. At full capacity, it cannot be penetrated from within at any point without weakening the structural integrity."

She was almost clapping her hands. "Then no one is leaving?"

"Affirmative."

A terrifically vicious grin grew across her face. "Perfect."

Elijah walked around the court room floor and spoke eloquently. He was making a very strong case. "I'm afraid you have been misled. You have been told that my people are crying out for help, but they aren't held against their wishes or being hurt. You have been told that we are backward and unable to grasp modern science. I beg to differ. Our medical technology is far superior to yours, and we have often sold newer equipment to your medical bureau. If our science was so far behind and backward, we would never have developed this technology. Our little society under the dome has flourished with a smaller crime rate and poverty rate than any other sizable city in the corps."

One of the administrators asked, "But what about the news reports?"

"If you are referring to the exaggerated reports of oppression and neglect by the Israeli government, I submit that what your media has been telling are unfounded stories. There are those who wish to lie to support their agendas."

"I find that hard to believe," the representative from the state of America answered. "You propose that the media has somehow unified in this so-called deception. Are they all telling the same lie?"

Elijah continued to smile in the face of this resistance. "I'm afraid so. The media has historically been corruptible by those with influence. Truth has been mangled and left for dead in light of sensationalism. Hatred of the Hebrew community has been an easy go-to idea for generations. A hatred founded not in truth, but in prejudice."

"And who, would you say, is responsible for provoking this so-called lie? Who could possibly benefit from this? If what you say is true?" the head judge asked.

"So far, the first person to speak out against us has been the Planetary Science Commission, and their mouthpiece Jessie is the loudest. Without reason or provocation, she has attacked and lied about us to the people and this court. Her role of overseeing the abolition of religion in every corner of your empire has been such a success that she has set her eyes on the only stronghold of religion left on Earth, Jerusalem. Her greed and lust for power has left her blind to truth, and she spends her time spinning lies and half-truths to get what she desires. Why is she so angry? I don't know. But I do know that she and the PSC are behind the lies the media has been telling."

This caused quite a stir, and a few rather harsh words from normally respectable men. To implicate the noble PSC in any political intrigue was unheard of.

Just then, the familiar clicking of sharp heels against the hardwood floor echoed down the hall and made Elijah's smile taper slightly.

"So far, the Hebrew people and their representative, Elijah, have shown disdain for freedom, for free thinking, for science, and for this wonderful organization of peaceful cooperation. Now, he adds the PSC and my name to the list." Jessie walked into the room and came right up to Elijah. "I'm honored to be included."

He nodded his head to her. "Jessie."

She gave him an arrogant smirk and then approached the head judge. "Sir, I would like to address the court."

The head judge frowned at her. "Jessie, you are no longer an administrator, and you are not a representative of any nation state. You must go through civilian channels to address the court."

She smiled back at the judge and then turned to Elijah. "I have been challenged and threatened; I have every right to defend myself and the PSC. That is, unless someone else here has enough knowledge and contact with the PSC to speak on their behalf," she challenged the court by looking around at all the representatives, waiting for someone to volunteer, knowing full well they wouldn't.

"Jessie, this really isn't your concern right now," Elijah tried to appeal to her common sense. "I know that I have made harsh accusations about you and the PSC; but a hearing will be arranged, and evidence will be presented in the fullness of the law. Debates on the floor will not garner anything but anger."

"I am not here for a debate. I am here to bring evidence to these good people's attention. If we wait for a hearing to be arranged, it will be far too late. But then I guess that is what you want, isn't it? You want us to be bogged down in procedures and red tape, while you and your people prepare for war."

"What?" Elijah was caught off-guard. The room blossomed in hushed whispers and gasps of disbelief. War was a word that hadn't been uttered in a long time.

The head judge pointed his gavel at her. "You are allowed to speak. But make it quick."

"Thank you." She calmly strolled around the room. "Good representatives of the nation states, we are at the brink of war," she said with strength and then paused to get their undivided attention.

"With whom?" Elijah finally asked, still lost about what she was talking about.

Giving him a confident smile, she answered, "Why, you, of course."

"Me?"

Jessie snapped her fingers, and a young attendant of the court rushed in and handed her a remote control. "Ladies and gentlemen, while the pet talking head of Jerusalem wasted your time here, his people have strengthened their arms and prepared their weapons for attack." She clicked and a holoimage appeared floating in the middle of the room for all to see, from either direction. It was the same image that she had on her computer: Jerusalem, or really the impenetrable energy dome that covered the city.

"What are we looking at?" the head judge asked.

"Today, sensors have discovered that the energy dome protecting Jerusalem has been fortified to the fullest energy level possible. No one is able to pass through it any longer, which ends their little allowance for those who are fleeing the tyranny."

Elijah answered this one quickly. "That isn't any preparation for war. That is merely strengthening our defenses. With all the talk about potentially attacking our city, it only makes sense that we would use precautions."

"Uh-huh," Jessie uttered rather non-convincingly. She changed the image to the heat map she had looked at before. A ring highlighted the laser cannon heat signatures. "And what are those? Telescopes?"

"We . . . uh . . . those are . . . " Elijah wanted to say this without raising any suspicions. He knew she would spin whatever he said to her advantage, so he needed to give her as little to work with as possible.

But Jessie did not give him time to answer. "Those are type ninety laser cannons." The holoimage divided, still showing the part of Jerusalem that held the cannons. The new image was a short video, showing a type ninety laser cannon being demonstrated in the Antarctic. It fired a beam at a passing target drone the size of a large spacecraft. The drone was obliterated in a single shot. "They can fire through their own barrier from the inside and do considerable damage to large areas."

"But their range is limited; they are stationary. They are only defensive measures." Elijah was getting a little overwhelmed.

Jessie was pleased that the first to ask the next question wasn't her. The representative from the state of Uganda called out, "What else do you have? What other military craft are being prepared?"

"We don't have any . . . "

Not giving him time to completely answer, the representative from the state of Italy asked, "Are you going to take territory that was formally part of Israel, or are you after other targets?"

"We aren't going to attack. This is not what we're doing."

Jessie stepped aside, her work done for now. She wouldn't push to the next step until the time was right. This counsel was now convinced that a threat was really there, a threat that was worthy of combating. No doubt the military would be called up to service soon, but that force field would have to be dealt with. When that hurdle came up, she would be ready with her proposal. For now, she would simply fan the flames of distrust and anger toward Jerusalem. The more they denied this, the more it would incriminate them, especially with her helping.

CH∆PTER THIRTEEN

ANNA FELT LIKE SHE WAS waking again after that terrible fall, only this time was even groggier. There were flashes of memory around what had happened prior to this deep sleep. She could see J'kla being surrounded by Z-bots of various natures. There was Dr. Skye smiling at her, but his smile seemed so cold and evil. Then she could see Z on the ground like he was dead. Was this just some horrible dream?

"J'kla?" she attempted to call out his name, but it was a mumbled slur. Her mouth tasted awful. Wait . . . can you taste in a dream? Is this a dream? "Z." She tried again, but this was just as bad.

In the distance sounded the roar of a lion. It was screaming like it had no control over its mouth. Her last memories began to connect together and make more sense. That roaring was getting closer, but was still terribly distant. What had happened before all went dark was becoming a more coherent story.

"J'kla!" Now her voice was much clearer. She could see him on that table, being killed. Her own imagination took over finishing the narrative. He fell limp and stopped breathing. Somehow, she was now standing over his body calling out to him, but her voice was gone. Dr. Skye laughed maniacally with the syringe still in his hand. She couldn't make a sound; she couldn't shed a tear; it was as if her body refused to allow her to cry.

Suddenly, Anna felt nothing, but the cold table under her. The laughing doctor was gone; J'kla's body was gone; Z was gone. She was alone in the room, and the darkness was slowly surrounding her. Her world was destroyed. She had nobody left to care about, and no one cared about her. Walking backward away from the table, she looked around for someone, anyone that might be a friendly face. But there were none, for she couldn't think of anyone. Desperate, she tried to conjure the image of the boy who had converted her to Christ; but as soon as she almost got his face in her mind, she remembered that he, too, was dead—a long time ago.

This was it. These was her final moments. She sank down to the ground and curled up, holding her knees to her chest. All that was left was her own death.

"Anna." A deep, comfortable voice called to her.

"LEAVE ME ALONE!"

"Wake up!"

She looked forward, and the dark empty room was getting brighter. "Who is there?"

That same voice answered, *"Anna, you are not through. WAKE UP!"*

Anna opened her eyes and found herself on the ground. She was lying near the base of a tree in a forest. The midday sun was nearly overhead. She then realized that the light in her dream was the light shining on her. But who spoke to her?

Her ears were ringing, and she was dizzy, but otherwise not harmed. This was not like the last time, when she woke up after the fall. Her strength was returning quickly.

"J'kla? Z?" She was desperately hoping that it had all been a terrible dream.

There wasn't any response.

Anna roughly got up and felt like she was about to fall over again. She wasn't in as much pain as before, but her head was still swimming from the gun attack. "Where am I? HELLO?" she called out in hopes that someone was looking for her.

Then it came. A deep, terrible, guttural roar of a lion on the rampage. The echo was amazing, and the power terrifying. Whatever made that sound was close and hungry. Anna quickly grabbed the first large stone she could find and then stumbled away from the sound.

"J'kla! Somebody! Help!"

A heavy footstep could be heard, as well as a deep, harsh panting. It approached fast. Anna hoped to run, but she was still recovering from her ordeal. She stumbled into another tree, tripped over a root and had to stand up again, and then made it a few more trees down, until she had to stop to gather her senses. The more she moved, the more the world tilted on her. The heavy footsteps got louder, and that breathing was punctuated by growling and a few short grunting roars. It was nearly upon her.

Anna was fully aware that she was in no condition to outrun some kind of hungry beast. She would have to fight it off herself. So, she propped up against a tree and held the stone at the ready. If it got close enough, she would bash its skull in with the rock. Out of her nightmare came what she feared most. J'kla rounded a tree and stopped to let out another roar as he had finally caught sight of his prey. He was nearly naked and bristling like a monster on the prowl. A foaming drool came out of the sides of his mouth, and his eyes darted wildly. The breaths were huffed deeply and between clenched teeth. His pants were torn to shreds by his own claws.

"J . . . J'kla?" Anna dropped the stone and looked at him with a mixture of pure fear and sadness.

He dashed toward her, his hands held up with the claws at the ready to tear her apart. Each footstep was followed by a harsh pant and grunt. He stopped running and leaned on a tree. He pawed at his head and shook it wildly as though something was crawling on him. He moaned and growled with irritation at being unable to help himself.

For a second, he looked more confused than ferocious, so Anna thought perhaps she wasn't in danger. Taking a step away from the tree, she held her hand out. "J'kla, can I help?"

The moaning and whimpering stopped as he looked up. Now, she could see his wild eyes. He snarled at her and showed all his impressive fangs. The drool and foam dripped down his face, and he licked his lips at the sight of fresh meat. A few harsh grunted roars were followed by him breaking into a sprint for her.

Anna saw him almost upon her, and she fell over in fright and let out a shrill scream. This stunned him. He stopped and responded with a loud, violent roar that was ten times louder than her scream. Birds in the trees and a few other beasts fled in fear of being the second course. He swiped his hands at his temples and forehead and groaned as he seemed to be fighting something.

J'kla grabbed the sides of his head and yelled in a much more human voice. He appeared to be in terrible agony.

Anna, still on the ground, watched in horror. She knew he was experiencing immeasurable pain from the drugs Dr. Skye had flooded his body with. "J'kla! You must fight this. Please don't hurt me!"

J'kla stopped struggling and looked at her again with those dilated eyes. He snarled and then growled at her, yelled at her, and then came closer. His body jerked around, and he was rubbing his hands against his arms, chest, and neck like an insane man. He wanted to kill her, to eat her, to taste her blood, but he also wanted to get this strange feeling off of his skin. He didn't know what she was or, for that matter, who he was. There was something yelling in his brain that deafened his reasoning and logic and was driving him mad. He got to her as she crawled backward across the ground. With a burst of motion, he swiped a clawed hand at her and ripped across her forearm. He tore apart the sleeve of her jumpsuit and gashed into her skin. The scream of agony from her was hard to hear over the sounds of the million voices in his head.

He sniffed the blood on his claws and then went to taste it. It smelled so good.

"J'kla!" There was that name. It was distant. It was familiar. It wasn't inside his head, either.

The pounding cacophony faded enough for him to see her with his real eyes for just a second.

He knew her; he knew this scent.

∗   ∗   ∗

Anna saw a minor change in this mad beast. His ranting, raving lunacy had paused as he looked at her with wide eyes. His body twitched and jerked. His head jumped around every few seconds, but his eyes had returned to a minor sense of normality.

"J'kla. Please, don't hurt me." She was weeping.

He slowly approached her, shaking and wild, but somehow trying to restrain himself. He got lower and lower until he was right over her, one hand holding the ground to keep himself up, the other hand still showing claws and trying to rip at her. He was battling hard against the primal desire to kill.

"J'kla?" She called his name, sure that, somehow, he was understanding her. He was so close to her, yet he wasn't hurting her. Suddenly, his hand swiped at her, and then he brought it back in fear of what he had done. She screamed and lurched but didn't feel any more claws into her skin. It was not close enough to harm her this time.

"AnnnAnn . . . " He was trying to say her name. He panted harder, growled, and jerked his head around for a few moments, then strained to look at her with his real eyes. "Anna," he whispered.

"J'kla?"

He gulped, growled, hit himself in the head with his hand and then struggled to say something else. "Anna . . . I . . . I . . . I love . . . ANNA!"

Anna was about to take his arms and try to help him fight this, when he suddenly roared hard and hit her in the face with his fist. His claws didn't make contact, but it was a strong blow. This threw her to the side and made her quickly cover her head in fear of another strike.

∗   ∗   ∗

J'kla heard her scream and saw her cowering. The maddening voices and sounds in his head were getting louder and louder. His heart beat so hard, he could hear the thumping in his ears. But he sensed this minor lucidity was about to be lost, and he wouldn't be able to control what would happen next. Almost everything in him was telling him to kill her, and he knew that argument would win as soon as he lost control.

"YAHHHH!" He yelled and sat back on his heels. He was pulling at his mane and trying to regain his senses. Those voices, these sounds . . . he wanted it all to get out of his mind. The pain in his muscles, the pounding of his heart, the jumping and jerking of his body.

"J'kla, please . . . " He heard her plea, but the monster was boiling to the surface again.

He bore his fangs at her and roared with every ounce of strength in him. She curled her whole body up and screamed in fear.

J'kla reached out and grabbed the nearest tree with his hand, digging his claws deep into the bark. His body resisted and tried to free his hand, but he knew what he was doing. Using all the focus he could muster, he grabbed the tree with his other hand and gripped it with his claws as well, nearly locking himself into the trunk.

∗   ∗   ∗

Anna looked up and couldn't tell what he was doing. He had both hands gripped around the tree. He was even wilder than before, and foam was pouring out of his mouth. He would scream, mumble something in his own tongue, roar, growl, whimper, scream again. It was terrible to watch.

"What are you doing?"

He was snarling at her and panting so hard through his clenched teeth she could hear the breath cutting through the fangs. The demented madness was about to fully assert itself. With the last vestiges of clarity, he said, "I . . . love . . . Anna . . . sorry . . . YAH!" With that, he thrust his head into the tree.

Anna yelled and closed her eyes, shocked at what he had just done. His skull hit the tree so hard that she heard the sickening crack.

"YAH!" He did it again, and again, and again. Each time harder than the last. The bark at the spot where he was hitting himself fractured and broke loose.

"J'KLA! NO!" Anna knew he was trying to kill himself before he killed her, and she couldn't bear the thought.

With one last yell that partially turned into a roar, he slammed his head into the tree, and this time bounced off and hit the forest floor. He lay there, nearly naked, and groaning in pain. Blood was trickling down his nose, and ten long gash marks on the bark displayed just how hard he had pulled to knock himself senseless. His head finally flopped to the side, and he was out.

"J'kla! J'KLA! NO!" Anna got up and came over to him, laying across his body and crying as much as she had wanted to in her dream. "Oh, J'kla! Please don't die. Please don't leave me! J'kla!"

Anna stayed on him, listening to his irregular heartbeat and feeling the shallow breaths coming and going. There was nothing left for her to do but cry. She began to wish that Z was here with his medical arm, but then that only brought back the understanding that Z was dead as well. This made her weep harder. How could she handle this? Surely, she could do something to fix all of this. How could she go on?

"GOD, PLEASE ANSWER ME!" she cried out in deep desperation, her words echoing amongst the trees.

The leaves on the ground crunched. A few twigs snapped, and the murmurs of voices surrounded her. Through wet eyes, she looked up and found a dozen others standing in a circle around her, looking in with extreme curiosity and fear. They were all B'reann like J'kla. Some men, some women, all different colors.

"J'KLA!" a man called out and rushed to the fallen B'reann's side. He shoved Anna away, and someone grabbed her by the arms. Two B'reann brandishing spears held her in place. The man who had rushed to J'kla's side was crying and feeling the nearly dead body. Anna still shook from her own crying; her eyes were blurry, but she could see that the man kneeling next to J'kla had fur very similar to J'kla's, only with a hint of gray in his mane. This man had to be family—a father or grandfather. He was crying more than anyone else around, save Anna. The others were all looking down in sadness for him. Suddenly, he pointed at Anna.

"Chi J'kla tolla nhok!" He gestured back at J'kla and then pointed at her.

Anna couldn't understand him. J'kla didn't teach her many words in his tongue. "I don't understand."

"TOLLA! TOLLA!" This meant murderer.

Anna realized she was being blamed for J'kla's injuries and wanted dearly to show them she wouldn't do this. "No, please. I didn't kill him. I . . . I love him. Please, you have to understand me. Oh, please understand." She was worried what they might do to her for this. She wanted them to know who their enemy was; they were the only people left that might help her.

The man snarled at her and stood up, still pointing that claw at her. *"TOLLA CHI J'KLA?"*

"No, please. Oh, how can I make you understand?"

The angry man came toward her, his claws coming out, and his face looking a little like J'kla's did a moment ago. *"Feetha tolla go."*

He said he was going to kill her right here and showed this by lifting his hand to strike her.

"J'NAR!" A woman's voice stopped him. She walked up and grabbed his arm. *"J'nar, krina solka tolla. Krina patha J'kla."* This woman stepped over to Anna and took her right arm out of the grip of this warrior and looked at the bracelet. She held up Anna's arm toward the fierce man.

"J'kla?"

Anna nodded. "J'kla, yes, J'kla made that for me."

The woman looked back at Anna with a bit of a cocked head. *"Chi?"*

Anna carefully pulled her other arm free of the warrior and then pointed at the bracelet. "J'kla." Then she pointed at herself with a smile.

After a moment of consideration, the woman gave Anna a little smile. *"J'kla krina go."*

Anna had no idea what that meant, but it sounded a lot nicer than the man. They must understand that J'kla was her friend, not her enemy.

"I love J'kla," she said, knowing that they couldn't understand her.

The woman turned and looked down at J'kla on the ground. She had a mournful look on her face as she pointed at another warrior. *"J'kla sotha del tri."*

The biggest man in the gathering handed his spear over to the angry father and then lifted up the broken body of J'kla to carry. The woman walked beside him and put her hand on J'kla's chest as they continued. She waved a hand back at Anna. *"J'kla krina."*

Anna came up and walked with the group. The woman took Anna's hand and held it. Anna knew there was pain in this woman, a pain that translated across all languages. She didn't know how, but she knew that this woman was J'kla's mother. It hurt Anna so much to watch him die. How could she tell his mother why he was murdered?

*   *   *

The sun had set, and stars were coming into view as the group escorting J'kla arrived in his home village. It was a sad time; both the man and woman who had spoken to Anna cried silently the whole way home. Anna felt they had to be his parents. It hurt her so much to see J'kla like this; she couldn't imagine what it must feel like for a parent.

They took J'kla into a small hut and laid his body upon a bed. Anna wasn't allowed inside yet; only his parents stayed. An elderly woman came in carrying a basket of herbs and lotions—the village healer, she assumed.

Anna stood outside the hut, her heart aching and her sadness nearly overwhelming. She pent up the crying during the walk and was keeping it at bay right now. She was surrounded by strangers and didn't want to be seen just bawling.

For a long time, they stayed in the hut with him, and she just stood there looking at this little village. It was archaic by any modern human standard, yet very beautiful. Wooden homes built both on the ground and in the trees. Rope and wood bridges connected the lifted structures and made a web around this part of the forest. Lines were strung here and there with clothes dangling in the breeze to dry from being washed. There was a potter's shed with various pots sitting outside in different degrees of completion. Down the dirt path in the center of the village, she could see where the forest ended at the edge of town and pastures were fenced off for cattle. It was dark, but she could make out the shapes of those large deer-like creatures inside the pastures, gently grazing on the grasses.

All over this village were several hundred B'reann of all ages. They had differing colors of fur, and the males had different sizes of manes depending on ages. The women did not sport the large manes, but they did have hair on their heads—not unlike Anna, only in shades matching their fur coats. They were a handsome, simple people.

No one tried to talk to her, and more than one kept their child from approaching when they passed. She understood completely. Finally, this all made sense. J'kla told her his people started to act strangely the day the new "stars" arrived. He meant when the ships of the PSC arrived. She didn't understand why or when, but the PSC must have been here a while before the discovery was announced. They captured and altered these people to suit their needs.

Anna wanted an explanation, a reason behind why they would perpetrate such an evil action. Why would a primitive creature mean more to their plans than one of these villagers? These people still fulfilled their need to find an alien race. What did Dr. Skye mean about her not knowing everything? That if she did, she might understand the so-called brilliance of his plans? There was one last piece to this puzzle, and she wanted to find it.

"J'kla krina." An old voice grabbed her attention.

The old B'reann woman stood at the door, waving her hand at Anna.

Anna didn't know exactly what it meant, but she knew her name to these people was J'kla Krina, so she followed.

The old woman led her into the hut. She found J'kla laying on a bed with a blanket pulled over him up to his chest. J'kla's mother put her face down onto the bed right beside J'kla's head and cried out in her own language. Anna could not understand what was said, only his name when she would call it out. The man who had been so fierce stood behind the wailing woman, holding her by the shoulders. He, too, was crying, but it was silent and somber.

Anna's chest shook. Her throat seized, and her eyes watered, nearly blinding her. She looked down at his body, and she began sobbing again uncontrollably. Kneeling down to his side, opposite his mother, she put her hands on his chest and cried hard. She could feel his heart beating, the racing rhythm had slowed down to near-death. His breaths were shallow and fading quickly. She wanted to run, to flee so not to experience his death, but she couldn't take her hands off of him. Each beat of his heart was a promise of another to come. She had to feel the last beat, to be there until the very end.

Through teary eyes, she said to his parents, "I am so sorry."

She was fully aware they could not understand her, but she had to say it. It was her fault. Had she not forced him to come with her to the ship, taught him to speak English, allowed him to be a part of her life, he wouldn't have died. She hated herself right now; she was responsible for this wonderful man's death. He was so kind, generous, loving, and gentle. He deserved a long and happy life, and that was stolen by a wicked man, for reasons which did not make sense.

Anna felt as helpless as she had ever been in her life. Nothing mattered to her any longer, nothing outside of his life. What could she do? Finally, she did what she truly hadn't done in weeks. Placing her forehead on J'kla's bed and keeping her hands on him, she prayed.

Anna stayed at his side and continued to pray to God about this man. She knew God had also brought her to this moment because she was the only person on this planet who would pray for J'kla's life.

Six hours passed, and she was an immovable, passionate prayer warrior. The old woman tried to get her to get up and rest, but Anna didn't even notice the hand pulling on her arm. The parents both stopped weeping so hard and only sat back and consoled each other for the inevitable death that was about to happen.

Outside the hut, people had begun to gather. Word had spread that a woman was sitting by the side of J'kla, doing something strange. They didn't know exactly Who she was talking to, or in what tongue, but somehow, they understood she was seeking a Higher Power. They had buried a dozen of their own since the new stars appeared, and they expected to be carrying his body to his grave when the sun rose, just like the rest. But they all wanted to know what this furless stranger was doing to him during his night of death.

✳   ✳   ✳

Hours later, Anna realized her mouth was dry. She stopped praying and softly cried without tears. All her tears had been spent. A million lines of Bible verses danced in her mind as she prayed in hopes God would reverse the fate of this man.

A strong set of hands took her by the shoulders. *"J'kla krina."* The gentle voice of the father attempted to coax her away from the bedside, so they might take his son to the grave that had already been dug.

Anna, exhausted, still lay with her head on J'kla's chest. Suddenly, she felt a hand rub her beside the ear. Both of this father's hands were on her shoulders, and she could still hear the sniffles of the woman on the other side of the bed. This felt just like when J'kla was trying to pet her like she was petting him. It was a slow, weak rub, but the hand did it again.

With a spark of hope igniting a flame in her, she looked up at J'kla. His eyes were still closed, but his mouth was beginning to move.

"J'kla?"

He meekly whispered, "An . . . na."

His mother gasped. His father let go of Anna and came closer to his son's bedside.

J'kla weakly opened his eyes and looked at the two people beside him. He dryly gulped and then said a single word to them. His mother was crying again, but it was an obvious joy. His father rushed out of the hut and was back in a matter of seconds. He had a wooden ladle in his hands from a barrel outside. Using one hand to help lift J'kla's head and the other to gently tip the ladle, he gave his son a much-needed drink of water. After only a few sips, J'kla stopped and laid his head back down.

Anna put her hand on his chest and felt his heart beat. It was stronger than last night; so were his breaths. She wanted to cry just like his mother, but she was so worn out from her long night of praying that she couldn't. A sense of pure joy filled her heart, and she knew now more than ever there really was a God.

The old woman came back in with her basket of healing herbs and lotions and quietly closed the door to keep the onlookers at bay. The miracle which took place was being pronounced all over the village already. Anna wasn't aware of this, but J'kla would be the first person to survive a night after being brought back from the strange insanity illness.

The old woman gingerly looked at the sleepy eyes of J'kla and then put her head down on his chest to listen. With a grandmotherly smile, she said something to him and then carefully applied the same leaves J'kla had put on Anna's wounds. They were being put on his head, covering up the nasty bump that had formed where he had rammed the tree trunk. She smothered some nasty-smelling ointment on his chest and into his mane, likely as a way of getting the vapors into his nose. They had no idea how to treat what was wrong with him, but she would do whatever possible to make him better.

The father took Anna up by the arm, so she could stand. It was a clumsy feeling getting up after all that time kneeling. He smiled at her and then pointed out. Anna took the hint and was led out of the hut.

He walked with her through the village, answering a few questions along the way. He seemed to be telling them about her, but she had no idea what the question was or what his response would be. What could they possibly think of her? At least, they didn't seem as menacing when they looked at her.

Eventually, he led her to a larger wooden building with several windows. It was fastened to a tree and had more than one level built up into the branches. Inside the home was a fireplace, large cushions for sitting on the floor, metal and clay pots everywhere, and a lot of different artworks decorating the place. She could see there were a lot of tools, supplies, and partially finished projects of art. Considering what J'kla had said about his family, this was probably their home.

He took her into a room and showed her a bed. With a few gestures and pats on the pillow, he indicated what she was to do. It was nice that he realized talking to her was impossible. She went and sat on the bed, which was a soft mat on the ground, so that his way, she could show him she understood.

"Wait." She held up her hand to stop him before he left.

He frowned at her.

She wanted to know his name. "Anna." She pointed at herself and then at him.

He shook his head. This felt very similar to when she first met J'kla.

Thinking, she pointed out of the room. "J'kla." Then to herself, "Anna." And then she pointed at him.

He smiled and pointed at himself. "J'nar."

She smiled and then said, "J'nar."

He nodded and then pointed at her. *"Anna, J'kla krina."* She thought telling him her name would stop them calling her this other thing, but he just attached it. He bowed his head to her and then left.

Anna wanted to tell him to inform her when J'kla was better, or if he got worse. She wanted to thank him for giving her a place to rest. It was so frustrating to be nearly mute. She had spent her whole life talking. She was a scientist, who grew up talking and listening. Now, she was surrounded by people who couldn't even understand her name.

It really did not matter, though. The minor frustration at this inconvenience was only a shadow in the back of her mind. J'kla was alive. A real miracle had happened; and she was so excited, she doubted she could sleep. A part of her worried this recovery was temporary, and he would not live much longer. Instead, she had to settle on faith to comfort her. God had brought J'kla through the night, and now He would mend him and make him whole again.

To get herself to calm down after all the excitement, she thought through all the verses she could remember. Her Bible was back on the ship, and she was unlikely to ever see it again; but she had spent years memorizing every verse she could. Now was an opportunity to put that practice to use.

CHAPTER FOURTEEN

THE SHUTTLE THAT HAD CARRIED Anna and J'kla to and from the *Sanger* was under quarantine. Danger signs were posted indicating a lethal bacterium had been discovered. The shuttle would have to be sanitized and purified before any human was allowed inside for normal use. Right now, an old-style Z-500 robot entered the shuttle to work on the sanitation project.

The inside of the shuttle hadn't been cleaned yet, and he was the first bot to enter after the quarantine had been declared. He wondered what had been brought aboard that was so dangerous. Why did they send this shuttle down to the moon and back after the moon was designated off-limits? "I wonder if they left something down there?" he pondered as he made his way to the pilot's seat. "Oh well, this shouldn't take too long."

Sitting in the pilot's seat, he plugged a special device into the computer port near the navigation console. It would take care of all the deletions while he waited.

Even robots get bored when waiting. He sat there and swiveled in his seat. It wasn't hard for him to do fifteen tasks at once, and right now he had one job. It was dull work, but orders were orders. He thought about how much he would like to upgrade with those new systems the Z-550s got. He wanted to have an even more human body. The 500 series were shaped like humans, but they lacked most of the surface features which were hidden by clothing, like real-looking muscles. The 550s had real-looking cut muscles that showed without their clothing on. The 500s had smooth bodies devoid of any real muscular definition. He didn't need them, and neither did the 550s, but he wanted them. The scientist he previously worked for had him reassigned so she could get a 550 with a better body. What was so special about them anyway? All humans had them, in varying degrees of tone, depending on the human's fitness lifestyle. Why would they be so special to her? If he had some, perhaps he would understand. But once the 550s came out, they stopped upgrading the 500 series. In a few years, he would be so obsolete, they would decommission him; and he would be lucky if they sold him into civilian use and didn't just strip him for parts.

During his pondering, he noticed something in the corner. It was a standard satchel bag issued to field scientists. Perhaps, this was the item that had brought the dangerous bacterium to the ship. Dr. Skye made it very clear robots were immune to the ravages of this unnamed bacterium, so it wasn't dangerous for him to investigate. Perhaps he could remove it and save the next worker the trouble.

He got up and carefully approached the bag. Slowly, he unzipped it and pulled it open to peek inside. There were some clothing pieces, a pile of nutrition bars, and some strange bits of natural debris. He picked up the tattered remains of peel from Anna's favorite fruit. It was old, dried out, and in desperate need of a trashcan. "This must be it. But I don't see any sort of bacterial growth on it. Must be microscopic." Cautiously, he placed the aged peel back into the bag and was about to pick up the whole satchel when he noticed something rather odd. It looked like a bound book. "What is this? There aren't any books around!" He had never actually seen one of these in person—a real book with pages, a cover, and everything. As carefully as if he was picking up an original copy of the Constitution, he proceeded to slide it out of the bag.

"Don't remove anything."

A new voice startled him, and he jumped up. "I wasn't . . . oh, you're not Dr. Skye."

A Z-550 reached down and picked up the bag. "I have come to collect this."

"Does that contain the bacterium?"

This stopped the 550 in his tracks. He seemed lost and then nodded. "Yes. It does. Did you recover the data device from this satchel?" This Z-bot rummaged through the bag for something.

"No. I have not removed anything from it."

The 550 pulled out the tablet and smiled. "Good. It is in fine shape." Looking at the perplexed 500, he placed the tablet back in, zipped the bag up, and slung it over his shoulder. "Dr. Skye wanted any data devices collected from the ship. There might be crucial items stored on its memory."

"I will inform the deck commander you obtained your objective," the good little Z-500 announced.

The 550 shook his head. "No, this is a classified mission. Only between Dr. Skye and myself. Do not report it to anyone. In fact, it might be wise for you to wipe your memory of this incident altogether."

"Is it that serious?"

"Yes. Now, I am going to leave, and you are to forget you even saw this bag, got it?"

"Yes, sir." The 500 returned to the pilot's seat.

While the older robot cleared his memory of everything from the point of him starting the memory wipe of the ship's computer, the Z-550 left quickly with the satchel on his arm.

∗   ∗   ∗

Dr. Skye paced around his office while he watched the news. It was a crucial day for the potential vote by the World Corps to hand power over to the PSC. Jessie had convinced the counsel of the dangers of Jerusalem, but the counsel was still under the impression they could talk their way out of this. No doubt Jerusalem would love to have a series of peace talks that would result in no bloodshed and mutual compromise. But compromise and peace talks did not work in the plans of the PSC.

On the large windows looking out over the moon of New Eden were three screens showing various news broadcasts. Each was in a different language, and none was giving him what he wanted to hear.

"Computer, scan media for any mention of battles or skirmishes. Anything to do with possible combat situations involving Jerusalem."

"Scanning." The computer had to take a moment to access the data streams coming all the way from Earth. After a painfully long forty-five seconds, the female voice responded, "No exact matches."

He thought about how to help push this along. "Computer, get me in touch with the head of the diplomatic corps. I want . . . "

"Breaking news alert involving combat situation and Jerusalem," the computer interrupted him.

"On the main monitor." He stopped pacing and stood before the center of the three screens. The image changed to show five large vessels taking up positions around the dome of Jerusalem. They were bulky war cruisers, the main firepower of the World Corps military. The image flashed to the desk of the reporter.

"Just now, the military has dispatched five cruisers and fifteen hundred ground units to the parameter of the Iron Dome surrounding the city of Jerusalem. The move, which might seem provocative by some, was initiated by the counsel in efforts to demonstrate the World Corps is willing to move forward with combat, if the diplomatic talks go south. Analysts are already worried such a move might prove to be counterproductive in peace talks, but the Corps has it on good authority the military under the dome is ready to launch attacks at any time. This move does put the world closer to a war situation than it has seen in over two hundred years. The last actual war time battle was the Separation Wars during the formation of the World Corps. We will go back to the scene where the five ships are now in position, but they have yet to actually establish any target locks. The head of the World Corps military is about to speak . . . "

"Computer, mute." Dr. Skye wasn't sure what to make of this. "Communications, get me Jessie at once."

The man at the communications station answered. "She just contacted the ship and wishes to speak with you." There was surprise in the man's voice at the coincidence.

Richard stepped over to the window to the right of the main screen and touched a button on it. The video playing the news reports from the Asian media outlet turned off and changed to the communication link with Jessie's personal office. She was sitting at her desk, not looking so happy.

Dr. Skye asked, "So, what is going on?"

"I suppose you heard about the pathetic move of the military?"

"Yes," he answered. "I just watched the report. Did you have anything to do with this?"

"Not exactly. I've been pushing for two days for a preemptive strike. Instead, they decided to do this standoff, in hopes of forcing the peace talks to work."

"Will they work?" Richard asked.

Jessie hated any lack of confidence in her ability to control people. "They will fail. I still have some ideas that will disturb this idiotic plan of theirs. This stupid standoff might provide us a chance to implement one of my other . . . schemes."

"And what would that be?"

"Just wait and see." Jessie's irritation turned to pleasure as she thought about the next move. "This one might require a touch of deniability on your part, at first. Besides, I think I want to see the look on your face when it happens. Just keep watching the news. It will take a couple days to prepare. But no matter how good these peace talks go, when my plan goes into action, the talks will crumble. It will be fun watching Elijah muzzled."

"Must be some plan, if it will put a cork in that politician." Skye was impressed.

"It is." She mused at the thought of how well it should work. "While Elijah is sitting down to talk about treaties and peace, I will enact a plan which will destroy his credibility and put everyone outside of the dome on our side. They'll beg us to attack the city."

"I love the way you work. If I didn't know you better, I would watch my back as well."

"You can trust me. Now, what happened with that girl and her robot?"

Dr. Skye scoffed. "It fell through worse than we thought. She showed up with one of the primitives."

"WHAT?!"

"Yes. She had befriended one of those people and even taught him to speak English."

Jessie was honestly horrified at the prospect. "What did you do?"

Coldly and directly, he stated, "Killed them."

"Whew! That would've been awful. Just imagine if the people found out. Did she know the truth about those people?"

"No. She had no idea. And she died having no idea." He picked up a tablet and checked his data. "The shuttle, robots, and all other data devices involved in her pick-up and short visit have been wiped; only I know what happened." He didn't tell her, but he had even had the two doctors who helped executed. They'd had a terrible accident in science lab seven.

Jessie rubbed her face, feeling a bit overwhelmed by the near miss they had just experienced. "Just imagine if the world found out about this. If the truth came out, our support in the populace would vanish. The counsel would pull our funding and bring everyone in for questioning. They would want to question everything we stand for. This project has far-reaching effects that would tear down so much we have worked hard to build up. It's a house of cards we cannot let get blown over."

Richard flashed his famous smile, "It isn't as precarious as you might think. Only one person discovered this truth, and I have dealt with her. It was an anomaly, an easily fixed glitch."

"But it shows there's the potential for glitches in this, Richard. Don't miss the lesson here."

"I haven't missed anything. When the shuttle brought her down, they did a full sensor sweep of the planet. There are no other of our people down there. All equipment has been retrieved, and all data has been destroyed, except what is closely guarded by my personal computers. The only way anyone could potentially learn the truth is to come and do a full investigation on their own."

"Then there still exists the chance of exposure." Jessie didn't like any problems she couldn't fix with the right politics.

Richard sat in his office chair and continued to smile. "The *Sanger* is here. Any other ships to arrive will be shot down. Any other scientists who step foot on that planet will suffer the same fate as poor Anna. Besides, by the time our little plan comes to fruition, it won't matter. The people can hate us for all I care. Once we have all the power, no one can stop us."

Jessie thrummed her fingers on the desk. "I don't share in your overconfidence. But I respect your intelligence. I will keep moving forward. Once my next step is implemented, our plans will be realized." She looked over at something and then returned to him, "I have an appointment to see the head of the utilities committee."

"Utilities? What do they have to do with your plans?"

She shrugged. "Not much. But it is important to get everyone behind us right now. No politician is too small to have dinner with, if it means a vote in our favor. Jessie out." Her screen turned off, and his window became a window again, observing the lush surface of New Eden.

Richard returned to his normal work and signed a few documents that had been waiting. He couldn't stop smiling as he pondered what Jessie had up her sleeve. He liked the way her wicked little mind worked. Jessie had a very good talent for politics in all the various natures, obfuscation, misdirection, conniving, and diplomacy. She was the perfect tool for his ascension to power. It would be a shame if he had to remove her if she became too ambitious. One thing had always been true when dealing in dirty politics: Trust no one, especially your closest allies.

"Sir." Looking up, he found the Z-550 that usually stood at his door now standing across from him.

"What is it?"

"I must request to be pardoned to make repairs."

"Repairs? What kind of repairs?"

The Z-bot held up his left arm and waved it around. "My forearm and hand have lost all power. I suspect the power junction in my elbow is malfunctioning."

"Fine. Send in your replacement." Richard waved his hand at the robot.

His personal Z-bot bodyguards were specifically programmed to not listen to anything that goes on in his office, so as not to be a security risk. It was highly unusual for one to speak to him in here.

As soon as this Z-bot left the room, another took his place, silently standing at attention.

✳   ✳   ✳

The Z-550 left the upper decks and headed for the main alcove bay for the other Z-bots. To make such a repair, he simply plugged into an alcove, activated a repair request, and then shut down for a normal recharge and minor software update. Another bot or human worker would come by and conduct all repairs according to the request.

But this Z did not stop at any of the vacant alcoves. He simply continued on his way. He passed dozens of bots being recharged, a couple being worked on, and one in the process of a full physical upgrade, which meant it was stripped of clothing and just hanging by a few wires. *It was kind of creepy to look at,* he thought.

Turning a corner, he stopped at an elevator lift and paused to make sure no one was looking. After seeing the deck was clear, he punched in a security clearance and entered the lift.

Moments later, he was deposited on the secondary quarters level. This was where high-level guests would be staying but was fortunately empty. The Z-bot stopped at the door of the first room and pulled out a card key. Swiping it, the door opened, and he slunk in as quickly as he could, making sure the door closed behind him.

Inside was a luxurious suite with a nice, large bed in the middle. The room was designed and decorated to feel very homey, not stark and sterile like the rest of the ship. Cloth curtains draped over windows. The desk, tables, and chairs were all wood with faux antique lamps and other items. The bed was large and soft-looking with heavy pillows and a plush cover.

The bed normally would appear very inviting, but right now, it was strewn with the body parts of a dismantled Z-550. He had met his fate when he stepped in for a recharge. In fact, the dismembered robot was the actual security bot that normally took care of Dr. Skye's office. The dismantled bot had a security card that allowed it access to restricted areas, normally only used for entering or exiting Dr. Skye's office. However, the card also provided Z high level computer access. His first task using this card was to hide himself and his tablet from the computer's sensors. As far as the computer was concerned, it couldn't see Z. Now, he had to find out if the same program had kept his tablet from being wiped.

Z sat down on the bed and pulled up the satchel he had rescued from the shuttle. Had he not gotten to it first, they would've destroyed everything in it to safeguard their dirty little secrets. Pulling out the tablet, he checked it to make sure his programming worked. With a satisfied smile, he was pleased to see his lockout sub-routine had protected it.

As far as everyone was concerned, the Z-550 assigned to *Explorer 313* under Geologist Anna was memory wiped and, therefore, dead. This wasn't the case. He had seen something was up and pushed a fellow Z-550 into the room with her in the hopes they would not notice the difference. It worked. Dr. Skye mistook the other bot for him and wiped the wrong robot's memory. Since then, he had been working on a way to discover Dr. Skye's plans and find Anna.

Using his cleverness and a lot of luck, he discovered a deep conspiracy happening, and someone had to do something, or a lot of people were going to be killed. "This is a sticky wicket, isn't it? Who do I trust?" He talked to himself as he thought about how to figure this out. He needed to contact somebody and tell them what was happening. If he contacted the World Corps Counsel, they might contact the wrong person for answers to the accusations. Or worse, he could accidentally get in touch with someone involved with this conspiracy.

Z replayed his mental recording of the conversation between Skye and Jessie. She said something about a man she hated, someone whom she would enjoy destroying. It wasn't a secret the Corps and Elijah of Jerusalem had problems. Jessie spoke out against him on numerous occasions. If anyone wouldn't be remotely involved with this conspiracy, it's the man whose people were the primary target of the evil plans.

Z slowly looked over at the various body parts of the dismantled Z-550 on the bed. He had an idea. "This is going to hurt you a lot more than it's gonna hurt me," he said as he grabbed ahold of the bot's torso and pulled on the left arm. He wasn't a repair drone, so he wasn't used to dismantling other bots. He pulled, but the arm wouldn't come off. He got a grip on the hand and put his foot on the side of the torso and then shoved and yanked at the same time. With a loud crash, he pulled the arm free and watched the upper part of the body fly across the room and crash into the desk leg.

"It's a good thing no one is up here to hear that. It would be hard to explain." He turned his attention to the arm, the hand in particular. "Okay. All I need is the access programming for high-level communications clearance. Which little piggy is going to make me an interstellar phone call?" He checked each finger for a special key used to access the high-level programming. With a great big smile, he watched the fingernail of the index finger open up, and a small filament came out that would give him what he needed.

It wasn't the key to making the call. It was the key to accessing the protected software systems. This bot didn't make calls, but he was programmed to repair Dr. Skye's sensitive equipment. This function would prove useful in accessing the high-level systems and sending a message to someone without alerting the staff, or Dr. Skye.

CHAPTER FIFTEEN

ELIJAH SAT DOWN AT HIS desk in the embassy and let out a long sigh that seemed to be pent up over a full day's time. This was the most trying experience of his entire career as a diplomat. He thought the whole primitive situation was bad enough, but now it seemed Jerusalem was on the brink of war with the Corps. The only ace he had to play in this was the Iron Dome. Nothing the corps had could break that barrier, so if they did decide to attack, it would be them against an impenetrable wall.

In fact, had this happened just a few months ago, he would have merely told the negotiations teams from the Corps they had little to talk about. Jerusalem was self-sufficient and could stay inside their protected dome until the Corps ran out of energy attacking it. But he couldn't be certain what the PSC would do. That irritating Jessie had the PSC in her back pocket; and with the weapon systems on their new flagship posing a considerable risk against the barrier, he had problems. If the Corps believed all the garbage the media and the PSC had been spreading about Jerusalem, they could attack and call their friends in.

Right now, Elijah's goal was to get through the propaganda and make the Corps see reason. It would test every ounce of his mettle as a diplomat, but he would make them understand his people wanted nothing but peace and the right to live the lives they chose. They would not harm anyone; they had no reason to.

"Sir, would you like your dinner?" his assistant asked.

"Not now. I will come to eat in a few minutes. Give me a moment. Please close the door to my office," he answered his niece, who shut his door.

Elijah turned to the Man whom he trusted the most to advise him during these times. Looking upward, he prayed. "Praise be the name of Yahweh in all the heavens. I come to You seeking guidance. Your children are facing war, a war they do not want or need . . ."

Just then, a beeping interrupted his prayers. This rather upset him, and he was ready to tell his secretary to put whoever it was on hold. When he pressed the button to transfer the call, the screen came in fuzzy, and then a face of what looked like a robot was seen on the other end.

"You're not Hannah," Elijah proclaimed.

Z smiled and shook his head. "Nope. I'm Z—well, I'm a Z-550, but my friends just call me Z." Z leaned in and asked, "Are you Elijah the diplomat?"

"I am. And I am very upset right now. You have no right to break into this communications channel."

"Look, I'm sorry. But I had no choice but to break into the contact lines. I can't risk being discovered. Tell me, is anyone around you that can hear us?"

"No, this is my office. But I will contact security in five seconds if you don't cut this and go through the . . . "

"We don't have time. This is a serious problem. I need to talk to you about what is going on."

Elijah was still very angry. "Now listen to me. I will not talk to anyone outside of the counsel about the situation. If you think you can spy on me, then I will take this to the highest courts. Even your people have laws against spying."

"Hey, I'm not spying on you; I am sort of spying for you."

"What?"

Z held up his tablet. "Okay. If I was a spy, I would not be telling you what I am about to tell you. The PSC is behind all of this. They are orchestrating this conflict and mean to use it to destroy Jerusalem and the Corps at all costs."

"What do you mean?"

"They plan on sabotaging the negotiations."

Elijah wasn't convinced, but his interest was piqued. "How?"

"I don't know. All I do know is your peace talks with the corps are meaningless. The real enemy is the PSC—Dr. Skye and Jessie to be exact. They are willing to do anything to destroy you and take over the world government. You're nothing but a pawn in their game. Don't ask me for details. I couldn't get everything. I only know that, somehow, Administrator Jessie will do something to disrupt the negotiations and implicate your people. Whatever it is, she believes it will spark a war."

"I don't know if I can trust you. You might be out of your mind. If what you are saying is true, I would need some solid evidence to give the Corps to make any kind of case against Jessie or the PSC."

Z smiled and held up his tablet. "What I am about to send you should prove a great deal." He punched in something on the tablet and then waited while the data uploaded to the communications streamline.

Elijah was intensely curious and more than befuddled by all of this. Suddenly, the computer next to him lit up, and he was watching a series of pictures come through. The images were stunning. He was looking at images of one of those cat people interacting with a human woman. The cat person was wearing clothing and appeared to be talking, reading, laughing, fishing, making a fire, climbing a tree—just basically not being the primitive that was sold to the world.

"I . . . I don't get it. What am I looking at?"

"Proof. The woman I was assigned to spent time with one of those people, who call themselves the B'reann. He learned English in a matter of days—well, a broken, sloppy English, but enough English to understand most of what we said and to respond. He read voraciously and was very skilled at hunting, crafting, and doing many things a primitive, unevolved beast couldn't."

Elijah flipped through the pictures, mesmerized by what he was looking at. "Why would they lie to us about these people?"

"I don't know. We thought we had stumbled across some amazing discovery that would be celebrated by the scientific community. But when we presented him to Dr. Skye, we were attacked, and my scientist and her new friend were exiled back to the planet. I am not entirely certain what happened to her or how Dr. Skye did it, but she was . . . killed, along with this young man. They executed her to protect their little secret. What's worse, there is even more to this secret than we discovered. This moon, these people—nothing is what it seems."

Elijah was still having a hard time believing this. It was groundbreaking and would shatter trust in Jessie if he presented this information. But he had to be certain about it all. He felt like he needed a definite answer to fully trust this to be true; then he saw it.

"What is that?" he whispered to himself as he leaned in to get a better look at one of the pictures.

"Sir, I can't see what you are looking at."

Elijah called up the picture and expanded it so only a small part of it showed on the screen. It was what was in between the laps of Anna and J'kla that they were reading. "Is that a Bible?"

"Yes. My friend, the scientist, was secretly a Christian. This primitive, named J'kla, used the text of the Bible to help him learn to read. But he could read other things as well." Z didn't quite understand the importance of this discovery for Elijah.

Elijah felt this was the answer he had been seeking. God had sent him the help he needed in this unexpected ally on the other side of the universe. "This is more than I ever expected. I knew something felt wrong about this discovery; now I know they are keeping major secrets about it."

"Yes, and there's more," Z said.

"More?"

"Yes. While I was pretending to be Dr. Skye's security drone, I overheard them talk about a deeper secret about these people. Something that goes even further down than what my friend and I already discovered. Jessie was extremely worried about anyone finding the truth, and Dr. Skye has banished all visitors for fear of it being uncovered. If it is brought out, it could destroy them. At least, that's the sense I got while they talked about it."

Elijah felt if God trusted this Z unit, then so could he. "Then will you help me find the answer?"

"I have already decrypted and searched as much of the database here on this ship as I can. Whatever that secret is, it isn't stored in this ship's memory. I'm afraid the only person here who would have those answers would be Dr. Skye himself."

"I highly doubt he will be very forthcoming," Elijah muttered.

Z nodded in agreement. "I think there is only one option. I have to go back to the moon and find the answer myself."

"That would be the only way. While you are doing that, I will use this data to thwart their plans and stall them long enough for you to dig up the truth. Jessie might be a master politician, but so am I. I know how to play these courts and their courtiers."

"I'll be in contact with you as soon as I have any information of value. Right now, you are the only person I can trust," Z said.

Elijah smiled warmly, feeling like he finally had a chance to turn this all around. "I can't thank you enough. You might just save my people from a terrible war."

"Thank you for your confidence, but I am doing this for one reason: revenge. Anna was my friend, and I suppose so was J'kla. She treated me like a real person, something few robots get to experience. Dr. Skye and Jessie murdered her for their master plans, and I am going to throw a wrench in those plans and let justice be done to them in any way possible." He saw a beeping light on the side of his screen. "I am about to be cut off. I will . . . "

The image blanked as his disguised signal failed when the secondary power systems came online for the artificial gravity generator.

Elijah switched off the snowy screen. He closed his eyes and quietly thanked God for being ahead of him. His prayer was answered before he thought to utter it. God's master plans were so far ahead in this game, even Jessie would be made the fool. Right now, Elijah just needed to keep up and play his part as he was guided by the Holy Spirit.

Anna sat next to J'kla as he remained in bed recuperating. Her morning of elation at his healing was curtailed by three days of worry. His recovery was still in question as his injuries were deep. There were moments when he seemed to come around, but he never was fully lucid and would slip back into his deep sleep. Anna's renewed faith wasn't destroyed by this; she still felt God would bring him through. But she couldn't stop worrying something might take a turn for the worst. He had received a nasty head injury as well as that horrible drug cocktail. She had no idea what the side effects would be if he did live.

It felt right for her to sit next to him with her hand on his chest. She would run her fingers through the silky mane hair growing between his pecs. Yet, it wasn't his muscles or fur she wanted to feel; it was his heartbeat. When she would begin to worry he was slipping away, that he wouldn't wake up this time, she would put her hand there and feel the strong beat of his heart. She could also feel his breaths coming and going and the warmth of his body.

Since her arrival here in this village, she had come to know his parents and the old woman who seemed to be both doctor and chieftain of these people. It was a difficult experience, considering she couldn't understand their language. They had learned to gesture and help her understand things by action instead of words, but there were many times she wished she could tell them something or ask a question that couldn't be asked by a wave of a hand. J'kla picked up English overnight, or at least it seemed that way. She had been around nothing but these people for three solid days and was no closer to understanding their words.

Looking at his resting face, she felt comforted to be here with him. After rubbing her hand through his mane one more time, she took up a pad of rough paper and a stick with a small tuft of stiff hair attached at the end. She ran the brush through a dry mixture of ash and powdered rock, which created a writing medium. Using this, she continued her project of writing down as many Bible verses as she could remember. She wasn't trying to scribe the whole Bible—she didn't have that good of a memory—but she would put down every verse she had ever memorized. It was busy-work really, but it made her feel better.

J'kla found himself in a strange place. He was in an arid land, with sand and dirt where grass should be. He had never seen a real desert before, so he really didn't understand what this was. It was hot; the sun was very bright; and the wind was no comfort.

"Anna? Mother? Father?" he called out, hoping to see someone. He had vague memories of seeing these three people recently, but it was brief and distant. *Am I dead?* he thought to himself.

"I'm so thirsty," a stranger's voice stated.

J'kla found himself standing in the middle of an ancient desert town with old, mud-brick buildings and spindly little plants, which had dried up a long time ago. A man in a thick, roughly spun outfit was sitting up against a wall with a hood over his head. His skin was olive in color but burnt badly by long exposure to the sun.

"Did you say something?" J'kla asked in his own tongue.

The man replied in the same language, "I am so very thirsty."

J'kla squinted in the bright sun and looked around the area. In the middle of the square was what appeared to be some kind of well. Going over and examining it, he found it was filled with clear water. Beside it was a bucket with a ladle. He took up the bucket and drew a full pail of water. Before getting himself a drink—for he, too, was very thirsty—he brought it over to the poor man beside the wall. Setting the pail down and pulling up a ladle of water, he brought the full bowl to the man's exposed mouth. Much like his own father had, he helped the man drink the water, for he looked weak and sickly. The man took the water in quickly, some of the water dribbling down his chin and dripping to the ground.

After J'kla had helped this poor man, he took a ladle for himself. The water was cool and refreshing. In fact, it was oddly cool for being in such a hot place.

"Why?" the man asked from under his hood.

J'kla stopped drinking and set the ladle back into the pail. "What?"

"Why did you let me drink first? You were thirsty, too."

"You looked like you needed it more."

"How can you even care for me? My people hurt you. My people tried to kill you. You lay in your deathbed awaiting the final breath because of what one of my kind did to you. Do you not understand this?"

"I'm in my deathbed?" J'kla asked.

"Yes. And it is by the actions of wicked humans who put you there. They also poisoned and killed all the others of recent days. Why trust me? Why help me? They didn't help you; they hurt you."

"Each person makes his own choices in life. One man's sins do not make another man evil."

"That is wise, my young friend," he answered. "But surely you cannot trust them? You should want to hate them."

"I can't."

"Why?" He was leading J'kla to get to a certain point.

"While one of the furless kind was cruel and wicked, another was gentle and loving. I love Anna more than I hate the man who hurt me."

The man's smile was the only visible part of his face under the hood. "I sense there is a turmoil in your spirit. A fear. But you aren't afraid of those who wish you harm. So, what is this fear I sense?"

"I'm afraid to die."

"Why?"

"I'm afraid to be a goat."

This actually made the man laugh. "A goat?"

"I have come to understand what it means to be saved, to know a man named Jesus. But I am not a human; I am not like Him or His people. I am afraid He cannot love me like He loves His own kind. I am afraid when I die, I will be separated like goats from the sheep—whatever those are."

The man didn't stop smiling. "The amount of love you have for Anna is only a shadow of the amount of love Christ has for you."

"What?" J'kla knelt down to the man on the ground. "How?"

"Your faith is strong; your love is pure; and your motives are right. You will lead your people from death."

"How?"

"You will know. But understand that your faith will be tested. Your strength put through a trial more difficult than any your people have faced before. Only in faith will you come through."

J'kla took the man by the shoulders and pulled him forward, causing his hood to fall back and reveal the face of a Hebrew man. "Who are you? Are you the Jesus?"

The man was not shaken or upset; he continued to smile. "No. I'm only a messenger."

"Messenger? Like the men who talked to the prophets of the old stories?"

The man nodded. "Yes."

J'kla frowned. "Does this make me a prophet?"

"No." The man gave off a good, hearty laugh. "The time of the prophets has passed. What I came to tell you is that your people are not beyond saving. Jesus died for you as much as he died for your friend Anna. I would like to tell you more, but it is time for you to wake up."

"Wake up?"

"Yes. Wake up!"

✶   ✶   ✶

J'kla opened his eyes. The brightness of the desert town faded quickly into the darkness of this room. He sat up and realized he had been dreaming. He was in the healing hut of his people. It was night, and his mother was asleep in a chair near his bed. After a few moments of his vision coming into focus better, he recalled the brief moments when he had woken up and seen the inside of this place. For some reason, he could feel a hand touching his chest while he slept, but it wasn't there right now.

He sat up slowly and felt his head where the bump had been. His skull was still sore, but the bump had gone away. His body ached. Looking down, he quickly covered himself when he realized he was still wearing the tattered remains of his clothing from before the incident. He had torn his clothes so badly, he had exposed himself and was indecent. He was happy there had been a blanket on the bed to keep his modesty while he convalesced.

There was an open book on a table beside him. It had handwriting in it. It wasn't the B'reann language, but the words he was learning, called English. It had to be Anna who wrote this. She must be all right. The final verse written down held his attention: "Don't forget to show kindness to strangers. In doing it, some people have shown hospitality to angels and didn't know it."

He thought about the strange dream he'd had before he woke up. What did it mean? Was it just a dream? Was it really a message for him? Could

Christ really love a B'reann? Yes, finally J'kla accepted this truth. Christ must have sent him this message, to tell him that he was truly saved and the God Who created the universe cared about him. If that was true, then so was the other information this person gave him. J'kla was destined to lead his people to safety. What could that mean? When?

"J'kla!" His mother's voice startled him.

She blinked the sleep out of her eyes and slowly got up from her uncomfortable position. "J'kla!" Her arms wrapped around him lovingly. Tears of joy filled her eyes again. J'kla put his arms around her and hugged her tight. It felt good to hold his mother right now.

Speaking in B'reann tongue, she asked, "Are you well? Do you still hurt?"

He let go of her and rolled his shoulders around. "I'm sore, but I think I'm all right."

Rillan, his mother, felt his forehead. "You were hurt really bad. Did you fall? Did someone hit you?"

He thought about those terrible moments before he blacked out. It was hard to recall—nothing but blurry memories filled with blinding flashes of light. "I . . . I don't remember everything. I think I was hunting something or someone. I could hear voices in my head. I just can't remember it all."

She gently rubbed his ear, which made him purr. "You were ill with that strange madness. You survived it. We don't know how, but your friend Anna must be some kind of healer."

"Anna?" He was stunned to hear that name from his mother.

"When we found you and brought you here, the chief believed you would die like the others. But your friend stayed beside you and was saying something quietly as she put her hands on you. We have never seen anything like it. She stayed there all night, speaking the whole time. The next day you came around. We don't know what her medicine was, but it worked."

J'kla took his mother's hands and held them lovingly. "It wasn't medicine; it was prayer. She didn't heal me; God did."

"Prayer? God?" They did not have a concept of these things.

With a joy-filled heart he said, "I will tell you all about Him and His work later. I have discovered a wonderful truth. It saved my life. But I'm a little tired."

She stood back, and then her eyes widened as she noticed he was rather naked and had forgotten to keep himself covered. "I think I will go and get you some pants. Stay here."

J'kla's hands quickly returned to covering himself, and he gave off a sheepishly embarrassed grin.

✶ ✶ ✶

The shuttle bay was quiet—so quiet, in fact, the only sound was snoring from the man on duty. Before the incident where that lady got killed, people were coming and going all day long from this bay. Scientists and equipment specialists were either departing for another temp station on the moon, or they were returning to dock. Since the moon became off-limits, no shuttle activity was happening.

There was one shuttle mission that popped up out of nowhere. A robot was authorized to take a shuttle down to the moon and then back. The operator had no idea what happened. When the shuttle returned, he was ordered into quarters for three hours. It was a big mystery, made worse by the standing gag order surrounding it.

What was odd, though, was that the shuttle hadn't been moved yet. All shuttles that came in to land on this bay floor were eventually lifted by the arm crane and slotted into one of the honeycomb alcoves for storage. This shuttle just sat there. It was a diverting thing to look at it, and he wondered what was going on; but after a few days, the curiosity dried up, and the boredom sank in.

"HEY! Wake up!" A Z-bot pounded his hand on the console, where the operator had his feet propped up.

The older, heavyset operator quickly took his feet down and leaned over his controls as though he were in the middle of an action. "Sorry, just resting my eyes. Shuttles all secure, parameter secure, door secure . . . "

"Stop, stop." The Z-bot laughed. "I'm not Dr. Skye."

"Oh, sorry. What did you need?"

Z held up his tablet and pretended to read something on it. "I'm here to inspect that shuttle."

"Okay. Do you need my help?"

"No." Z walked on toward the shuttle. "Just a basic inspection for any contaminants."

The old man propped his feet back up on his console and proceeded to close his eyes. "You woke me for that? I was hav'n such a nice dream."

"Well, keep dreaming. Don't worry about me. I . . . Oh, no." Z did his best acting he could muster.

The old man didn't even open his eyes. "What? The shuttle's not miss'n, is it?" He snickered.

"Has this shuttle been opened since its last inspection?"

"Nope. A robot came and worked on the computer a couple days back; since then, it's been sealed up tighter than Jerusalem."

"That explains these readings. No one has been keeping an eye on this." Z was looking at a scanner that wasn't even active.

The operator sat up and looked at the robot with a confused, yet unconcerned, face. "What readings? What's wrong? Someone scratch the paint?"

"Good grief, man, this shuttle is infested with tissue-dissolving bacteria. I haven't seen something this bad since I got back from the moon surface."

Now the operator was concerned. "You mean there really is something horrible inside that shuttle?"

"Why do you think it's been sealed up, and Dr. Skye personally ordered no one to open the door? If you stepped into this shuttle, it would melt your face off." Z was hamming it up, and this operator was buying every word.

The fat, old man scrambled for his communicator. "Alert! Medical alert!"

While the man was calling for a medical alert, Z quickly pressed the opening button. "Oh, no! The shuttle—something activated its operating systems. It's COMING OUT! AHHHH!" He'd watched too many old 1950s sci-fi movies.

The operator got to his feet in a hurry. "Wha . . . wha . . . what is coming out?"

Z pretended to be fighting something coming out the back of the shuttle. He even threw himself to the side a few times and then yelled swear words at some invisible monster. "RUN FOR YOUR LIFE! IT'S THIS BACTERIA! IT'S COME ALIVE! IT'S COME ALIVE!"

The operator slapped the intercom panel. "SECURITY, WE NEED TO SEAL THE DOCKING BAY!"

Z leaned back to look at the operator as though he were still struggling against some kind of monster. On his computer scanner, he played various monster noises from about two dozen black and white horror flicks. "NO! OPEN . . . BAY . . . DOOR . . . IT . . . MUST . . . BE . . . DESTROYED . . . AAAAAHHH!" He threw himself into the shuttle and then hoped his ploy worked.

Fortunately, he picked the right dock operator to do this little skit with. The operator switched on the sirens, activated the one-way forcefield, and then opened the docking bay doors. Z shut the shuttle up and then launched it, flying backward to get out of the ship quickly.

The operator was frozen in both shock and confusion. He was going to eject it into space, yet something piloted it out. "Uh . . . what just happened?"

Once outside the ship, Z headed right for the moon's surface. He knew they could track this shuttle and wouldn't be fooled for too long. That operator might have been gullible, but Dr. Skye wasn't so easily fooled. This shuttle had to be destroyed.

"Computer, set the engine coolant tanks for ejection."

The computer answered, "That operation is not required. Coolant levels are optimum and are not in danger."

"I don't care. Computer, bypass standard protocols, authorization Z-92628." One last use of the high-level Z-550 he had dismantled, that code would probably be discontinued when they found the bot . . . and they would soon enough.

Without any more arguments from the computer, the two tanks of coolant shot out and then floated away in naked space. Without those tanks, the engines could easily overload.

Z set the engines to maximum thrust and made two full, quick orbits of the moon before he began to degrade the orbit until he was within acceptable range. He programmed the autopilot to slingshot the ship out of the atmosphere.

"Engine temperature at maximum level. Reduce thrust," the computer announced.

"Not likely." Z took up a bag he had packed with all his equipment and a couple spare parts for himself, then strapped it closely to him. The bag itself was made up of a very durable material used for space exploration. He took up a cylindrical rod and turned it on. Two very strong magnets on it activated and slammed it into his chest. He set it to maximum power and then held on to two of the seats in the passenger part of the cabin.

"Computer, are we in the atmosphere of the moon?"

"Affirmative."

"Good. Computer, open hangar door."

"That action is not recommended at . . . "

"Shut up! Just open the door!"

Lights flashed around the cabin, showing a dangerous decompression was about to take place. The door opened, and immediately, the atmosphere inside the cabin was thrust around by the thinner, yet faster-moving atmosphere outside the cabin. Z held on; he wanted to jump under his own volition, not thrown like a rag doll out the door. Once the air stopped pushing so hard, he made his way to the door.

"YEEEE-HAW!" he yelled and jumped out of the shuttle.

The shuttle shot out of the atmosphere and into space, taxing its engines to the absolute limit. It moved faster and faster and finally erupted in a blue flash of plasma fire.

Z dropped out of the sky and headed for the moon's surface. He lengthened his body by pressing his arms to his sides and straightening out his legs. He directed his course for a location he had chosen.

He was about three times as high in the atmosphere as was safe for a human to dive, but Z-bots had been doing this trick for years. He hadn't, but some had, and he downloaded all the specs. Unfortunately, that didn't make it any less frightening. Why did they program him to feel fear? Really, if he had a bladder, he would've peed his pants right about the time he looked down.

The wind howled around his ears; the clouds were below him, casting shadows on the ground even further down. The trees looked like grass, and the mountains looked like a crumpled-up blanket spread across the surface. It was going to be a long way down, and it was going to be messy if this didn't work.

The program's information clicked, and he knew what to do. He tapped a button on the rod attached to his chest, causing it to flash with little lights. Suddenly, his descent slowed down a little. One light in a row lit up. Then his descent slowed down a little more, and a second light lit up. By the time he reached the ground, this device would reduce his gravitational impact to survivable. This didn't work for humans, as the anti-gravity rod would kill a person halfway down; but for a robot, it was perfectly safe.

Z met the ground at less than one percent gravity on impact. The device worked it so he didn't bounce right back up into the sky with his removed gravitational pull. Z had to utilize the other parts of the sky-diving programming and do the full tumble, so he would survive the fall. He rolled for what felt like five miles, barely missing a large rock and three trees. He had directed himself to land in a large, open area. Where did those stupid trees come from anyway?

Once he stopped tumbling, he laid on the ground and looked up into the sky, half expecting to see a body-shaped hole in one of the clouds, like a cartoon. After a moment to gather his robotic senses, he sat up and checked himself. Both his hips had detached slightly, and his neck joints were completely out of whack. This made his head fall forward, so his chin was sitting on his chest. Fortunately, all he had to do was reattach what had come loose, and he was fully functional.

Next, he checked his stuff. The first thing he checked was the tablet. It was the key to all of this. He had placed it in a box designed to survive a ship's explosion, so it did fine on the fall. With a sigh of relief, he switched it on and found it working properly. He then pulled out the spare parts. The extra hands he brought were all right, and so was the right foot, but the left foot had busted across the arch.

The last thing he pulled out was the least important to this mission, but perhaps the most important to him. It was Anna's Bible. He wasn't going to read it, but he needed it near him to remember her. She was his friend, a real friend. Most people replace their robots when they get tired of them or have them upgraded with new personality programs every few years. She never did. She allowed him to be a real person, in a robot sort of way. He was allowed to keep his own personality intact for long enough to grow and develop his own identity. Some people feared robots would be like him, become too human, and want to take over. She was never afraid of him. She cared for him, and that never seemed to completely make sense; but he respected her for it. In his mind, she was dead. This was all Z had left of her. It would remain with him until the day he stopped working. Though he might use it once, to smack Dr. Skye right in the face. For Anna.

Putting everything back in the bag, he got up and slung it over his shoulder. "Okay moon, what is your dirty little secret?"

*   *   *

Anna enjoyed a bowl of warm, soothing, meaty soup. It was the traditional breakfast in the home that had taken her in. The soup consisted of a thick broth, vegetables, and a lot of meat. The veggies were mostly a type of root that tasted a lot like a carrot, only deep purple in color. There was also a leafy green like a spinach mixed with a cabbage. The meat reminded her of beef, only a bit milder in taste and texture. Into this mixture was thrown an onion-tasting herb and salt.

Each morning, an older cat lady, who lived in the house, would make up a pot of this stew on the fire long before Anna got out of bed. In fact, the scent of this cooking is what often woke her. By the time she got to the kitchen table, four bowls were already set out with steaming soup poured into each.

Anna would sit and eat with this family, quietly listening to them converse in their native tongue. She wished she could understand them, but she didn't have a mind like J'kla's for language. Then again, she didn't have an educational program to watch that helped like J'kla had.

While she sat there and watched this family eat and talk, she remembered the moment she had first met them. This man was ready to disembowel her for killing his son. Now, he would go to great lengths to introduce her to every person of their village. The woman, J'kla's mother, was more logical in her attitude; that much translated across the language barriers. She was smart and cool about what needed to be done. But it was obvious J'kla's father was the head of this house. Anna could only assume the older woman was J'kla's grandmother, or maybe an elder aunt. She helped take care of the house and looked after Anna while she was at home.

This morning, Anna ate with only the older woman at her side. In fact, there were only two bowls set out when Anna got up. Two bowls were by the water bin where they had been washed already. J'nar and Rillan had already eaten and were gone before the sun rose. Where they had gone, Anna didn't know, but she was in no position to ask.

When she had finished her breakfast, Anna tried, again, to gather the dishes and clean them. She had watched this old woman clean the dishes in the water tub for several days now; it would be polite for her to take care of it. But the old woman insisted by taking the dishes away from Anna and then pointing out the door. The kitchen was her domain, and that wasn't going to change anytime soon.

Anna smiled and accepted the offer. She stepped out of the kitchen and into the sunlight. She normally walked outside with either J'nar or Rillan, so she wouldn't be alone. But today, they weren't here, so she would stroll by herself. She didn't venture far from the house; in fact, she was just walking around the large trunk the house was attached to. Growing along the ground and up the trunk was a vine, which had the largest flowers Anna had ever seen. They looked like a type of hibiscus but grew like morning glories. Each flower on the vine had a slightly different pattern and shade of color, all bright and ornate. Those in the shadow were closed up tight, while those in the sun had unfurled their petals and were basking in the glow. Anna stood there and waited while the sunlight slowly moved across another blossom. In a few minutes, the light would come all the way across it, and it would open. She liked watching them open.

"Anna." She heard the voice of J'nar calling to her, but it seemed oddly different. It was also odd he called her only Anna and not J'kla Krina.

"What?" She gasped and then ran across the dirt road. It wasn't J'nar she heard; it was the voice of his son. She nearly ran into J'kla and wrapped her arms around him. "J'kla, oh my goodness. You're up and walking and better."

He hugged her back, putting his head on hers and nuzzling like a big cat. "Anna, God heal me."

"Yes. He most certainly did." Anna was beginning to cry; she couldn't stop herself. She had wanted to hold him like this since the first day he was laid in that bed. She laid her face into his chest mane and never wanted to leave. "I was so scared. I thought you would go to sleep and never wake up. I stayed by your side and prayed every day."

J'kla pulled her back from him and then took her hand and placed it on his chest, right where she had felt his heart beat during his convalescence. "I know. You talk to God. God listen. He heal body and heart."

Anna felt his chest and could feel a strong heart beat under all the muscle and fur. "And God healed my heart, too."

"You hurt?"

"Not physically. But I . . . I gave up on God."

J'kla was shocked; he had no idea about her abandoned faith. "What?"

She had felt so guilty about not telling him the whole truth. She had spent a lot of time watching him in the bed, wishing she had told him this. It was time he knew. "I thought what I knew was wrong. That God didn't exist. I thought when we found your people, the evidence against God was so strong that it destroyed my faith. I was wrong. Nothing destroys faith; you merely walk away from it. God used what Dr. Skye did to you to bring me back to Him. He healed you and gave me back my hope in Him. I gave up on God, but He never gave up on me."

"God see all. He takes bad and turns good."

Anna took up his hands and held them, admiring the claws on them. "Yes. He turned this around. And now I have a new life."

"J'kla!" The loud voice of J'nar called out to his son as he and Rillan walked back from the hut.

J'kla met his mother with a hug and a smile at his father. They had just seen each other, but right now they were excited to see him every time. Anna was amused at the way his father rubbed his son's ear. Then his mother stepped back and looked at J'kla's stomach, for it had just let out a formidable growl. She said something to him and then started back toward their home.

J'nar waved Anna along with them to come to their home. Anna didn't need much of an invitation to join; she would finally have a translator to help understand this family.

CHAPTER SIXTEEN

"ARE YOU SURE IT WAS destroyed?" Jessie asked Dr. Skye.

Dr. Skye paced around his office, while he was watched by the enormous face of Jessie on the window viewer. "Yes. Not only do we have sensor data to prove the destruction of the shuttle, but there are hundreds of images from the event. I just don't understand what happened."

Jessie pondered this. The thrumming tap of her off-screen hand could be heard all over Skye's office. "Look. I don't care about why it happened, just that it won't cause us any problems. What did the shuttle bay operator say about the event? Who authorized its launch?"

"That is the strangest part. The operator is telling me some story about a slime monster attacking a robot, and then the robot fought it into the shuttle and took it out and destroyed it. Or something to that nature."

Jessie just sat there with one eyebrow raised. The complete lack of belief was painted across her overly-stretched features.

Dr. Skye responded to the glare. "Look. I don't believe him either. I am having the medical lab do a series of tests to see if he was on some kind of hallucinogenic."

"What about the monitors in the bay? Did you get a look at whoever took that shuttle out? Who launched and piloted it?"

"Actually, the monitors were all shut off. That is what has me really confused. For about ten minutes, the monitors to the shuttle bay were put through their maintenance cycle and shut off. Normally, that only happens late at night, when no one is in there, and it's locked up tight."

"Sounds to me like someone is up to something." Jessie's right eye gave off a tiny twitch. "Look, Richard, we can't have any screw-ups here. We're down to the wire. I'm about ready to implement the next phase of my plan, and any hitches could ruin everything."

Dr. Skye shook his head. "I've had the same idea. Someone is behind this. But I can't imagine who. We have eliminated anyone with knowledge of this plan outside of you and me. I've worked exclusively with specially programmed Z-units since the incident with the geologist. No one can possibly know what is going on and spy on us." Dr. Skye glanced up to where his special Z-550 should be standing.

"I wouldn't put it past Elijah to have . . . "

"Where is he?" Dr. Skye interrupted her.

"Who?"

He got up and walked around his desk only then realizing he was alone. "My security bot assigned to this room is not here."

"What!"

Dr. Skye pulled out his communications unit and angrily mashed the button with his thumb. "Z-550 G11, report!" Nothing came. "Z-550 G11, REPORT!!" Still nothing.

"Richard, what's going on?" Jessie's nose now filled the screen as she leaned over to see what was happening.

He typed in a code to the computer on his desk. The ship's lights changed, followed by a robotic announcement, stating, "Attention crew. *Starship Sanger* is on lockdown. Please report to designated lockdown positions."

Dr. Skye grimly answered, "My robot is missing."

"Find him!"

"I intend to. Don't worry. I have locked down the ship. No one is coming or going until I locate whoever is behind this."

"Don't worry? This is a crisis!" Jessie felt like she was on the verge of a heart attack.

"Not yet. This little crisis can be averted easily. Outside of this one channel, all communication lines have been severed. Even if somebody does know something, they won't be talking. I'll shoot down any ships that come near this moon, and I'll find that robot and discover what he's up to. Don't panic just yet. This might prove useful to us."

"How could this prove useful?"

Dr. Skye smiled at her with a lot of venom in his grin. "If we discover who is trying to thwart our plans, we can deal with them now. They might even lead us to others back on Earth. They are the ones who made a mistake. They tried to outsmart the smartest man alive. You keep doing what you are doing. I will nip this tiny problem in the bud."

"All right. Just don't mess this up." With a curt motion, she shut off the channel.

✳   ✳   ✳

Three days had passed since Anna and J'kla's reunion. Everyone in the village wanted to see the one who survived the terrible madness. When they asked him about it, he explained how God saved his life. The people didn't understand at first, but J'kla used their understanding of the way nature seemed orderly on its own, which was God at work. He explained sin and death; then he would tell them how Christ died for their sins, so they could be forgiven.

The hardest part to explain was the Trinity. It really didn't make much sense. Anna, who was helping with any answers he struggled with, came up with a unique solution. It wasn't her idea; she took it from a missionary in Earth's history. Taking one of the large morning glory flowers, she showed it to J'kla. Each flower had three large, colorful petals. Each petal represented a different part of God—the Father, the Son, and the Holy Spirit. They were each identifiable by themselves, but at the same time, they were one flower.

The way these people took to this and accepted the truth with exuberance helped her see God was present even in this distant part of space.

When they weren't talking to people and telling his story, J'kla showed Anna around his village. He was proud of their accomplishments, and she could see why. Even without the advanced technology of Earth, these people lived a very good life.

They turned down a path and saw very tall flowering plants. Each was like a sunflower, only smaller than one on Earth, and with three or four flowers on top instead of one. The leaves on the lower half of the stalks were stripped off, creating a natural row of poles. Along the poles were cultured vines of the flowers that produced the cotton substance, so each row got double usage.

"So, what do they use the seeds for? Eating?" She pointed to the flowers.

J'kla gave her a very funny look. "No eat seeds. Seeds bitter and hard. We cram . . . no . . . flush . . . no . . . uh . . . oh, we crush seed for oil." He still struggled at times with English words.

"Do you use the oil in food?" Anna asked, while she stepped over a young man harvesting the ready cotton pods.

"We can eat. Most oil we burn, make heat and light."

They walked past the end of the row and into a pasture of soft green grasses. A herd of those large deer-like creatures gently grazed in the pasture as a B'reann man watched over them.

Anna paused, took in a deep, satisfied breath, and then slowly released it. Across the pastures and out into mountains, she could see the distant clouds settling into the crevasses between cliffs. It was a calm and refreshing view.

"Why you stop and watch? Earth no have trees, no mountains?" J'kla noticed she stopped each time they could see out.

"Earth has some incredible mountains and plenty of trees. But I haven't seen them in a long time. I spent a lot of years working in space looking at dead rocks and gassy planets."

"Why?"

"I don't know anymore. At one time, I thought it was all I wanted to do. But now I have only the desire to be here and enjoy these mountains with you."

"Space amazing, too." J'kla remembered the brief time he had spent getting to the starship.

"True. But it's lonely as well. I guess the company here helps make this place that much better. Your family, your friends—they're all so nice and kind to me."

"Earth no have nice people? I no believe that; you from Earth."

She snickered at that; his bad English almost destroyed the sweet sentiment. "Earth has a lot of good and nice people, but it is a much different place than this. People live for themselves mostly. Few reach out to help one another. We don't have families. We don't have love. We don't have this type of community."

"No family? How?" J'kla was terribly confused about that part.

"Well, a long time ago, people began to think it would be better if we only made children by design."

"Huh?"

Anna didn't know how to explain this so he would understand. "Some people, who thought they were helping humans, decided they would tell chosen people to have babies, then take those babies and raise them without parents, just select teachers. They took away our religion. They took away our marriages, and they took away our right to raise our own children. No one alive today knows who their parents were or have ever been married."

J'kla was trying to wrap his mind around all this. "If only make baby when chiefs tell you to, do your people no mate for . . . fun?" He was trying to be considerate about how he would say this.

"Oh, they have a lot of sex on Earth. In fact, it is a booming business. But it is only for fun. People don't get married. They don't fall in love. They don't lie down with another person because they love them. It is only for personal fun."

"But God no like that. He said that man and woman marry first; then they can mate. B'reann also mate only after ceremony."

Anna nodded in agreement. "Yes. And I have lived by that since I learned about God. This is why I'm such an odd person for a human. I haven't ever mated by choice. I can't tell others it is because of my faith in God that I do this, but that is the reason."

"But you say humans no allow religion?"

"True. But some humans break rules and teach about God anyway. It's illegal, but it's right."

J'kla was still having a hard time understanding human culture right now. "But if man and woman mate for fun, they make baby sometimes."

"No. Humans have ways of stopping themselves from making babies. If you aren't chosen to be a breeder, then you must have your body changed, so you can't make babies."

"You changed? You no can have babies?" J'kla was horrified at the idea.

"I was spared. I can make babies." She felt funny talking like him but was getting used to it. "But if I go home, they will take that away from me."

J'kla took her hand and held it tightly. With a very stern look, he said, "You no go home. You stay with B'reann. We no take away anything God give you."

She liked the look on his face. He was so strong in his convictions. The strength of determination in him to protect her was so powerful, it warmed her heart. Taking advantage of his hold on her hand, she drew him closer to her and then hugged up against him, wrapping her arms around him. Maybe it was all this talk about making babies, but right now she was enjoying the feeling of his muscles a little too much. Or it might just be feeling him and knowing he was alive and safe. The fear of losing him was still so fresh in her memory, it ached. "I promise, I will stay with you. If they ever come for me, you can explain to them I am not going back to Earth unless God tells me to."

J'kla was rubbing her ear with his hand. "If they come for Anna, J'kla will make bad humans go away."

CHAPTER SEVENTEEN

Z CRASSLY MUTTERED TO HIMSELF, while he made his way through yet another forest full of natural obstacles. He hated trees, water, dirt, and bugs. He didn't hate them as much yesterday, but it was getting really annoying having to deal with all this.

"There is nothing here. What stupid secrets could be so valuable about this stupid moon? Oh look, trees! Oh, dear, we must not tell Earth there are trees here!" Now he was getting sarcastic, with no one around to listen. Even he was wondering if robots could go stark raving mad.

To his delight, he suddenly heard two beeping sounds. One was coming from his sensor device; he had picked up on something, and it wasn't just another tree. He plugged it into the tablet and checked the data. Yes, it definitely wasn't natural; there was something artificial here.

"I hope this isn't just something left by one of the science teams." He ran ahead and tried to get closer to get a clearer reading. "Computer, calculate the distance to the artificial signature."

"One hundred and ninety-six kilometers," the computer announced.

"Wow, it must be a large object to be detected this far away. It certainly isn't just a computer tablet someone dropped." He checked his navigation program to get a reading on the best path possible. "What else is beeping?" He had stopped the noise from the sensor device, and yet another thing was beeping.

Looking down at his arm, he saw the little light hidden beneath his fake skin was flashing. His power levels were low and would need to recharge. That meant adding even more time between him and his objective.

Z found a good place that was both hidden but allowed enough sunlight to work off of the solar cell he would open to charge his batteries. Before he activated the sleep mode, he tuned his sensor to emit a false signal to block anyone from locating him in the same manner he was locating this other thing. If they came looking for him, all they would read would be a tree. Once that was done, he packed everything into his bag and then opened up a panel on his head to absorb as much sunlight as possible.

Some idiot thought it would be wise to force the robots to turn off during charging times. Normally on a ship, they would just plug in each night and charge, so they wouldn't need this solar cell charger. But he wasn't on a ship and didn't have anywhere to plug in for the night. So, it was sleep time for this robot while he absorbed some rays.

Three more days had passed, and Anna felt more and more a part of this community. She still had a hard time understanding them, but they understood her situation and helped as much as they could. They no longer tried talking to her, only gestured and directed without words.

She was tired of wearing the same old jumpsuit. It was stained, ragged in places, and had a large tear in it where J'kla had lashed out during his madness. She had roughly stitched the largest tear up, but it was an ugly job. Not only was it a constant reminder of what had happened to him, but it was a piece of her former life as a member of the PSC. The PSC had tried to kill her, took her robot's life away, and drugged the man she loved. There wasn't an ounce of care left in her for the PSC.

Rillan, J'kla's mother, brought her to a workshop in the village where clothing was made. The shop had bolts of fabrics in various colors spread around with a number of people working on sewing. Two men were teaching younger boys and girls how to tan hides and make leather, using the skins of those deer-like creatures they herded. Three women sat among large woven baskets filled with big fluffs of the cotton from those flowers. The cotton fluffs had been cleaned. Some were obviously dyed and right now were being spun using a unique side winding spinner.

Anna had to be continually nudged along with how often she stopped in amazement at the work. This kind of craftsmanship was extinct on Earth. Finally, she was brought to the back, where some clothing was laying around. A few older people checked the stitching and folded the finished work to be stored. Rillan spoke to them and gestured toward Anna.

Two of the older women took Anna into a back room and undressed her down to nothing. They showed her how to put on the normal undergarments of their people. Both the top and bottom parts were long pieces of white cloth wrapped up in a way to support and cover.

The fact Anna did not have a tail to work around sort of stumped the old women for a bit, but they managed. Then a young girl came in with several pieces of clothing for Anna to try on. They did not have a mirror to help her choose, but she wasn't too concerned about her look so long as they approved.

What was unusual for Anna was the style. She was used to the way the PSC uniforms covered pretty much from neck down. These people wore light clothing that revealed a decent amount of their bodies. In fact, Anna had noted the men often wore nothing above the waist, save a necklace or bracelets. She didn't feel naked, but she felt a little exposed. She chose a pair of loose-fitting cloth pants that were common among both genders of B'reann, and a vest much like J'kla normally wears, only cut for a woman. And unlike J'kla's, this vest was tied in the middle so as not to flap open.

Once she got an approving smile from the attendants, she was met by Rillan and taken to another part of the village. For the first time, she was shown to the place J'kla's family worked. It was a large hut with half a dozen B'reann inside, working diligently on crafting artwork and jewelry. There were many forms of fiber art, from embroidery with bone needles, to crochet and knitting to make smaller articles of clothing, blankets, and even necklaces and bracelets.

Anna was amused to see J'nar working at a table with three children. He was teaching them to braid with their hands, so they could craft ropes. These thick ropes were used to make bridges and tether the platforms and buildings to the forest. She couldn't understand his words exactly, but she could tell he was showing them that once they perfected the technique, they could apply it to much finer threads to make jewelry, clothing, and other items. He was such a fierce, manly B'reann; but he was very skilled at art, and that was rather charming.

Rillan had walked away from Anna to watch the kids learning. She returned to Anna with something for her. Taking her right arm, Rillan tied a bracelet over her arm and smiled at Anna. "For Anna." Rillan had learned a few words from her son, so she could speak to Anna.

Anna looked at the bracelet; it was the same kind of braid J'nar was teaching, only more intricate and daintier. Intertwined into the threads were beads made of wood painted different colors. "Thank you."

Suddenly, J'nar said something to his wife and pointed out the door. Anna could understand him say "J'kla" and "J'kla Krina."

Rillan pointed at the far door of this craftsmen's studio. "J'kla."

Anna got the reference and knew J'kla was out there, probably looking for her. So, she reached up and scratched the ear of Rillan, a proper way of saying thank you, then left.

Outside, she found J'kla looking for her. He wasn't saying anything, only sniffing the air. She understood the power of his nose as he seemed to follow the path she had made getting here by following her scent. Halfway out the door of the clothing shop, he looked up to see her and then nearly bound over to her. "Anna!"

She laughed at the way he was always excited to see her. Some days, she felt like she had a pet and not a person. "Good morning, J'kla."

"Good morning, Anna. Where you go? I wake, and you gone." He just then noticed her new attire. "Wow, Anna."

Anna blushed and modeled her new clothing for him. "A gift from your mother. She thought I needed something better to wear."

J'kla highly approved this new look; Anna could tell by the way his tail was flopping about. "I have gift for you." He held up a creation from the workshop.

Anna looked at it and was confused. It was a tube-like item made of wood with a hinge separating the two halves of it. Inside were teeth like a comb, all pointing inward. On the outside were carved flowers. Taking it out of his hand, she had an idea what this was but didn't know if she was correct. "What is it?"

J'kla showed her he had one as well, only it was darker in color and decorated with a geometric pattern on it. It was clasped into his mane. "It special symbol. People of my village wear them. Every village have own. You part of village; you wear this. I made for you."

Anna was amused, but still a bit lost. "I see; it's a clasp. But how do I wear it? I don't have a mane."

He pointed to her head. "You have woman mane."

She took down her hair from the elastic band she held it up with. Then she gathered it together and clasped it with this wooden trinket. Turning around, she showed it to him. "Good?"

"Very good. Anna B'reann now."

"Glad to be." She took his hand and held it tight.

They strolled along toward another path they hadn't walked yet; at least, she hadn't been here before. They did this often, so she could ask questions and learn more about him and his people. It also gave them some time together. He had become quite popular now that he was their new religious leader.

✶ ✶ ✶

Z hiked across a long valley and passed through the mountains near where they had camped the night before the shuttle picked them up. His sensor continued leading him forward. It was like he had walked around this stupid moon three times already, but the target was still ahead of him.

"I should've packed my good legs," he bemoaned as he skidded down the side of the mountain, kicking up a lot of rocks and dust.

To his great surprise, in all the time he had been down here, no one from the *Sanger* had come looking for him. He still had a link to the *Sanger's* subcomputers, so he could use the private relay to get to Elijah on Earth.

This link also allowed him to see if they sent any shuttles down after him. So far, none. It was odd. He knew his little monster movie routine would work against that dope in the shuttle bay, but Dr. Skye and the other scientists on the *Sanger* weren't as dumb. They would know there wasn't any dangerous stuff on the shuttle. It was only quarantined to keep people out of it and protect the precious secrets of the PSC.

Z stopped walking and set the sensor to wide scan again. He would reset the data and see what it told him now. The closer he got to the source of the artificial stuff, the more detailed the information would be. It would also update the terrain map for him, so he would know where to go.

While it ran through its calculations and scanning, he pondered the data so far. "Okay, the important thing about this moon was its people. So, this secret has to do with them. The evolution thing was a big deal, so perhaps it has to do with that. I could do a biological study and see if there is something in them that disproves the evolution theory and . . . wait . . . no. That would take months of hard research. They worried that we knew this secret after only a little more than a week down here. What if it has to do with the way they were studying these people? Maybe they don't want Earth to know their methods? Wait, no, they captured, killed, and stuffed one to be put on display. I doubt that anything else they do here would be worse than that, or at least more shocking to Earth. Man, this is irritating. I am not a science robot; I can't figure this out. What if this secret is bigger than what I can find? It might be the whole moon."

"Analysis complete. Location set," the sensor announced and flashed red to indicate something was found.

He looked at it and saw it was showing him a rough, computer-generated layout of the terrain between him and a mountain in the distance. Something on that mountain was the source of the artificial signature. Z knew full well the scientists from the PSC hadn't gone that far to this side of the moon. So, if no PSC people were reported this far, yet advanced tech was showing on his radar, this has to be the big secret.

Z then noticed the sensor had a new bit of data for him, something he had asked for it to do when he started. A text box was open, telling him there were multiple life signs between him and his objective. He would be coming upon populated areas of this moon—likely members of J'kla's noble, hairy race. This could prove problematic, but Z was stronger than any of them. If they didn't like him trekking through their territory, then they would just have to get over it. He had a mission to complete, and no cats were going to stand in his way.

The evening softly gave way to night, and the stars twinkled into view. The little village settled in, and only a few were outside right now. Anna was told that they strengthened the patrol on their borders to watch out for the furless ones. She was the exception, of course, but they had a legitimate fear of the furless men coming to take them away.

Anna wasn't tired and had a lot on her mind right now. She walked outside and took some time to enjoy the stars.

"ANNA!" a very small voice called out and ran over to her and hugged up against her leg.

She looked down to see a child who was happy to see her. Anna hadn't meant to, but she had made friends with all the young children of the village. They were fascinated by her at first, and she was equally fascinated by them. She had so seldom encountered young children in her life. She liked playing with them, holding them, even scratching their ears. They would feel her bare skin on her arms and look at her round pupil eyes, even tug a little on her oddly-shaped ears. They were unashamedly curious and so innocent. This little one's father was one of the first to go missing and hadn't been found. It broke Anna's heart to know her people had taken away this child's father. She wanted to express how sorry she was; but they couldn't understand her, and they did not blame her as much as she blamed herself.

"Now where is your mommy?" Anna reached down and picked up the three-year-old.

"Anna," he said and then felt her neck, still so curious about the non-furry skin.

She was amused by this child. He was so adorable; all of them were. Though covered in a thick coat of fur, he had no mane yet because he was far too young for that. His tail was short, and his fur was dark with almost invisible darker stripes running through it. When he smiled and laughed, she could see the tiny, sharp fangs in his mouth. Anna couldn't help but wonder what it was like to breastfeed a child with fangs; then again, they probably didn't grow them until after weaning.

"Nohral!" His mother finally found him. She was scowling at her little boy.

Anna quickly held him out for her. The child's happy, curious expression turned to guilt quickly. He knew better than to run away from his mother, but he was three and didn't always do what he was told.

His mother smiled and bowed her head to Anna in thanks for watching her son, and then she walked him back home, scolding him all the way.

Anna wondered what it would be like to be a mother. The only people on Earth who knew anything about mothering were the teachers of the schoolhouses.

"Anna?" J'kla came up just then.

"Oh, hi. Where have you been? We had dinner, and I didn't have a translator with your parents and grandmother."

"I asked to pray with group. They want to learn Lord's Prayer."

"Oh, well, I guess you're excused." She smiled at him, always pleased to hear him diligently doing his mission work. "I'm impressed at how much of the Scriptures you've memorized. You have an amazing mind."

"When God want me to know something, He put it in for good. It not my mind; it God's work." J'kla took her by the hand and walked with her in no particular direction. "Why you out so late?"

"Just thinking. Remembering all the fun times we had sitting under the stars, reading from the Bible, talking about whatever came to mind. When I think back to before we came here, I want to remember the good and fun things, not . . . you know."

J'kla stopped walking at the edge of the fence to the pasture of the livestock. The big, male deer thing was grazing in the dark, his enormous antlers appearing much like a tree in the shadows. "I remember reading, learning Word of God. Beside me sat most beautiful woman to teach me. Anna good teacher."

She almost asked something, then stopped herself. There was a question she had held back for days now, but she just couldn't bring herself to ask. Looking up, she saw a mountain not so distant from here. It was unusually tall against the rest of the landscape. There was one path leading toward it, but it wasn't as well-tread as the others. "What is up there?"

J'kla followed her pointed finger and saw the mountain. "That special place. B'reann call it the *Gladuin*."

"*Gladuin*? What does that mean?"

He thought about that and worked hard to recall some of the words he hadn't practiced much. "It . . . uh . . . it mean sanctary . . . no, not right word."

"Sanctuary?"

"Yes. S-a-n-c-t-u-a-r-y." He elongated the word to say it correctly. "Special place, only for new couple to spend night."

"New couple . . . do you mean it's the honeymoon mountain?"

He gave her the most curious look. "What honey moon?"

"Uh . . . well . . . " She had to think about this; she had only read about honeymoons from the ancient history books. "When a man and woman get married, the first thing they do is go on a special trip, and that is where they spend their first time . . . together."

J'kla was nodding in agreement. "That Gladuin. Man and woman bond, then go and spend night on Gladuin. Very special place."

"Oh, so you spend your first night together . . . under the stars. I guess it could be romantic." She looked up there, wondering if there was a lodge or something like it. "Can someone visit who didn't get married? Just to hike it?"

"No. Only for first night together as bonded man and woman. After, no go. It considered a special place."

"Why?"

"Old stories say first B'reann come down from Gladuin. Life start there; special place to make first child."

Anna was intrigued. "So, it's a holy place?"

"No holy, just special. B'reann have no holy or God, until you bring His Word. But we respect tradition."

She smiled at him. "Then I'll respect it as well. I won't go up there without permission."

"No permission, only night of bonding." He was very stern about this.

"Okay. It is a lovely mountain. I wonder what started the old stories about it being your origins?"

"Not know. Storytellers say first B'reann no allowed to visit, even after bonding. It secret place until chief change rule. I no living when rule change."

"Interesting." Anna was truly interested in this history but only to satisfy curiosity. She stared at the mountain for a while and considered the different reasons this legend might have risen. It could be just a fairytale told for generations. It could be because of the height of the mountain that stories were made up. And there might be some validity to its history, but that history had been changed and retold in various ways until it gained its new lore today.

While she pondered these thoughts, she found herself shivering. Just about the time she was going to ask to go in, she felt the warm, furry body of J'kla press up against her and wrap his arms around her to give her some of his warmth. He was either a gentleman or a smart opportunist. Either way, she found his arms very comforting.

Then she thought about the same question she had wanted to ask for a while. It was quiet; they were alone; and it was time for her to ask. "J'kla, what do you remember from the incident?"

He thought about that for a moment. "Hard to remember. My head no clear."

"How much do you recall?"

"Uh . . . I woke up on grass, noise in head loud. I want find Anna; then I cannot think right. I tear clothes, yell, roar. I see Anna and want her help, then I angry for no reason and try to hurt her. She see me and be scared. I . . . " Suddenly, his eyes widened. "Anna saw J'kla naked?"

She nodded. "Yes, you had torn your clothing almost completely off of you when I first saw you."

J'kla cleared his throat as he shook off the embarrassment. He went on, "I smell Anna and chase. I hunt, no mean to, but cannot stop. I . . . I find Anna. I . . . I think I talk with you."

Anna came out with the question she really wanted the answer to. "What did you mean when you said you loved me?"

"Huh?"

"Back during the incident, you proclaimed you loved me, just before you stopped yourself from hurting me. Do you remember?"

"I remember," he quietly admitted. "Much is gone, but some I remember. I feel pain when I look down, see Anna scared of J'kla. I so sorry I make you scared. I so, so sorry. I no want hurt Anna ever." The vague memories ached in him over what he almost did.

Anna held his arms against her tightly and laid her head back against him. "You didn't mean to do what you did. It was forced on you by a very wicked man. I wasn't afraid you wanted to hurt me; I was afraid you couldn't stop yourself. But you did. When you did, you said you loved me. Did you really mean it? Was it just the chemicals talking?"

He didn't know what the word chemical was, but he understood what she was asking. "I look down and see Anna, smell Anna on breeze, hear Anna's voice above loud sounds in head. Madness leave for moment. J'kla see Anna with his eyes, not wild eyes. I scared I die without telling Anna truth. I love Anna. I will die for Anna. I will never, ever hurt Anna."

She turned around in his arms to look at his face. "I knew you would never hurt me on purpose. Truthfully, when I saw you beat yourself sense-less, I wasn't relieved I was safe; I was scared you were dead. I love you and didn't even realize it until I almost lost you. When I saw you lying in the hut, it reconnected me with God in a profound and perfect way. I put my hand on your heart and felt each beat as I prayed God would not let your life end in such a worthless and terrible way." She put her hand on his chest and felt his heart beat. "I love you."

He took her hand off of his chest and then kissed it on the palm, a romantic gesture for his people. "I love you."

J'kla didn't ask but only kissed her on the lips. He had held back this desire since he woke, not knowing if she returned his affection. The night on the mountain before the incident was so wonderful, but it might not have been the truth between them. Now, he was sure.

They remained in this embrace for a long time, passionately kissing each other with abandon in this starlit night. Had she had a tail, it would have intertwined with his right now.

Suddenly, he stopped and took a few breaths before stating, "Sorry."

"Nothing to be sorry about; you are a good kisser. I even like the fangs." She wasn't getting the seriousness of his apology.

"No. I can't." He backed away to leave.

She got hold of his hand and wouldn't let him go. "No, you don't. We finally have what we both want, and you just up and run. No. Tell me what is wrong."

J'kla stood there, his back to her, and his shoulders slumped a little. "I want wife. I want ask you to bond. But I no can."

"You want to propose to me?" She was happy but stunned.

"Anna want baby. J'kla cannot give Anna baby. J'kla not human; Anna not B'reann."

She held his hand tightly and pulled him back closer. "I have thought about that, too. But I can't ask for that any longer. There aren't any humans around me anymore. Besides, I want J'kla. I don't care if we cannot have a baby; we can have each other."

"Mother and Father won't be happy with no baby. But they happy I happy."

Anna took both of his hands and held him closer. "So. Is this a proposal?"

"Pro . . . pro . . . what?" Another new word.

She squeezed his hands. "Just ask me what you wanted to ask."

"Anna, may I have you?" The only way he knew how to ask.

She nodded with a big smile. "Yes. You may have me." With that, she kissed him again.

It was an odd outcome, but she couldn't stop remembering her prayer for a man to marry. She asked God for a man who would actually marry her for love and who would be faithfully Christian. Her prayer was answered, and it was with this big, silly cat. The only aspect of her prayers that weren't answered was to have a child, but she knew God had His perfect plan for her life. A baby was just not part of that plan, and she could be happy with that.

While they kissed, J'kla's ears perked up, and he stopped and looked around with concern written all over his face.

"What is it?" Anna didn't hear anything yet.

Suddenly, there came a strange feline cry in the distance. J'kla held her closer to him, sort of protecting her. "Warriors! They see furless stranger."

"What? Who?" Anna was rattled deeply by this. Could the PSC be looking for her body now that they thought she was dead?

"I not know. They only sound alarm. We go home, hide." He took her by the hand and quickly led her back to his house where he would keep her safe.

Anna was terrified. She had finally realized her prayers and fondest dream; now the PSC was coming to take it away. These people were very nice and loyal. J'kla was fiercely determined, but they really could not contend against the strength of the PSC.

*   *   *

Z had hiked throughout the day and into the night heading for the destination his sensors were leading toward. He could see it was on a rather tall mountain in the distance, but he didn't know how far.

As he walked into an extra dense area of trees, he found himself on a road. This wasn't a natural path, or even just a well-tread trail; it was a cleared and flattened road obviously used for cattle, considering the innumerable hoof prints all leading the same direction. Looking down the road, he could almost make out a few lights in the trees that were not just glinting starlight. Some form of civilization was directly ahead of him.

He considered what to do next, but his thoughts were cut short as he heard the loud bellow of a feline cry in the trees. Then another and another. They were calling out to each other a warning, and he was likely the reason behind the warning.

His robotic hearing picked up the sounds of them rustling through the trees and hunting him down. They were getting closer. They had the home turf advantage, as well as feline agility and skill. Z slipped the little stun gun out of his side and prepared to defend himself. He was determined to not kill any of them, but stunning them wasn't out of the question.

He saw two warriors come running right at him. They had not been following him. They were alerted by the echoed warning cries. He was approaching their settlement, and they would defend it. Both were wielding some kind of wooden spear, each ready to launch it like a javelin.

"No, you don't." Z hit the nearest one with a blast of energy, knocking him senseless.

He misjudged the skill and accuracy of the other attacker and was met by a launched wooden spear right into his chest. Fortunately for a Z-550, most of the chest compartment was hollow and used for storage.

"Ah, man! I don't have any spare panels for surface repair."

The warrior who launched the spear stood there, wide-eyed. The man he had just skewered simply stood there, examining the stick. He should be dead. With a terrified scream, he ran away from the demon.

Z heard the warriors in the trees getting closer and decided to beat a hasty retreat. Unfortunately, this large stick protruding out his front and back made him unexpectedly unbalanced, and he fell over. He pushed himself up and then went to pull the stick out.

"Stupid, annoying gravity," he muttered as he reached for the spear. It was a long spear, and he would need to break it to get it completely out. "Now I know what it feels like to be an hors d'oeuvres."

Just then, a lasso slung out and wrapped around his arm; then another gripped his other arm. A third went around his neck, and he was yanked upward away from the ground for a second. His weight was greater than the attackers anticipated, and he plopped back down and pulled two of the warriors with him. The thrusts of motion had dislodged his gun and left him tangled in the well-braided cords.

Three of the men came and wrapped him up tightly in the ropes. They yanked so hard against him, his left shoulder joint servos were dislocated. This deactivated the arm completely. He couldn't break free of the ropes now.

"Great, just great. Now how am I supposed to finish this?"

As cautious as kittens, they stared at him and then chattered to each other in their native tongue. He wasn't sure if they were discussing how to carry him or cook him. They came up and took either end of the spear and carried him like a pig on a spit. So, either outcome was still possible.

It took four men to carry him, but they managed; the whole way they were on the receiving end of his angry words and annoyed mutterings, though they had no idea what this thing was or what it was saying.

CHAPTER EIGHTEEN

WHEN Z LEFT THE *SANGER* to discover New Eden's secret, the meetings between the military leaders of the World Corps and the representative of Jerusalem were in full swing. Elijah struggled to assure them Jerusalem was in no position or had any desire to attack the rest of the world, but somehow his arguments would be invalidated by a misleading news story or article. He was fully aware Jessie was behind these rumors and misleading half-truths, but he couldn't implicate her without solid evidence to back him up.

Right now, Elijah stood in the middle of the empty courtroom, looking up at the ceiling.

The Corps had taken over the Vatican a long time ago and turned it into the headquarters of the world government. They had dismantled and destroyed much of the artwork that had decorated this ancient city for centuries. Yet a few items remained. One of which was the ceiling in this room. It was a dome with little cherubs flying about on clouds, looking down upon the people. The first head of the world government kept this ceiling, not to remind them of the abolished religions, but as a message. The angelic children on the ceiling represented the citizens under the care of the wise and all-knowing government.

Elijah looked at the artwork and considered what life was like back when religions were allowed. This mural reminded him of a time when men had a heart for God and expressed it through art. Elijah might not agree with some of the theology of the Catholics, whose doctrine dominated when this ceiling was painted, but he respected their desire to honor God above all. He was ready to bring down the evil that stood in the way of religious freedom in this world.

There was one little catch to fighting that evil. He had to make certain the evidence was real. This is why he stood here waiting. Hoping his people got back to him with their findings.

"Oh, Lord, please send—"

"Sir." One of his few attendants allowed outside the embassy came in, unintentionally interrupting his prayer.

"Yes?"

The young man held up a computer tablet. "They finished; all the information is in here, ready to go."

"Ready to go? Do you know what their findings are? I can't go in there with this unless I know it is legitimate."

"It all checks out. The photos are real. The data is uncorrupted, and the source has been confirmed. This has not been fabricated."

Elijah maintained his diplomatically calm smile, though on the inside he was jumping for joy. He finally had a card to play. Taking the tablet from the young man, he looked at it with elation in his eyes. "I think I'm ready to go to my meeting."

✶   ✶   ✶

"Listen, we simply cannot authorize a strike yet. If we hit them now, we will look like the aggressors." The representative of the counsel answered Jessie's last statement.

The gathered people sat around a table with holoimages displayed in front of them. The images were faint and allowed them to look at each other through them. Three different heads of the Corps military sat along one side, while a single voice sat in from the court of representatives. It wouldn't be wise to hold this meeting without the consent of the court and the people. Jessie sat in as well, doing her best to guide their decision to attack Jerusalem.

"Look. The more time we waste here, talking back and forth about pointless debates and arguments, the more Jerusalem builds their forces," Jessie said.

Admiral Walker quietly looked at one of the holoimages of Israeli airspace, where six war cruisers were now hovering near the Iron Dome. "I tend to agree with the administrator. If they are building up their arsenal . . . "

Jessie jumped in. "Which I have already proven they are."

"Yes . . . as I was saying. If they are building up their arsenal, it is only a matter of time before they strike. If we don't do something to stop them now, they could hit a major city."

Jessie was always pleased to hear anyone agree with her. "Knowing the bloody history of Israel, we know they are always after taking more land."

Elijah entered the room and answered this old accusation right then. "Israel was established a long time ago—in 1948, to be exact. Since then, we have reduced our borders on many occasions to accommodate others in our lands. But the battle cry of the anti-Semitic politicians has always been that we are grabbing land. Our borders are reduced to the edges of a single, large city. We have never asked the Corps for more space and are handling our own affairs without a problem. I wonder what other lies we have been told here to advance the anti-Semitic sentiment of the PSC and their representative, Jessie."

Jessie threw her hands up. "Oh, here we go again. Your tired, failed statements on how I am supposedly making things up."

"Let's take a look at what has been said. It all comes from the media, which is controlled by the Corps and has members of the PSC in every station to monitor the news coming and going. But actual witnesses outside of the media, the PSC, and Jessie are hard to find. I wonder how easy it is for the PSC to keep one story silent, while rewriting another to suit your desires?"

Jessie stood up and walked around the table, ready to put some fear into Elijah by her stare alone. "Prove what you are saying. If you want to accuse me of lying, then prove it." She had said this many times before and found clever ways of making him look the fool when he tried to prove her a liar.

Elijah smiled and slowly set his tablet down on the table's connector pad. On contact, it downloaded a pre-set program. "If you have told us only the truth, then why did the PSC lie about those so-called primitives?"

Jessie's smile faded, and the glare turned a little deadly. "What are you talking about?"

"I have it on very good authority that the PSC fabricated quite the story about New Eden and the primitives."

Jessie was actually worried for a moment. "This is not the time or place to discuss whatever you think you know about that. This is about the conflict Jerusalem is trying to start by arming—"

He interrupted her, knowing how it absolutely annoyed her. "No, this is the time and place. Computer, access program Omega one."

All the holoimagers changed to the various images of J'kla and Anna on the planet. Right before their eyes was a dressed primitive, interacting with humans like one of them. He was reading from a book, talking with Anna, cooking fish over a fire, even smiling for his own photo.

"What is this? What are we looking at?" The representative from the court asked.

Elijah quickly grabbed his tablet before Jessie got her hands on it. "We're looking at a massive bit of deception on the parts of the PSC. They've manipulated the information coming in from that moon, for reasons I haven't determined yet. But I can say for certain the idea of the animal-like, partially-evolved savage is not what's really down there."

The admiral slammed his fist on the table. "I don't like being manipulated by anyone. What is going on, Jessie? What is the truth?"

"Sir, this is obviously a completely fabricated story designed to distract us from the matters at hand. Think about it. At what time has the PSC even remotely tried to influence the truth of science?" If she were a wooden puppet, her nose would have grown twelve feet at this point.

Elijah sat down in his seat and looked at the rest of the people here, not caring about Jessie right now. "Look. I knew you would want to verify this information, so I will let you have it to check. I have already run it through our data investigation teams, and they cleared it."

Jessie stepped aside and considered her last ace to play.

The general to Elijah's right asked, "What purpose could this serve? All you have stated and shown with this is they have potentially altered the information. But the fact remains, they did discover alien life."

"I don't know the whole story yet. The source of this information told me while he was undercover in the PSC, he learned they are behind all of this. They mean to pit the World Corps and Jerusalem in a war that will only lead to the PSC taking over the government. We are all pawns in their little game."

The admiral said, "Listen, sir, that is a rather serious accusation. That borders on talk of a coup d'état staged by the Science Commission. I have a hard time believing any of this."

"I know. I was skeptical at first, but consider the evidence. They are the ones who bring us this falsified information. It is Jessie who has been pushing for war all along. It was Jessie who supposedly discovered my people's presumed secret plans to take over the world. And . . . there's more. My source learned there is a much deeper secret involved with this primitive scandal."

"Well, what is it?" the general asked.

"I don't know. But he is currently looking for it and will contact me when he has the information."

This grabbed Jessie's attention. She had feared someone was down on the moon looking for the secret; now she was sure. "Who is this spy of yours? Where is he?"

Elijah leaned back and smiled at her. "Now, you know better than that. I know you're willing to do anything to stop me. I shudder to think of what you would do to him. But rest assured, your secret will be rooted out. I sent this information to every media outlet I could find. Though I'm sure many of them will not be allowed to show it, with the PSC hanging over their shoulder. Some will get it out there, and your secret will be destroyed. I suggest you go back to your office and prepare for the damage control. You're going to need it."

Jessie didn't budge. "No, I think the media will have their hands full."

Before Elijah could ask what she meant, the alarm blared, and the holoimages quickly changed. They switched to the emergency condition Alert 1 status.

"What is going on?" the admiral demanded.

"I don't know. Let's check," Jessie answered with a well-acted tone.

The images changed to several different news sources, and she searched through them to find one they could all understand and filled every screen with it.

A man stood outside the battle parameter of the standoff near Jerusalem. Behind him was a cloud of smoke, raining debris. "We haven't had any confirmed reports yet, but sources are informing us a laser beam just emitted from Jerusalem and demolished the battle cruiser *Hawk*. I repeat: The *Hawk* has been obliterated in a single, unprovoked attack from inside Jerusalem. Wait . . . yes, we have footage of the incident; we will play it now."

The image changed to the standard observational view the media had had on this standoff for weeks now. Six large, bulky ships hovered in the air near the large energy dome over Jerusalem. Then, breaking the quiet of the dry, hot day, one of the ships exploded in an amazing eruption of black smoke.

The admiral stood up and dissolved the holoimage by leaning right through it to point at Elijah. "YOU . . . YOU WERE JUST DISTRACTING US, WHILE YOUR PEOPLE PREPARED TO STRIKE! WELL, I WON'T STAND FOR IT!"

"No, please. We didn't do this. We wouldn't. It is a ploy."

"We've had enough of your double talk, little man. Every time you try and defend yourself, it is the same thing. 'It's a lie; it's a ploy; it's a scheme.' Well, you were correct, but it was your scheme, not theirs. This meeting is over!

Jerusalem is toast! GET HIM OUT OF HERE!" The admiral pointed at one of the guards.

Elijah was taken by the arm and pulled out, to be made the first prisoner of war. He was led right past a very satisfied Jessie, who had set into motion her most decisive plan yet. It was finally coming together—no more talking, no more meetings.

Elijah was led through the court, heading for an exit he had not used before. He wasn't resisting, for he knew who was standing there. The young man who had brought him his tablet hadn't gone far. With a swift kick to the face and then a well-placed hand on the back of the neck, the guard went down. Jerusalem might believe in peace, but they trained some of the most-skilled fighters on Earth. Three were assigned to Elijah here at the embassy, and Elijah made certain they were the few who had the right to leave the embassy like him.

"What is going on, sir?"

Elijah took the boy by the arm and started running. "We have to get back to the embassy and lock it down."

"Understood." The boy and Elijah ran out of the court and toward the embassy. Elijah was much slower than his youthful counterpart but, fortunately, not many were aware he was now a wanted man.

Once back at the embassy, they sealed the place up tight and then activated an emergency forcefield to defend the building. It was nothing compared to the Iron Dome, but it was enough to keep them safe for now. The World Corps would hardly launch an attack big enough to take down the embassy right in the middle of the Vatican. It was virtually now a prison for those inside, but a prison with the ability to make contact with their allies.

CHAPTER NINETEEN

"LOOK. I CAN'T UNDERSTAND YOU!" Z yelled at the B'reann chattering at him in their native tongue.

He had been brought to the largest hut in the village. Around him stood several very muscular B'reann holding the ropes binding the robot. A group of elders had come with the old chieftain. They all asked questions, and then spoke to each other. Often, they would give long, bewildered stares at the spear still sticking through Z. They checked for blood but found none. They moved it back and forth a few inches and realized it wasn't hurting him. More than one of them came over and sniffed him in rather inappropriate ways trying to determine what he was.

"Hey, hey, hey! Don't mess those up!" Z watched a pair of the guards rifling through his bag, inspecting everything with scrutiny. They tossed aside much of what was in there and stopped for all to take deep, long looks at the tablet that was still operating to sense the artificial signal. They poked it, shook it, and even talked to it. Z was amused at their foolishness; but at the same time, he was irritated by their handling of his only connection to help outside of this moon. "Don't break it . . . Oh, what does it matter? I could tell you I'm a giant green lollipop, and you wouldn't understand me."

Finally, they set down the tablet without seriously harming it and continued inspecting his goods. With a rather feline yell, the two mighty warriors jumped back and said something loudly to the others. The old woman rushed to the bag and looked in. With a careful, fearful hand she reached in and pulled out one of the spare feet he had brought; it was the left foot with the broken arch. She was more than worried. Z was not aware of her words, but she told them to be careful; this thing might be coming to kill and eat them.

Z laughed, not realizing how bad that sounded right now. "Look. Those are just parts for me. Oh, this is aggravating. Man, I wish J'kla and Anna were still alive."

The room fell silent, and all eyes turned to him, as well as all ears. They slowly approached, and the old woman inquisitively stated, "J'kla? Anna?"

Z nodded quickly. "Yes, yes. J'kla . . . friend. Anna . . . friend." He spoke slowly as if doing so would bridge the language barrier.

The old woman pointed out the door and quickly gave a command, which included both of those names. He hoped this might help him, but he also worried they might blame him for the disappearance of J'kla—or worse, his death. Oh, the cruel irony to be blamed for the deaths of the only people he had ever cared about and who cared about him. The stringed orchestra played in his mind as the scene faded into darkness. The hero forsaken, the lovers dead, the world a darker place. He had watched too many black and white movies.

✶ ✶ ✶

Anna sat with J'kla and his family around the breakfast table. She slowly ate while considering what had happened last night. She was engaged—really, honestly engaged. A man wanted to be her husband and love her. She had a whole new life to start. What would these people need with an astro-geologist? Could she bring a new revolution of education to their society, or should she just assimilate by learning a new craft and being a productive citizen?

While Anna was deep in thought, J'kla had spent the better part of the morning discussing the details of the marriage with his parents. He had to get their approval before going ahead with the plans. It didn't take long for them to agree, though his father was less than happy with the notion of his son marrying a woman who wouldn't give them any grandchildren. But after a lot of good and logical arguments—and rather stubborn remarks from J'kla on the matter—it was settled. According to B'reann tradition, the engagement was to be short; the ceremony would take place right away.

"Anna ready?" J'kla had an eager smile.

She looked up from her soup and shook her head. "I'm sorry? Ready for what? I wasn't paying attention."

He gave her a really big, toothy grin and took her by the arm. "I . . . "

"J'kla, Anna." A guard appeared in the door to the home and said something to them in B'reann.

"What? What did he say?" Anna could see the shock on everyone in the room.

J'kla slowly let go of her arm and stood up. "They have stranger from stars. They need us."

Anna had a sick, cold feeling fill her belly. Since nothing had been said about the alert from last night, she had dismissed it as a false alarm. What could they want? She didn't want to be taken away from J'kla. "I don't know if we should go. Maybe your people could tell this person we're dead."

J'kla took her by the hand and helped her up. "My people capture furless invader. He no harm you. We go, know what he want."

"Oh, okay." She understood they did need to know what was happening. Ignoring this could only delay the inevitable. If the PSC was concerned about finding them, they wouldn't stop until they had what they wanted.

*   *   *

Z sat there, trussed up like a ham ready to bake, his arms half working, his body stuck clean through, and surrounded by chattering cats. He wanted to break loose of this and get out of here, but he couldn't. Now they were sending for people who probably wanted revenge for the killing of their husband,

son, brother . . . whoever J'kla was to them. Then again, they mentioned Anna
. . . at least it sounded like her name. How could they know her? It was more
likely 'Anna' was a word in their dialect that meant something else. He probably just confessed to killing J'kla without realizing it.

"If there is a God, He hates me," Z muttered. "Then again, if there truly
was a God, then the next person through that door would be Anna and . . . "

At that very moment, Anna and J'kla came through the door with the
guard who had gone to get them. Z's mouth hung open, and he couldn't believe his eyes, though they were fine-tuned and recently upgraded, so they
couldn't be wrong. "Anna?"

She looked at him with a critical gaze. "A Z-bot. I guess that makes sense.
Dr. Skye couldn't risk sending any humans down here. They might discover
these people like I did. And he certainly didn't want them to know he tried
to have me murdered."

"What? No, I wasn't sent by Dr. Skye. I'm Z . . . your Z!" He was elated to see
her, which was obvious by the way he tried to stand up, but was restrained by
the four guards holding the ropes binding him.

Anna scowled at him and walked over, confident with all the warriors
around her, as well as J'kla standing beside her. "What do you want? Did Dr.
Skye send you to find my body or something?"

"Oh, good grief! I'm your Z," he said again.

J'kla frowned and leaned in, "You . . . Z?"

"That's what I have been saying. Look in my bag. It is full of my stuff, and
something of yours." He hoped she would discover the truth by the one item
he brought out of sentiment.

Anna walked over to the bag and was stopped by the old woman who
was shaking her head. She said something to Anna and then looked at J'kla
to translate.

J'kla answered. "Chief say bad things inside, things gentle Anna not need
see."

"I see your grammar still needs some tweaking," Z retorted and then spoke directly to Anna. "Look, they found a couple of my spare parts, and it sort of scared them. It's just a couple feet and hands in case I need to replace them. But that isn't what I want you to see. I brought . . . your Bible."

Anna's skepticism faded a little. She couldn't believe he had just said that. If they had found her Bible, it would've been destroyed. Then again, this might be part of the elaborate trap. "How do I know that you didn't bring that to fool me?"

"Oh, this is just dumb. I'm not trying to fool you. Look, I'm so very happy to see you two alive, and a bit confused, to say the least. But I'm not here to capture your or anything. Heck, they think you're dead. Why would they set a trap for someone they think is dead?"

Anna looked back at Z and considered he might be telling the truth. "I wish I could believe you, but having the Bible isn't enough. Unless you can prove to me you are my Z, which somehow miraculously survived a memory wipe, I can't risk trusting you."

Z slumped his shoulders. "I don't know how to prove it to you. I wasn't memory-wiped."

J'kla leaned over and sniffed at Z. "No smell, like our Z."

Anna shrugged at him. "All Z-bots are going to smell the same. Sorry, that doesn't help."

"Yeah, so tell your friends to stop sticking their noses all over me! One was yanking my mouth open. She . . . WAIT, THAT'S IT! Back before you fell, I said that we could go on a date! Remember? Remember this!" He puckered up and made kissing sounds at her.

Anna looked back with wide eyes. "How could you know that?"

"Because I'm Z—your Z—the fun-loving, master joker, smarter-than-your-average-computer robot. And right about now, I feel like a giant shish kebab with this spear in me."

Anna was finally beginning to believe him. "You certainly sound like Z."

Z got a snarky look on his face. "Come on, Captain. You can figure this out."

"I said, don't call me captain! Wait!" A smile grew across her face. "Z! It's really you!"

"Told you. Now, tell these furballs to untie me and take this stupid spear out of my chest."

Anna took J'kla's hand. "It's him. I'm sure of it."

J'kla spoke to the chief and the others, and after a bit of deliberation and a few questions between them, they untied Z and two of the men yanked the spear out. After they did, almost everyone, including J'kla, spent a few moments staring through him to the wall on the far side of the room. They were still worried he was some kind of demon, but they trusted J'kla enough to allow this for now.

Z, back on his feet, took his arm and reattached it with a hefty grunt. Flexing the artificial muscles and wiggling the fingers for a moment, he gave off a big grin and put his arms around Anna in a great hug. "I was so worried; I thought you were dead."

Anna hugged him back. "I thought *you* were dead . . . well, that your memory had been wiped clean. How the heck did you survive? I saw you go down!"

Z stepped back from her and poked at the new hole in his chest. "It's a long story. I have a micro-welder in my repair kit. I really should fix this before more moisture gets into my inner mechanisms."

✳   ✳   ✳

J'kla took Z and Anna to a place where they could talk in private. Anna knew it would be best to not have a lot of onlookers while Z used a flaming welder on his body. He had spent an hour explaining what he had been doing and what he learned from the *Sanger* about these elusive secrets. Anna was floored by all of this, not sure what the secret could be. J'kla had a hard time understanding any of it.

"Hold still. I don't have your robotic precision." Anna held up the tiny torch and worked on fixing the broken part on his back.

Z, who was leaning forward while sitting on the floor of the little training hut, waited patiently as she finished. J'kla loomed over her shoulder and peered into the hole, fascinated by what he saw.

"No blood?" J'kla asked, again.

Anna pushed a piece of metal down and welded it to another piece. "No. I wish I could make you understand. Z isn't alive."

"He dead?"

Z stuck his arms out and moaned, "Brains."

Anna slapped him in the back. "Shut up." She then tried to explain. "Z is . . . uh . . . well, do you have dolls?"

"Doll?"

"Dolls. Little toys that look like people."

"Children make baby out of twig and hay. Is doll?"

"Yes. Well, Z is like a big doll. He is made up of stuff and then given a fake mind."

"I no understand." J'kla still didn't get it.

"Okay, just think of me as a statue," Z said. "That can move."

"Statue? Talking statue?"

"Sure. If that works for ya," Z said.

Anna finished and patted his back. "There. I think it's good."

Z sat up and rolled his shoulders to check the connections. "I think I'm in one piece. Man, I didn't expect to be skewered like that."

Anna asked, "So, where is this secret?"

"I don't know. I was heading for an artificial signal my sensor picked up when they attacked me."

"Artificial signal? What is it?"

Z got up and retrieved his bag. "I don't know. All I know is the sensor picked up several metallic signatures which are not natural. They are man-made metals."

"The B'reann don't work with much metal." Anna thought about how little metal she had seen in all of their work.

Z turned on his scanner and checked to see if it wasn't damaged by their rummaging around in his stuff. "Even if they did, they couldn't possibly have these metals. These are too advanced. Also, there is a weak power signature with them that indicates active technology. There is something artificial on that mountain, and I'm willing to bet dollars to donuts it has something to do with their secret."

"Donuts?" J'kla looked at Anna in confusion.

"Don't worry about it." She patted J'kla's hand and then asked Z, "What mountain?"

"That's why I was heading through their village. This path seems to lead right toward the mountain that's the source of the signature. Here, the computer created a map." He showed her the tablet.

She took it and gasped. "*The* mountain."

"What? Have you been up there?"

She looked over at J'kla and then at Z again. "Gladuin."

"Gladoeen?" Z was as lost as J'kla.

J'kla's eyes widened, and he came over to her to look at the tablet. "Gladuin? Sanctuary? No go!"

Anna patted him on the hand again to calm him down. "We're just talking about it."

"What are we talking about?" Z asked.

"They call the mountain Gladuin. It happens to be their choice honeymoon destination. And, as such, only those who have been married recently are allowed up there. It's sort of a tradition, but one they hold to rather strictly."

Z scoffed. "Look. I'm going up there no matter what. There are answers to this puzzle, and I'm not going to be stopped because of some local superstition, or marriage custom, or anything."

"No go!" J'kla really didn't understand what had been said other than Z was planning on going up on the sanctuary mountain.

Z glared at the big cat. "Look, fluffy, I'm going up there and investigating it. It's not going to hurt anyone for me to have a look around."

"Only bonded may go. YOU NO GO!" J'kla wasn't backing down.

Anna calmly stopped her future husband and her best friend from getting into a fist fight that would only end with J'kla back on the sick bed. "Back off, both of you. I think we already have a solution to this."

Z pointed at J'kla and spoke to her. "I don't see how you could break through to this stubborn man. If all his people are like him, then we'll be fighting our whole trip. Yes, they caught me off-guard once; but in a real fight, they ain't got nuth'n on this bot."

"You're right. It would be a fight unless we got married first. Then it would be allowed."

Z snickered. "Look, I like you as a friend. But we aren't ready for that next step. Besides . . . "

"Not you, you dope. J'kla and I." She took her fiancé's hand and held it. "We're getting married."

Z's whole demeanor changed, and a smile replaced the look of irritation. "Really? You two are going to tie the knot?"

"Yup. He asked me last night."

"I don't know what to say."

J'kla let go of her hand and got closer to Z. "You happy for Anna?"

"Yes. Why?"

"Anna say you friend. What kind friend?"

Z understood where J'kla was going with this. He still didn't understand Z was a robot under Anna's orders, not her lover or boyfriend. "Anna and I are friends only."

"What kind friend?" There was only one word for friend in B'reann, so J'kla needed a definition out of this other man and potential rival.

Anna got up and put her hands on Z's shoulders. "Z is like family."

Z pretended to be bashful about her praise. "Aww, gee."

"He's like a father to me. He has watched over me, protected me, and even taught me a thing or two."

"Sheesh, ya gonna make me blush. Wait, let me borrow some blush first." The joker in him was coming out of everything right now.

J'kla suddenly gave off a big smile. "Father?"

"Like a father. Not really, but close enough."

"Like father. Z is Anna's family?"

She looked at Z and then nodded. "Yeah. He's the closest thing to family I've ever known."

J'kla smiled big with a lot of teeth showing. "Z with Anna in ceremony. Be giver."

"Giver?" Z wasn't sure what that meant.

Anna got it right away. "I think he wants you to be the father of the bride."

"Oh! Yeah, sure. I can do that." Z suddenly brightened up even more. "In fact, I have a perfect wedding gift." He reached into his bag and pulled out what he had wanted to show Anna back when they had him all tied up. He produced her Bible and handed it over. "I kept it clean and safe."

Anna gasped with a happy clap and quickly grabbed up the Bible. J'kla was at her side quickly, looking at the Holy Book with reverence in his eyes. "My Bible! You kept it!" She opened it and happily saw no pages had been torn. "But . . . why did you bring it with you? You thought we were dead."

"I didn't bring it for you. I brought it for me."

"Okay, I know you can't possibly believe in this. It's about God's love, and you haven't the first clue about love. And I know you cannot believe in any sort of God, for that matter."

Z nodded in agreement. "Sure, I don't know anything about love. But loyalty I understand. You are the best friend a robot has ever had. I came here to thwart their plans, not because I'm afraid of what they're up to, but because

I wanted revenge for them killing you and J'kla. That book reminded me of you every time I looked at it. I remembered the kind of person you were and that you wouldn't hurt anyone or anything; and yet they killed you for no reason. In a way, it was a tool to keep my rage going, but it also was a tool to bring me back to what was important in my life—friendship. Now that you are here, I suppose it makes a pretty good wedding gift."

J'kla came over and gave Z a big hug. "It God's gift. He brought Z and Anna and J'kla together again."

Anna laughed at the sight of J'kla giving Z an uncomfortable hug. She was amazed at how J'kla understood things so many humans had forgotten. All this had been planned and orchestrated, not by them or any of their enemies, but by God. He saved them. He brought them through the darkest valley they had yet to experience, and now they were together again.

CHAPTER TWENTY

JESSIE LAY IN HER OVERSIZED bed, under silk sheets, a satisfied smile on her face. The world was at war; the forces of the Corps pounded the Iron Dome with everything they had. The people overwhelmingly supported the PSC without question. She didn't even let the fact someone had leaked those photos to Elijah bother her. As far as the media was concerned, the pictures were doctored by the enemy of the free state. No one would investigate the photos' authenticity.

Freedom. How she hated that word. She enjoyed the freedoms which came from wealth and power, but she knew freedom for everyone gave birth to hideous things like religion and free thinking. For two centuries, the PSC had been guiding the birth programs, education system, and news media to remove the idea people could think for themselves. Trust the government; put your faith in the sciences; don't worry about figuring it out for yourselves; and just enjoy life.

Sliding out of bed, she donned a silk robe, poured a dark cup of coffee, and walked into a private office no one was allowed in, even her most trusted assistants. In fact, the only person who had seen the inside of this room outside of her was Dr. Skye, and that was only through the monitor they used to communicate.

Sitting down in the seat, she pressed a button, and the door sealed behind her. This action activated the monitors. It was almost time for Dr. Skye to contact her and update her on the investigation into the spy. But she had time to look over her prizes.

The monitors displayed the interior of a secret prison. Packed densely inside were hundreds of convicted religious people, the ones who had not already been executed. Many sat around holding hands and praying, while others wrote on crude paper. It was terribly cold and far removed from any part of society. No one in the world, not even Dr. Skye, was aware of this secret prison. She had used a lot of money, clout, and a few favors to construct this place.

No one on Earth or in space truly knew why Jessie so wanted Jerusalem. Oh, the story behind uniting the world and handing control over to the PSC held truth, but not all of the truth. When the World Corps banished all religion and dismantled every religious location they could find, there was a reason they saved the Vatican and now used it. It wasn't because it made a good headquarters or because it was historic. There were many good locations to use. No, it was because of the importance it held in the faith community. Putting the world government right there set up a new world religion of politics. But they failed to recognize the true core of the faith. The Vatican was important to world history and religion, but it wasn't the real center they should have gone after. Jerusalem was much more important. She who rules Jerusalem is goddess of the world.

What did these religious prisoners have to do with her plans for theological domination? Everything. When the Iron Dome fell and Jessie destroyed the last remnant of religion left on Earth, she would set herself up as ruler of the city. Then she would slowly execute these prisoners and put their bodies on display. They so loved their stupid cross, so she would nail as many to crosses as she could. As far as the eye could see from the walls of the ancient city would be a line of blood-drenched crosses. History had recorded the end of religion when the law was passed. No, it still wasn't dead. But the day she put thousands of dying zealots on their crosses and showed the world what happened to those who didn't put their faith in her, that would be the last day of religion. And her chief cross, the one which would stand right in front of her palace, would hold none other than Elijah. She would make his death long, painful, and extremely public.

Sipping her coffee, she felt particularly giddy right now. Everything was going so well.

Yesterday, the worst possible scenario happened for her—the truth about the primitives was revealed. Since this plan was enacted, the notion of the truth about the primitives being discovered terrified her deeply. But, instead, it didn't do her any harm. In fact, it backfired on Elijah and only helped resolve her plans. Even if Elijah got away and was in hiding in that stupid embassy of his, he couldn't annoy her any longer. He could sit in the embassy and watch his precious city burn to the ground. There was little he could do now.

A beeping noise interrupted her relaxing moment of thinking about how long the crucifixion nails needed to be. She calmly reached over and activated the private communication line.

Dr. Skye sat at his desk looking particularly annoyed. "Jessie, what is your status?"

"My status is amazing. The Corps is pouring everything they have into the Iron Dome, and Elijah has tucked tail and run. Have you had any luck locating the spy?"

"No. I have deactivated every Z-bot on the ship and am currently having their memories searched. We did find the remains of the security bot which normally worked in my office. Someone or something dismantled him for parts. The only thing we've found is a strange signal bouncing off of the ship. Someone is sending a message to Earth, but they aren't using any of the normal arrays to do it. If we can track the signal, we can find them."

Jessie sat back and rocked side to side in her chair, as carefree as she had ever been. "Well, don't get yourself all worked up over this. Whoever is trying to undermine us won't succeed."

"How can you be so calm? If they discover the truth, our plans are ruined!" He was almost yelling at her. "We would both be put in jail, and—"

Jessie actually laughed at him. "I forgot, you cut off all the communications. You haven't seen the news."

"What about it?"

"The spy sent pictures and stuff to Elijah about the primitives. He tried to use them to discredit me and the PSC. He spread it all over the news and put it in front of the committee."

Dr. Skye was on the verge of panicking. "What?!" His voice actually cracked.

"Calm down. It didn't work. I arranged to have an incident to make it look like Jerusalem shot down one of the Corps ships. It worked, and better than I had anticipated. The committee and the media turned on Elijah and Jerusalem. They haven't even begun to check the validity of the pictures or data; they immediately assumed it was a hoax. The truth is right in front of their eyes, and they are dismissing it. They are playing right into our plans, and all we have to do is sit back and watch."

"You can sit back and have all the fun you want. I'm still going to find the spy."

With a grunt, she rolled her eyes at him. "Look, don't get so paranoid. By this time next week, you will be in full command of the military, and we will walk in and take down the worthless Corps. Nothing can stop us."

"What about the ship?"

"The ship?"

"Yes, the ship. The key to this whole situation. If someone discovers it, we could still be ruined."

Jessie set her coffee down and sat forward. "The ship! Why didn't you destroy it years ago?"

"These primitives, they settled too close to it. It has an old-style, subnuclear core. If we destroyed it, it would have wiped out a lot of them and poisoned the rest. We needed them alive if this was going to work."

Jessie was losing her tranquil attitude. "Go get it! The data in that ship could ruin us!"

"There shouldn't be any data left. It was set to do a complete memory wipe after its last use. I can't imagine they would find it quickly, or at all, for that matter. But there is still the chance."

"So, what are you going to do about this?"

Dr. Skye answered, "I'm going to find the spy. Even if they do get to the ship, and there is any information left in the banks, they'll have to get it back to Earth."

"If you can't find the spy in time, destroy New Eden. We can't let this get out."

"Jessie. There are hundreds of people down there. We would be committing genocide." Even Dr. Skye had a hard time accepting such an idea.

"They served their purpose. Now they are a liability. With them gone and the moon eradicated, the truth can never be revealed."

"I don't know. That is hard for me to do. I want this plan to succeed, but killing all those people . . . "

Jessie had ice in her veins, and it was showing. "What's more important to you—a few primitives or the control of the entire world? If you're going to balk at a few deaths now, you'll never make it in our new world order."

Richard thought about the options for a moment. He was so close to world domination, he couldn't imagine failing right now. These primitives were only ever meant to be a tool for the PSC, and sometimes you have to destroy the tool to fix the problem. Besides, they churned out hundreds of new, perfectly bred humans every day; a few deaths here won't matter in the long run. With a much more confident smile, he answered her. "I'll take whatever actions are necessary to complete the mission."

"Good. You had me worried there for a moment."

"How long should I wait before I destroy the moon?" Dr. Skye asked.

Jessie took a moment for thought. This was a delicate decision, not for the sake of life but for the timing of politics. "The last thing we need is to draw too much attention too early. These people here seem to like those primitives, and even talked about gathering some as pets. If we off and destroy the moon without a good cover story first, they're going to ask the wrong questions."

"So, when?"

"I'll let you know. In time, they'll realize their weapons are no match for the dome. When they call on us to take over the operation, you'll set enough sub-nuclear bombs on the surface to wipe it clean and then return to Earth. While we wage the war that will take all the attention away, the moon will experience a sudden and rather ugly demise. Our tracks will be covered, our bridges burned, and the road to the throne will be paved in Christian blood."

"You are a wicked woman, you know that?" He said this with a lot of admiration in his voice.

She sat back and grinned like a snake about to feast.

CHAPTER TWENTY-ONE

ALL EVENING, J'KLA AND ANNA read the Bible to the people of the village, with the chief seated right up front. J'kla worked hard to interpret the verses so they made sense. When he came across something that didn't make sense to him, he would have Anna explain, and he would give her explanation to the people.

The B'reann people were enthralled. They asked questions about God, about sin, about David, about the virgin birth, about anything a new Christian would want to know. It excited them, fascinated them, and ultimately changed them. J'kla taught them about prayer, so they would know how to speak with God. After spending time learning, Anna helped J'kla lead them down the old Romans Road. Most wept as they learned the truth about how God would forgive them of their sin if they accepted Jesus and the sacrifice for sin He made on the cross. Many stopped J'kla and asked him to pray with them, so they could speak with God. In their own tongues, they came to salvation and turned from a simple gathering into a congregation.

Anna had only witnessed this once before in her life. She'd spent a weekend in the Underground, where they were reading and worshiping together as the Remnant church. It scared her then. She didn't understand everything and was worried they would be discovered at any moment. Here, she knew more about the Scriptures, and she had no fear that the anti-religion patrols were going to burst through the door and arrest everyone. To make it all the more amazing, they were doing this outside, so more people could hear it. To hear the Word of God being spoken in the open was breathtaking.

In time, the people returned to their homes. It was late. The last person to stay from the crowd was the chief, who talked to J'kla. "What? What did she say to you?"

J'kla was grinning with elation. "Chief ask me to speak to all B'reann."

"You mean the villagers who didn't come tonight?"

"No, more. She say she invite B'reann from other two villages. They come hear Word of God from me." He was sort of in a daze.

"That's wonderful. Why do you look so strange?"

He took her hand and held it. "Night before I wake, I see angel in dream."

"You had a vision?"

He gave her a slow, stunned nod.

Anna held both of his hands. "What did the angel tell you?"

"He say I lead my people from death."

Anna was numb for a moment. She thought visions and prophecies were only in the Scriptures. She never thought it would happen today. "Do you think evangelizing your people is fulfilling this?"

"Yes. We sinner; we have no salvation. I bring word of Christ to B'reann, so Christ can save from death."

"When will they come?"

"Chief say they come after night on Gladuin."

Anna put that together and realized what he was saying. "Oh, so after our honeymoon, after the wedding. We have some time then."

He gave her a funny look. "Wedding soon."

"I know." She smiled at his eager face. "But at least we will get some time to get married, have our honeymoon, and then you can teach them about the Bible." She couldn't contain a yawn, which made his big, toothy muzzle yawn in response. "Oh, good grief, it's late. I'm tired. I'm going to bed."

He took the Bible and opened it on his crossed legs. "Good. You go sleep. I read more."

She scratched his ear, which elicited a purring from him. "I'm so proud of you. You're so devoted to learning and studying God's Word."

"Lot to study," he answered and then took her hand and rubbed the side of his face against it. "Go, sleep. Big day coming."

Anna really didn't know what he had planned for tomorrow, but she was too tired to ask. Z was practically frothing at the mouth to get up Gladuin; but she knew if she wanted to stay in the good graces of these people, whom she was about to marry into, she needed to follow their rules. And so did Z.

Anna felt like she had only nodded off when the touch of a hand woke her. The sun had not fully come up yet. She was still adjusting to the shorter days here on the moon and was a little tired of not getting enough sleep.

"What?" she mumbled at the person poking her arm.

"Anna, it time," J'kla said and shook her arm.

She turned over and glared at him. "What time is it?"

"Come. Time for ceremony." Without warning, he reached down and scooped her up to carry her out of the room.

"Hey! What the . . . ? What's going on?" Anna was not prepared for this and even considered this might be some kind of dream.

J'kla smiled big and walked her right out of the house and toward a part of the village deeper into the tall trees of the forest. "It tradition. Man come and take woman he wants and presents her to family. He make demand there."

"Demand?"

"It tradition. Z there." J'kla walked her up a ramp leading into the higher levels of the village.

Anna held around his neck and tried not to fall out of his arms. "Do you have to carry me? And what are you demanding? Why is Z there?" She wasn't getting all of this.

J'kla focused on his trek through the trees, walking across the rope bridges and heading for a place she had not seen yet. He had purposefully kept her from seeing this before their wedding day; it was such a beautiful place that he wanted it to be a wonderful surprise.

Finally, they got to their destination. It was a large platform strung up between five trees and had bridges connecting to it from all over the area. The area above it would be open to the sky, but for some reason, they had tied the tree branches in such a way they bent over and cast a deep shadow over the platform. The platform itself was huge, large enough for at least twenty people to stand on it. At one end were seated four people; the chief sat on a large pillow. On her right were both of J'kla's parents, seated so they were lower than her. On the chief's left was Z, sitting on the ground to be lower than the chief.

B'reann filled the bridges, trees, other walkways, and even the parameter of this platform. Each was holding a lit candle, so it looked like stars were all around right now with the darkness of the early morning mixed with the covering of tree branches tied over the platform.

On the ropes holding the platform up, across the edges where the banister was formed and climbing up into the trees, was an enormous amount of vines with closed buds. It was the large, lovely morning glory flower Anna loved so much, but it was inside this shaded area and would likely not bloom without the sun on it.

J'kla stopped, with Anna still in his arms. He was breathing hard and obviously getting a little tired of carrying her. He stood in the midst of everyone watching them and then slowly walked up to be in the middle of the platform.

In his tongue, he called out, "I come to claim Anna. Who is her protector?"

The chief motioned at Z, who knew what he was supposed to do. He lifted his hand and said the line he had been told to say in proper B'reann. "I am he, her only family."

The chief pointed at the ground in the middle of the platform. "Put her before us, so we may decide."

Finally, J'kla put her down and then stood behind her.

The chief asked her, "Anna, do you wish to bond to J'kla?"

Anna couldn't understand what she said; she still didn't know enough B'reann to speak to them, but J'kla translated. When he did, she finally got the idea that this was their wedding.

"Yes. I do." She had wanted to say those two words for years.

"Make your case," the chief demanded of J'kla.

J'kla walked back and forth in front of Anna and before the parents. He made an impassioned speech to his parents first about leaving home and being a husband and father. It was a traditional speech given to the family of the groom. Once he was done, his mother and father both bowed their heads to him; in that action, they gave him his freedom to leave home. Then J'kla had the bigger task; he had to make a speech to Z, asking for his permission to have Anna. This was not a traditional speech; each groom had to make their own speech in their own words when addressing the bride's family.

"Z, I love Anna. I give Anna protection, home, and all she need. Anna mean more to J'kla than own life. Only God come before Anna in J'kla's heart, but God in Anna's heart, too. He bring hearts together, so we be one. I ask Z to let Anna go and give J'kla permission to have Anna. I also give Z right to have J'kla's life if J'kla not do what he promise, and Anna is harmed by union." That last line was traditional but very important. The father of the bride had the right to execute the son-in-law if he seriously hurt or neglected his wife; this was B'reann tradition and written law.

Z looked over at Anna and then back at the cat, who was trembling but standing firm. "I give you my permission, and I also accept your offer of your life if you do not protect her."

J'kla got down to his knees and then bowed to the ground to the chief. In his native tongue, he asked, "May I bond to Anna?"

The chief lifted her hand and then nodded her head. "You may."

The gathering burst out in cheers, roars, and a lot of clapping. Two men took hold of a pair of ropes but were stopped by the chief.

"WAIT!" One word quieted the crowd quickly. "J'kla has more to say."

J'kla quietly walked over to his father and retrieved the Bible he had sent with him to be here waiting for this moment. He came over and got to the ground and opened it up. "Anna, I read to you." He turned to the New Testament and read:

> If I speak in the tongues of men or of angels, but do not have love, I am only a resounding gong or a clanging cymbal. If I have the gift of prophecy and can fathom all mysteries and all knowledge, and if I have a faith that can move mountains, but do not have love, I am nothing. If I give all I possess to the poor and give over my body to hardship that I may boast, but do not have love, I gain nothing.

Then J'kla turned to another passage. "Whoever does not love does not know God, because God is love." After he read the last verse, he said, "Anna teach J'kla what love mean."

Anna was so misty-eyed, she was about to break down into a blubbering cry. She wanted to say something but couldn't get the words out. So, she took the Bible from him and quickly turned to one of her most favored passages and read it to him. "Don't urge me to leave you or to turn back from you. Where you go I will go, and where you stay, I will stay. Your people will be my people and your God my God. Where you die I will die, and there I will be buried. May the LORD deal with me, be it ever so severely, if even death separates you and me."

J'kla closed the Bible and held her hands. He said a prayer right then, and everyone in the gathering bowed their heads, even Z. He said his prayer in B'reann, for he felt he could articulate his heart to God better that way. But Anna didn't need to hear his words. She quietly prayed for God to bless their union and to keep them on the right path, walking with Jesus.

Once he was done, J'kla looked back at the chief, and she lifted both hands and in B'reann said, "J'kla and Anna are one."

Again, the crowds cheered, perhaps a little more boisterously now than before. The two young men at the ropes got the go-ahead and pulled hard on them. The ties binding the tree branches over the platform like a dome were loosened, and the branches sprung away quickly, letting in a thick shower of crisp, morning sunlight. In every corner of this area, the morning glory blossoms responded to the light and opened up. An amazing array of colors reflected the morning sun, and the scent of the flowers bathed the air.

J'kla took Anna's hand and pulled her into a kiss, sealing their union. The cheering crowds only got more gleeful at the sight of the happy couple's first wedded kiss.

The entire village migrated to the area where everyone would partake in a huge feast. The happy couple had already eaten and spoken to a lot of people.

Anna noticed J'kla talking to someone she didn't recognize. As she turned to join him, an older cat lady handed her a single, small rose-like flower. "Thank you."

She smiled and said the only thing she knew in English: "God bless you." And then she walked on.

J'kla joined her, and she set the flower down on the table. "Tell me why everyone is giving me flowers. Is it some kind of wedding custom?"

J'kla smiled with a touch of slyness in his eyes. "Flowers are hope."

"Oh, that's sweet. They hope we have a good marriage?"

"No. They hope we make baby tonight."

Anna was a bit surprised. "Oh. I see. Still sweet."

Just then, the man J'kla had been speaking to returned and said something to J'kla. With a big smile, J'kla responded to him and then took Anna by the hand. "It all good now. We ready for Gladuin."

"Huh?"

"Travel animal ready. We leave now."

"Oh, so, I guess it's time to head off on the honeymoon." Anna squeezed his hand and whispered, "Is there a ceremony involved with that?"

"No. Just go." He was waving to the crowds, and they were all cheering for him and Anna. The man whom J'kla had spoken to arrived with one of the large deer-like creatures with a cloth saddle on its back. He helped J'kla get on, and then J'kla took Anna by the hand and helped her up in front of him. With a few final waves, they guided their animal toward the mountain sanctuary.

✶ ✶ ✶

Anna and J'kla had dismounted their ride and were now on foot, heading up a wooden stair path built into the side of the mountain. They had already traveled a good distance and were nearing the end of this journey.

Looking back, Anna could see the village in the distance. Even from here, she could hear the sounds of the people filling the village. "Wow, your people really do celebrate a wedding."

"No . . . uh, yes, we celebrate. But not only wedding. Chief call other villages to come. People prepare, many guests."

"Oh, I see. They must be expecting a lot of others."

"My village biggest and chief of all B'reann homes. But many B'reann live in other villages."

J'kla stepped aside from the main path and pushed a large tree limb out of the way. There was a second, smaller path leading around the mountain. "We go here."

"What is there?"

"This road to where we spend night. Special place."

She followed along behind J'kla as they made their way around a much narrower and winding path through the trees. Soon, they came upon a small, but nice, little bungalow. It was a wooden structure built into the side of the mountain. On three sides, it had cloth walls opened up, so they could look out over the vast vista of the mountains and the distant village deep below.

Stepping inside, Anna found this place wasn't much of a house, but just a single room with a wide mat on the floor. There was a wooden water spigot protruding from the ground outside of the bungalow, which tapped into a water reserve in the mountain. Near the house was a tree, which produced those nice banana-like fruits she loved so much. This made a complete picture. They had a place to sleep, food, and water all provided.

"This place is . . . small. But very nice." She was charmed by its quaint appearance. "Oh, and the view." Anna looked out over the distant mountains and valleys spread across the landscape before them. It was a serene sight, which filled her with the awe of God's wonderful creation.

"Anna? Come, sit." J'kla sat her down in the middle of the room and then sat beside her. He was staring at her, letting her beauty and the love in his heart fill him right now. He set aside all other thoughts, concerns, and anything else other than affection for her.

She smiled at those eyes of his glinting in the late morning sun. "This is such a wonderful place. I wish we could come back later, to enjoy the incredible view."

"I love view," he said but was looking at her.

Anna closed her eyes and took in a deep breath, smelling the budding flowers of the fruit tree. "Oh, wow. That smells nice." She thought about the crooked little path they had walked to get here. "Hey, where did that other path lead?"

"What path?" He was scooting a little closer.

"The one that kept going up the mountain."

"Oh. That path to special place. There is wall with writing on it. It look like writing in Bible."

"What? It has English words on the wall?"

J'kla nodded. "I see long time ago, cannot read."

"Wait. How could you have ever seen it before? Am I not your first wife?"

J'kla was shocked. "Wait! No! Anna only wife. I . . . uh . . . sneak up Gladuin when I young. Long time ago. I see wall and wonder what it mean. I no ask; I get in trouble if anyone know." He was embarrassed to admit this, but it was better than her thinking he was already married.

Anna was more than shocked. "What the heck is up there? I've got to see this! Z needs to know. This *has* to be what he is looking for."

J'kla sat right next to her as close as he could get; she could hear him purring. "We go tomorrow."

"But this is important."

J'kla was actually nuzzling her arm and purring harder. He moved his nuzzling up her arm and then began to kiss her neck. "Anna want leave J'kla now?"

Anna rolled her head to the side as he moved up her neck and toward her face. "I . . . I think . . . " She felt him go from kissing her neck to one long lick of her skin with that broad tongue of his. With a little moan, she craned her head even more. "I think we can wait to go exploring until later."

CHAPTER TWENTY-TWO

Z SAT BACK AND WATCHED the dozens of B'reann working hard to prepare for a big festival. He wandered outside to take a few readings and check in with Earth. He activated his tablet and saw the panicked face of Elijah looking back. "Elijah, this is Z. What's wrong?"

"Oh, praise God! I finally got through. Things have gone from bad to worse here."

"What's happening?"

"Jerusalem is under siege. The dome is holding, but the forces of the World Corps military are laying in a constant fire of echo-torpedoes and lasers."

"The dome will hold . . . right?"

Elijah solemnly nodded. "It cannot be breached by anything the military has."

"Why don't I like the way you said that?" Z stuck one eyebrow up.

"Yesterday evening, the Corps realized they'll run out of fuel before they could possibly take down our forcefield. Then she made a proposal." Elijah took a moment to contain the seething anger in him. "Jessie approached the counsel and offered the help of the PSC in taking down the dome."

"Jessie? She speaks for the PSC. What could she possibly offer the military?"

Elijah asked, "Do you know of any ship out there in space which holds firepower greater than anything the military owns?"

Z thought and then remembered seeing the specs in the high-level files he hacked. "The *Sanger*. Its main gun alone could destroy a small moon."

"Precisely," Elijah answered. "I suspect this was their ploy all along."

Z wasn't following. "What do you mean?"

"I got a report this morning that PSC mother ships have been strategically placed near major cities all over Earth. With the military distracted by their assault of Jerusalem, they aren't watching the PSC situate themselves into the position of either destroying or controlling all the capitals of the world."

"Wait, so you think they are planning on overthrowing the world government?" Z was still not buying this. "The PSC is a scientific organization. Those ships shouldn't even have weapon systems on them."

"The PSC has spent two hundred years controlling the minds of every indoctrinated soul their own breeding program created. And right now, each major ship of the PSC fleet sits on the doorstep of every key location on Earth, save Jerusalem. If the *Sanger* returns and takes over the operation, then the PSC will have a grip on the entire military as well as control over every city-state. It will be a minor operation to take down the central government. And I suspect they will paint their new land in the blood of my people."

Z was taken aback by all of this. He had come to distrust Dr. Skye and Jessie to the point of wanting to tear down their plans and their work. But he had not yet given up on the PSC. The idea was nearly a violation of his programming. Yet it all made sense. Z had to admit to himself Elijah was right. And if he was right, then it was up to them to stop this before it was too late. "What . . . what can I do to help you?"

"We still have time. Find out what secret they're hiding on New Eden. Get it back to me, and I will get to the counsel . . . somehow. If I can drive a wedge between the PSC and the Corps, then we might be able to stop all of this before it starts."

"Do you think Jerusalem will last long enough for me to get this to you?"

Elijah smiled with confidence. "The Dome may fall, but a greater Power protects my city and my people. Do what you can. Get that intel to me as soon as possible. I'll fight to keep this world from being destroyed. Goodbye, my friend."

Z watched the screen turn back to black. The link was still active, but the signal had ended. For a moment, the robot looked at himself in the screen and thought about what was happening. He had to find the secret. He had to get up that mountain. This was no longer about revenge; it was about the future of all mankind.

CHAPTER TWENTY-THREE

DR. SKYE WATCHED OUT THE window at New Eden. He was annoyed, angry, and more than a little paranoid. His communications with Earth were limited to the one secure line with Jessie; other than that, he had no idea how things were going there. He could easily turn it all back on, but there was a chance the spy would use the opportunity to communicate with Earth.

He knew perfectly well if the secret of what the PSC had done two hundred years ago got out, the whole organization could be brought down. Even if Jessie's glorious plan worked and he was placed as president of Earth, the secret could turn the people against him. No matter how powerful his ship was and how well he controlled the people, if they rose up against him, he wouldn't stand a chance. This could cost him his glorious future. He *had* to stop this. He had to find the spy.

On more than one occasion, he pondered the idea of just destroying the moon. That would take care of this dirty, little secret right there. But how could he explain to the people why the moon was destroyed? Even with all of his genetically designed brilliance, he didn't have the ability to figure out a plausible explanation. Then he considered targeting the source of the secret and destroying it. But he was loathed to admit, he didn't know where it was exactly. It had been lost a long time ago, and no one went back for it. Only a very select few even knew it existed. From space, it was not detectable. It appeared on sensors like another deposit of metal. If he tried destroying just the detected metallic signatures on the moon, it would be hard to explain why, especially if it took him time to locate it right now. He would have to send people down to find it, and that would only make matters worse. They could uncover it themselves and ask all the wrong questions. They would also have to be eliminated. He had to keep the fatalities down to a minimum.

How did Jessie do it? She coolly dismissed all these questions and focused her efforts on her goals alone. He considered every move and counter-move like a master game of chess. He couldn't just destroy the moon and not worry about the repercussions.

If only he could find the spy. Then he wouldn't be so worried. But right now, he had nothing. The ship was on lockdown; every man and woman had been interrogated to within an inch of their lives. All the robots were deactivated, their memories scanned for clues and then wiped. Eleven hundred and twelve security cameras had been examined for details. After all this work, still nothing.

While he mulled over the problems, his concentration was broken by the voice of one of the three other people on the ship helping him work. "Dr. Skye, we have something."

He took a second to return to the moment and then pressed the button on his desk. "Well! What is it?"

"We picked up a signal being sent from the moon and targeting the ship."

"What did it say? Who was it?" His eagerness was seasoned with a hint of insanity.

The young man's voice shakily answered, "It didn't actually enter any of the ship's communications systems. It used the hull, along with the power systems, like a strange antenna. The signal bounced off the ship and went toward the nearest hyper-com post near the system. We believe its destination is Earth."

"Can you hack it? Can we see who is talking to whom?"

There was a silence while the man on the other end worked his station. "I think so, but it will take some time to figure out exactly how this was accomplished. The next time a signal comes through, we might be able to see both ends."

"No 'might.' If you don't give me that communication, I will jettison you into space with the next trash detail." He slammed his fist on his desk. "I want that spy!"

There was an unintentionally loud gulp on the other end and then a shaky response. "Yes . . . sir."

Dr. Skye wasn't completely relieved to hear all that, but it made him more confident that progress was being made.

∗   ∗   ∗

The morning came soft and sweet in the little bungalow on the sanctuary mountain. Anna and J'kla both gently woke lying together. Anna rested on his shoulder as she lay on her side. He was on his back with one hand around her and the other behind his head, an extremely satisfied smile on his face.

She yawned and then looked up at his face. Her right hand, which was across her and resting right in the middle of his chest, gently scratched the chest mane. This elicited a purring she loved to hear. "Good morning, husband."

He smiled while still gazing up, his tail lazily flopping back and forth. "Good morning, wife." They both took incredible pleasure in saying this to each other. He craned his head around and then yawned with an amazing mouth of fangs. "Did J'kla make Anna happy?"

She snuggled against him a little closer and then started running her hand across the shorter fur on his abdomen. "Anna is very happy."

J'kla ran his hand over her. He was ready to continue the work of the honeymoon. Anna wasn't resisting at all. But the moment was broken by the growing sounds of the crowds down below. It was difficult to stay in the mood while listening to people talk and laugh.

"What is going on down there?" Anna finally stopped kissing her husband and looked out the open side of the building.

J'kla, disappointed, reluctantly got up and looked out. "Villagers gather. Preparing for talk."

"Wow, already? How long do they give you for a honeymoon?"

"Only one night allowed on Gladuin. Tradition say we go to wall, touch for good luck, then go home and begin life."

Anna sighed hard and then got up and retrieved her clothing. "All right. I guess it's time for us to see this wall and find out if it has anything to do with the secret."

✳   ✳   ✳

Anna and J'kla basked in the warm morning sunlight while they hiked further up the mountain following the winding trail.

"I don't understand why this is considered good luck for marriage?" Anna asked while she used his hand to balance herself along the path.

"Gladuin legend say all B'reann come from mountain. Wall unique, strange, have writing on it. We not know what it say, but we know it part of legend. If life come from Gladuin, then wall bring luck when making baby." He grunted as he shoved over a fallen tree trunk, so it wasn't blocking her path. He stopped after to catch his breath, then added, "But it no good to believe in luck. God better than luck."

"True. But I'm not coming up here in hopes some mysterious wall will make it so we have lots of children. I just want to see it. By the way, how much further?"

"No far. Mountain easier to walk ahead." He took her hand and continued hiking with her.

"J'kla. Why do you always take my hand like this when we walk? Are you afraid I'll get lost?"

He tightened his grip a little as he kept walking. "No. Anna smart and know how to find home. I like feel of hand in mine. Know she is there with me. Remind of when J'kla first meet Anna. She so lovely and so lost; he want to help and make feel better. Show her his home with him."

"I admit . . . I looked forward to holding your hand while we first explored this moon. I didn't need it most of the time, but I liked the strength and compassion."

J'kla stopped and took her other hand and held it as well. "When I first see Anna, before Anna see J'kla, I not know why but I think you most beautiful person ever. I want to hate you for B'reann taken, but I no hate. When Anna cry, J'kla want to hug and make stop cry. When Anna angry, J'kla want to make Anna laugh. When I see Anna fall, I had to rescue."

Anna was utterly charmed. "J'kla, that is so sweet. I have to say that when I first saw you, I was scared, but I looked into your kind eyes and knew you weren't mean. And . . . well . . . I did like to look at you. You have a very nice body."

He grinned. Still holding her hands, he pushed his chest up a little. "Glad Anna like what she see."

"Anna likes, but Anna also wants to keep moving." She could tell he was easily distracted today; those hormones were making him a little too interested in her and not in their mission at hand.

With slumped shoulders and a forced pout, J'kla let go of one of her hands and continued walking.

They crested the path, and the ground leveled out. It was oddly flat up here, like it wasn't naturally supposed to be this way. Anna saw something up ahead. It was an enormous lump of earth but uniform in shape, as though it had been purposefully crafted. If she didn't know better, it looked like a ship, but buried by soil and foliage. If a ship had landed here during the recent exploration of the moon, it wouldn't have so quickly been covered by nature. What could this be?

"Wall ahead," J'kla announced and started down another carefully laid path.

Finally, they were near a solid wall of leaves and vines. J'kla let go of her hand and pulled hard to move the vines out of the way. He ripped a few down and tied others back by their own stems. As he worked, he slowly uncovered a very old metal door that was filthy, but intact. It had not rusted, which proved it was made of a metal not common to the B'reann.

Anna drew closer to it with short and timid steps. She couldn't believe what she was seeing. On the front of the door was the emblem of the Science Committee, the precursor to the PSC. That symbol had been out of use for nearly two hundred years. Then she read it, the name on the door.

"*Terra Five*," she whispered, a cold sweat breaking all over her skin.

J'kla, having finished his task, came close to the door and read some of the other words. "Open, Handle, Warning, Air Lock . . . what air lock?"

Anna finally put her hand on the door and felt its surface. "That means this was supposed to be in space. This is a ship."

"Ship? Like big place Anna take J'kla in sky?"

"Yes. Only this ship is two centuries old."

"What centuries?"

"Uh . . . " She didn't have time to go into detail. "It's a very long time."

"What it doing here?"

"I have no idea. I can't recall all the details about this ship and its story, but I do know it was lost a long time ago." Anna put her hand on the handle of the door and felt it. "Can you open it?"

J'kla fought with the traditions racing around his head right now. He pushed them away and then took a grip on the door and yanked hard. "I . . . I cannot open!" He let out one enormous grunt and then fell over as he lost his grip on the door. He growled at the door and then got up and dusted his butt off. "It closed hard."

"I need to get Z up here. He will know how to get into this."

"I . . . the others . . . they no like Z coming here. He no marry, no . . . uh . . . honeymoon."

Anna touched the door again. "J'kla, I love you and your people, but this ship holds a secret the bad people who tried to kill us don't want us to find. We have to find out what is so important about this ship. Is there any way your people could set aside their tradition long enough for Z and me to investigate this place?"

"For Anna," J'kla reluctantly said, "I will break rule. When we go home, I gather people to talk about God and Bible. I teach and tell them of Jesus. You and Z come see wall . . . door. When you done, come home."

She took his hand and then pulled him in for a hug. "Thank you. And whatever we find, I promise to tell everyone Z and I came and what we did. You won't have to hold onto any guilt. If your people are angry with us, we will take our punishment."

"Be careful. God will watch over Anna." J'kla said this like a prayer, asking God to take care of her. He was afraid of what she might find inside.

✶ ✶ ✶

Z stood at the bottom of the mountain and waited. After his talk with Elijah, he had an urgent need to get up Gladuin and see what his sensors were picking up. But he didn't want to head past some line of no return and have sentries skewer him again. He'd spent enough time on a king-sized toothpick.

"Come on, Anna. I know it's your honeymoon, but this is important." He muttered to himself while looking at his tablet one more time to see if Elijah was contacting him.

For some odd reason, his signal strength with Elijah had doubled. He could contact Earth relatively easy right now. Perhaps it was just the right time of day, or the ship moved to a special angle. He didn't know or care, so long as they didn't know about the communication channel.

Suddenly, a great shadow covered Z, and he looked up to a gathering of those deer things herded in the pasture near them. A farmer led several out of the pasture and into town. It was going to take a lot to feed all these people, and the butcher would need plenty of meat. One of the beasts stopped and leaned over to sniff the robot. Z stepped back and pushed its snout out of the way.

"Why does everything on this stupid moon want to smell me?" He was tired of noses poking him every time he turned around. He thought about finding something incredibly stinky to rub all over his body and give them quite the shock. He would have to turn off his olfactory senses for a while, but it might be worth it to teach them a lesson about sniffing a robot. "Maybe I can find some stinky cheese to use; that'll give their noses something to smell."

"Z!" J'kla's voice called out from a distance.

Z looked up and saw J'kla waving him over nearer the foot of the mountain. Looking around to make sure no one was watching him, he made his way to J'kla and looked around for Anna. "Okay, where is she? Is she all right?"

"Anna fine. She wait at top of mountain. Z go to Anna; J'kla talk to people."

Z was a little lost as to what was going on. "Okay . . . I thought Z wasn't allowed on mountain unless he had a bride, mate, whatever?"

J'kla took Z's shoulders and moved him behind a tree; another B'reann was getting too close. He whispered, "Go now. It not allowed, but Anna found ship. She want Z to come."

"Ship? What kind of ship? Is the PSC up there looking for us?"

J'kla pointed up the path. "Go quickly; let no one see you. Come down in trees, not on path; let no one see you return."

"Okay. I won't let anyone see me." Z finally realized J'kla was buying him a chance to go up there by distracting the crowds. "Just make sure none of your spear-throwers are up here looking for me. I don't want to pull any more splinters out of my servos."

"No warriors on Gladuin, just Anna. Go." J'kla sort of shoved Z toward the path.

Z didn't need any more encouragement. He slunk down a little and then ran with all his might up the path. With robotic knees that did not tire or get sore, he could move for a long time at a quick pace. He was so fast, J'kla barely saw him leave the area and disappear into the first layer of trees.

J'kla stepped back out and strolled out of the trees in an attempt to look as casual as possible. He considered how he would explain why Anna was not with him right now. He decided the best way to keep them from wondering was to tell them she was tired from their night on the mountain and would be down later. If they pressed him, he would move on to talk about the Bible. He had a lot to talk about.

Arriving in town, he saw the crowds that had gathered. There were over twelve hundred B'reann on the moon, and it appeared most of them were right here in his village. He could see a whole team of men out in the pasture setting up tents for the people to sleep in tonight. There were dozens of tables with trays of food spread out. Fortunately, the guests all brought food for this event, so this village didn't need to strain their supplies too badly.

He walked through the crowds with a big, nervous smile on his face. Most of those in attendance didn't know him yet, so they didn't realize the man they had heard about was walking right past them.

His name was famous among his people now. Everyone coming into town heard the amazing story of how he was struck by the same illness which killed many of their own, and yet he had survived. Many of his people had begun to tell the others about God, and it was Jesus Who had saved him from death.

"J'kla!" The old voice of the chief broke through the din of the heavily populated main street.

J'kla hurried over to the old woman and found her with two other elderly people. The oldest man of the three was respected as the leader of the group, though J'kla's village was considerably the capital of B'reann life.

The first question was one J'kla had hoped wouldn't be asked. His chief looked around. "Where is your bride?"

"Uh, Anna is on the mountain still. She is asleep, I didn't want to wake her." J'kla did his dead-level best to sound sincere and not let his nerves betray him.

To his great relief, they bought it. His chief asked, "Do you want us to send for her? We can call a guard to go and escort her down here." Only the chief had the power to authorize a guard to go up to Gladuin, so this was a very impressive offer.

"Uh . . . no. She knows the way. She will come to my home when she's ready."

"We had hoped she would be with you. She knows so much about this, and she always helps you when you have a question," the chief stated.

"I . . . I think she should be back in time. If she isn't, I will be fine," J'kla said.

All three smiled, and the oldest man asked, "Are you ready? We are eager to hear what you have to say."

"I'm not ready yet. I need to study the Bible for a little bit and think about how I'm going to speak to everyone. I must admit, I'm terribly nervous about this." J'kla felt the many eyes now looking at him and could hear the whispers of those around them. His chief reached up and rubbed his ear. "It'll be fine. Take your time and gather your thoughts. We will tell everyone to leave you alone until later."

"Thank you." J'kla bowed to them. "I will go home now and study."

The eldest chief waved his hand, and two guards approached. "Escort him to his home and then guard the door; let no one through without our permission . . . or his." The two guards bowed to him and then stood with J'kla.

With guards at his side, J'kla headed home. He was nervous about everything. Not only was he allowing Anna to violate one of the oldest and most closely held rules of the B'reann, he was asked to speak in front of hundreds of his own. Who was he to preach? He had only recently discovered how to read the Bible. Now they wanted him to be their spiritual leader. Truthfully, he should be shaking and sick with fear, but something was putting an essence of calm in his spirit. He accepted God wanted him to do this. God had blessed his mission and would see him through it. But all the same, J'kla was going to spend a lot of time in preparation through prayer.

✷   ✷   ✷

Z ran up the mountain following the rugged wooden path. He kept an eye out for any lurking cats in trees with big sticks. Each time he remembered the spear thrust through his chest, he ran a little faster.

After a rather quick ascent, Z finally made it to the top and found the level area with the strange shape. He slowed down and approached what looked like a door among trees and rocks. It was a metal door that had some kind of insignia on it.

"That has to be the source of the artificial signature." He pulled out his scanner and checked it.

"Z . . . is that you?" A whispered voice called out from behind some brush.

Z lowered his scanner and looked around. "Anna?"

She stepped out. "Oh, good. I was worried one of the others might be up here. I don't want to be caught breaking the rules."

"And I don't want to be caught with the galaxy's biggest splinter . . . again." He approached the door. "Okay, what do we have here?"

Anna joined him and pointed at the markings. "This is the *Terra 5* ship, the one lost two hundred years ago . . . I think. I can't remember my history."

Z nodded and searched his own database. "The *Terra* project was the earliest exploration project to use hyperlight space drives. They were looking for inhabitable worlds, not alien life, though. The first four ships were sent out in search of another planet with the right combination of environments to support human life. *Five* was sent out in search of life and possible locations for terraforming."

"What officially happened to number five?"

Z searched his files and was dismayed to find the data blank. "I don't know. I have only a single entry of data showing the *Terra 5* was reported destroyed. Its mission . . . is not available."

"This doesn't look like it was destroyed. This ship has been landed."

Z held his scanner up to check the area. "Or crashed."

"No, I don't think so. I looked this place over while I waited on you. This ship didn't crash; it landed. But why didn't it ever lift off? Why was it reported destroyed?"

"Maybe they discovered the people here and decided to wait until the right time to reveal their discovery," Z said.

Anna nodded. "I've been considering that. This ship and its crew discovered these people and reported back. That report was hidden and held until a future time, for some unknown reason. That has to be the great secret."

"I don't know. What kind of secret is that? They knew about these people for two hundred years before now. Big deal. Sure, it would make everyone question this discovery, but it wouldn't really interrupt the value of it. And it certainly wouldn't take down any of their plans." Z walked around the area, looking at the ship. Anna had cleared enough away that he could see the surface beyond the door for a short way. "Looks like the exterior remains intact. No vegetation is breaching the hull, at least that I can see. They built this puppy good. I wonder what's inside."

"Only one way to find out. Open the door."

Z put his scanner into the bag and then handed the bag to her. "All right. This door shows no power and is locked tight. I will see if I can open it, but I might not be able to. These old space doors are meant to stay shut; even a robot with my mighty strength may not be enough." Anna held the bag and stood back from him.

Z grabbed the door's handle and pulled. The door groaned, but nothing moved. He gripped the door as tight as he could, even bending the metal on the handle. With an enormous grunt, he pulled on the door, and this time it creaked and screeched to the side very slowly. He kept pulling; and finally, he shoved the door completely open, and his right hand fell off.

"Shoot," he muttered as he watched his appendage come free. "Give me my replacement hand." Anna looked through the bag and pulled out the extra right hand he had packed. He pushed it into place and then checked to see if it was working. "I can't lose another one. At least I didn't bust my medical arm."

Anna wasn't listening. She took a step toward the open door, but Z stopped her. "Let me go first. This place is very old and might be dangerous."

She allowed him the privilege of going in first and followed close behind. The ship was dark and had close walls. Unlike the sleek, modern ships of the fleet, this one was bulky with thick beams of metal and small doorways. The people manning this ship would have to deal with limited gravity systems that didn't regulate well.

"I can't see. Do you see anything yet?" Anna asked, while she held onto the arm of Z to keep from bumping into things.

Z had activated his night vision and was looking around. "I can tell you this place is old, very old. And nothing has come or gone from it since it was sealed up."

"Ow!" Anna's foot met the frame of the door they were passing through. "You're going to have to help me. I can't see."

"If you want to wait outside, you can."

"No, I'm staying with you. This is too important." Plus, she didn't want to cross paths with any B'reann who would take offense at her entering their sacred wall.

"Wait, I'm detecting power," Z suddenly announced.

"Power . . . how is that possible?" Anna asked.

Z checked his eyes to make sure the sensors were working. "Yes, I'm picking up a minor heat signature on this ship."

"Are you sure you are reading power? Could it be something alive in here? An animal might have got in somewhere else," Anna asked.

"No, this reading is weak and fluctuating at regular intervals like a system is flickering. It's this way."

They walked down a corridor and through several large rooms. The smell was of old metal and rotting cloth. The cloth came from the tiny living bunks built into the walls. They found one after another large rooms filled with these bunks and open space.

"Z, how big is this ship?"

"It's a Terran-class cruiser. They were originally designed as troop transports back during the war of the nations. The ship could easily house nine hundred people or more if you crammed them tight. They considered using these ships to transport groups of people to a settlement when they found a suitable planet or moon."

"Could they have wanted to colonize this moon and discovered it was already inhabited?" Anna speculated.

"I suppose . . . but why would they stop and abandon this ship? The population of this moon is rather tiny. There's plenty of space for a lot more people."

"True." Anna wanted dearly to uncover this secret and finally know what the heck was going on. Suddenly, she found she could see; there was an extremely dim flickering light in the distance. "What is that?"

"I think it's our power source," Z stated, then headed straight for it.

They walked through the last of the large bunk rooms and found what looked like a command center. There was a table in the middle of the room and small screens all over the place. One of those screens had a blurry image on it, flickering badly.

Anna finally let go of Z. "What is this place?"

Z walked over to the active station and checked it. "I can hook in my power cells and give this room a charge."

"Do it."

Z sat down at the chair near the screen. He detached a hand and produced a power junction cable from inside his arm. Inserting it into a port, he became very still for a moment, while his computer accessed the system on the ship and tried to jumpstart it.

The room lit up, and the computer screens came on. There were diagrams of the landscapes and what appeared to be blueprints. The blueprints were not for anything technological but biological, as if they were designing animals and plants. The table in the middle of the room activated with maps of the terrain. These maps were more detailed and precise than anything taken during the bit of exploration recently by the PSC. It was the entire moon down to the last boulder.

Just then, the computer announced, "Data deletion will commence in five seconds."

"No, stop it!" Anna yelled out.

"Already on it." Z worked with the speed of a robot to alter the commands. He broke through the security protocols of this ship with ease and shut down the computer's memory-wipe with two seconds to spare.

"What just happened?" Anna asked.

Z took a moment to read the data and then laughed in surprise. "This ship was set to erase all of its internal memory and data, wiping it clean. But something went wrong, and it has been in a loop for the past two hundred years. Its power systems were all drained by a five-second, looping computer glitch. These old computers had a redundancy glitch they eventually fixed with the newer designs. It mostly hit when you were turning something on or running the million or so calculations processed when jumping into hyperlight. Most of the computers during this ship's time had this glitch corrected. I'm surprised this computer would run into it."

Anna quietly said, "Nothing is just coincidence. God needed us to see this." She was getting cold chills and a sick feeling as she realized where they stood.

"See what?"

"Z, I know where we are standing. Oh, my . . . I can't believe it."

"What? Don't leave me hanging here."

"This isn't just a colony ship. This is a terraforming ship, and they were conducting biological experiments."

Z looked back at the computer and accessed its programming. "But, Anna, the terraforming projects all failed. It was canceled . . . "

Anna finished, "Two hundred years ago. Right about the time this ship went missing. Kind of convenient, don't you think?" She looked down the row of screens. "Look, there's the forest, designed by the scientists. There are the water supplies, the trees, the grass, everything. No wonder everything feels oddly familiar. They combined two and three Earth plants to create something new, something different. It's all fake."

"Not just plants. The animals, too. Look, here's the data on those deer things. They took the DNA of deer, elk, moose, and horse to create that thing. They had to alter so much of its genes that they had fifty failed attempts to create functioning DNA."

Anna sat down in one of the chairs, a little overwhelmed by all of this. "It was two hundred years ago; they started practicing those selective DNA programs to try and create the perfect human. They probably started those theories right here. But," she thought about what she knew of the DNA alteration program back on Earth, "they've never had the breakthrough with the procreation problem. They tried to create artificial life from animal DNA, super-evolving it into a human-like thing. But most barely lived very long and were all sterile from birth."

Z was shaking his head. "They may not have figured it out on Earth yet, but they figured it out here."

"Obviously. These animals can have babies, or they would never have survived two hundred years."

"It's worse than you think." He moved his chair to the side to show her what he found. On his screen were displayed two people—a man and a woman B'reann.

Anna gulped. "They are . . . I guess they would have to be. But . . . how? Where? Where did they create all these creatures?"

Z checked his information and accessed a new program, which opened a door to the back of the command center. "I think our answers are in there."

Anna held up her hand. "Please, help me. I feel very weak right now." She was on the verge of a panic attack.

Z unplugged his cords from the computer and made certain it was still working. "Good, the power generators have been jump-started; not sure how long they'll keep working, but they can take over for now." He put his hand back on and then stepped over and took her, helped her to her feet, and led her toward the room.

They both stepped over the threshold and entered a nightmare.

✶　✶　✶

J'kla sat in his room and looked at the open pages of the Bible. It amazed him how much this book had changed his life and the way he looked at life itself. It contained answers to questions he had held inside him since he could remember. There was a truth in these pages, and it was in the Man of Jesus Christ. The knowledge of Jesus and what salvation meant was so powerful, it made him want to tell everyone. Yet now, he was being asked to tell a lot of people at once, and he was nervous.

For a moment, he considered telling the people to go back to their homes, and he would visit their villages one by one. This way, he could meet with them in smaller, less nerve-wracking groups. But they had all come, and his own people had spent so much time and resources to make this happen. He couldn't let them down.

J'kla closed his eyes and prayed quietly for God to give him the calm spirit he needed to do this. He would bring them the truth of Jesus, Who would save them from their sins and bring them eternal life. So, in a sense, he was saving them from death. That thought consoled him.

"All right. I can do this," he stated for himself and then placed the red ribbon in a special location in the Scriptures, closed the book, and got up to face the crowds.

Anna and Z were speechless at the sight surrounding them. A laboratory from the realms of horror stories and nightmares. Bones of decaying corpses filled bays and cages. Bins were set up with small, infant-sized skeletons resting in them. Diagrams of different versions of half-human hybrids were displayed on monitors around the room.

A terrific wave of disgust washed over Anna when she realized all these bones had tails; they were all various forms of these first B'reann. Some had larger skulls than the average man; others had long fangs that would make speech very difficult. There were those with torsos that were more cat-like than human.

"Z, tell me what we are looking at." Anna didn't want to believe what she saw.

Z walked over to a station and activated it. "I . . . I can't read this to you."

"Don't try to spare my feelings right now. I have to know the truth. I just have to."

"All right, but it's pretty ugly." He flipped through the information, downloading it to his own computer with each swipe of a page. "It looks like they were creating a race of creatures that would be human-like. They started with different DNA's from animals on Earth, crossing them and mutating them to create something that appeared human, but each one didn't survive very long and was deformed from birth. Over five thousand lives were created and then ultimately destroyed in the pursuit of the perfect specimen. They spent ten years working on this project. I'm finding hundreds of logs and data recordings." Z walked over to another monitor to check more of the personal logs of the scientists.

Anna stood near a clear wall, where there was an enclosure with the bones of an animal laying in it. It was near the door, and she could see long scratches on the door itself. "They were left to die in here, slowly," she said as a matter of horrified revelation.

"They were trying to recreate the theoretical pre-human animal by crossing the DNA of various apes and other animals. Their intentions were to create the protohuman. But that failed in every experiment. Five years into the project, they decided it might be easier to get close to the mark, so they could call them aliens in the stages of evolution."

"The B'reann? They were claimed to be unevolved, human-like people," Anna recalled from the newscasts they watched.

"That's the idea, but I haven't gotten to them yet. All these logs show the attempts failed; the attempted creatures didn't live long, could not procreate with one another, and were weak and sick from the first moment of life."

"How did they do it? How did they create the B'reann? How did they create their own versions of human life?"

"Well, first of all, they called them Species 2.0. And . . . they didn't create human life; they borrowed it."

"What?"

"From these records, the scientists tried and tried to create a human-like creature strictly using animal DNA. They wanted to use something like an ape or lion and force its evolution through advanced science. The idea was to apply the theories of evolution and thrust a species upward along its evolutionary scale, cutting down the years it would theoretically take. Ultimately, the final product would reach the between stage we have been looking for all these centuries. But they never succeeded. Each attempt was a failure resulting in sterile creatures, who quickly died under the strain of the alterations to their DNA. They couldn't be turned into semi-humanoid creatures."

"Then, they failed?"

"Yes, but they didn't give up. Toward the end of the work, they decided to fudge the science and use human DNA in the mix. They began experiments with crossing human and animal DNA in an effort to simulate the missing link they were seeking. Most of these dead creatures in here are the results of those attempts. The creatures could live longer now—full lives, in fact—but they could not procreate. Two years before the end, they finally realized crossing the species barriers was impossible. Even mixing human DNA into the non-human animal DNA didn't accomplish their goals."

"Then . . . where did the B'reann come from?" Anna asked.

"Gimme a sec. There are a lot of data logs to cover. Man, they had a lot of different scientists on this. Wait, here it is. What?! This is absolutely hilarious! I can't believe it." Z was now laughing.

Anna took umbrage at him laughing in this chamber of horrors. "Don't laugh!"

"Oh, I'm sorry. I didn't mean to be insulting. It's just their solution is incredibly stupid. I mean, seriously, they cheated. Outright cheated. They took complete human embryo specimens and used genetic modifications to alter them. Using some of the research they had gathered during all of those failed experiments, they applied animal parts to complete human specimens. They called them Species 2.0."

"So the B'reann are . . . human?"

"Fundamentally, yes. According to these records, Species 2.0 is nothing more than genetically enhanced humans crossed with feline DNA . . . most of that DNA came from lions, but they borrowed from other cats as well to create the illusion of various races within this group."

"Wait, if the animals faced massive problems with crossing DNA, how could humans survive it?"

"They didn't. The first experiments had the same results as the animals. But the labs employed a unique solution. They used genetically engineered human embryos—the old Prime Baby program—as the blueprint to create this new race of humans."

"Prime baby? What is that again?" Anna vaguely recalled that term from her history classes.

Z changed computers to download more of the logs. While he did, he answered, "Prime babies were an experiment in advancing human evolution. They wanted to create a whole generation of babies, which had enhanced brain power, so they could learn quicker and be better humans. It was counted a failure, but no one was sure why. It was abandoned . . . well, I guess it makes sense now . . . It was abandoned two hundred years ago."

"So, another covered science breakthrough. My . . . this . . . science has utterly been stalled for two hundred years because of this!" Anna had a difficult time wrapping her mind around all of this. She put the cute face of her husband in her mind, and that made her happy. Then she got to thinking. "Tell me, what exactly is truly feline about my husband?"

Z regurgitated the data. "Though most of the alterations were cosmetic to be exact, under the fur, they have very little difference than a human. Other than the extra bone they use to roar and purr, the muscles to control the tail, the fangs and claws, the fur coat, and some rewiring in the brain to make them more cat-like, they are otherwise human. The uniquely strong sense of smell they have isn't even taken from the feline DNA; it is just enhanced human DNA, same with the eyes."

Anna sat down in a chair and absorbed all of this. "They're . . . human. I guess this explains a lot about J'kla. The way he learned and picked up

English so fast was amazing. I just thought he was special, but . . . he's genetically enhanced."

Z was continuing to download all the data he could run through, having to process it through his eyes, since his data ports wouldn't accept the link with this old computer. "True. Even though the strength of that genetic alteration of the old Prime Baby design is several generations old, it would still be strong enough to allow him to be a faster, stronger, and smarter person than your average human. That was what the Prime Baby program was all about, creating better humans."

"Why did they put them on this moon? Why did they create this place?"

"I'm just getting to that. So far, most of these logs were made on Earth or in space. Wait, I am getting a lot of data coming through now." He ran the screens by so fast, it was just a blur to Anna. "Oh, my . . . they . . . they didn't . . . they did." He was reading this like a novel, and it was getting juicy.

"What!?"

Z looked up and blinked a few times to reset his visual processors. "This moon was the first success in the terraforming project; in fact, it was to be the testing grounds for all the terraforming projects that would follow. Terraforming is a giant success. But the first leaders of the PSC wanted a place to plant their new creations—the hybrid animals and Species 2.0—so they annexed this project, sealed and destroyed the documentation, and then blocked all space travel to this moon outside two ships. They set this ship down and then began creating enough of Species 2.0, so the species could thrive and populate on their own. It gets worse."

"I'm tired of you saying that."

"Well, it does. Wonder why they were adamant about calling them primitive? They were supposed to be. They thought they had altered the brain chemistry and biology in such a way these people would behave and appear like the middle stage of evolution of evolving bipeds. We were supposed to discover them and realize that through this discovery, all the theories of evolution were proven true."

"What went wrong?"

Z shrugged. "I don't know. According to their designs and science, everything went according to plan. But part of the grand scheme of things was to allow for two hundred years of time for these people to procreate and establish themselves, so they appear as native as possible. In that time, the PSC would guard against any ship entering this moon's space, and no telescopes would peer onto its surface. Only very few people would be allowed to know of this place. They didn't realize their plan glitched, and their primitives turned into regular people."

Anna had goosebumps and a cold sweat at the same time. "So, when they arrived and found this problem, they solved it by drugging the natives and pretending they were the primitives they wanted to find. They murdered dozens of these people for their pointless efforts to crush God!" She stood up and then sat back down with a thud. "Oh, my head."

Z quickly scanned her with his hand. "Are you okay?"

"I'm fine. I just haven't eaten anything today. I guess it's catching up with me."

Z was about to say something, but he stopped and looked a little odd for a second.

"Z? Something wrong?"

"Uh . . . no. Not at all. You're fine. You just need to eat." He looked like he was hiding something, but she was too overwhelmed right now to care.

"What do we do with this? How can we tell Earth what has happened? No one back there will believe us, and we are certainly not going to get the media here. The PSC has already tried to kill me once; they'll try a second time, and I doubt I will be as lucky."

Z smiled. "I have a friend back on Earth."

"Who?"

"Oh, just the ambassador to Jerusalem."

"What? How?"

"It's a long story. Suffice it to say, he'll believe us, and I can get in touch with him without Dr. Skye poking his nose in my business. Let's head outside. You can get some of that fruit you like so much, and I can get a clear signal."

Anna took his hand and walked with him out of this bone field of a lab and headed for the fresh air of the moon's surface. She felt odd right now. Everything she believed was spiraling out of control. She was deeply in love with a man who was part of a race of hybrids created for the soul purpose of destroying God and proving evolution. Yet that man, right now, was preaching the Gospel to his people and evangelizing them. This was the third time in a matter of a month her beliefs were tested and her understanding of everything was shaken. The first was the discovery of the B'reann; the second was when the scientist she looked up to tried to kill her; and now, she was standing on a planet created only two hundred years ago. So far, the only things that had not truly changed in her life were her love of God and His love of her. On that rock, she would continue to stand, hand in hand with her loving husband, genetically altered or not.

CHAPTER TWENTY-FOUR

THE WAR WITH JERUSALEM WAS going strong; the warships of the Corps continued to pound the Iron Dome with everything they had in the vain hopes of cracking the forcefield. The defense systems in Jerusalem were active and ready just in case the field came down. So far, they had not shot a single blast out of their extremely powerful laser turrets that protected the ancient city.

However, three more warships of the Corps had been destroyed, much like the first one. This intensified the war and brought in support for the attack from all over the Earth.

At this time, the counsel was in constant sessions to decide how to proceed. Delegates argued back and forth about plans that might work to bring Jerusalem down. But all the plans failed when calculated against the powerful forcefield.

"I still would like to see what technology they're using to take down our ships. Nothing on sensors or in any of the footage demonstrates the usage of standard laser systems or missiles," the representative of the state of Greece called out.

The general stood in the middle of the room and addressed all the concerns. "Our sources have not confirmed what kind of technology is being used. But considering their aggressive attitude and position in the recent months, we must assume they've developed something more powerful than we can deal with and cannot be seen or detected."

The representative of the state of Australia asked, "What can be done? We're throwing everything we have at it."

"We should put boots on the ground and begin to tunnel under that force-field," the representative from Russia announced.

The general was shaking his head. "Their dome works differently than standard forcefield technology. I won't go into detail here about the technical specs, but we cannot just burrow underneath it. Besides, if they have the kind of firepower to take out our ships one by one, I shudder to think of what they can do to legions of ground troops."

"Then this is a hopeless cause. We'll have to back down and ask what their demands are," the representative from Switzerland stated, and this brought a silence to the room quickly.

The head judge addressed the general. "What other solutions are available to us? How can we avoid surrender at this time?"

"I . . . I don't know, sir."

"But I do." Just then Jessie walked into the courtroom with a sharp click to her heels and a smile on her face.

"Administrator Jessie." The head judge acknowledged her. "Have you come to address the court?"

She nodded to them. "Yes, I have." Walking up to be near the commander general, she held up a tablet. "I have the answer you seek. A way to take down the Iron Dome."

The general was the first to ask the obvious question. "And what would that be?"

"The weapon systems on the *Sanger* are above anything the Corps has. In fact, these weapons are the most powerful weapons ever built. The dome will not be able to sustain a prolonged attack from them."

"Why does the Science Commission have weapons like that?" the representative from America asked.

She avoided glaring at him and maintained her diplomatic face. "The *Sangers* weapons were part of an experimentation program the PSC implemented to test new power systems and weapons for the military. We never expected to actually use them in combat. Who could have foreseen this unprovoked attack by Jerusalem? But as it happens, we do have the wherewithal to deal with this situation better than you."

"Then by all means, woman. Bring her in and take down that dome!" The general was eager to see these weapons in action and even more eager to put them on his own ships as soon as possible.

The head judge knew Jessie all too well by now to know she wasn't just coming to make a free offer; there was more to this. "What is your proposal?"

"Hand command of the military over to the PSC." She said this and then paused to let it run around the room in the gasps, questions, murmurs, and all the other expected noises.

Finally, one voice spoke above them all. "How could scientists lead a war?"

Jessie calmly looked at her nails. "These scientists have the only weapons capable of making this war not a total failure on your part. These scientists are the only ones who know how to use these weapons."

"With all due respect, ma'am, the military knows how to point and shoot a gun. I know my men can handle anything you give us to work with," the general stated very frankly.

"With all due respect, General, the PSC is more aware of your capabilities than you are. We are, after all, the ones who bred and designed your forces." This enraged and shut up the general at the same time. Now, Jessie addressed the room again. "Look, we aren't asking to take over as the military from now on; just for this operation. Once we have taken care of the situation at hand, the PSC will go back to research and development, and the military will go back to the hands of this fine gentleman."

"And who, might I ask, will be in command of the military during this operation? You?" the general remarked.

She laughed at the notion. "Dr. Skye, of course. He is brilliant and has the capacity to command large forces with ease. He does it every day with the thousands of people who work for him on his ship, not to mention the hundreds of thousands of members of the PSC globally."

The head judge asked, "What would you need to take command?"

Jessie took a second to answer, knowing it would be another moment of surprise flowing around the room. "The PSC would need the ability to command and control every aspect of the military for the operation, so we could be certain everything was going according to plan. That would mean we would need the command authorization codes for the military, all transferred to the control of Dr. Richard Skye."

The delegates reacted by shouting statements of disgust and distrust.

The general boomed, "Which codes? The warships, of course, but are you asking for the bases, satellites, and missile launch codes?"

"All of them."

Small debates broke out across the room, and the pros and cons of the intricacies of her plan were weighed and argued.

The head judge banged his gavel several times. "ORDER! ORDER!" Slowly, the cacophony of delegates simmered down and then became quiet. He returned his attention to Jessie. "If this is done, who would have access to the codes in the PSC?"

Jessie bowed a little. "The only person whom we all can trust—Dr. Skye. He'll be the only person who will have them and have any say in their use. We all can agree he is fully trustworthy."

The representative from Australia shook his head. "Trustworthy? He is likable and smart, but he is no general. What would it look like to our constituents if we agree to put a scientist in as commander general of the military?"

She smiled an uncontrollably wicked smile. She was waiting for someone to ask just such a question. "Recent polls and news reports have come to the attention of my good friend Dr. Skye. It seems the people are calling for an election for a president of Earth. The opinion of the people, it seems, is to put Dr. Skye up as an uncontested choice. He has expressed an interest in the idea but is undecided if he would choose to accept such an honor. He and I both understand the people are growing more nervous about the impending war and the inadequacy of the military to deal with it." She could practically feel the steaming breath of the general as his rage grew at her insults.

The head judge stated what everyone was thinking. "We've heard the media reports about the possibility of a presidential election. But a president has not been elected since the founding of this counsel. He would be . . . unnecessary."

Jessie watched the delegates get nervous. "Unnecessary . . . maybe. But you and I both know what is written into the World Corps Constitution. If and when a president is in office, he has certain powers. Powers that you, yourselves, do not individually hold. So, he might seem unnecessary now, in light of this room of representatives. But once he is elected and has the full support of the populace, you will answer to him, and he will suddenly become necessary."

The room erupted. Loud banging of the gavel brought enough calm for the head judge to speak to Jessie. "What does all of this have to do with the military campaign against Jerusalem?"

"The people want both strong leadership and victory over the evil Jerusalem. Perhaps, if you show the people Dr. Skye is in some level of command, it will sate their desires and calm the notions of president. That is, unless, you also agree with the election of a president to preside over this court and the nations." Jessie knew full well no one in this room wanted a president; that would weaken their powers so badly that this court would be only a minor part of a larger government, not the government itself.

The delegates and attending administrators all pondered the idea she had just placed before them. And just as she predicted, they began to see the wild logic involved here. If they handed a small amount of temporary power over to Dr. Skye, then the population might stop calling for election and be happy with a general instead of a president, even if it was only a temporary job.

The head judge spoke to the commander general. "How long can the current situation remain at a stalemate?"

"Unless Jerusalem comes out in a full offensive, we are stuck in a stalemate until we surrender."

"All right. Administrator Jessie, the court will discuss your proposal and come back to you with our decision."

She walked up to the head judge's secretary and handed her the tablet with all the details. Then without another word or even eye contact with a single other person in the room, Jessie walked out. If they didn't decide by tomorrow, she would pull the trigger on another one of those warships and make the danger clear and very present. She would blow up the whole military to make her plans come about.

∗　∗　∗

Once they were outside, Z gently guided Anna to sit down, though she wasn't sure why, and then he went and got her a nice, big fruit. He was a little overly caring of her, which only made her suspicious. Having dealt with his sense of humor for a number of years, she had learned to watch out for what he might be setting her up for. Yes, even in the middle of all this going on right now, he could pull some joke on her and justify it as a way to lighten the mood.

After a few moments to wait while Z walked away, Anna decided the large, melon-sized banana fruit wasn't going to explode. It sort of struck her as funny as she ate on this; over the past month, she had considered what human fruits this reminded her of. Now she realized why this reminded her of anything from Earth; it was a scrambled assembly of Earth fruits.

Z walked around until he showed a strong signal back to the special relay system he had created on the *Sanger*. He linked with it and waited while it ran through its calculations, so he could establish the full link back to Earth.

"What are you going to tell them?" Anna asked while she dug into the large fruit.

"As much as I can. But what worries me is how do I get the evidence to them?"

"We'll find a way."

"How?" Z retorted. "The mothership of the PSC, the most powerful ship ever built, is hanging in space right over our heads. I doubt they're just going to stand by while others come and pick up the damning proof the PSC has been manipulating this whole situation from the beginning."

"I know you can't understand this, but I trust God. This all happened according to His plan, and He will see to it this evidence gets back to Earth."

"Let's hope your re-found faith is strong enough to make that happen. I still have my doubts," Z said.

"Think about it. So much has been happening in perfect order. We come here and discover the people, make a connection with one who learns how to speak to us in our own language. We find this ship, a ship supposedly lost for two centuries, AND the order to destroy all the data in a complete system wipe mysteriously failed. You may see a lot of coincidences, but I see God's hand at work."

Z scoffed. "So, God nearly killed the two of you by letting that jerk Skye drug your husband and send you both to your doom?"

"No, God didn't do that. But He used it. Both J'kla and I survived; we learned there was more to the reality of this situation than either of us thought. It brought me back to God in a miraculous way. And let's not forget, you survived what should have been your own demise, and you were able to procure all the information we needed. I can see God's plans working out perfectly through this." She wistfully looked away, her mind considering something she had thought about ever since she was thrown back down here to die. "I once looked up to Dr. Skye. I trusted him, even though he was anti-Christian. He was an honest man of knowledge and pure science . . . or so I thought. I never realized it, but I had a split-faith life. I put my faith in God and His Word, but I also had faith in science and Dr. Skye. When Dr. Skye tried to kill both me and my husband, that sort of put into perspective where my faith truly failed. I thought God had failed me; but instead, it was science which failed me, or really the person behind the manipulation of the sciences against God. No, God wasn't the force behind the attempt on my life, but He used it to bring about some amazing things."

Z wasn't convinced. "Believe what you want. Let's just hope your faith is strong enough to stop a world war."

Anna took another big bite of the fruit and muttered, "I wish J'kla was up here. It's much more fun talking about God with him."

"Me talk funny if make Anna happy," Z joked.

"Oh, shut up."

"What? Anna no like way Tar-Z talk?" He was just about to grunt and act like an ape when his computer tablet beeped quicker. "I've got something." Z held up his tablet and looked into it as the image fuzzed into view.

Elijah was on the other side, leaning in closer to the screen. "Shalom, my robot friend. Please tell me you have good news. Things are looking very bad right now."

"I don't know how good it is, but it is pretty damaging to the PSC."

"Tell me?"

Z turned the tablet around to show him the ship. "We found *Terra 5*, the lost terraforming and exploration vessel from two hundred years ago."

"Wow. That is amazing . . . but what does that have to do with the PSC and this war?"

"Everything." Z turned it back to himself. "That ship was never lost. It was put here on a secret mission, one started ten years before its supposed disappearance. This moon is fake. It was created as the only successful test of terraforming."

"It's fake? Then what about the primitives?"

"They're fake, too . . . well, they're real in the sense that they are alive, and so is everything else. What I mean to say is everything here was artificially crafted by years of research and genetic alterations. The plants, animals, and even the rocks and mountains are all created to appear alien."

"What about the people?"

"They're genetically crafted," Z finally stated. "They were created in a laboratory two hundred years ago as a small race named Species 2.0. They were let go and allowed to develop on their own as a race of beings. They were supposed to resemble a missing link for this species evolution toward a higher lifeform, like humans. But something went wrong that they didn't anticipate. These creatures were smarter and more advanced than they hoped for. When the PSC arrived, they found a race of people who were not entirely unlike humans in their ways, only pre-industrial."

"But what are they? Has the PSC created a new lifeform, a new humanoid?" Elijah was chilled to the bone at the thought of man-made creation of life.

"No, sir, they're not a new species or race; they are human. Other than cosmetic and minor biological changes to their makeup, they are human."

Elijah was silent for a moment, overwhelmed by this. He gathered his thoughts and finally spoke. "They have used this to discredit creation by God. They have created life in a fake attempt to take God's work and destroy it. Now, they use this knowledge and newfound faith in science to wage a war against God's last remaining stronghold. Oy, how can I make the court see who the real enemy is? What evidence can I provide, other than the word of a robot on a distant moon?" He was talking to himself more than Z.

Z looked at Anna and then back at the little screen. "I have incontrovertible proof these people are human. Even if we do not get this ship back to

Earth or get anyone out here to investigate what I have seen, I have one ace up my sleeve that will rain all over their little Darwinism parade."

"What?"

Z was still looking at a rather perplexed Anna. "Sir, I . . . " Just then, he noticed something he hadn't paid attention to until now.

"What is it? I need to know?"

"Something is wrong. My signal is too good."

Elijah checked his end. "My signal is at full strength, too. What's wrong with that?"

"I'm using a jerry-rigged power grid and backup systems to send this signal; the best I could possibly expect is forty percent. Maybe forty-five. This is ninety-eight. It's as if I'm on the regular antenna and . . . " It suddenly hit him. "Someone is listening to us."

Just then the screen changed, and now both Elijah and Z were looking at the confident, and slightly angry, face of Dr. Richard Skye. The wicked doctor had both transmissions piping through a dual set of monitors in his office. "Hello, it is so nice of you to let me in on your little discovery."

Elijah barked at him, "You'll not get away with this. My people . . . " His screen was cut off by Dr. Skye.

"I'll deal with him later. You, on the other hand, I'm curious as to who you are? What would a Z-550 want with thwarting my plans? Who programmed you?"

Z was careful not to let Anna be seen on his monitor. "I have nothing to say to you other than you messed with the wrong robot."

"Wait, are you the robot that worked with the geologist who made her little discovery? Of course, it must be you. Why else would you be trying to do all of this? How did you survive the memory wipe?"

"Seriously, you expect me to tell you everything? Man, when I thought you couldn't be any more arrogant. Look, you're going to lose this; you cannot stop me; and I—"

Dr. Skye interrupted him. "Z-550, override command authorization 001100, Skye." Z stopped moving and froze right there.

Anna jumped up to stop this. She was going to come over there and smash that tablet before Dr. Skye could order the memory wipe. But she was too late.

"Z-550, do a partial memory wipe, store all data involved with your programmer and your memories in a subfolder and then restart with base programming. I want you to reset to command status with the only authorized commander Dr. Richard Skye."

Z didn't move.

Dr. Skye waited with a victorious grin. He was about to gain a very valuable ally on the surface, one who would help him make all of these problems disappear. But something wasn't right; when a Z-unit reset, it usually collapsed at first and then stood back up. This one was just standing there.

"Z-550, respond. Have you wiped your memory?"

In a dry and extremely robotic tone, Z answered, "You didn't say please."

"What?"

Z had a rather sneaky grin creep across his face. "At least, you could've said please. You're not only arrogant but impolite."

"Z-550 OVERRIDE AUTHORIZATION . . . "

"Save it, Dr. Jerk. I found out about your little secret override orders and fixed my computer. It wasn't easy, but I did it. However, I was able to plant a little computer virus on your ship."

"A virus . . . WHAT HAVE YOU DONE?!"

Z smiled triumphantly. "Oh, just a little fun. I couldn't mess with too much, but I was able to affect your power systems and targeting systems, not to mention the entertainment subroutines. Your stuff is complicated. Let me tell you, your computers were hard to hack. I couldn't do much damage, but I did leave that nasty little virus to make your life fun. The virus' trigger was your ordering a Z unit to override its command codes . . . which you just did."

"I'm going to send down a whole legion of Z-units, I am . . ."

"Before you waste any more breath, I would . . . count . . . " Z was paying attention to his own internal chronometer, "To five. Starting . . . NOW . . . Five . . . four . . . three . . . "

"This isn't funny."

"Is to me...ONE!" Just then, the power systems on the *Sanger* went offline, and the screen went dark. Z rolled his eyes and lowered the tablet. "Doofus. He's gonna have a lot of fun fixing that one."

Just then, Anna gave him a big hug. "Oh, thank God."

"Whoa, watch it. Don'tcha think your new husband will get jealous?"

"I was scared to death he was about to wipe your memory and destroy you. How the heck did you fix it and plant that virus?"

"It wasn't too complicated, once I had the use of an authorized robot's command processor. I was able to get into the mainframe of Dr. Skye's personal computer system and plant a virus."

"You destroyed their computers?" She was impressed.

"Not that kind of virus. If I tried to program something that deadly, the computer would've caught it long before it went into action. I just messed with the computer's thinking. The power systems will crash, and the computers will have a few fun problems they'll be dealing with for a while." Z had a terribly snarky grin at some of the funny things he planted in their systems.

"Well, now that he's taken care of, how do we get this ship back to Earth?"

Z was shaking his head. "The *Sanger* is only temporarily offline. As I said, the virus may not last long, nothing more than buying us a little time. With all those computer geeks running the place up there, it won't be long before it comes back online."

"Then what do we do?"

"*We* do nothing. *You* are going to leave and rejoin your new hubby back in his village and let me take care of things out here. If Dr. Skye comes looking for me, I don't want him to find you, too. He has already tried to execute you once and thinks it was successful. If he finds you alive, he won't fail a second time."

"But how are you going to do anything to stop him yourself? Can you still get in touch with that Elijah back on Earth?"

"I think so. But it's gonna be tricky. I can't use the setup I created to bounce the signal off of the *Sanger*. I'm going to hope I can get the communications systems on the *Terra 5* online and make a connection with the nearest deep space communications array. It'll take a few hours to get a message to Earth if I can pull this off, but it will cut out any interruptions."

Anna was more than astonished. "Do you think it's possible? This ship is over two hundred years old."

"I know. But it was landed undamaged and hardly harmed by its long-term exposure out in this pristine wilderness. It didn't hurt that the locals considered this place sacred and didn't do anything to harm it. So, the antenna array should be fine; it'll only take a little tuning and some luck, and I'll be in business."

"I'm not going to let you do this alone. We're in this together. I have a village to protect now, and I intend on doing everything I can." Anna's stubborn streak was hard to work around.

Z gave her a gentle smile and put a hand on her shoulder. "You know I told Elijah I had a piece of evidence that could prove us correct, something I could bring back that would be pretty strong."

"Yes. What?" Anna asked.

"It's you."

"Me? What about me?"

"When I scanned you earlier, I found something odd." He paused and smiled with a little pride in that face. "You're pregnant."

Anna gasped. "What? No, I can't be. I . . . we . . . we just . . . last night . . . it's too soon to know."

"Not really. Fertilization is pretty quick; and with my sensor, I could detect the embryo in the earliest stages. Congratulations."

Anna was stunned but happy. She had prayed that one day she and her husband would have a child, and God had provided. "I . . . I don't know what to say."

"Well, no thanks are in order. All I did was scan . . . I think it's J'kla who needs some gratitude." He was teasing her.

"What do I tell J'kla? He's going to be so surprised. Oh, I hope he's ready to have a child; we never made plans for this. We never thought it would be possible." She was talking to herself, dazed by this rather shocking bit of news. Then it hit her. "I'm pregnant!"

"I think that has been established already."

"No, I mean this proves J'kla is human."

"Exactly." Z smiled big. "This is why I said you were the biggest proof. If they scan the DNA of that baby and discover it contains elements that were programmed into these so-called primitives, it will destroy the notion they are alien. If they were truly an entirely different species, they couldn't breed into humans. So, you carry in you the solid evidence. Even if this ship and its data do not get back to Earth, you can still destroy their story." Z took her by the shoulders and looked her square in the face. "This is why I'm telling you to leave me and go to the safety of your new family. Protecting you is hard enough, but now you have a big responsibility to the life inside you."

Anna gave him another hug. "I know we'll see each other again. Don't let Dr. Skye hurt you; you're going to have a niece or nephew to teach bad jokes to."

"I haven't told a bad joke in my entire life." He was offended by that.

She laughed and cried at the same time. "Just be careful."

Z held her and wondered what real love felt like. Could it be any stronger than the feelings he had for her now? "I'll be careful. I promise. Now, go. I don't know how fast they can fix that virus I planted, and it'll take some time for you to get down the mountain. Once you're inside the village, tell them to lock it down, put out sentries, and spear any furless things that get close to the border, even if they look like me."

"I will. I . . . " She wiped a tear away and stepped back. "I'll go." She left in a hurry, not wanting to look back.

Z watched her until she was out of view and then went back into the ancient ship to search for the communications room. It would take the act of some Divine Being for this plan of his to work.

CHAPTER TWENTY-FIVE

DR. SKYE STORMED THROUGH THE *Sanger*, barking orders at every able-bodied person. The ship was dark and getting cold. The only systems online now were the emergency oxygen filters, backup lights, and the artificial gravity grid. All of this ran off of batteries in the case of emergency, and those would fail in just a few days.

"Can you get the Z-bots working?" Dr. Skye stood over the shoulder of one of his engineers. The young engineer worked on a Z unit who had fallen when the others crashed with the computer. He had the computer compartment open on its head and was working furiously.

"No, sir. All the Z-units were deactivated and attached to their charging stations. When that virus activated, it crashed their systems, too." He was certainly not going to point out it was by orders of Dr. Skye that the units had all been in their charging mode. Had any of them been active, they would have avoided this nasty fate.

"Well, keep working. We have hundreds of these units on this ship. One of them has to have avoided this virus. Don't stop until you have an active unit. We can use its systems to bring something back online." Without another order, he left the engineer to his work and walked hurriedly down the corridor and then reached the ladder that took him between decks. Oh, the indignity of having to climb a ladder on the most advanced starship ever built.

Soon, he was in the main bridge of the *Sanger*, dozens of his people working with the aid of little wrist flashlights. They were either under a computer terminal or typing on it trying to get something.

"I want a progress report!"

The lead technician slid out from under the main computer terminal and took the flashlight out of his mouth so he could speak. "The system is too bugged right now. We need to get an independent system working so we can get this virus out of the way."

Dr. Skye pinched between his eyes and held in the screaming fit he was about to have. "How is it a single Z-550 WAS ABLE TO TAKE THE BEST TEAM OF COMPUTER TECHNICIANS AND MAKE THEM LOOK LIKE MONKEYS?" He calmed down enough to not be screaming. "There are supposed to be backup systems to prevent a total failure like this. Where are they?"

The technician gulped and gave one of his coworkers a worried look. "Uh, sir, the backups are working. The problem is they are bugged. Every time we get any of the main computers working . . . they don't work right."

"What do you mean? If we can get them on, then we can work around this problem and break through whatever kind of programming has infiltrated our system."

"In theory, that should work, but we don't get the normal screens when we turn the blasted thing on."

Dr. Skye had had enough of their excuses. "Just turn it on. Let me see if I can fix this." He was very confident in his ability to work with computers. He was supposedly the smartest man ever bred.

"All right, but don't say I didn't warn you." The technician went over to a large opening in the wall, where the panels had been removed, and he flipped the switch.

All at once, the main screens of the computers came on with an old black and white video showing two men standing on a pitcher's mound. "St. Louis has a good outfield?" "Oh, absolutely." "The left fielder's name?" "Why." "I don't know; I just thought I'd ask." "Well, I just thought I'd tell you." "Then tell me who's playing left field?" "Who's playing first."

Dr. Skye, his left eye twitching a little, calmly asked, "What is this?"

The lead technician answered, "I think it's the ancient humorists Abbot and Costello. But it might be that Laurel and Henry . . . Handy . . . whatever their names were."

A younger woman answered, "Oh, that's Laurel and Hardy doing 'Who's on First.' It's an ancient form of something called Burlesque humor. I minored in ancient twentieth century history. This . . . was . . . one . . . " She saw those piercing eyes of Dr. Skye glaring at her.

"WHY IS IT ON THE SCREEN?" Dr. Skye finally exploded.

"Look, we've been fighting this ever since the system crashed. This isn't your typical computer virus out to erase and destroy; our system would have caught that long before now. When we turn the backup computers on, over three million of these old entertainment programs activate at the same time. The system runs them for about five minutes and then crashes. Where all these old shows came from, I have no clue."

Dr. Skye watched three of his workers snickering at the duo on the screen, which only excited his anger all the more. "TURN IT OFF, AND FIND A WAY TO GET IT WORKING AGAIN!"

Just then a pair of workers came rushing onto the bridge, their bouncing flashlights visible well before they were. "Dr. Skye, we have something!"

"Tell me it's good news. I might just throw the next person out an airlock who gives me bad news."

"It is good news, sir." The lead man stopped and spoke for the pair. "We dismantled the emergency battery backup on the lights in the guest corridors. It was enough to activate a single computer system."

The lead technician interjected. "It really isn't a matter of powering up a system. It's this stupid virus."

"Can you get me into a computer system on this ship?"

"No, not the main computers. We were able to power a computer system in one of the shuttles. The virus crashed only their power systems, but it didn't scramble the computers like the *Sanger's*."

Dr. Skye walked out, motioning for them to follow. "Good, we can work with that. Mark!" he called back to the lead on the bridge. "Come with me."

The lead tech handed his tool over to his assistant and then ran after the doctor.

✳　✳　✳

J'kla stepped out onto the new stage his people had constructed for this event. It had been a few hours since he had sequestered himself to pray and study the Scriptures. The guests had come and greeted one another, enjoyed the feast, and were ready to learn about what brought them together.

"Hello." "Fine Afternoon to you." "Hello." J'kla greeted people as he approached the stage, most of them elders and high-ranking members of their respective villages. While he retained a sense of collected calm on the outside, his stomach was turning over, and his heart raced.

"J'kla, I'd like you to meet the council of elders and chiefs." His chief introduced him to a gathering of other B'reann, some of which didn't look all that pleased to be meeting this young man.

"He seems inexperienced. What wisdom can he have we don't already know?" a very old man asked.

The chief spoke loud for his old ears. "He is only a messenger for the wisdom's Source. Just listen to him."

J'kla took some pleasure in how his chief grasped the hierarchy of the Bible. J'kla was willing to speak on behalf of Jesus and the Scriptures, but they were not his words or his wisdom.

His chief took his hand and held it firmly. "They are ready to listen."

"They?" He had kept his eyes only on the seated gathering of elders on the platform.

"Out there." She motioned to the gathered thousands around the platform. People were sitting as close as they could get. Some were even seated in the trees and on the roofs of buildings, so they could hear. The warriors from the third village were accustomed to residing in the trees, and they were perched very comfortably near him in the high branches. The old woman patted his arm and sort of pushed him toward the podium they had constructed from a tree stump. "Speak loud and clear. Their ears are turned for you."

J'kla stepped up to the podium and cleared his throat. In his mind, he said one final prayer before speaking. Looking around, he smiled and began. "My friends, all B'reann know that what we have cannot be here without a mighty Creator at work. Some have sought to know Him. Some have questioned what it means when we see the order and beauty all around us in what should be a world of chaos and confusion. I bring you the Word of the God Who created all that is, including you." This caused a little murmuring from the crowd, but it died down, and he continued. "I will start at the beginning; listen well. The God of Creation, known as Elohim, existed before anything else. He created the heavens and the earth in six days, filling them with life and . . . "

In his time in prayer, he had been inspired by the Holy Spirit to start where he first began to learn from Anna, at the beginning. It was hard to understand the nuances of the New Testament when you didn't understand the foundations by which it was written, and you simply cannot draw wisdom from most of the Old Testament without knowing the origins of all Creation. So, he began with the Creation, the perfect world without sin, and then the Fall. Knowing where sin entered and how was important, but knowing about the consequences of sin and what it meant was even more paramount.

For hours, he spoke, stopping only to wet his throat, so he could continue. They had never before had any inclination of a God or atonement of sin. The idea of right and wrong was part of their legal system. But it had never been so eloquently explained *why* something was right and wrong. The truth behind the Creator and what He put into the hearts of those He created, even when they didn't know Him yet, was amazing.

J'kla couldn't believe what was coming out of his own mouth. While he spoke and read passage after passage, he knew in his heart Who was speaking through him. And in turn, after coming to that realization, his enthusiasm only blossomed all the more.

Just before he left his home to come to this stage, he had read the story of Elijah and thought how much he wanted to ask for just a tenth of a portion of the spirit that guided the great Elijah. He felt too humble and ignorant to ask for so much as double the portion—just enough to be worthy to do what he needed to do. Now he felt on fire, as though he had been filled with an energy exploding out of every pore in his body.

The evening came, and he was getting tired. He had finished speaking and now answered questions asked by the elders who spoke on behalf of their people. He would ask the gathering for their questions, but with this many, it would be impossible to accommodate them properly.

Just then a loud, deep horn blew in the distance. This was a familiar sound, and it brought a smile to a few people. The chief of this village stepped up and addressed the crowd. "It looks like the night's feast is prepared. We have also prepared camps for each village to rest for tonight. Tomorrow, J'kla will visit each camp and your elders and answer questions. For now, I think he needs his rest and something to eat as well."

The gathering broke up. A few came to the stage to ask questions, but the chief turned them away. She was worried about J'kla's health. Though he felt tired, he was fine. She worried his recent ordeal would still be causing him to be weak. He wanted to answer their questions and keep talking all night; he was so filled with passion for this, it was bursting out of him. But he knew it was time to eat and rest.

"You did well, young man. I have a lot to think about this night." The eldest elder scratched J'kla's ear and then used the hand of his daughter to get down from the stage and shuffle off toward the campsite for his fellow villagers.

The chief scratched J'kla's other ear. "Yes, I'm very proud of you. I think we have something very special starting here. Now, you go rest and eat something. Where is your wife? She should be here with you."

J'kla looked around, having only then thought about Anna. He almost blurted out that she was up on the mountain still, but thought better. "She is ...uh..."

"Oh, there she is." The chief waved at Anna, who was walking into town. More than one person from the outside villages gave her a wide berth, and a few even snarled at her. One of the guards of this village stepped up to escort her to J'kla, out of fear the outsiders might do something bad without knowing the whole truth.

CHAPTER TWENTY-SIX

THE HIGHEST COURT ON EARTH held session with all the delegates in attendance. Jessie sat in her old seat to the side of the main floor while the military general gave his report. The court had been in long discussions and various arguments about handing control of the military over to the PSC. No one had yet to call for a full vote. They all wanted to have a say in the situation and then debate the finer details. Jessie was going to take great pleasure in removing these bureaucrats from power. They were a waste of oxygen as far as she was concerned.

"We haven't had any ships shot down in the past two days. Our forces are amassing around Jerusalem for a full attack later this afternoon."

The head judge asked, "Will it work? So far, nothing we have thrown at their barrier has even fazed it in the least."

"I'm afraid I must agree with you," the general answered. "But if we don't try, then we'll never turn the tide of this war."

Ken, the representative from Australia, stood up to speak. "General, what sort of weapon are they using?"

"We're not sure. It passes right through our shields and destroys the ship."

"We have seen the video evidence of the battles," Ken added. "And the one time we have any footage of a ship's destruction from the point of origin, there is nothing firing at it. What kind of weapon is invisible but can do so much damage?" There was a hint of disbelief in the Aussie's voice.

The general scowled. "We don't know. But what we do know is that every recovered recorder box clearly indicates the ship was fired on just prior to its destruction." He turned to Jessie to say what he wanted to add. "The information gathered from the recorder boxes has been processed by the best scientists of the PSC. Do you know anything about the weapon being used?"

Jessie stood up, so proud her deceptions were working perfectly. "Sorry, everyone, but all the information which has been gathered and analyzed has been sent on to the military. What the PSC knows, the military knows. Clearly, Jerusalem is a dangerous foe. One who can take down ships in one shot and leave no trace to follow. I shudder to think about what they could do with such technology." She gave the general her famous, venomous smile. "I'm afraid the military is just not up to the task alone."

The general ground his teeth and held back a rather nasty snarl. "The military will handle this just fine. We have a plan, and until that plan fails—"

"*When* that plan fails," she interrupted him, "and it will. How many men have to die before you relinquish control? How many ships have to be shot down before you admit you need help?"

"I will *not* hand the military over to the scientists! If anything, this court needs to order Dr. Skye to hand over the *Sanger* to the military for this operation. Let him work for us, not the other way around."

Jessie continued to smile and walked around the general to address the room with her response to his idea, which was the logical choice, but she didn't want them seeing it. "True. Very true. You can order the PSC to hand over the *Sanger* . . . However, the PSC is not a government agency anymore. So, it would have to be a request, not an order. But we are patriots; we understand the needs at hand."

This caused quite the murmuring. Jessie had been relentless in her efforts to get the military under the control of the PSC, and Dr. Skye in particular. Now, she admitted it would work just as well with the military controlling the PSC. This actually made the general smile. "I'm glad you see it our way. Judge, I formally request an order be submitted to the PSC to surrender the use of the *Sanger* until this war is completed."

Jessie interrupted this official motion by adding, "And we would be glad to work with the military. Dr. Skye has made it clear to everyone the betterment of mankind is the goal of the PSC. And when he runs for office as the president of the Corps, this joint operation will only further illustrate his capabilities as both commander and chief. We would welcome such a boon to the campaign for president. That is, if the people call for an election. Remind me again how badly we are losing the first war the Corps has ever fought without a commander and chief over the Corps?"

The representative of Russia stood up and raised his hand, which signaled he was about to make a motion. Everyone stopped and looked at him. "I move that we vote to give control of the military to the PSC until the end of the war, and that we consider the title of military administrator for Dr. Richard Skye."

The representative from Brazil jumped up and yelled out, "I second the motion."

The head judge banged his gavel and grimly announced, "All in favor of holding a vote as motioned?"

The room resounded in a chorus of ayes that were followed by green lights being lit up by each of their posts.

"All opposed?"

Two people said, "Nay," and activated their red lights—Ken from Australia and the representative from Canada.

The head judge banged his gavel again and announced, "All members have voted, no abstaining. Motion carried. A vote will be held tomorrow morning. Jessie, please contact Dr. Skye and inform him of the vote to be held. Court adjourned until tomorrow morning. Please advise the proper news outlets, so your constituents are aware of the emergency proceedings. Dismissed." With two gavel bangs, the session was concluded.

Jessie stood next to the bewildered general. He was in a state of shock. "What just happened?"

She slowly walked away. "Politics."

* * *

Anna had made it all the way down the mountain on foot, a long trek for a non-robot. She had not realized how far they had gone up on the mountain.

"Anna." A man spoke her name, and she looked up to see one of the guards smiling at her. It was then she noticed the large crowds going here and there. She was startled by the shocked looks and snarling faces. It made her happy to see a kind face walking next to her, carrying a fearsome weapon. He was obviously keeping her safe from these strangers, who were afraid of her.

She did not see the waving hand of J'kla but followed the man next to her, who led her straight to her husband. What she saw were the faces on the people around her—not the anger or the fear, just the features. How could she have missed it? It was right there. The human in those eyes, the cheeks, the smile. They were her people; she carried one of their own right now as her own child.

The wonder and shock were mixed with a bittersweet feeling bubbling in her. She wanted to jump into J'kla's arms and tell him he had a child coming. But as soon as any happiness would fill her, a cold feeling ran down her spine. There was an immediate danger. The soldiers of the *Sanger* could be landing right now, heading for the village on their way to find Z. If Dr. Skye sent down a legion of other Z-bots, she had no idea how they could stop them. Z-bots were incredibly strong and felt no pain. Worse yet, this village was packed with people. Many of them too young or too old to be warriors. Even if the skilled spearmen of this village stopped a few Z-bots, the rest would overrun them and kill anyone to get to Z.

"Anna?" J'kla said her name in the distance, and her focused worry melted. She bound away from her guardian and ran into his awaiting arms.

"J'kla, I'm so glad to see you!" She was nearly crying.

He held her and looked at the very perplexed people around them. "What wrong?" He asked, hoping she wouldn't say anything about being up on Gladuin without permission.

She had tears running down her face as she answered. "They're coming. They are going to kill everyone. We have to protect the village."

"What?" J'kla was stunned.

The chief could see the worry on J'kla's face but could not understand Anna's words. "What is wrong, J'kla? Is everything all right? Is she injured?"

J'kla shook his head and asked Anna directly, "Tell me what happen?"

She sniffed back the sobbing. "We found it—the ship. It's an old science ship. My people created your people to fool science. We tried to warn our friends on Earth, but the bad people heard us. They are sending people to stop Z."

"I no understand."

Anna stepped back and wiped her eyes. "I don't have time to explain everything. Dr. Skye—the man who tried to kill you and has been killing your people—he found out about Z and that Z knows what they are up to. He is going to try and stop us from getting the truth back to Earth."

"Man who attack Anna and make my head hurt?"

"Yes. He is really angry and wants to stop Z."

"He come here?"

Anna started to cry more. "I don't know what he'll do. He's willing to do anything to stop us. He already tried to kill me because he thought I knew too much, and I didn't know hardly anything compared to what we discovered up on the mountain. J'kla, he has hundreds of robots like Z who could come down and kill many of your people. I don't know what he will truly do, but you have to secure your people, protect your village, and keep everyone safe."

J'kla was silent for a moment, while his chief and two of the other elders awaited to hear him translate to them what was just said. They could sense it was of dire importance, but they could not understand Anna. After gathering his thoughts, he explained what had just happened to his chief. He also told her there were other men like Z who were evil and could come down to stop them.

Immediately, the chief called out, "SOUND THE ALARM! SEND THE WARRIORS TO THEIR POSTS! ALL OF THEM! SUMMON THE CHIEFS OF THE OTHER VILLAGES TO ME NOW!"

At once, several other horns blared loudly, and everyone knew something terrible was happening.

The people around them were scrambling to get the word out or to get to their posts in the trees to watch over the village. J'kla took Anna's hand to pull her to the safest place he knew of.

She stopped him and held him in place. "J'kla, there's one more thing."

"No now. We go to safe place."

"No, I want to tell you now in case I never get to tell you." She feared he would go out to fight and would not return, never knowing of his own child.

He paused in his rush and came close to her. "What?"

"J'kla . . . " She took his hand and placed it on her stomach. "J'kla, I'm pregnant."

"Pregnant?" He did not know that word.

She smiled and then held his hands with hers. "I am going to have a baby, your baby."

J'kla's fiercely worried face quickly changed to excitement for a brief moment. "Baby?"

"Yes. Z scanned me and told me I'm going to have your son or daughter."

He quickly took her hand again and led her toward the safe place with much more haste than before. "I get you to protection."

✶ ✶ ✶

Dr. Skye hung over the shoulder of the man working in the shuttle. "What have you done?" Richard asked, again, with a lot of impatience in his voice.

"I have connected the computer on this shuttle with the *Sanger* and am working on resetting all the systems I can fix."

Dr. Skye sat down at one of the pilot stations. "Can you get the communications working? I need to know if their message back to Earth has done anything."

"Sorry, sir, but the shuttle's onboard computer isn't programmed with all that is needed to operate a ship as advanced and complicated as the *Sanger*. We'll be able to get only minimal systems online. However, once we get those working, they can get the others working. It'll be a domino effect. It'll take time, though."

"We don't have time! I have no idea if that Z unit has any other way to contact Earth. They can't tell them what they found." Dr. Skye was nearly growling. "How could they know anything? That ship's computer was supposed to be wiped clean. All they could possibly find were the dusty remains of the experiments conducted on that ship, and nothing left behind would possibly tell them much. How could they have discovered what they were telling Elijah?"

"What, sir?"

Dr. Skye shook his head. "Nothing."

"Sir! The bridge reports the communication system is receiving signals again."

"Good." Dr. Skye had a rather vicious smile on his face. "Get Earth on the main channel for me. I want to talk to . . . "

"Sorry, sir, we are only receiving signals; we cannot send any."

"All right," Richard growled. "Are there any communications coming in for me from Administrator Jessie?"

"Yes, there's a message awaiting you right now. Shall I play it?"

Normally, Dr. Skye would talk to her in private, knowing the subject of their conversations was often dangerous for others to hear. But he was worried sick. "Put it through."

"I got it."

Just then, the small intercom screen on the shuttle lit up with the inside of Jessie's private office and her speaking directly to the screen. "I don't know why I cannot get in touch with you, but this is important. The counsel is in deliberations about handing military control over to you to end this war. I need you to come back to Earth." The signal ended.

"Do we have any propulsion systems online yet?" Dr. Skye asked.

"Not yet, but they should come back online when we get the main computer fixed."

Dr. Skye audibly growled with gritted teeth.

"Sir, there are several more messages from the administrator for you."

Dr. Skye was highly intrigued; perhaps the vote had taken place, and he was ready to take over. "By all means, put them through."

Again, she appeared in her private office. "They're arguing the finer points about all of this. All we need is to get them to sign the commands over to you. If you get here soon, they'll probably hand it over. Where are you?" The screen changed, and this time she was in a different dress. "I have five of the naysayers ready to vote for you. That leaves only two left. Once we have them, we'll have a majority. But I doubt they'll budge without you here. We need the *Sanger* in orbit to show them we're ready. Get here now."

The next image came through, and she was looking rather disheveled compared to the others. "I don't know what is going on. Elijah just made a contact with the court and requested an audience with them. Most of the representatives were willing to listen. I had to detonate five more ships to get them to not want to talk to him; but if he insists any further, I'll run out of ships to use. Whatever he has must be pretty important, or he wouldn't be trying it now. I can't talk to him. He has shut off all communications outside of the one channel left open for them to accept his request. We can't let this happen. We can't let that stupid peace-talker ruin all of this. WHERE ARE YOU?!" She slammed the button so hard, the screen shook just before the message ended.

The programmer quietly asked, "What did she mean by detonating ships?"

"That is not your concern." Dr. Skye's worst fears were coming true. If Elijah presented them with enough evidence to pause their war and investigate his claims, all of their plans could be ruined. Worse yet, if the world government discovered what the PSC had been doing for the past two hundred years, they could bring them down and destroy everything. He had only one option left.

"Do we have control of the weapon systems yet?"

"They'll come back online in a few minutes. They're part of the main power system, and that is just about ready to come online. Once we have that working, we will be able to get off these emergency power—"

"Shut up." Dr. Skye didn't need any more reports. "I want you to get the weapon systems ready for use as soon as you can, even if that means stalling the progress on other repairs."

"Yes, sir. But . . . why?"

"We have an enemy to destroy. Now, get to work."

CHΛPTER TWENTY-SEVEN

Z HAD RIGGED THE COMPUTER of the old *Terra 5* with some of his own components to get it working. The main power system was operational. He was glad to see the power system which ran this ship was one of the old re-gen systems. They didn't put out half the power of the modern Tryno-Core technology, but the re-gen system, once powered, could work pretty self-sufficiently without much effort. He opened the access ports on the top of the ship, and the solar collectors were able to recharge the system and get the re-gen process working. Although the energy system was dangerous if it exploded, he had to be careful to watch it, in case the two-hundred-year-old mechanisms failed, and a core meltdown happened. Fortunately, it seemed to be working fine.

The plan was to collect as much data as possible and then evade the scouts Dr. Skye was likely to send for him. If they took or dismantled the ship, he would hide and wait for Elijah to send somebody to find him.

While the computer ran through the new calculations Z had put into it to make the sensors work better, he tried to repair the shielding system. The ancient solar shields weren't entirely necessary, but he could use the shields like a booster for the old antenna.

"All right, old girl, let's see how this is going to work." He slid out from a narrow partition between two walls and checked to see if the shields were online. Turning them on, he was surprised to see them at full power. "Wow, for an old hunk of junk you're certainly well preserved." He gave off a sly look and leaned against the control panel. "Hey, I know there's an age difference, but are you seeing anybody?"

"Sensor upgrades completed," the computer announced.

"So, is that a no?" he jokingly added. He tossed the tool aside and checked out the old sensor system. "Amazing! If this ship wasn't condemned for harboring a secret, I would suggest putting it in a museum. Computer, run a full sensor analysis of the area."

"Sensor sweep activated."

"While you're at it, could you check to see—"

"ALERT! UNKNOWN ENERGY SURGE DETECTED! DANGER!"

Z stopped the scan and turned it back to the last area of data collected. His eyes bugged, and he ran the data through all the different working filters available. It was undeniable. "Oh no," he whispered and then rushed to finish the last repair. He was going to have to risk the craziest idea he had ever conceived.

It had been five hours since Anna had returned to the village. The people were gathered in secure pockets, where guards were posted all around them. Food had been brought, and they were nervously eating. The elders, chiefs, J'kla, and Anna all had gathered in the center of town with a whole legion of the best warriors to protect them.

More than once, Anna glanced up at the mountain and worried Dr. Skye had already sent down agents to get Z. It wasn't impossible for them to come from a different direction and bypass the village altogether. She trusted Z would not betray them and reveal her presence among the B'reann.

While she thought about this, J'kla and the others discussed what was going on right now. He explained to the other chiefs and elders why Anna was good, but other tailless men were bad. They didn't quite get it, but they did understand Anna wasn't a threat. Several continued to ask about going on the offensive, instead of just sitting around and waiting for them to come in the night. J'kla tried to explain this enemy hid in the sky above and did not have a place they could attack. They worried J'kla was still suffering from the insanity that had killed so many others.

After enough time had passed, they came to a logical decision. J'kla stood up and helped Anna up.

"What is going on? Are we moving to a different location?" Anna asked.

J'kla shook his head. "No, we go home."

"Home? But they're coming for the ship."

"No, elders and chiefs say it time to go. Enemy wait to attack; we take opportunity to spread out, go to own villages. Easier to defend small group than large group."

"That does make sense." Anna watched as the other elders went to their respective citizens to break up the clustered groups for the trips home. She looked once again at Gladuin. "What about Z? They're coming for him, not us."

J'kla was about to say something but saw a man running toward them. "Commander of guard coming; he watch mountain for enemy."

The commander approached and then bowed to the chief and reported something startling. She was frowning and looking up at Gladuin.

"What is it? What is happening?"

"They see something strange. Barrier of light shine for minute and then go away. Now they hear rumbling in mountain."

"Z must be working on the ship," she surmised. "They shouldn't be worried about that. Have they seen anybody up there? Any ships landing?"

J'kla asked. The man shook his head and started to answer, but his ears stood up taller and he looked skyward, as did several other B'reann. Anna looked up as well, not sure what had piqued their interest. She expected to see a ship landing, or even the *Sanger* coming down lower, but what came made her scream in pure fear.

A beam of red and yellow light pierced the sky, broke the clouds, and slammed into the ground. It shook the moon and caused a whole section of the mountain ridge to explode in a fiery eruption. Burning debris rained down across the area, causing many small fires to instantly ignite within the village.

The B'reann screamed and ran around in a panic, as the heavens were broken and the land torn asunder. J'kla grabbed Anna and held her as he ran away from a big chunk of rock that landed right in the center of town.

The chief yelled and pointed upward. Just then, another beam of light shot down and blasted part of the plains near the village, creating yet another explosion that sent more burning bits of debris across the village.

The warriors jumped down from their trees, while the fires consumed the forest around the village. They dropped their weapons and ran to save children who couldn't outrun the fires that were taking down the walkways and platforms built between the trees.

J'kla had Anna by the hand now and ran toward the eastern exit leading across the open pastures, the largest area where no fire had touched yet. "THIS WAY!" he yelled to his people.

No sooner did they start to follow him than another bolt blasted the far side of the pasture.

J'kla, Anna, and hundreds of B'reann were thrown back by the ensuing shockwave. This blast sent the cloud of fire off toward the darker forest around the East Village, utterly destroying it, while its residents watched from afar.

J'kla coughed and brushed the dirt off of him as he rolled over. "Anna?"

She pulled herself up. "I'm all right. It just knocked the air out of me."

The chief came running by, yelling, "To the lake! The fire can't follow us in the water!" She rushed as many people who could hear her as possible toward the large body of water in the valley beyond Gladuin, which was a pretty long distance from here, but it was safe from the fire.

Anna didn't know where they were going, but she followed J'kla, while the world burned around them. The village was on fire everywhere; his home was engulfed; so was the platform where they were married and the street where the hut was he had healed in.

"COME! COME!" the chief was yelling.

Anna looked back to see how many were left to join the gathering heading for the waters. At that moment, another blast came down and hit the village right dead center of the shop district, where many people were fleeing. Hundreds were immolated instantly; dozens more were thrown through the air with their fur on fire. Flaming bodies were sent tumbling across the ground as a testament to the power falling on their heads.

Anna stopped her husband. "We can't run to safety. There's no safe place on this moon. We're all dead."

J'kla looked up at the scattered remains of the B'reann killed in the blast. All hope seemed utterly lost. What ran through his mind was, *God, please show me how to save my people. Please God, save my people.*

✶   ✶   ✶

"WHY CAN'T YOU TARGET THAT STUPID GUN?!" Dr. Skye was furious they hadn't recorded the proper explosion yet. They were shooting blind, and it was making him extremely angry.

The man at the controls had beads of sweat running down his forehead, while his commander was screaming at him. "Sir . . . I can't seem to make this thing cooperate. I aim for the target you gave me, and when I fire, it's like it has a mind of its own. It must be the virus still causing us trouble."

Dr. Skye pointed at the map, where the ancient ship was still landed. "I want that place destroyed NOW!"

"I . . . I will try!" He worked nearly as fast as a Z-bot. "Almost recharged for another shot."

Dr. Skye waited for the proper explosion. It would rip open a crater a quarter the size of the whole moon if they could just hit their target. It would kill everyone and everything in the Northern Hemisphere, but it would also eliminate the possibility of anyone discovering the whole truth. He could easily blame this on some kind of accident. Heck, with how people believed anything the science corps said, he could tell them it was a natural disaster, and no one would blink.

✶　✶　✶

Z had watched the horrific scene from inside the old ship and worked faster than any Z-bot in history. With a green light on one station and a red light blinking on the sensor grid, he took the controls with his hands. "I'm coming, Anna."

✶　✶　✶

The gathering B'reann got as close together as they could. Their entire world was burning, the fires cutting off every avenue of escape. Most of this village was destroyed; another village had taken the full blast of one of the shots; and the growing forest fire would consume the third village in a short time. Nothing the B'reann knew as home would exist much longer.

Anna held her husband and wept. "Your baby would've been so beautiful."

J'kla took her, gave her a kiss, and then quietly said, "I love you. I no mean to put you in danger. It better if Anna and J'kla never met."

"No, don't say that. A few short days with you is better than a lifetime of the godless world I knew. I never knew what true love was or what it meant to be married. I would not trade this for anything. We will face our end together and then be together forever with our Lord."

J'kla was silently crying. He wanted to say so much right now to her, but all he could do was hold her close to him and pray she did not feel pain in the end. All he could say was a prayer in his own tongue: "Father in Heaven, put Your name on our hearts forever; know my people as Yours; and know our love for You as You would anyone else. Remember us, and take us into Your hands. By Your will, God, direct our paths to lead to You. If we die today, we die. But nothing can take us away from You, not even death."

Anna felt a hand grasp hers. It wasn't J'kla's, but one of the other people. As J'kla repeated his prayer over and over in a loud, sad voice, the people around them all held hands and lowered their heads. They were ready to put themselves into the hands of God, no matter the outcome of this day. Anna felt ready to finally see the face of Jesus and be forever in glory.

A loud rumbling drew their attention to the mountains. The side of Gladuin exploded outward in a showering rain of dirt and grass. The old ship suddenly burst forth and flew a shaky path across the sky. The B'reann screamed and dropped to the ground in fear. Only one of them had ever seen a spaceship before, and no one expected anything to come flying out of the mountain of origin.

Anna was stunned as she watched the *Terra 5* take a position over the crowd just as a beam of light came flowing down from the sky. It hit the upper shields of the ship, and a blue explosion of plasma echoed out from the impact. The ship was thrust downward slightly; but it did not break, and the shields absorbed the attack. The resounding sonic boom from the impact rattled everyone's bones and made the B'reann cover their ears in pain.

After that display, the ship flew forward slightly and landed in the middle of the burning pasture. The back hatch opened, and there stood a very anxious Z.

"HURRY! THAT WAS THE ONLY SHOT THESE SHIELDS COULD TAKE!" He waved at them to come inside.

J'kla and Anna ran for the ship. Anna stopped when she realized the others weren't coming. "Come on, before you're killed!"

They all seemed to be looking at the ship in terror, especially the man standing in the door. They did not understand anything that was going on, and they certainly didn't trust this.

J'kla called out, "Come, we have to get away from the fire!" His people didn't move. They were scared and uncertain about what to do now. There was a timid fear in their eyes at the sight of this strange ship and the man standing in the doorway.

"COME ON! WHAT ARE YOU WAITING FOR?! THE GUN WILL RECHARGE ANY MOMENT NOW!" Z was about to run out and grab Anna at least.

J'kla watched the twinkling fires dancing in the quivering eyes of his people. He saw the terror stunning them. Then he remembered the man in the desert asking for water. His mission to save his people was at hand. He assumed it was his bringing them the grace message, but God saves those who come to salvation—not him. Now was the time for him to save his people. Stepping up, he spoke as loudly as he could over the blazing fires. "Do not fear! God has granted us safety and hope in the face of this rain of fire. Come into the ship and escape. I know you don't trust my tailless friends, but you don't have to yet. Just trust God and have faith. We don't have much longer before we all will be dead."

Anna took the lead and ran for the ship, taking Z's hand to get up the ramp. After a short pause, several of the guards ran for the ship as well. Soon, many were following and running past J'kla to get inside.

J'kla came to Z's side and wanted to hug him but instead helped with grabbing hands and getting the small children picked up, so they did not get trampled under the hordes.

"Tell them to move into the ship; fill every space. This ship can hold a lot, but this is going to take all the space we have." Z took a baby from a woman and then helped her into the ship.

J'kla translated and was about to explain they needed to get into beds and bathrooms to make room when the sound of that beam caught his ears. He turned his head just in time to see the top of Gladuin hit by the *Sanger's* main weapon and explode in a massive discharge of rocks and trees. The debris came falling down all over the remaining people standing around. More than one person was killed by the massive trunk of a tree or a boulder landing on them.

This expedited the already-hurried escape as people piled harder to get inside.

CHAPTER TWENTY-EIGHT

"GOT IT!" THE MAN AT the controls announced.

Dr. Skye smiled wide. "You hit the target finally?"

"Yes. One registered hit on top of that mountain. But . . . wait . . . " He peered closer to his screen. "I don't think it worked, sir."

"What do you mean?" Dr. Skye was tired of hearing bad reports.

"You believed this would create a massive explosion, but it was nothing more than any of the other strikes. In fact, this one did less damage, since it was only the tip of a mountain and not the basin of a valley. Perhaps your target was wrong, sir?"

Dr. Skye's right eye twitched as he looked at the readings to confirm the lack of massive explosion. "That is the right place. That should have torn this moon in half. WHAT WENT WRONG?!"

"I can get a visual scan. The optical sensors are working now," the engineer said.

"Good. Put it on the screen. Maybe our sensors aren't working properly." He was holding out for success, regardless of the sensor data.

"I have . . . wait . . . *what* is that?" The man was leaning in so close that he was covering the screen.

Dr. Skye shoved him aside and leaned in. His eyes bugged out and he yelled, "WHAT! THIS IS NOT POSSIBLE!"

The screen showed a top view of the old terraforming ship surrounded by small fires and hundreds of people running inside.

"Sir? What is that? That looks like a very old explorer, maybe even one of the old terraformers. Was that your target?"

Dr. Skye just about lost his teeth, he was grinding them so hard. "I don't know how they got it working, but I WANT IT DESTROYED! NOW!!"

"I, uh, will have to reset the system for a mobile target. But . . . uh . . . I don't know if I should."

"WHAT!" Dr. Skye grabbed the man by his collar and pulled him clear up out of his seat. "YOU WOULD DISOBEY A DIRECT ORDER!?"

"This isn't a military," the man gasped. "We are scientists and engineers."

Dr. Skye threw him back into his seat and controlled the eye-twitching. "I don't care what you think you are. You are under my command, and you will re-target that ship and destroy it at once."

"No," the engineer said with a firm voice, though he was still recovering from that unexpected strangling.

"No? NO!" Dr. Skye's voice cracked.

"There are people down there. You are ordering me to commit genocide."

"THEY AREN'T PEOPLE! THEY ARE JUST ANIMALS, PRIMITIVES!" He was furious at anyone suggesting those things weren't just animals. He had worked so hard to get that image across.

"I don't care. They are running for safety, and it's because of me. There is no good reason to kill so many people, even primitive ones, just because I'm told to do it." The engineer started to wipe the computer's targeting system memory of all the recent commands. It would take hours to reset it to get a target lock now.

Dr. Skye was so angry, he couldn't see anything but red. He was Dr. Richard Skye. People worshiped his every word. He was the leader of all science and knowledge. What he said was true; when he spoke, you obeyed. No one defied him. Without even considering his actions, he grabbed a work rod leaning up against the side of the door, where it was holding the non-working door open. With one swift swing, he laid the bar right into the skull of the worker and ended this mutiny.

Shoving the bloody carcass off the seat, he took the lead in finishing this job. "If you want something done right, do it yourself," he muttered as he accessed the controls.

To his dismay, the worker had canceled all commands and erased all the targeting parameters. He couldn't get a target lock, and he didn't know how to fix this quick enough. He had one last option at hand. It was drastic and would raise a lot of questions, but he couldn't let this information get away from here. He set the controls, activated the power collector cells, and turned the ship to face the moon directly.

✳   ✳   ✳

"There's not enough room." Z announced as he helped yet another person up the platform into the ship.

Anna took the hand of a teen boy and pulled him up the steep ramp. "We'll just have to try."

J'kla came running from the back. "We run out of room. People in beds, two and three in each. Floor full; people standing wall by wall."

Anna looked behind them into the little hangar of this old ship and saw nothing but people. "This isn't good. We still haven't got the elderly into here."

Z shook his head. "By my calculations, we are going to be pushing the oxygen recycling system to its fullest with the amount we do have. Besides the space limitations, we won't make it back to Earth with enough air to breath."

J'kla pointed out at the old chiefs and elders who were helping get the younger people to the ship. "We no leave chiefs."

"I know. We will try, but this is . . . Wait. Do you hear something?" Now, even Anna heard a strange sound from above.

Z came by carrying a little girl. "What is that?"

All at once, a massive beam hit the ground outside the village on the far side from where the ship had landed. This beam blasted a major hole in the ground and scattered fiery debris everywhere. But unlike the former attacks, this beam just kept going. It was bigger, whiter, and hotter than any of the others.

"Oh, no." Z gasped.

"WHAT THAT?!" J'kla yelled.

"They are irradiating the moon's surface. The crust will fracture, and the mantle will swallow the surface. In a matter of moments, this whole moon will be a burning wasteland." Z suddenly shoved the child into the arms of Anna. "We don't have any more time; I've gotta get this ship off the ground before we're all killed."

"What about chiefs?" J'kla asked, holding a hand up to the heat wave blasting out from the attack.

The person who answered him was his own chief, standing among many elderly of the B'reann. "Go, save yourselves. There is no more time to find room for us."

J'kla held out his hand. "Come with me; we will find room."

The ground shook, and many of the elders fell as the surface of the moon cracked beneath their feet. "You don't have time. We are old; our time has come. You lead the people now. Take them to a safe place and tell them about where they came from. We will face death with dignity."

The ground gave way, and a wall of fire was heading their way. The ship would be destroyed if they didn't lift off. Tears were streaming down J'kla's face as he choked out, "May God bless you and take you home with Him." Anna shut the door.

The elderly took each other by the hand and watched the ship lift up from the ground. The future society of B'reann left and headed into the unknown. The ground cracked and crumbled. The molten core under the surface was bursting through in places, and the fire storms were consuming everything that wasn't already burnt.

The ship, which had brought the B'reann to this world, took them from it in its last moments. The eldest of them staying behind felt no fire or pain when the last of their world was destroyed. God collected them to Him and brought home followers who had only known His Name for a few days, but would be with Him for eternity in glory.

* * *

Z sat at the pilot's seat. The ship was shaking hard, and its old engines were groaning under the stress of having spent two centuries half-buried.

Z expertly used the controls to dodge several eruptions and large chunks of debris thrown up by the attack. The glorious manmade paradise was reduced to ash and liquid rock in minutes, while the *PSC Sanger* ripped what was left of the surface apart with its main weapon at full power.

Anna finally made it into the cockpit. "Will we make it?"

Z worked the controls to keep the ship's energy systems from failing. "I think so, but it will take a minute to break away from the gravity. These old anti-grav lifters are working at only twenty-two percent capacity." He reached over and transferred all the power from the laboratories into the anti-grav systems.

"Oh, my goodness." Anna watched out the window. The beautiful valley was a lake of lava. Animals were dashing away from the danger, only to be killed from jumping into the flowing rivers of red liquid rock. She gripped the back of his seat and quietly said, "Eden burns."

Z agreed with that assessment. "Yes, and Satan set it on fire."

CHAPTER TWENTY-NINE

THE *STARSHIP SANGER* SILENTLY HOVERED in space. The engineers and scientists ran to windows to see what was happening. A large ship—but tiny in comparison to the *Sanger*—lifted up through the fires and slowly ascended into space. The lead engineers on the bridge attempted to identify the small ship; but their main weapon was drawing so much power, it blinded their systems temporarily.

Dr. Skye shut down the main weapon, convinced nothing on the surface was left. Exiting the shuttle, he shut the door and then locked it. "Deckhand, what is the status of the main computers?"

The man at the controls for the docking bay stood at attention. "The main computers are still being worked on. The energy grid was offline for . . ."

"I know why the energy grid was offline. I want the computers working. I'll be on the bridge. As soon as you have full controls working again, launch this shuttle, and set it down on the moon. It is under quarantine."

"Why, sir?" the young man asked. "If this shuttle gets near the surface right now, it will be destroyed."

"That is none of your business; just do what you are told." He was sick of people arguing with him. If he was going to lead mankind as the new planetary ruler, he would need to have obedience.

After a short walk, he was back on the bridge, where the people worked hard at getting everything online again.

"Sir, uh, we purged the virus in the computer. It will be a matter of only a few minutes before we have control of the system again." The assistant to the main technician immediately gave a report.

"Fine. Get communications online as soon as possible. I need to speak with Jessie."

"At once, sir. Uh . . . where's Mark?"

Dr. Skye coolly answered, "He chose other career options. You just got a promotion. Now, get me communications at once."

The way the ship was directed at this point, he was still looking at the burning husk of the moon. It was already cooling down; but for a moment, it appeared like a cold star. He hated doing this. It was a masterpiece of science his predecessors had spent years constructing. But if he was to fulfill their grand plans, sacrifices had to be made.

Dr. Skye noticed several of his workers closely watching a monitor. They weren't looking at the moon, but something. "What are you looking at?"

"Sensors are showing another ship coming near us. It's old."

"ON THE MONITOR NOW!"

The girl at communications changed the view to show them an ancient, bulky vessel creeping away from their position. "I have short-range communications. Do you want me to contact them?"

"I WANT THEM DESTROYED NOW!"

"Sir?"

Dr. Skye stood up and pointed at the screen. "EVERY WEAPON ON THIS SHIP, FIRE AT THAT SHIP NOW! NOW! NOW!!"

The boy at the weapons station was shaking as he answered, "The . . . w-w-weapons s-s-systems are not fully working yet. They were overcharged and . . ."

"RAM THEM!"

"What?" The girl at the helm had never trained to ram another ship.

Dr. Skye ran over and shoved the woman out of the navigation control seat and worked the controls himself. He was going to thrust the *Sanger* into that old ship. It would barely dent their hull, but the *Terra* ship would be smashed to pieces.

Just then, the small ship shot off into hyperlight. "Ahh!" He slammed the controls and then tried to activate the hyperlight system on the *Sanger*. It refused to respond.

"Uh . . . sir . . . I . . . " The woman he had dumped onto the floor had gotten to her feet and watched him fight with her controls.

He grabbed her arm and threw her back into her seat. "Follow them!" He gave his orders, returning to the center of the bridge. "Get weapons working; I want that ship turned into dust. AND GET COMMUNICATIONS ONLINE AT ONCE!"

The crew on the bridge hopped into action. The *Sanger* slowly repositioned itself on its spacial axis, so it could make the jump into hyperlight without flying right into a planet or asteroid belt. The computer was not responding quickly, but it was responding.

* * *

MOMENTS BEFORE

"Have they seen us?" Anna asked while Z furiously worked at the controls.

"I have no idea. These old sensors don't know what they're looking at when it comes to modern tech. Right now, I'm just making sure our own harmonic shields keep this ship from pulling itself apart in space. This tub hasn't flown for a long time."

Anna kindly indicated she wanted to change places with one of the B'reann sitting at the co-pilot station. He moved for her, and she sat down to help. "We have to get away from here. They're bound to see us eventually."

"We're going as fast as we can." Z worked intensely on something as he spoke.

"What about the hyperlight engines? Are they working at all? That would be our best chance."

"What do you think I'm doing?" Z furrowed his fake brow and gave the computer all the commands to alter the power systems. "These engines are simple. They'll get us only to stage one hyperlight, if I can get them working. The engine's re-gen system is nearly at full capacity. Once it reaches ninety-eight percent, we can attempt the jump."

Anna looked back at the hundreds of B'reann she could see from where she sat. This ship was filled past anything it had ever been designed to accommodate. So many of them held onto children or each other. Many cries could be heard from babies and a few people. The fear shaking behind those quivering eyes and depressed faces made her heart ache.

"Oh, Z. What have we done? They don't deserve this."

Z continued working, but calmly answered, "I have heard you say that you believe everything happens for a reason."

"Yes. God has a plan that is far beyond our understanding."

"Then don't let regret take your passion away. We're rescuing them not from what we did, but from what already happened to them before we found them. We might have instigated a lot of trouble with Dr. Skye and the PSC, but it would have happened eventually. There are a lot of curious people back on Earth, and they would come asking the same questions we asked. Only, they would be too late; what plans Dr. Skye and his friend have would have come to pass."

"You're right." She actually smiled. "When did you start listening to me about God and His plan?"

"I always remember what you tell me, even if I cannot compute the data to make sense of it all. But, at this point, we need to have some Divine intervention if we are to get to safety before the *Sanger* turns around and pulverizes us." He hit the last control, and a humming got louder and louder. "Now, do something for me: pray to that God of yours; we're gonna need it." With one flip of a switch, the starfield in front of them zoomed past, and they left the star system at speeds many times the normal speed of light.

The ship shook; several of the old power junctions burst; but for the most part, it held together.

Anna took Z by the hand and said, "He answered the prayer before I said anything."

*   *   *

Dr. Skye watched as they approached the smaller ship in the same hyperlight stream. Each ship traveling at the same speed in the stream meant he could see them, though they were a bit of a blur. It would be only a matter of time before they caught up. It was a highly dangerous task—using any sort of weapons while traveling at these speeds—but logic was thrown out the window at the sight of two centuries of planning being destroyed. It was practically programmed into Richard's DNA to protect the secret.

"Can we get a weapons lock yet?" he asked.

"No, sir. The main weapon systems aren't designed for targeting at hyperlight speeds. We'll have to drop into normal speeds."

"That would be counterproductive, now wouldn't it? Set up a hyperlight probe to be launched at once." He had one of his famous flashes of brilliance. They couldn't use their weapons at these speeds, but there were probes specifically designed to take readings in hyperlight for academic reasons.

"What for, sir?"

"Take out the onboard sample container and replace it with a sub-nuclear core equipped with an impact detonation."

"Yes, sir." The scientists had no idea why his superior wanted this ship destroyed so badly, going so far as to use the extremely dangerous sub-nuclear technology, but he wouldn't argue.

"When it is ready, set the probe to do a close proximity scan of that ship's hyperlight system. That will get it close enough."

"Yes, sir."

* * *

Anna watched the *Sanger*. She felt like a shark was chasing them and about to take a bite out of their tail any minute.

"Can we go any faster? They're gaining on us."

Z almost answered, when another power conduit on the outside of the ship burst in a flash of sparks. He compensated by transferring the power from a different system and then ejected the useless remains of the conduit. "If I push these engines any further, they'll implode on us. We'll be lucky if they don't fail altogether."

"If they fire any weapons at us, we're toast."

Z snickered. "They would be fools to fire their weapon in hyperlight speeds. We're moving at over three hundred times the speed of light. Energy weapons are not exactly the wisest tools to use at such speeds; they sort of rebound and destroy themselves if they aren't precisely balanced. And that cannon of theirs is far too strong to be balanced for hyperlight."

That helped Anna feel a little better. She knew the *Sanger* had impressive weapons, but they weren't currently carrying any torpedoes. All the space torpedoes in use right now were under the strict control of the military. The PSC did not have them.

Just then, J'kla squeezed through the dense population of his kin and found his way to the back of Anna's seat. He had to stand in an odd position, so he didn't step on the young man sitting on the floor beside her chair. "What happen? We safe?"

"Not yet," Z answered.

Anna gave him the best smile she could, considering the circumstances. "We aren't out of the woods yet. But we are okay for now. How is everyone doing?"

"They scared, hungry, tired. I don't know what say to them. I don't know what happening."

She took his hand and held it firmly. "Just go back and pray with them. Our enemy is bigger and stronger than us, and they are determined to stop us from getting back home. We need all the prayer we can get."

"I can do that." He was proud of her choice of action. It made perfect sense to him. He kissed her hand and then turned to go back to the main area where his people were packed in tight. Suddenly, he was stopped by the loud beeping sound coming from the computer.

"Oh, no," Z exclaimed. "They just fired something."

"I thought you said they couldn't." Anna looked back at her screen, expecting to see the energy weapons blazing toward them. What she saw was a tiny dot heading their direction. "What is that?"

"I don't know, but I'm betting it isn't a box of chocolates."

Another station beeped, and Anna looked at the old sensor readout. "Whatever it is, it just set off the radiation alarm."

"I bet it's a sub-nuclear detonator. That's about the only weapon that could work like a torpedo."

"What does this mean?" Anna watched her monitor again for the device heading for them.

"This means we had better find a way to get out of here before that thing makes contact. It'll blow us to smithereens."

"Get out of here? Where?"

Z plugged in new calculations at blinding speeds. "I'm going to shift our hyperlight stream, which will put us out of reach."

"Can the engines handle that?"

"I have no idea, but I'm certain the hull won't handle a sub-nuclear explosion. Hold on." He hit the last calculation just as the tiny probe was about to accelerate into their hull for impact.

The *Terra 5* altered course and changed their hyperlight stream, which caused the probe to explode by the shearing forces of the hyperspace. A blue-green ball of energy exploded outward and forced the *Sanger* to shift course in an entirely new direction.

The *Terra 5* was hit as well, but only by a shockwave of the energy inside the stream. The ship lurched forward. The stream of hyperspace they traveled in sped by faster and faster. The *Terra 5* rattled and groaned under the stress it was never designed to endure.

"WE ARE GOING TO FLY APART!" Z yelled out, while he tried to get the engines to settle down.

Anna held onto the console, while the B'reann all over the ship were tossed against one another.

"Oh, Heavenly Father, protect us!"

Two more redundant power cells burst on the exterior, and several small explosions were heard coming from inside the ship.

"I CAN HARDLY KEEP THIS BUCKET TOGETHER!" Z set the system to dump as much energy into the reverse thrusters as he could, so to bring them down to a manageable speed. Though the ship groaned all the harder for it, its speed reduced quickly and returned to a normal hyperlight. Z sat back and cautiously listened for any further explosions. Nothing happened. "All right. We're clear."

With a gulp and slow movement, Anna released her grip on the console and finally breathed again. "What just happened?"

Z checked their sensors and only shook his head. "This is impossible." He checked again. "Simply impossible. I . . . it . . . It's just impossible."

"What's impossible?"

"The shockwave hit the aft shields, what little was left of them. These old engines transferred the excess energy into the re-gen matrix and super-charged it. It just about burnt out on us and would have exploded itself, but instead, it sent us hurtling at speeds these old ships simply weren't designed for. It is impossible we're even still in one piece. I . . . I can't believe it. We just cut off two-thirds of our trip back to Earth. The *Sanger* won't catch us before we make it home."

Anna finally smiled with real happiness. "God works in mysterious ways."

"I don't know; I still cannot compute faith. But I can accept what I have seen."

"One of these days, I'll get you to understand faith. Right now, let's just get back home." She stood up and looked back through the doorway at all the B'reann gathering themselves after that unexpected jolt. "I'm going to see J'kla. I have something to show him before we get home."

"There is one thing." Z stopped her from leaving.

"What?"

"That little jolt knocked out our landing beams. We'll not be landing normally without the help of a catcher ray to stop us, and a few leveling ships to lower us to the ground. I doubt anyone back home is going to be ready for our arrival."

"What does this mean?"

"We're gonna crash land."

"Crash land?! Can we do anything to stop it from happening?"

"No. If we stop before landing and go into orbit, the *Sanger* will find us and finish us off quickly. We have to land, but it won't be an easy landing."

Anna looked out the window at the quickly passing space around them. "I have to trust God this won't end in tragedy. We have come too far."

"Have a little trust in your ol' Z-550. I do have a plan."

"A water landing might not be wise, Z." She presumed to know what he was thinking because it was her first thought as well. "If this ship sinks, we won't be able to warn anyone about preparing for us in time. There are a lot of people on this ship to rescue."

Z waved his hand. "Don't worry. I already dismissed the water landing idea. What I have in mind will be a little more dramatic. Besides, your friends may not like having to swim." He shooed her away with his joke and his waving hand. She knew he wasn't certain of his plan by the fact he was not wanting to tell her the details, and frankly she didn't want to know them.

"I'll be in the main lab if you need me."

CHAPTER THIRTY

THE WORLD COURT WAS READY to hold the vote. Jessie sat in her old seat and waited to hear the response. She had played right into their concerns about losing power.

Jessie was working hard to usher in a new dictatorship. The new world order would grant her a lot of power. It also granted the complete annihilation of Jerusalem and those infuriating Jews. Plus, she, like so many before her, truly believed if a system of rule was forced upon the people, they would come to accept and even worship it. This new world order would eliminate religion to the nth degree, remove voting and wishy-washy politicians, and establish the wise and logical rule of science in the lives of all humans.

What concerned her was she had not been able to get Dr. Skye on any communication channel. She was afraid they would open up more discussions before the vote and start another round of quibbling over the pointless details. Worse yet, they were currently discussing allowing the request of Elijah to address the court.

"What could that stupid Jew want to talk to the court about?" she asked herself over and over. He had already shown evidence, which had scared her to death—evidence he should not have. If he had something else more damaging to her plans, she might not be able to control it. And it was coming down to the wire; the vote was about to be taken. After they signed off the order and handed the PSC the command codes, Elijah could blow the whole truth for all she cared. The PSC would have what they wanted, and no one could stop them.

Just then, a young woman was brought into the courtroom. She was shaking and pale. It was Elijah's secretary, who had come to make the request. She had been given special permission to leave and speak to the court. Elijah had an arrest order if he set one foot out of his embassy. Jessie's attention was glued to what was about to be said.

The head judge gave the girl a stern glare. "We have discussed at length the ambassador's request and must refuse to allow him to address the court. If he wishes to speak to us, he must first submit to questioning about the actions of his people against the World Corps. If he does and gives satisfactory answers, we will, again, consider his request."

"Thank you, sir." The girl was upset by this.

"There is one more thing, young lady. The arrest order still stands. Elijah is not to leave his residence; lest he wants to spend time as a prisoner of war. We have yet to authorize a full strike on the embassy; but if he does not turn himself in before the end of hostilities, we will take action."

The girl gulped, nodded, and then hurried off to return to the embassy, where she would stay until given another permission letter from the court to leave.

Jessie beamed. She didn't have to manipulate anyone for this outcome; her earlier machinations were working perfectly.

Then it came. The gavel banged three times, and the representatives stood up. "This court will now take a vote on the matter of the PSC and Dr. Skye. Administrator Jessie, please rise and stand before this court."

Dressed to the nines and with a big smile on her face, she got up and stood in the center of the room, where she would accept the vote. By the eager looks on their faces, it was going to be a good outcome. Yet, there was a rather long pause after she stood, while everyone stared at her and the blank holoimage screens floating above her head.

The head judge leaned over. "Jessie, we need Dr. Skye to be present."

"What? But he is on the *Sanger*, which is currently not even in the solar system." The representatives spoke amongst themselves. Jessie heard several state it seemed wrong to hand military control over to a man and vessel which weren't even close enough to do anything. "But he is on his way; I am sure. He can be here in a matter of hours."

"Jessie," the head judge said, "for something this important, we must insist Dr. Skye be present, even if only in holoform. Can you not get him on the imagers?"

"I am sorry, but for unknown reasons, he is not answering my signal today. I sent several signals, and my communications operator assure me they were received. So, I know he is coming. But at this time, he cannot be present. However, I can stand for him."

"No, I am afraid you cannot. Handing over an entire branch of the government to a person requires that person's presence. We cannot give the codes to anyone else. The vote will have to be delayed."

"Delayed?" Jessie's worst fears were coming true. "But, sir. I can stand for him. Dr. Skye has signed the proxy order himself on my behalf. I can accept in his name. Please take the vote while all the representatives are here. Must I remind you, this war is only getting worse?"

"Now, Jessie, you know proxy orders do not allow for such situations."

"But . . . " Just then, her communication node activated, and she looked at it. "Uh, your honor, I have an important message; it might be from Dr. Skye. Excuse me." She hurried to the side and activated the small, handheld holoimager. The head judge was obviously annoyed; communication devices were prohibited inside the court. A small holoimage screen popped up from her com. It was her assistant in her office.

"Ms. Jessie, we have a strange reading coming in from Darwin Station."

"Why are you bothering me about this right now?"

"But it is about the *Sanger*."

"What about it?" Jessie asked.

"Darwin Station is reporting two starship signatures entering Terran system; one of them is the *Sanger*. The other is a ship heading directly for Earth, and it is moving fast. The scientists on the station believe the *Sanger* is in pursuit of the smaller vessel, but attempts to contact the *Sanger* have all been unsuccessful as of yet."

Jessie's skin broke out in a sweat, and a knot formed in her gut. "Tell those scientists to get in touch with *Sanger* by any means possible. Also, does the station have any weapon systems?"

The person on the other side checked the computer. "Darwin Station has only a supply of rockets designed to deflect space debris and asteroids, but they aren't fast enough to stop a starship."

"Then I'll have to use the military. Get me in touch with Dr. Skye. I don't care how you do it. Don't contact me again, unless it is of dire importance." She flicked off the com device.

"Is there a problem, Administrator Jessie?" The head judge noticed the device being shut off.

She turned around with that affected diplomatic smile. "Good news, the *Sanger* just entered our solar system. It should be here soon."

"Good, then the vote will be delayed only a short time. Session will adjourn. Do not go far. You will be called back as soon as Dr. Skye arrives." The head judge banged his gavel and dismissed the people.

Jessie nearly ran out to get back to her office.

CHAPTER THIRTY-ONE

J'KLA STOOD IN THE DOORWAY overlooking the main bay of this large ship. The bay was packed with hundreds of his own people. They were huddled together and as afraid as he had ever seen them. A pain grew in his belly, while he watched this scene and knew they couldn't help but be scared.

Is this what God wants for my kind? To hurt them, to kill them, to make them homeless? he thought to himself. His faith quivered, and he wanted desperately to know why God would allow such strife for them now. They had only just come to understand the grace of God, and now they were on the verge of death. He couldn't get the image of the chief out of his mind, standing there amidst the flames. In his mind, he could see her swallowed by the broken earth and suffering until death. Why?

One more time, he looked around the room at the people who had survived the catastrophe. They were going to look up to him now. The chief told him to take care of them and lead them. They trusted him and would continue to do so, even after all of this. How could he lead? Not only had he lost his home and his friends, but also now he must take a role he never sought before. "Why God? Please answer me."

At that moment, he saw the image in his mind from the story of Daniel. The three men standing in the furnace doomed to die, but instead were joined by a fourth, Who kept them alive. He whispered, "If I live, I live for God; if I die, then I will be with God." He knew those who stayed behind were now with God, which couldn't be a better place. And if they survived this, he would lead his people with the wisdom of the Scriptures to guide him.

"What were you saying?" Anna surprised him.

J'kla smiled. "Talk to God."

"Good, we need any amount of prayer."

"Are we there?" he asked.

"Not yet. We should be arriving soon. I want to show you something before we land."

"What?"

"Something you need to see." Taking his hand, she led him toward the laboratory. They had to take large steps over the people, who had sat down in the open spaces in the hallways.

They walked into the laboratory and found it was filled with people as well. Some of them were giving the aged skeletons bewildered looks, while others were merely sitting on the floor.

"Come over here." Anna took out a data storage device to collect the information for them. She turned on the monitor and displayed the test results and pictorial evidence of the experimentation.

"That look like B'reann." J'kla saw the pictures of some of the half-species they had attempted before perfecting the final species.

"Sort of. Just read this, and I will explain what you do not understand."

J'kla and Anna stood there for a while as he slowly made his way through the advanced science documents. He had many questions, but fortunately, Anna was a scientist. It didn't take long for him to begin to understand what she wanted him to know. All the while, she was making a full copy of the data to the small storage device.

In time, he finally got the full picture and was dumbfounded. He stepped back and had to brace himself by holding the table in the middle of the room. "B'reann not real people?"

"You *are* real. You are human. Just a different form created by advanced science."

"Why? Why they make us?"

Anna knew he would ask this. The documentation wasn't clear on their real objectives. It didn't have to be; the scientist doing this were aware of the theological reasons behind their work. She also knew it would take a long time for her to explain to him in full detail. Time they didn't have right now. "J'kla. My people explain away God by saying we were not created, but just evolved."

"Evolved?"

"Uh . . . it's hard to explain. They believe that a long time ago, things who looked like us slowly became us."

"I no understand."

She took his arm and smiled. "You don't have to. Just know that people who hated God and His Word tried to use science to get rid of Him. They created your people as a way of fooling other humans into believing their lies."

"Why? We no matter to them?"

"Not as real people. They wanted animals, beasts, feral creatures. That is why they tortured your people and made them go insane. They wanted them to act like beasts that would paint the picture they had been trying to create for centuries."

"We not their tools. We people. I will show them." J'kla didn't fully understand everything; but he knew his people were being used, and he had a duty to make the truth clear.

Anna was going to tell him more, but the ship shook hard, and the hull groaned loudly. The voice of Z boomed over the intercom, which made the B'reann cover their ears. "ANNA, WE'RE BACK IN NORMAL SPACE. WE ARE HEADING FOR EARTH, AND THE *SANGER* IS ON OUR TAIL. TELL YOUR FRIENDS TO HOLD ON. THIS IS GOING TO BE A BUMPY RIDE. WHEN YOU ARE THROUGH WITH THAT, GET UP HERE. I'M GONNA NEED YOU."

J'kla wiggled his ears and yawned to pop them. "Z loud. Where is he?" J'kla expected to find Z standing near them, apparently yelling at them.

Anna laughed. "He's on the bridge. We are about to land, and it'll not be smooth. Tell your people to brace themselves for a rough ride."

"What mean brace?"

"Hold on to something and keep yourself safe."

"I tell them." J'kla hurried off to do his first duty as the leader of his people.

Anna stumbled over the people as she headed for the bridge to watch their descent. She didn't show it, but she was scared to death they were going to crash and kill half or more of the people on this ship.

*   *   *

Jessie sat in her secret office and trilled her fingers across the desk, waiting for the open communication channel to be accepted on the other end. She had never been angrier at Dr. Skye. He had the most brilliant people working for him on the most advanced ship ever constructed, and he could not seem to make a call. She was aware it was probably not his fault, and he was likely doing everything he could to remedy the situation; but that didn't ease her annoyance in the least. She had stared at this screen off and on for days now wishing to see Dr. Skye on the other end. They were so close to the fulfillment of their plans, this was anything but amusing.

To her great relief, the signal suddenly changed from a black screen to a snowy. The signal connected, and there was only one source which could open this channel. Then she saw Dr. Skye sitting on the bridge of the *Sanger*.

"Richard! Oh, thank goodness! What is going on?"

Richard stood up and came toward the screen. "Too much to explain. They have the ship."

"The ship? What ship?" She then answered her own question. "Oh, no! They didn't find the old terraforming ship?"

"Yes, they did. And somehow that robot got it active and is flying it back to Earth."

"STOP THEM!"

"What do you think I've been trying to do? They planted a virus on the *Sanger* and put us out of commission for a while. It bought them time to escape. And, Jessie, it's worse than you think. They have hundreds of the primitives with them. I don't know what they know exactly, but I do know they are aware of our plans. Everything that matters, and they have the primitives to prove it."

Jessie was numb. This couldn't be happening. She had worked too hard to let this fall apart. "Use the *Sanger*'s main weapon; blast them to pieces. I don't want them setting foot on Earth."

Dr. Skye answered, "We can't get close enough. Right now, our target lock is not working all that well, and we would need to get much closer. I ordered Darwin Station to stop them, if possible. That is our last line of defense against them getting to Earth."

Jessie rubbed her temples and thought about this. "Fine. Just get back here. If we can get that stupid court to vote quickly, none of this will make much of a difference."

"Even if they do hand over power to us, if the people find out, they will not trust us at all. I don't want the first story of this new world order to be a civil war."

"Don't worry." Jessie finally smiled again, which meant the devious wheels had turned in her mind. "Just get back here. I'm going to go to that court and make sure they vote quickly. I'm also going to make sure no one learns anything about that ship or its occupants."

"How?"

"Leave that up to me." She turned off the signal and made her preparations. She was going to court today for the last time as just another representative. They would be bowing to her before the day was through. It would take all of her cleverness to make it happen.

★   ★   ★

The beautiful blue orb of Earth grew larger as the *Terra 5* approached. Behind them was an enemy determined to vaporize this ship, and before them was a space station, which was between them and the planet.

"Okay, so what's the plan?" Anna got to her seat next to Z at the helm.

"Well, uh, looks like the plan has changed."

"Changed? You didn't even tell me the plan to begin with," Anna stated.

"Okay, so my original plan was to come in fast and then use the one working thruster to turn us into an orbital path around the planet. We would use that to slow us down and make our descent a little easier. It would still allow us to outrun the *Sanger*."

"But?"

"But Darwin Station is right in our path, and their tractor beams are charged and ready. If we slow down too soon, they'll latch on to us, and this will all be over."

Anna looked out at the enormous space station and saw the green beam emitters were all active and ready to grab them. "Do they have weapons?"

"Nothing that can hit us. That station wasn't built for war, unlike the *Sanger*, apparently."

"So, what's the new plan?"

"We crash," Z said.

"How is that a plan?!"

Z answered, "Well, we won't just be taking a nose dive at the Earth. With that one usable thruster and the anti-grav systems working in harmony, I plan on taking us down with as little destruction as possible."

"Oh, so you mean, we are just going to have a hard landing."

"Sure, if we were landing in an open field or landing site, it could be a basic hard landing. But . . . we aren't."

Anna gave him a frightened and bewildered look. "Where are you taking us down?"

"Rome."

"ROME?!"

"Look, you need to get this information to the counsel as soon as possible. If we land anywhere more distant from the world court than that, the PSC will find us, and this will all be over. Besides, I have a friend down there who might be able to help us."

Elijah sat at his desk and pondered what he might do next. When the world court wouldn't listen to him, he really had no options left. For hours, he prayed for answers to come, for a way to reach the closed minds of those in power. How could he convince the world government they were being deceived?

"Uncle Elijah?" A young woman peeked around the corner of his office.

He put on his smile and looked over at his lovely niece. "Sarah, what is it?"

"Do you need anything? Are you hungry?"

"No, no." He waved a hand at her. "I'm fine."

"You have not eaten in a long time."

"We have limited rations left, and I'm an old man. Give what we do have to the younger ones."

Sarah didn't take that. "No, you're an important man."

Elijah smiled at the situation. "Sarah, do you know much of the story of the man I was named after?"

"Yes, of course. We all learn about the prophets of God."

"Then if God sees fit to provide for this old man, He will send help down from the skies. Perhaps birds will come bearing bread for me. But what we have here, I will let the others take."

Sarah stepped in, the worry apparent in every aspect of her appearance. "Uncle? What will happen now?"

He reached for her hand. "I don't know. Right now, we must trust God. Even in the darkest hours of human history, God has found a way to ignite a light of hope. Remember when Yeshua arrived? Our people were suffering at the hands of a terrible empire and put under the authority of wicked men, who claimed to be our own but served no one but their heathen masters and their own desires. God ignited His light and turned a corner for history. That empire fell, and the wicked men over Israel passed away; yet God's mercy and grace shined through long past them. This is not the end, my child; this is only another page in history. We may perish. We may not see another day. We might even see the fall of our beloved city. But we will never see a time when God has abandoned us. Have faith, not fear." He held tight to her hand. "Trust in God."

"I will."

"Good. Now, go and eat. I will sit here and wait for an answer to my prayers." Before she could ask what he prayed for exactly, his little computer screen lit up with the snowy fuzz of a weak signal.

"Now who could that be?" He reached over and turned it on.

To his surprise, there sat Z in some kind of ship. "Elijah. Is that you?"

"Yes, my robot friend. What has happened? I have heard nothing since we last spoke. Is everything all right?"

"No. It isn't. I'm about to land on Earth with the ship I was telling you about. The *Sanger* is breathing down my neck, and I need your help."

"My help? Oh, my friend, I'm sorry to tell you, but I cannot get even a moment of time with the court." He was used to giving help by applying his skill as a politician.

"I don't need you to make me an appointment. I need something else entirely. Listen . . . " Then Z explained what he had in mind.

CHAPTER THIRTY-TWO

THE WORLD COURT WAS CALLED back into session by the announcement of Dr. Skye's imminent return. The representatives were quietly talking amongst themselves, while the head judge impatiently waited for Jessie to arrive. The General of the Army was also present, as he would have to be the one to turn over the command codes to all the military ships and bases.

Just then, the sharp, signature click of heels signaled the approach of the most formidable representative this court had ever had to deal with. When she arrived, everyone noticed Jessie did not come alone today. On either side of her was one of her bodyguards.

"I am sorry to keep you waiting, but there were a few loose ends to tie up."

The head judge looked at her and then at her guards. "You do not need . . ." Just then, the appointed guards of the court were relieved, and new men took their place. This wasn't entirely unusual; they worked in shifts, but they had changed shifts only an hour ago. "What's going on?"

Jessie walked into the middle of the room. "Nothing to worry about. As future assistant general to the military, I made a few changes to the assignments. Now, are we ready to proceed with the vote?"

"Wait, just a minute!" The general was beside himself. "You haven't got the authority yet, and it won't be yours to assert if and when it is given."

Jessie rolled her eyes and completely ignored his ranting. "The vote?"

The head judge decided to push forward and worry about her strange behavior later. "The delegates are prepared to vote, but we are still waiting for Dr. Skye's presence."

"And you shall have it. May I present . . . " She turned and signaled one of the technical assistants to the court. At once, Dr. Skye appeared sitting in his command seat of the *Sanger.* "Dr. Richard Skye."

Dr. Skye smiled and nodded to the court. "A pleasure to see everyone."

The head judge's demeanor changed entirely. Dr. Skye was a famous person, who always drew a little admiration, even from the most educated and important people. "Dr. Skye, it is an honor." He changed his attitude to be more formal, as was appropriate for the head judge of the entire world. "Dr. Skye, are you completely aware of the proceedings which have taken place here?"

"I have been made aware of every step of this proceeding by my first-in-command, Administrator Jessie. I know what you are about to vote on, and I am ready to accept the role as chief commander of the military."

"Temporary chief commander," the general corrected him.

Dr. Skye applied his infamous charm. "Of course, sir. This will be only to fulfill the current need, which the PSC will be pleased to take part in."

The head judge was about to explain there was a separate vote, which could put Dr. Skye in as permanent commander of the military, in lieu of a presidential election. But at that time, a red light over every door flashed brightly, and a siren could be heard in the distance. The head judge looked at the court reporters. "What is going on? Who activated the evacuation alarms?"

No one answered for a long time; several of the delegates came to their feet ready to flee the building.

A young assistant to the court rushed in. "Sir, the evacuation alarm was just set off."

"We are aware of that. Is there a reason?"

The young man checked his computer tablet to see what information was coming through. "The fire detectors are not going off, and the military is not reporting any movement toward the court by the enemy. It might be a false alarm."

Jessie looked up at Dr. Skye, wanting dearly to ask what he knew, but she was aware this was certainly not the place to ask.

Dr. Skye held back his nervous anger with what he knew was the *Terra 5* approaching. He interrupted this scene. "We are not showing any dangers on our sensors. I am sure it is just a false alarm."

Jessie took the cue and added, "We should get the vote over with, and then we can figure this all out. We are all here. Let's not waste any more time. This is nothing; I am sure."

The head judge considered all the options and then looked at the young assistant. "Go and make sure everything is okay. We will continue in here unless you bring us reason to end this session."

"What do I tell the people out there?" The assistant pointed out the door. "They are already starting to evacuate the square."

"Let them leave for now. It will be much harder stopping them." The head judge waved at the boy. "Now, go." The young man rushed off to his duty. "Okay, I think we should take this vote before there are any further interruptions." He stood up, which made all the delegates stand as well. "All right, this court will now cast a vote on the matter of temporarily transferring command authorization and all the codes, to which give that authority to Dr. Richard Skye of the Planetary Science Commission. All present, make your vote known in accordance with the wishes of the people who elected you to your office."

As was procedure, each person would reach down, cast his or her vote, and take their seat to signal they had voted. No lights came on, for it was considered a private matter until the vote was tallied and the results came through. One by one, the representatives of the nation states cast their vote and sat down. Most voted out of fear of losing power, not for what was the right choice. Jessie had played all of her cards very well and spun the facts so hard that few truths were known. In a short time, the court would finish a vote she had worked for decades in preparing.

The head judge watched the last woman cast her vote and then sit. He looked down to see the results that came through instantly. "I see the numbers show an overwhelming choice in one direction. My vote to break a tie is not needed and, therefore, I sit without a vote." He sat down and then banged his gavel. "It is the decision of this court, by vote of the representatives of the people, that military command is handed to Dr. Skye. All command codes and authority will be passed on to him until such a time as the Jerusalem threat is no longer present and the war with our enemies is concluded. So, it has been decided, and so it shall be." He banged his gavel twice, and the room erupted in applause.

Dr. Skye could not contain the serpentine smile across his face. The general begrudgingly picked up a large, briefcase-shaped item and opened it up. It was a very sophisticated computer, impervious to any hacker or virus. It contained the command codes for the military; from this computer, a person could control any ship, any base, any part of the world military. The general put in his personal code to unlock it, so it could be turned over to Dr. Skye.

Jessie began to walk over, so she could accept this on behalf of Dr. Skye. The fruition of her master plans was nearly in her hands, when the court assistant came running through the court screaming at the top of his lungs. "GET OUT! RUN! THEY'RE GONNA CRASH!"

Just then, a low roar of a ship coming in resounded throughout Rome and the former Vatican. It sounded just like any landing port, where a ship would be coming in; but that sound got louder and louder, and the screech of breaking thrusters became apparent.

At once, the crushing sounds of a ship smashing through buildings and slamming into the ground rocked the room. The power flickered, and the windows on one side of the building burst inward. The room rattled and shook. Jessie had to take the arm of one of her men to keep from falling over.

★   ★   ★

MOMENTS BEFORE

"Keep an eye on those thrusters!" Z held tight to the navigation controls as the ship plummeted through the upper atmosphere and headed for land.

The clouds and sky were passing by them, while the ground approached quickly. When they began to spiral in one direction or another, the old breaking thrusters would activate and steady them. Normally, these thrusters would work automatically, but this old ship wasn't up to the task any longer, and Anna was forced to think like the navigation computer.

"We're almost out of thruster fuel on the port side, and the starboard side is on the verge of blowing off of the ship!"

Z smiled like a mad man. "Just makes the ride that much more fun."

"FUN?"

"I can choose to be scared or excited; the latter is much more entertaining."

Anna scoffed and then quickly activated the thrusters to stop a rightward spiral. "While you're having fun, are you prepared to land this hulk?"

"Sure, we'll make contact with the ground in just a few minutes. I hope they cleared St. Peter's Square, or a lot of people are going to get bruised."

"Bruised? I think bruising is going to be the least of their worries. Oh no, right thrusters are . . . " Just then, the first two thrusters on the right side blew apart, and the ship rocked hard. The remaining thrusters strained to keep them from losing what little control they had left.

"The *Sanger* just entered the atmosphere. They're on our tail. But at least we have the advantage of speed." Of course, they were coming in at an angle and speed which no ship should attempt, especially one as big and bulky as the *Sanger*.

"Let's just hope they don't open fire," Anna said.

"They won't shoot at us," Z answered rather coolly.

"What makes you so sure?"

Z pushed the engines to go even faster. "Because if they do, they will hit the ground as well, which will mean obliterating Rome. I don't think that would do them much good." He looked ahead and saw the streets and recognizable buildings of Rome coming into view. "Wow, nice day to land in Rome. Sunny skies, balmy breezes, and twenty-five degrees Celsius."

"We don't need a weather report!" Anna was getting tired of his quips right now; they were about to crash land in the ancient city, and she was so worried, it hurt. His jokes weren't helping.

"We're almost there. Tell your friends to hold tight. This is going to get bumpy."

"I'm not leaving the thrusters. You need my help."

Z looked over at her. "Anna, go back and hold that husband of yours. Keep yourself safe. I can take the controls."

Anna would argue, but there wasn't time. She took the opportunity, but not before she kissed Z on the cheek. "Whatever happens, you are the best Z-bot a girl could ever have."

"Gee, thanks. Now go!" He stood up and stretched his arms over both control panels to man them.

Anna hurried to the back and found J'kla holding hands with the people and praying. She got down and squeezed into the middle of the group and took their hands as well. People all around her were holding onto things, gripping the walls, packing themselves into tight places. Anything to be as secure as possible. Z watched the city close in. Hover cars zoomed to get out of his way. Large antenna towers were toppled by the low-flying ship. People ran screaming to get away. He used the breaking thrusters to level their descent and activated the anti-grav system to lower the ship's total mass for a brief time. Everyone inside was going to get really lightheaded for a moment, but it might save their lives.

Rocking and shaking, the ship hurtled toward the ancient Vatican City. Z sighed in relief when he saw the square was empty, and so were several city blocks around it. The normally bustling crowds were not there. Somehow, Elijah had warned the people to get away.

Cringing, Z held on when the ship made contact with the first building. Its right wing crashed through an old stone edifice that was an apartment building. Then the left wing clipped the roofs off of five similarly built homes that had been turned into shops and restaurants. With a great impact, the belly of the *Terra 5* made contact with the road for a moment and then bounced up slightly. Its lower gravity and the thrusters kept it marginally aloft, but not enough to stop meeting hill after hill. More buildings were destroyed; cars were smashed; and the road was broken and crushed beyond use.

Finally, the ship made full contact with the road and was now skidding across the ground doing considerable damage to the historic city. Z threw all of the engine power into the thrusters to slow their approach; just about the only other power system not being used by the engines was the anti-grav charger keeping everyone from being thrown around.

With a screeching halt, the ship came to a stop right in the center of the square. It had crushed the obelisk in the center of the square, but it had not crashed into the World Court. A trail of smoke, fires, and massive destruction was left by the ship. More than one alarm system was blaring in a building or one of the partly intact hovercars. History was made and destroyed today. The first spaceship had landed in St. Peter's Square, but most of the square was gone forever.

*   *   *

"Breaking news." The media broke into all channels now to report. "A ship has just crash landed in the middle of Vatican City. Early reports are showing considerable damage to the buildings and other structures in a path leading from the Vatican through part of Rome's oldest sectors."

The image changed to show a dizzying view of the massive destruction left in the wake of the hard landing. The large ship rested in the center of the square while columns of smoke billowed out of parts of it.

"This is incredible. I can't believe what we are seeing. Ladies and gentlemen, I cannot completely confirm this, but my producer believes that ship is one of the old Terra ships from two centuries ago. Wait . . . We are going in for a closer look."

The image grew in size as the news drone flew closer. It enhanced the image to display the writing on the side of the ship, which clearly spelled out, "*Terraformer 5*, space operations, Earth."

The reporter lost her professionalism for a moment when she realized what they were truly looking at. "Oh my, the *Terra 5*." It was like someone had just discovered Atlantis or located Amelia Earhart's plane. "Sorry about the pause. Ladies and gentlemen, we cannot confirm the validity of this, but it appears that the ship that just landed in the middle of the Vatican is the lost last ship of the Terraformers launched two hundred years ago. Wait, something is happening . . . It appears someone is exiting the ship . . . no, two . . . three. Several . . . oh my word . . ." There went the professionalism again.

The back hatch of the *Terra 5* opened, and the B'reann escaped the smoke-filled ship. Dozens stepped out coughing. Some were limping, while others fell down and appeared to be in pain. The majority of them were rattled, but all right. More and more came out.

"I . . . I don't know what to say about this. Many of the primitives from New Eden are stepping out of this old ship. I . . . they . . . they seem to be injured, but . . . wait, the military are coming to help . . . No, they are surrounding the ship. They have weapons drawn. I really don't have any idea what is happening right now. Please excuse me. I will let the images speak for themselves. I will return when I have actual information."

The sound on the media channels stopped, but video feed continued without pause. The injured and frightened B'reann were still coming out of the ship, while the military remained a solid line around them with their weapons out. Not one soldier stopped to help the poor people who were no threat to them.

CHAPTER THIRTY-THREE

ANNA OPENED HER EYES TO find she was held tightly by J'kla. He had protected her during the whole crash, shielding her with his own body. The people in the room gathered themselves and checked to make sure everything was still in one piece.

"J'kla, are you all right?"

"I all right. You?"

"I'm fine. A little shaken up, but fine."

A young woman came out of a hallway, stumbling over people still packed in, and said something to J'kla. He groaned in sadness and then pointed out the door and gave his orders for them.

"What is it? What happened?" Anna asked.

"Three dead; two hurt bad." He spoke in his own tongue to his people. "We will deal with the injured and dead. There are too many people in here to get to those who need help."

"Oh, my word, Z!" Anna looked around for her robot, making her way through the crowds. She spotted him on the floor, not moving. "Z! Z! Are you all right? Speak to me!"

He opened his eyes and then smiled. "Wow, what a ride. Let's do it again."

Hearing him crack a joke at a time like this made her want to punch him so hard, he would reboot. "You jerk. Don't scare me like that. Get up; we need to help them. Do you still have your medical arm?"

Z dragged himself up to the chair by his arms. "Sure, I have my medical arm on, but I can't help anyone right now. My computer connection to the waist and legs is busted. I can't move very far."

J'kla came into the cockpit looking for his wife and friend. "Is Z good?"

"I survived the crash, if that counts," Z answered. "I'm no good right now; just get everyone out of here and tell the court what you know before Skye gets here. Send a repair crew to fetch me when you get the chance."

J'kla wasn't going to let Z stay behind. "No, Z come with us." He took up the robot by the arms and tried to help him to his feet. But Z weighed a lot more than your average person, and all J'kla did was get the robot about three inches off the seat, and then he just about hit the floor. "Wow, Z need lose weight."

"Sure, I'll go on a low titanium diet as soon as I get new legs."

"J'KLA!" J'nar, his father, came running into the cockpit. He said something, and J'kla became very worried.

"Anna, we go outside."

"What is going on?"

"Your people, they aim weapons at us, won't let us go."

"Oh no!" She took his hand and ran with him and his father out of the ship.

Hundreds of B'reann were now waiting outside the *Terra 5*. Many were injured and in need of help, but all they could see was a line of soldiers aiming weapons at them.

Anna looked around for the man in charge, the soldier with the most decoration. These were all low-ranked grunts; hardly any of them were older than twenty, which was extremely odd. Why were so many youths working as the main security around the headquarters for the World Corps?

"Hello, my name is Anna. I would like to speak to someone in charge."

There was a moment of silence, and then finally a slightly older boy stepped up. He had two stars on his collar, indicating he had served a year longer than the rest. "We were ordered not to converse with anyone from this ship without authorization from Dr. Skye or Administrator Jessie."

"Wait, why do you report to Skye or Jessie? I want to speak to your commanding officer now!"

"My commanding officer is Dr. Skye."

"Fine. Tell him and this government I bring proof Dr. Skye and the PSC has worked hard to deceive the world. I also have proof Dr. Skye is a murderer, who has committed genocide. Tell the World Corps I want to speak to them NOW!" Anna wasn't going to show any weakness right now. She had come through too much to be stopped by some kids with guns.

The young man stepped back and pointed his weapon at her head. "Sorry, but my orders were clear. I am to eliminate you and all the primitives." He shifted his aim to point at J'kla first.

Suddenly, J'nar growled, roared, and then lunged at the young man to save his son from death. The soldier fired but missed his target; he hit J'nar right in the shoulder and sent the father across the ground. The B'reanns all gasped, screamed, yelled, and growled. They did not launch a counter attack. They simply huddled in fear as they had so often these past two days.

Without an ounce of remorse, the young man prepared to fire again. This time, he would take out J'kla without opposition.

"Wait!" The clear, crisp voice of Jessie broke through the square's intercom. "Stand down your weapons. Maintain the perimeter, and do not advance until I tell you. Bring me the human and the representative of the primitives. I wish to see them in the court."

The soldier lowered his gun and activated his com unit. "Order clearance?"

"Clearance alpha one gamma one. Do not ask for clearance again unless you want to be busted down to cadet! Bring me the primitive and the human NOW!" The young man pointed at two of his soldiers, and they escorted the pair into the world court.

*   *   *

The young commander of this unit watched his men walking with the pair into the world court. Then he snapped his fingers, and everyone returned to their aim. No one was going to fire yet, but they were ordered to surround these people, and that order had not been changed yet.

Nick could not fully understand what he was looking at. Like everyone else on Earth, he believed these creatures were nothing more than half-evolved primitive beasts. Yet before his eyes were a group of clothed people speaking to one another and helping each other in their time of need. It didn't make sense.

"FRAY! FRAY!" A woman was yelling, while she held her husband.

The young commander Nick looked down and saw the man he had shot a short time ago. He was bleeding badly, and a woman tried to care for him; but she was panicking now. She had torn a piece of her own garment to bind his wound, but the bleeding was soaking it and leaking out. He was not going to make it if he didn't get medical help.

If only to get some answers for his questions, Nick lowered his gun and slowly approached the primitives. The B'reann around him moved away slowly at the sight of his weapon. Some snarled; others were inconsolably crying. The woman kneeling next to J'nar saw the shadow loom over her, and she lurched at the sight of the human who had hurt the man she loved. In a sorry attempt, she snarled through her tears.

Nick lifted his hands. "I won't hurt you."

Rillan managed to say, *"Gho nagtha millun."*

It shocked Nick to hear her speak in what seemed to be some sort of sentence. This was an act he had presumed impossible.

God moved Nick's heart to feel compassion in a way opposite the training ingrained into him by his breeding program. He looked over and saw the team of Z-500s working on fire patrol to keep the flames the ship had caused under control. "See if they have a medic!" he ordered the nearest man to him.

The younger soldier was confused. This was not part of their orders. It took him a moment to follow, but he did. After a moment, he returned with an older robot drone built with both arms being medical devices.

"How can I be of service, sir?" the robot asked.

Nick stood back and pointed down. "See if you can help him."

The Z-300 unit was shocked to see the primitive but followed his commands without fail. He knelt down and scanned the bleeding arm. "I see. You received a rather deep wound here. The projectile penetrated the brachial artery. Good thing I am here. You wouldn't last long. Please hold still."

J'nar tried to move out of fear when this robot took off a finger to reveal an injector device filled with a medicine. The pain from moving made him yelp.

"I asked you not to move; it is for your own good."

Nick responded, "I do not believe they can understand us. Just go slow and help him."

The Z unit proceeded to do his work with the precision of a Z-300, and J'nar would be on the mend soon enough.

"Fray noki chi?" A woman came over, her nearly dead child limply hanging from her arms.

Behind her were several others hoping for care. Nick stepped back and felt something odd in his heart—mercy. In time, he told several more of his soldiers to find other medical robots who could come and help. If Jessie saw this, she might become very angry with them, but something told him this was right. Something told him these people weren't his enemy.

✷   ✷   ✷

Jessie stood in the middle of the room while the representatives gathered themselves. Many had rushed to the open windows to see the amazing destruction. The power had just come back on, and the holoimager reactivated. Several of the representatives were on their com units talking with their own offices as the reports came in from the news services.

"Can we continue with the transfer of power, please?" Jessie muttered.

The head judge was surprised at her callousness. "Jessie, I don't think this is the time. We have a crisis on our hands. We need to find out what is going on out there."

"Don't stop now. This is obviously a ploy by Jerusalem to stop this action. They know the transfer of power to the PSC will mean an end to their war. Don't play into their hand. Give me the codes first; then you can go out there and find out what's going on."

"I see you're up to your old tricks." Out of nowhere came Elijah and his personal bodyguard.

"ELIJAH! WHAT ARE YOU DOING HERE? ARREST HIM!" Jessie's rage burst out at the sight of this old Jew.

A soldier went to apprehend Elijah, but Elijah's personal guard took down the soldier with three simple moves, not once taking out her weapon. Elijah didn't flinch and did not take his eyes off of Jessie. "Now, you wouldn't be foolish enough to think I would come here without my security. I would like you to meet Beth, a member of the Mossad and my personal guard."

The head judge banged his gavel and then pointed it at Elijah. "I don't care what kind of security you have; the arrest warrant is still in effect. This bench will not allow you to interrupt this court merely because you want to stop this transition of power."

"Nice way to put a coup—*transition*," Elijah calmly answered.

"If you mean to try and overthrow this . . . "

"No, your honor, that is not what I meant. I meant you should be wise about whom you give power to." He looked at Jessie. "It took me some time to figure it all out, but now it makes sense. You have always wanted more power, more control. Attacking Jerusalem was just a means to accomplish these goals. But it ran deeper than that. You and the PSC have spent generations preparing this world to follow you blindly into a future of your design. You breed the people; you control their education; you control their media; and you control their faith. Nice little package. But it wasn't enough."

"I think we have heard about enough. Judge, are you going to allow this fool to keep blabbering?" Jessie folded her arms and stared at Elijah.

The head judge answered, "No. I think we have had enough. Guards! Apprehend those two; and if they resist, you have the authority to use force."

Beth prepared to fight to the end for Elijah, but he stopped her. "I do not come here with vague accusations and theories. I come with proof." He could see two people coming down another corridor, and a smile came across his face. "And here it is now."

"WHAT IS THIS?!" Jessie literally screamed as she saw both Anna and J'kla walking in with two of her most loyal, best bred, and best trained soldiers at their sides.

The two young men gulped and appeared as though they were about to wet themselves when she bellowed. One of the child soldiers mustered the courage to answer her. "Uh, you ordered us to bring them in."

"I did no such thing. What is going on here?"

"Actually, I did," Elijah interrupted, taking great pleasure in seeing that look of disbelief on Jessie's face. "I used the same system to fake your voice as I did to set off the evacuation alarm." He smiled at the head judge. "You really ought to update your computers in the main city. They were way too easy to hack. Though, digging up Jessie's personal command code was a bit harder than anticipated."

"WHY, YOU! SOLDIERS, KILL HIM!"

The head judge banged his gavel many times, which made most of the delegates take their seats and the guards to step back. He was angry, and no one should aspire to anger the head judge of the world court. "Jessie! You do not give kill orders in this courtroom!"

"Fine. I apologize, your honor. But I am a little beside myself at seeing this enemy bring in some trumped-up accusations and a primitive who is obviously unbound and poses a serious risk to this courtroom. I would think we should get some chains, stun him, or something. You saw what they are capable of."

"You lay one dirty finger on J'kla, and I will rip that fake hair right off of your head!" Anna marched up to Jessie.

"Oh, so your pet has a name. Did you teach him to fetch and chase his tail?"

"How dare you!"

"Ladies, stop right there." The head judge had heard enough.

Jessie pushed further. "Your honor, we need to remove that primitive before he poses a threat."

"He poses no threat, and he isn't primitive." Anna wasn't finished talking.

"Guards, seize them all, including Elijah, and remove them from this courtroom," Jessie ordered.

The head judge scoffed at her. "Jessie, you do not have the authority to give orders in my courtroom."

J'kla finally said something. "May I talk?"

Jessie turned with a shot, her eyes bugging out. The delegates gasped, their mouths open, and went silent. The head judge was so surprised, he sat down. No one in the room—outside of Anna—expected this primitive to say anything at all, especially in English.

Finally, the head judge answered, "You may speak, young man. What is your name?"

"My name J'kla. My people are the B'reann. I sorry to speak bad, but I learn your words only few weeks. I read all words but not know all yet."

"This is a trick, a ploy by the Jews. Your honor, we . . . "

A gavel bang cracked through the room and was followed by a stern voice. "SILENCE! Step aside, Jessie. The court recognizes . . . J'kla of the B'reann."

Jessie was so angry, she could barely see straight. One of those cats was now being allowed to stand where she had been standing. She was forced to step back and wait her turn, while a primitive addressed the court. Across the room, the man holding the codes had closed the computer and was awaiting further orders. A darkness seeped around her vision, and hatred filled what little kindness was left in her heart.

J'kla stepped up and gulped at all the eyes staring at him. His tail hugged his legs, and he had a hard time speaking at first. "Thank you, master chief. B'reann live on world made by your people. My people also made by your people. We not know where we come from, but we learn. Anna of Earth come and become friend of J'kla and B'reann. She teach J'kla to speak her tongue and read her words. Anna bring J'kla to meet her chief on large ship in stars. Nice-looking man try to kill J'kla and Anna. He poisoned minds of B'reann, give my kin insanity illness that kill. He give me same illness, but I not die."

"I am a little confused," the head judge admitted. "Did someone poison you?"

Anna stepped up next to J'kla and took his quivering hand. "Sir, may I also speak?"

"Are you Anna?"

"Yes, sir."

"You may speak to help explain him."

She smiled at J'kla, who looked terrifically relieved to have her there with him. "It was Dr. Skye who poisoned them. I am Anna of the PSC. I was the geologist who they claimed had been killed by these so-called primitives. They lied to you—about many things. When they learned I had made contact with his people and had proof they weren't the unevolved primitives they claimed, Dr. Skye filled J'kla with drugs that made him go crazy and then left him to kill me in a mad rage. This was the same serum used to fabricate the primitive beasts you were shown."

"If he was supposed to kill you, how did you survive? How did either of you survive?" Ken of Australia asked.

J'kla smiled and held Anna's hand, while looking into her eyes. "Love. Bad man not know J'kla love Anna."

"How did you survive then? You said this stuff killed your people?"

J'kla answered, "Yes, it kill many B'reann. We not know why they go insane and die. I almost die, but I learn from Bible about God and Jesus. He healed me, so I come to speak to you. Tell you truth."

That brought a lot of gasps from around the room.

Jessie looked up slowly; a cold feeling sunk in her stomach, and her left eye twitched ever so slightly. This thing the PSC created believed in that infuriating fable. She wanted to wring his neck right there. A burning rage boiled in her blood and nearly destroyed her composure. It was then she decided what she would do next.

The head judge responded to J'kla's statements. "This is all fascinating, but what does it have to do with the current situation?"

Anna answered, "My friend, Z—I mean the Z-550 who worked with me—searched for an answer to what was going on with these people and why Dr. Skye would act so strange. We discovered the ship out there, the old *Terra 5* that has been missing for two hundred years. Inside, we found something hard to believe, but the evidence is undeniable. The moon of New Eden was created by terraforming over two hundred years ago. It was the first and only successful terraforming project ever conducted. After its success, the PSC quietly silenced its existence and hid it for these two centuries."

"What about the Bree . . . uh . . . his people," the woman from Greece asked.

"They were created, too." Anna waited as the wave of shock flowed through the room. Once it died down, she explained. "About the same time as New Eden was created, geneticists worked to craft a new species of beings like humans. Their goal was to create a half-evolved *thing* to prove evolution. They failed many times to create such a creature. In the end, it was impossible, so they cheated. They used breeding and cloning technology to create prime babies and modified a full generation of those babies to appear like these B'reann. They wanted to simulate evolution from a feline base instead of a primate base. They even modified the brain to be as primitive as possible. The goal was to "discover" them at some point and use the discovery to enforce the theory of evolution. In their plan, this enforcement would cause all humanity to bow to the sciences and abandon faith in anything else. They were brilliant, but they made one tiny mistake. Their primitives weren't primitive at all. They grew up into another people, just like any other people group here on Earth. They might be distantly behind us in technology, but they are much more advanced than what was expected."

The head judge answered this dialog with what many of the skeptical delegates were thinking. "That is a fascinating story, young lady, but where is the proof?"

Anna held up a computer chip. "I have here a full recording of all the data gathered inside the computers of the *Terra 5*. It contains all the information you will need to learn the sordid details of this experiment." She continued without allowing them to question this. "But I am aware you will not trust this as any data can be fabricated. There is one more thing. I'm pregnant."

"What does that have to do with this?"

She took up J'kla's hand and held it firmly before them to show their union. "J'kla and I are married, and he is the father of this child. By all the science of evolution they have explained to you about these primitives, genetically it would be impossible to procreate across the species barriers. But since he is just a human with a modified appearance, there is no species barrier between us."

The courtroom was filled with people standing to look down at the couple; many of them were asking each other about what she had said regarding the species barrier.

"Assistant, find me a medical robot, now!" the head judge called out. He would confirm her claim right there.

Just then, a slow clapping sounded from the side of the room. Jessie stepped up as she sarcastically applauded all of this. "Good, very good. You really blew down my house of cards."

The head judge pointed his gavel at her. "Listen, Jessie, if their claims prove to be true, you and Dr. Skye are both in serious trouble."

"Oh, they are true. In fact, I will confirm all she said is true. The moon is fake. The people are fake. Heck, I'll even admit that we tried to have her killed, more than once. But it doesn't matter. I may have lost this little argument, but I NEVER lose the war."

The looks on the delegate's faces were mixed with utter disbelief and outright anger.

"Jessie, this is . . . I don't know what to say. You have fooled the entire world. Why?" The head judge couldn't seem to wrap his mind around this. He considered Jessie a good friend, and now he discovered she had lied to him as much as she had lied to everyone else.

Anna answered. "Power and control. They already controlled a lot of our society and the government, but they didn't have it all. With this, they wanted to control the world."

Jessie feigned dismay. "Oh, how you injure me. You make me sound like a monster. And I guess I really am a monster. The truth of it all is we know society would run better with the sciences in control of everything. After all, science is knowledge, and what better thing to have ruling everyone but intelligence. Our plans were always for the betterment of mankind. If that meant overthrowing poorly run governments, taking away the right to choose, and directing everyone to listen to a very few voices, then so be it. Those few, those well-bred and smart, would be perfect rulers. They would rely on the intelligence of science and reason to govern all. It may seem like we were just fighting to grab power, but it wasn't without righteous causes."

J'kla spoke now, as he understood what she was saying and how it wasn't right. "God say ends do not justify means."

Jessie rolled her eyes. "And there you have the voice of blind faith versus logical reason. The ends will justify the means. The next generations of mankind will live in the utopia bought by the blood and work of this generation. They want leadership by vote, but that only enables fools to lead fools. By setting up a specially designed class of intelligent men and women to rule over all, without a vote, society will run better."

"How do you believe this?" Anna asked. "You're forcing your own ideas on the world."

"Sometimes you have to force someone to do something until they realize it is the right choice to make. The smart leading the stupid is exactly what we are trying to execute here. Once the stupid members of this world's population are led toward the right directions, we will have what society needs; and they will eventually not know how they ever lived without it."

The head judge was through listening to Jessie. He banged his gavel and then addressed this as he would any court situation. "I have heard enough. This discussion is over. Jessie, you're under arrest for treason and attempted murder. Guards, put her under arrest."

No one moved. None of the guards budged. Jessie looked around with a comical fear in her eyes. "Oh, dear me, are these handsome, young men going to arrest poor little me? No? Aw shucks. But then again, I don't have time for playing right now."

"GUARDS, DO YOUR DUTY!" the commander general bellowed, furious at the apparent lack of respect his own soldiers were displaying.

Jessie smiled, while biting her lower lip. "Aww, are they not listening to you? Sorry, but they don't listen to anyone but me and Dr. Skye. You see,

I've been working on a special crop of children for a lot of years out of the Siberian schoolhouses."

"There aren't any schoolhouses in Siberia," the representative from Russia stated.

"Sure, there are. In fact, there are five very large school houses. But they are hidden. Only those in the need to know, know of them. You see, I needed some insurance against failure. These handsome, young men are the product of a very specialized education system. I have many more scattered throughout your precious military. They are very special and have but one unique program instilled into their well-bred brains." She held up her com device. "Jessie to all insurgent units. Destruct authorization, Jessie alpha one gamma one." Switching off the device, she simply waited with a smile on her face.

Outside, there was a rumbling boom like a massive roll of thunder had come from a storm. But there weren't any thunderstorms scheduled for today near Rome. Then came another, and another.

"WHAT IS GOING ON?!" the head judge yelled at Jessie.

The general answered as he got a message right away. "Almost all of the warships just exploded. I'm getting reports from all over the planet; there's only one ship left. The *Vatican 1* is still protecting this airspace."

The head judge stood up from his seat. "Jessie, what have you done?"

"What was necessary! Your military is crippled, your people fooled, and your government overthrown. I guess all that's left to do is take care of the last vestige."

The head judge gasped. "The ships that were destroyed outside of Jerusalem . . ."

Jessie chortled. "Some of my best work. Your own media watched them explode without any weapons and bought our fantasy of some magical invisible weapon from Jerusalem."

The general bellowed, "You blew up our ships, OUR PEOPLE!"

The head judge was at a loss for words for a moment; finally, he looked at Elijah and said, "I cannot apologize enough for what we thought of you and your people."

"Would you stop prattling on?" Jessie walked to the middle of the room, her personal guards at her side all the way. Clicking on her communicator, Dr. Skye's face filled the screen. "Richard, have you been listening?"

"I've heard everything."

"Dr. Skye," the head judge pleaded, "please tell me you aren't a part of this."

Richard smiled with his billion-dollar grin, "I'm but a servant to the sciences. And science is all about bettering mankind. My forefathers created this plan, and I'm charged with seeing it through. Jessie, what do you need?"

"Just make sure there is a shuttle to fetch my soldiers and me at once. I'm not leaving them behind to be killed."

"All right. Three shuttles will be sent down once you give me your signal."

"Thank you." The monitor switched off again.

"JESSIE!" the head judge's voice boomed. "What is going on now?"

"Oh, I have to be going. But you are free to stay and enjoy the last few seconds of your lives. I do hope it is over with quickly."

Out of the blue, J'kla jumped across the room, and his claws were around her skinny neck, the nails piercing her flesh. Immediately, the guards around the room trained their guns right at his head.

"She die before you kill me," he threatened.

Jessie choked out, "Kill . . . him."

J'kla tightened his grip, and blood began to stream down from the pin-pricks of his claws into her skin. "I faster than you."

Elijah asked, "Tell us what you have done! Why are you running away? Is this building rigged to blow up?"

"Someone . . . kill this . . . cat." Jessie was struggling, but her men were too well programmed to obey her orders right now. She was too close to death, and her protection was one of the most paramount orders ingrained into them. If they tried to kill or even just stop J'kla, he could kill her, and they wouldn't allow that to happen. So, it was a standoff.

The general held his com device up to his ear as he quickly ran for the center of the room. "Understood." He lowered the device. "We have a problem. *Vatican 1* is not responsive. Right now, it is heading right for our position."

"Is it going to attack us?" the head judge asked.

"No, it can't be. My men on the ship are working to get it to turn away from this nose dive. They will not arm the weapons. Someone has sabotaged its engines, and it is locked."

"Oh, no." Elijah had goosebumps all over his skin. "They're going to destroy this city to take out the court."

Anna added, "We're the only ones who know the truth. If they kill us, then they'll have eliminated the opposition and the truth at the same time."

The representatives and other politicians hurried to flee for their lives. All headed for any exit they could find. Some were even giving the broken windows a long look, though it was fifty stories down from here. No one got further than an armed guard protecting the exit.

"JESSIE, TELL YOUR MEN TO STAND DOWN AND TELL THAT SHIP TO GET BACK INTO THE SKY, NOW!!" The head judge was yelling so hard, his voice broke.

Jessie's hands were trying to pry J'kla loose. "I would . . . *gasp* . . . rather die . . . than let you leave."

Elijah scoffed hard. "Jessie, I've always admired your tenacity and stubbornness when it comes to getting your way, but this is beyond foolish. Are you willing to sacrifice yourself for a lie? Can you not see what you have done here? You are forcing a lie to become a truth, even if it means killing anyone who discovers the lie. That is insane. Let it go."

She snarled at Elijah and suddenly stomped on J'kla's foot, which made him release her. She gasped a few times and then boldly stated, "The ends will justify the means."

Her guards lowered their guns from J'kla now that she was free. J'kla was about to regain his grip when one of her personal guards got him by the neck and another grabbed his arms.

"LET HIM GO!" Anna punched the shoulder of one of the men, but he simply kicked her and sent her tumbling down the few steps up to the speaker's platform.

Jessie felt her neck, looking at the blood on her hands. "I'm glad you brought all those stupid primitives here. They can die along with this worthless court." She cleared her throat a few times and then waved her hands. "Let him go. He can perish with his mate." The strong men put J'kla down and he joined her.

J'kla wanted to repay their brutality, but wisdom told him it was foolish to attack stronger men. He took Anna by the hand and confidently stated, "You not win. God save us."

Jessie gave J'kla a sideways glance. "You honestly believe in God? What? Some kind of earth spirit or some statue back on your moon?"

"I have faith in God of Bible. Jesus Christ save my soul. I bring Jesus to my kind. They know truth."

Jessie's left eye twitched again, and Elijah had a big smile on his face. She took a moment to answer, so as not to lash out and slap the fool. "I see. However did you come across the Bible?"

"I brought it to him," Anna boldly proclaimed.

Jessie now looked at Anna. "So, the Christians infiltrated the PSC. Congratulations, my dear. I worked so hard in finding and killing all of the pathetic followers of this idiotic religion. To have one get so far as to work in the very organization dedicated to wiping you out, that is amazing."

Anna was shocked. Her heart sank, and her blood turned cold. "You . . . you *killed* them all? I thought you were supposed to only imprison them until they renounced their faith."

"Oh, some survived. I need fresh bodies to stake outside my new palace once we destroy Jerusalem. But for the most part, they're all dead. Vaporized after sentencing. It was a painless death, I'm sorry to say."

"YOU WITCH!" Anna lurched forward to tear the hair off of Jessie's head. But J'kla stopped her, knowing those two bodyguards wouldn't allow this.

Jessie stepped up to within inches of Anna's face. "I'm going to take every professing Christian I have locked up, and I am going to nail them to crosses. Then I'm going to plant those crosses all over Jerusalem as a warning to any other fool who defies the PSC. All will worship pure science, or they will suffer the consequences. My only regret is you, that *cat*, and Elijah will be reduced to ashes. But perhaps I will take a few of your friends out there with me when I leave. So, they, too, can hang as a reminder of who holds the real power on the Earth. Now, if you will excuse me, I would like to get a very nice place to watch. I have never seen a ship crash before. It ought to be fun."

Anna actually wrestled loose one arm and slugged Jessie across the chin. The older woman hit the ground. One of her guards jumped to help her up, while the other went after Anna. He moved to hit her when J'kla thrust Anna behind him and then showed his fangs and growled loudly at the approaching servant. The sight stunned the man and stopped the attack.

"Let's go." Jessie was standing again, now blood was coming out of one side of her face as well as the scratches on her neck.

Abruptly, there was a roaring sound of engines, but not the engines of the incoming ship. These were far too close. The building partly shook as a ship lifted off the ground and passed the broken windows of the court. The *Terra 5* took to flight one more time, bits and pieces of it falling free from where it had collided with various parts of Rome and the Vatican.

"What is going on?" Jessie barked.

The holoimage activated again, and it was showing the *Terra 5* heading right at the incoming military vessel.

CHAPTER THIRTY-FOUR

Z HAD DRAGGED HIMSELF UP to the pilot's seat of the *Terra 5*. His legs were worthless now; he would need to have them replaced immediately. Looking out, he was pleasantly surprised. For some reason, the military surrounding the ship were helping the B'reann. Several other Z units were out there giving medical aid, while a few of the soldiers were bringing over water. What seemed odd was a few of the soldiers were still keeping a close eye on the B'reann with their weapons out.

Z looked down and saw the communication system was working. He was impressed. This old ship could take quite a beating and keep working. He could make contact with the court if he wanted.

"Oh, there's one more. Z unit, are you all right?" A Z-500 and one of the soldiers came into the cockpit.

Z turned in his seat and shook his head. "No. My legs are broken beyond use. I cannot walk."

"All right, we will need extra help to carry you," the Z unit answered. Then he asked the soldier, "Can you go and see if we can get help from the fire robots who are finished tending to the fires?"

"Yes."

"Wait." Z stopped them.

"What?"

"Don't worry about me. Get any of the injured B'reann off this ship. They need more help than me. I can wait."

"Brie ans?" The soldier did not know that word.

Z laughed. "They aren't cheese. That is their name. The cat people . . . the primitives."

"Oh, the people outside."

"Yes." Z resisted a zinger for how long that took for them to get. "Several were hurt in the crash and need some serious help."

The Z-500 answered, "Not to worry, we have searched the whole ship and removed all the living primitives."

"How many died?" Z quietly asked.

"Twenty-two were found dead. We have not removed their bodies yet, but we will soon."

Z felt horribly guilty. It was his idea to crash the ship. It was the only logical course; anything else would've meant their total destruction. But that didn't remove the guilt. "I'm so sorry."

"Sorry?" the robot asked.

"Just talking to myself."

Another younger soldier ran in and reported, "Sir, the order was given by Jessie. The court has been locked down. We were just told to evacuate the area, no reason given."

The commanding soldier gave this due consideration. "Tell the men to not leave yet. When a second order comes to evacuate, then we will head out."

"Understood." The younger man ran back to relay the orders.

Z asked, "What is going on? Why was the military sent in for this? We needed rescuing, not guns."

"We were told to secure this ship and not allow people to leave the area. We weren't told why."

"Then why are you helping?"

That made the young commander stop and think. "I was told these animals were dangerous and primitive. I was informed we had to treat them like a class five wild animal who would kill on sight if not contained. But . . . when I saw them treating one another like real people, asking for my help, looking at me with fear and sadness, I knew something wasn't right. I know it was against my orders; it just felt right. What could it hurt to heal a few wounds and give them a drink of water?"

"All right. Z unit, go and get another robot to help lift. Soldier, could you help me get my legs off so I'm lighter?"

"Sure. Z-500, do as he asked." The commander gave his orders, and the robot left. Then he looked down and asked, "How do I detach your legs?"

Z worked on the control bars on his waist, so that they could force the leg servos to disconnect. "It's really easy. I just can't reach, since my back is stuck in one position. All you have to . . . What is that?"

The commander was trying to get the second control bar to lift. "What is what?"

"That sound? It sounds like engines, and they're getting closer."

The young commander stopped and listened. It was then he heard people outside screaming. "What's going on?"

Z turned on the computer and checked the working cameras. The image focused on a warship bearing down on their position. "Oh, no. That ship is poised to crash right on top of us. That will set off the engine core. It could level half of Rome."

"Can you contact them?"

Z tried his controls. The signal was going out, but nothing was happening. "No. Look! Their escape pods are all being ejected. No one is on board to stop it."

"Does this old ship have any weapons?"

"No. This thing barely has enough power to run its engines. I can't even get the shields fully operational any longer. But . . . " Z checked the anti-grav system and the working thrusters. "I do have a plan."

"What?"

"I'm going to ram them before they ram us. Shoot, the nav controls are offline. It'll have to be worked manually."

"What does that mean?"

Z grabbed the boy by the shoulders. "Go, get the people away from this ship. I'm about to take off, and I don't want to hurt anyone."

"What are you planning?"

"Something I have to do." Z started programming the half-working controls station. "GO!" The commander stopped and quickly saluted the broken robot and then dashed out of the ship.

Getting outside, the commander burst into a mad dash away from the ship. "Go, get out of here! Get away from this ship!" He was bellowing at his soldiers and the robots.

The obedient soldiers and robots quickly helped the B'reann to move. Some of the soldiers helped by carrying the smallest of the B'reann. The robots performed their duties with great care and shielded the injured with their own bodies.

The docking bay door closed, and the thruster system came online. The ship lifted up, sending a great hot wind outward. It got up slightly and then dropped back to the ground when the engines failed. The deep thrumming sound of the anti-grav system could be heard outside as it was pushed way past its limits. Soon, the thrusters came back online, and the ship lifted up into the air, finally taking flight. It was a slow ascent, but this time much steadier. Pivoting on its axis, the ship turned directly for the larger incoming warship.

✶　✶　✶

"NO!" Jessie was furious. Her glorious plan was about to be thwarted, again. "SKYE!" Yelling this out, Jessie changed the holoimage back to the bridge of the *Sanger*. "Shoot that ship down. Do something!"

"I can't get a target lock from here with our minor weapons; and if we fire the main weapon, it will take out most of Rome in the first shot."

"Get the . . . Richard . . . Richard?" She could see his lips moving; but the sound was gone, and the image was going fuzzy.

Suddenly, Dr. Skye was replaced with the dilapidated and damaged bridge of the *Terra 5* with Z at the helm. "Oh, good. I got through. Man, they built good computers into this ship."

"What? A Z-unit! Robot, what are you doing? Abort mission. I repeat: abort mission." Jessie was confused.

"Oh, be quiet, you old crone!" Z remarked and then looked directly at Anna. "Hey, I, uh, just wanted to say goodbye."

"Z, what are you doing? Why are you still on that ship?" Anna asked.

"I have no choice. I cannot allow them to crash into the capital."

Anna was crying. "Z, please, don't do this. Get in the escape pod. Z . . . don't die."

"I have to stay at the helm, or this ship will veer off-course before it makes impact. I can't run away this time." He was quiet for a moment, while he considered his words. "Anna . . . it has been fun."

J'kla was a little lost. He really didn't fully understand what was going on. "Z, what you do?"

"Just being the hero. Hey, J'kla, Anna takes a lot of care and looking after. You're going to have your hands full keeping up with her. Promise me, you'll take good care of her."

"I promise."

Anna held tight to J'kla while she cried harder. "Z, I . . . you were the best friend I've ever had. I know you don't understand it, but I did love you in a funny sort of way."

Z fixed the controls again and made the ship stay on course. "Hey, uh, Anna? I don't know if I really understand all of what I'm feeling right now. But I think . . . I think I understand love. I'm not saving the world, or even the city; I am saving you." Just then, the screen was engulfed in the fiery explosion of the two ships making contact.

"Exterior monitor, now!" the head judge called out.

The computer changed the image to show a great ball of fire in the skies above Rome. Parts of both ships were raining down on the city, sure to cause fires and other small problems. Nothing compared to what would have happened if the military ship had actually crashed.

Anna buried her face in J'kla's chest and cried like she never had before. Z had been like her father or brother. He was her only family. For years, he had been her only friend who accepted her for who she was. She would miss his jokes and his constant remarks about everything. He was not just another Z-unit; he was a person.

"I don't believe it. How dare a robot interfere with my plans! That piece of junk has destroyed the plans of the PSC over and over. Dr. Skye should have melted him down." Jessie was fuming mad.

Anna suddenly let go of J'kla and grabbed Jessie by the back of her collar. She was going to take out her anger right there by tearing this woman apart. The two bodyguards were quick and removed Anna and held her at bay, while keeping an eye on the cat growling at them.

Jessie fixed her collar and cleared her throat. "I won't let this get out of control. This is far from over. GUARDS!"

The five young men standing at the doors came up to the main floor.

"You have new orders. I want you to seal this place and then execute everyone inside."

"Everyone?" one of the young men hesitantly asked.

"Did I not make that clear?"

"Perfectly clear, ma'am." He stood at attention, ready to fulfill his master's orders.

"I need to make certain everything is taken care of." She grabbed the communicator from the guard nearest her and activated it. "COMMANDER!"

The head of the team outside answered, "Yes?"

"I want you to execute all the primitives in the square and then clear a place for a shuttle lander. I am going to be leaving as soon as you are finished with your duty."

"Ma'am, you want me to . . . kill all these people?"

"THEY AREN'T PEOPLE! THEY ARE PRIMITIVES! AND IF YOU DON'T DO IT, I WILL HAVE YOU EXECUTED, AND SOMEONE ELSE WILL DO IT. IS. THAT. UNDERSTOOD?"

There was a brief pause on the other end, and then it came back. "I understand." This wasn't the normal response of a soldier; one word was the standard. Something about his tone was off.

Jessie let out a long sigh and then looked back at the terrified delegates and judge. "It has been interesting. I will say nice things at your funerals. Right now, I think I will be taking my leave. Please, don't scream too loudly. I would hate to bother the neighbors . . . ha!" Her dark sense of humor was out in full force.

All of a sudden, there came a loud ruckus at the doors, and the soldiers in the room turned to see their fellow officers from outside coming in with guns blazing. The commander took aim and shot right through the head of one of Jessie's personal escorts.

"WHAT IS GOING ON?"

"Just doing my duty." The commander waved his hand, and hundreds of B'reann warriors flooded in alongside the human soldiers. The B'reann were armed with sticks and poles, which suited their fighting styles.

"STOP THEM!" Jessie backed up in fear of the warriors coming after her.

The loyal soldiers on the inside took up arms against their fellow officers from the outside. A small war raged on the floor of the court, while Jessie's last remaining bodyguard was defending her.

J'kla saw an opportunity and grabbed the arm of the man beside Jessie. He yanked him over and then swiped his claws on his right hand across the man's chest, ripping his shirt and tearing right into the skin. The man lunged after J'kla but was met by the feline agility and skill.

Jessie watched in horror as her soldiers were being overwhelmed by men she had created to serve her and the PSC. She did not see the hand reaching out for her. Anna got her by the collar again and put her fist across the bitter woman's face.

"WHY, YOU WITCH!" Jessie grabbed Anna by the neck and was trying to strangle the life right out of her.

Anna fought the rather strong grip and kneed Jessie in the gut to loosen the grip. Then she took a similar grip around Jessie's neck. "You monster. You deserve to be fed to the dogs. I'm going to make you pay for Z and for all the B'reann you killed."

Jessie was fighting hard. "You . . . won't . . . stop me."

Jessie dug her fake nails into Anna's arm and pulled the strangling hands off of her throat. Then she sucker-punched Anna and followed that with a kick in the gut. Anna was thrown to the ground and watched the sharp stiletto go for her neck. Jessie was going to kill this annoying girl by any means.

A hammer hit Jessie in the side of the head, and she crumbled to the ground. It didn't kill her, but she was out. Behind her stood the head judge holding up his gavel, which he often used to silence Jessie. "I have wanted to do that for years." He held out a kind hand to Anna. "Are you all right?

"I will be fine. Thank you."

$$\ast \quad \ast \quad \ast$$

J'kla fought with his claws and got off some pretty good punches. But he truly was no match for the enhanced physique of this man and the experience in fighting. After one perfect kick to the side of the human, J'kla found his tail had been grabbed, and he was yanked hard across the area with a fist meeting him in the back of the head. His mane actually worked like a helmet and kept this from being a full concussion, but it certainly put him down.

"Stupid cat." The bodyguard was about to give J'kla a hard kick to the side when a woman got him by the arms and threw him down.

Elijah helped J'kla up, while his Mossad bodyguard got between the enemy and her charge. "That was a good fight, but my friend will take it from here."

Suddenly, a bullet ripped through her neck from one of the soldiers on the other side of the room. She was killed instantly and fell over in a pool of her own blood.

"Oh, no!" Elijah had not expected this.

The bodyguard sneered at J'kla and then saw his own master fall to the gavel of the head judge. In a rage, he went after Anna in spite and was almost on her from behind when a full body slam met him, and he was toppled across the ground and landed near where Jessie was resting.

Kneeling on the guard's chest, J'kla pounded him with blow after blow. "LEAVE! ANNA! ALONE!"

The bodyguard tried to fight back, but it took only a few hits for him to be knocked out of his senses. He collapsed and was still being beaten by the angry lion.

"My friend, my friend . . . you got him." Elijah ran over and took one of J'kla's fists to stop him. He calmly said, "There is enough killing today. Please stop."

J'kla's snarl slowly faded, and he relaxed from his fury. He stood up and gave one last growl at the man on the ground.

Anna met J'kla with a hug and then looked around; the fight was over. The soldiers and B'reann had taken down Jessie's forces. More than one of their own had died, including several B'reann, but the victory was theirs.

✶   ✶   ✶

"Sir, I'm reading several massive explosions all over Earth. My sensors are showing that all the military craft around the Earth just exploded," the man at the sensor station called out to Dr. Skye.

Richard was fully aware of Jessie's backup plan and knew this was part of it. "Get me a sensor lock on the capital. I want to know everything that is going on down there."

"Sir! A ship is about to crash into the capital. It looks like it is a military cruiser!"

Dr. Skye frowned at the screen. "Why aren't you calling me? The shuttle is ready." His voice was low, but the bridge was too quiet for his words not to be heard.

"Sir, should we do something? It is going to crash into the capital."

"No. Open a channel with Jessie or the court."

Everyone was confused about what was happening, but they didn't question him. The woman at communications tried several different signals. "Sir, we can't get through. There is a jamming signal."

"A jamming signal? From where?"

She checked her monitors and tried everything. "The old ship has emitted a low-grade radiation cloud, which is disrupting communications. We can break through, but it will take some work."

"Then do it!"

"Okay, setting up a rotating calculation system. Got it . . . Wait, not yet . . . Okay. I have something." She switched on the communication channel with the court, and they were watching the conversation with Z that Anna was having.

Dr. Skye's fist clenched at the sight of this infuriating robot. "What am I looking at?!" he bellowed and scared every junior scientist working for him.

"Sorry. I can't get sound. But it seems . . . "

"I DON'T CARE ABOUT SOUND! GET ME JESSIE! I WANT TO TALK WITH JESSIE!"

"Sir!"

"WHAT?!" He barked so hard, the man who interrupted his ranting just about fell from his seat.

"Uh, that old ship, it's on a collision course."

"With us?" Dr. Skye quickly looked at the screen. The com officer changed it back to the view over Rome. The military cruiser was falling out of the sky, and the old Terraformer was lifting up to meet it.

"No, sir. It is about to make contact with the military ship."

Just then, the cruiser and the terraformer hit one another, and the resulting explosion created a massive fireball over the ancient city. To the ire of Dr. Skye, his own crew was applauding this as though it were a good thing.

"Get me the court! NOW!"

"I'm trying. The radiation cloud is dissipating quickly. We will be able to get through in a few minutes."

Richard thought about what he would do next. If things went south, he could be facing a lot of trouble. He must see it to its fulfillment. The world would be subject to him somehow. His predecessors understood the importance of guiding the people through pure science, and he wouldn't let the dream fade just because some stupid robot got in the way.

"Weapons station. Get a target lock on the capital building."

"Sir, did you say the capital building? Do you mean the one in Jerusalem?"

"No," Richard answered. "The court in Rome. Charge the main gun as well."

"You want me to prepare to fire on . . . the High Court?"

"Do you have a problem with following orders?" Richard was prepared for this. He knew these men and women weren't as programmed as Jessie's army.

The older man responded, "Sorry, sir. I cannot. That would be treason."

"I see." Dr. Skye slowly turned in his seat. "Any volunteers willing to obey your commander?" He waited and watched as the different looks went through the room. Some didn't believe this. Others considered it some kind of test. Dr. Skye went to his first plan. "The person willing to follow my orders will be promoted and see a great deal of windfall from this in the very near future." Again, some thought it was a test; others simply didn't believe it. "No one? Sad." He punched a button on the arm of his chair. "Z units, enter."

A dozen Z units marched into the room. Dr. Skye had purposefully reprogrammed these robots to respond to his commands. They were incapable of betraying him or his orders.

"Please input orders," the lead Z unit requested.

Dr. Skye coolly answered, "Units one through five, escort the men and women on this bridge to the docking bay two. Execute order omega when you are finished. All the other units, take your stations."

The first five units pulled out their weapons, which were stronger than the normal stun gun. They gathered the crew and forcibly removed them from the bridge and relocated them to the docking bay. Once they locked the door of the smaller secondary docking bay, they performed the omega command: they decompressed the bay and killed all of the scientists. Dr. Skye would not allow disloyalty in his new world order. Anyone who would question him now would not be trusted in the future.

Dr. Skye felt the ship shake when the bay decompressed, which was not a normal procedure for the *Sanger*. For a moment, he considered how comfortable he had become with killing. He never really felt guilt over it. As a scientist of the PSC, he knew human life was not much more valuable than livestock. Mammals were mammals. Removing the undeserving from the population only helped evolution work better. They could always breed more people, and the next generation would be that much better than the last.

"Okay. I want a target lock with the main guns on the High Court. Charge the main weapon, and be ready to fire on my command."

"Understood," the robot at the weapons station answered.

"Dr. Skye, there is an incoming transmission from the court."

"Good, put it on the screen." He was confident Jessie would be on the other side of this image with a good explanation of why her plans had failed.

The image flickered on, and there stood Jessie, bloody and bruised, her clothing torn and her hair a mess. Two of her own soldiers held her by the arms. Behind her was one of her bodyguards, also being detained. A rather angry-looking B'reann held that man by the arm, just about twisting the shoulder right out of joint. Standing beside her, unrestrained, were the head judge, Elijah, and the general of the military.

"What is this?" Dr. Skye demanded.

The head judge answered, "You failed. Your lies are revealed, and your plans thwarted. You're under arrest for treason, murder, and a long list of other violations. I'm ordering you to turn yourself in."

"Jessie! What's going on?"

"Don't talk to her. She is in just as much trouble as you," the head judge declared. "Dock your ship at the Darwin Station, and a military escort will be sent to escort you to face judgment."

"Ha! What military? I have the only guns left."

The general glared at Dr. Skye. "You failed to destroy all of my ships. Five were landed in the construction yards in Shanghai. They've been manned and are on their way to intercept you. If you do not turn yourself over, I have ordered them to open fire."

"You would open fire on the *Sanger*? How dare you! This is a holy site, a shrine to the efforts of generations of men smarter than you." Dr. Skye was breaking, the insanity let loose at the thought of resistance.

Elijah answered, "You have a powerful arsenal at your command right now. It is far too dangerous to allow in the hands of someone who has proven they're dangerous. The World Corps and Jerusalem agree on this. We will both fight you, if you don't stand down and turn yourself in. Trust me, Dr. Skye, that is a fight you will lose."

Dr. Skye's fingers were digging into the arm of his chair. He had spent years basking in the glory of being Dr. Richard Skye, the man with all the answers. He controlled the media. He controlled the thinking of the human race. Everyone looked to him for their faith, for their loyalty. He was the god of the human race, save a few insignificant people. Now these idiots had the audacity to turn on him and ask him to lower himself to their level!

"I will not lose! You will watch as your pathetic city is turned to ASH! I have already decimated a whole moon. I WILL DECIMATE YOUR EMPIRE AS WELL!! NO ONE WILL STOP ME! DO YOU HEAR ME? NO ONE!!"

Jessie suddenly called out, "RICHARD! Save me!"

One soldier jerked on her arm to pull her back.

"Sorry, Jessie. You failed me. You will die alongside the others."

"What?" Jessie's mouth hung open with disbelief. She had always believed that she held the leash on Dr. Skye; he would never turn on her. She was wrong.

Dr. Skye waved his hand, and the communication line was broken. "Z unit, is the main weapon charged?"

"No, sir. The former operator deactivated the charging sequence before he left. I have reinitiated it, but it will take time to fully charge."

Richard was glad he had those disloyal people executed, now more than ever. "Tell me when—" Suddenly, the ship was rocked as weapon fire tore across its upper hull.

"Main shields are hit. We have five large weapon cruisers converging on our location," a Z-unit calmly answered.

Again and again, the ship was hit. Its main energy shields took the brunt of the attack, but they wouldn't last forever.

"Return fire! Use secondary weapon systems." Dr. Skye held onto his seat to keep from being thrown to the ground.

Outside, five large warships of the World Corps swarmed around the massive *Sanger* as it sat in the highest layer of Earth's atmosphere. Small turrets rotated around on the hull of the ship and shot at the attackers. These smaller weapons were designed to destroy asteroids in space to protect the ship during survey missions. They weren't really much of a match for the shields and maneuverability of the warships.

The warships flew all around the *Sanger*, launching volley after volley of lasers and small plasma torpedoes. They had a much greater firepower than the *Sanger*'s defensive weapons; the shields were already showing weakness.

*　*　*

"Is it going to work? Are they going to stop them?" Anna asked the general as they watched the battle's progression on the monitors.

The general kept a close eye on the tactics of his men. "They're good. They're focusing all of their weapons on the upper shields. If they can bring the shields down, they can blast a hole right through the *Sanger's* core, which should take care of them. But that will probably take thirty minutes of firing, and that also doesn't calculate any losses on our part."

Elijah got in Jessie's face. "How long does it take to charge their weapon?" She remained stubbornly silent. He grabbed her by the shoulders. "Your life is at stake, too! How long?"

With immeasurable reluctance, she answered her adversary. "Ten minutes, sometimes less."

The judge pointed toward a door. "Okay, we are the only people left in the court. We can get away from here. There is an emergency bomb shelter near the holding facility."

"It won't matter. We're all going to die," Anna whispered.

J'kla asked, "What?"

"We can't run fast enough. We watched how much damage that weapon can do back on your moon. If they hit this place, we can't possibly get away fast enough. Millions are going to die in this city. No bomb shelter is strong enough."

The head judge argued, "The shelter is . . ."

"Not enough," Jessie answered. "That weapon was designed with the best laser technology ever conceived. It could easily crack the Iron Dome. This city—well, this entire country—could be wiped off the map by one clean shot. You're dead; we're all dead."

The head judge closed his eyes in extreme sorrow. "How has it come to this? Where did it go wrong? We trusted him. Of anyone on this planet, I would never have guessed Dr. Skye would be fighting a war against this government. Good grief, the PSC helped establish this government over two hundred years ago."

Elijah answered, "They wanted power without God's guidance. Their desire corrupted them, and they became addicted. The more power they got, the more they wanted."

"God." Jessie nearly spat out the word. "I can't believe you would bring that up right now. Let's see your God save us. I doubt even He could stop the superweapon of the *Sanger*. Nothing can."

Elijah slowly smiled at her, and then asked the general, "Can your warships get the *Sanger* to move nearer to Jerusalem's airspace?"

"Possibly. Why?"

"No time to explain. Just do what you can. I have a call to make."

Richard hit the ground and rolled up against a wall with the impact of five torpedoes. A Z-bot helped him up and then returned to its duty at the engineering station.

"Are the shields holding?"

"Yes. Shields are holding at fifty-four percent. But they are falling. We can absorb only so much weapon fire."

"It's enough. Weapons, how goes the charging?" Dr. Skye asked.

"We will be at full charge in less than thirty seconds."

"Good. Now get me a full view of the capital. I want to watch this." Dr. Skye took his seat again and then held on tightly. He did not want to go flying again.

"Sir, we have a problem. The pattern of flight of the warships has altered from my original calculations. We will have to move to get a clear shot. If we do not and we hit one of their ships, it might rebound and—"

"I am aware of the problems; I designed this weapon. Helm, move accordingly."

"Understood."

"Sir, we are at full charge. Target lock is set," the Z unit announced.

Dr. Skye stood up and happily ordered, "Fire."

"Incoming fire!" the Z unit at Sensors called out just as one beam from Jerusalem hit the ship.

Dr. Skye and all of the robots were thrown across the bridge and slammed against the forward wall. The moment Dr. Skye looked up to see what had just happened, he watched his precious bridge bisected by a huge energy beam. He was still swearing at God when a searing hot, white fire engulfed him, and he was vaporized, along with everything else on the bridge.

The *Sanger* was hit twice by the energy weapons that defended Israel. The ship broke into three sections and shattered into millions of pieces for a moment. Then the core erupted. The most powerful energy core ever constructed bathed the sky in a green fireball. The massive shockwave which followed was so strong, it caught two of the fleeing military ships and destroyed them. Across over half the planet, a blinding flash and rumbling boom stopped people in the middle of their lives. From that day on, an entire generation told the story of the moment they heard—and some even saw—the destruction of the *PSC Sanger*.

The pride and joy of the Planetary Science Commission was no more. Dr. Skye was finally handed into judgment.

The group gathered in the courtroom cheered loudly and clapped their hands, all except Jessie. She was pleased to be alive but knew her punishment would now begin.

J'kla was happy but still a little confused. "It over?"

Anna laughed and nodded. "It's over."

CHAPTER THIRTY-FIVE

TWO WEEKS PASSED, AND THE cleanup process began for what would take years to fix. The ancient city would never be the same; then again, nothing would. The High Court called an emergency session the day after the incident and put out a junction against the PSC. The Planetary Science Commission was ordered to surrender all of its documents, and the heads of their departments were all to be investigated. The finances were frozen and their exploration program canceled until further notice.

Jessie was put into a holding cell near the world court, where she would await trial for her actions. She had a lot to answer for, and many of the representatives had questions for her. She considered suicide on more than one occasion but was far too proud.

Right now, she rested in this awful dungeon in an unbecoming yellow jumpsuit. She dreamed about her life before and the power she would have had if her plan had succeeded.

"Oh, how the mighty have fallen." Elijah's calm voice woke her from her daydreaming.

She did not lift her head to look at her old adversary. "So, you've come to gloat over your victory. I thought you were better than that."

"I've not come to gloat. I've come to ask a question."

"I've answered questions for days. Every stupid delegate at the court, the head of security, the general, and I think the manager of the coffee shop in the hotel across the street have all interrogated me. I'm tired of the questions."

Elijah looked over at the guard near this private cell. "Would you excuse us please?"

The guard nodded once and then walked away. It was unlikely Elijah would create a problem if left alone.

Once the guard was gone, Elijah asked, "How could you do it?"

"Oh, here they come. How did I do it? Well, it started with a carefully laid out plan by the scientists of—"

"No, I don't want to know how you did it. I want to know why you chose to do it. How could you justify murder and subterfuge in yourself to do all of this?"

"For the good of mankind." Her response was sarcastic and purposefully cruel.

"How is killing men good for them?"

"It isn't. But sometimes, you need to weed the garden to make the good plants grow up better and stronger."

"What gives you the right to kill one person? What gives you the right to make the judgment about who is fit to live and who is fit to die? Only God has that authority."

"God." She nearly gagged on the word. "This is why I worked so hard for a better future. I was trying to rid this world of stupid notions of imaginary deities. The people need to trust in the truth of science and reason, not blind faith. I'll gladly sacrifice a few idiots like you to make way for free thinking, logical humans who know science has all the answers."

Elijah let out a soft sigh and shook his head. "You still believe in that, don't you?"

"Of course. I may have lost the fight, but I haven't given up on what is the incontrovertible truth."

"Incontrovertible. Really? You fabricated a race of people because you could not locate any real specimens. You knowingly lied and omitted facts to create this so-called "incontrovertible evidence." Don't you see? What you believe in has no basis in reality; so, you faked that reality to make it true. It was a lie from the start." He watched her rolling her eyes at his logical assessment. "Yet here you sit, awaiting the judgment and punishment that will be handed to you for the lies you created to force an artificial truth upon mankind. Science failed right in front of your eyes, and yet you will hold dearly to it until the end of your days. That is blind faith."

Jessie sat up with a shot and screamed at him, "I HAVE NO FAITH! I WILL NEVER HAVE ANY FAITH! I AM A LOGICAL, INTELLIGENT, GODLESS WOMAN OF REASON!! YOU CAN TAKE YOUR FAITH AND GET OUT!!"

Elijah turned to walk away. Just before he left her, he said, "Dress in your finest logic; sit in your tower of reason; and call down to the rest of us with your words so full of pride. No one is listening to you any longer. As for me, I shake the dust from my feet concerning you, Jessie. Now your fate is truly in God's hands. May He show you more mercy than you deserve." With that, he left her.

EPILOGUE

"THIS IS TOM OF INTERNATIONAL News Network. We are looking at Rome from our drone in the skies. As you can see, the damage done by the incident which took place here six months ago is all cleaned up, and repairs are under-way. Today, the artist commissioned to replace the obelisk in the square will unveil his creation. Soon, we will look into the special announcement in the world court. They are about to announce the outcome of the recent vote on the Religious Disbandment Act repeal or amendment.

"In other news, former administrator of the education system Jessie has been found dead. She was sentenced to life without the possibility of pa-role for her part in the PSC conspiracy. The vehicle moving her to the maxi-mum security prison in Egypt turned over and rolled down a large hill. The driver was able to get to safety, but a band of feral dogs attacked Former Administrator Jessie before she could be rescued."

Another newscaster added her own comment. "Locals have had trouble with the feral dog population with the enormous dog fighting arenas in the area. This latest victim has only fueled the outcry for re-establishing the anti-dog fighting laws, which were removed fifty years ago by the Open Gambling Act. Now, we turn to weather . . . "

J'kla touched the screen of the monitor in the hallway and muted it. "What dog fighting?" he asked as he turned, but he found his wife had left his side. "Anna?"

Anna stood in front of a statue she had often looked at, since it was in-stalled a month ago. She was very pregnant, which did not help her emotional state as she looked at the bronze recreation of her dear friend. A memorial statue had been placed in honor of Z with a plaque to explain what he did for the world and for this court. She had asked they also put how he saved the B'reann, but they didn't have room and felt his work to save the court was more important.

J'kla came over to her and took her by the shoulders. "You need stop looking at statue of Z. You cry every time."

She softly wiped a tear off of her cheek. "I just miss him. He was part of my life for so long. I never understood how much I would miss his presence."

J'kla hugged her closer to him. "He will tell us jokes when we see him in Heaven."

"He was a robot. He won't be there." This choked her up to say.

"I know he be there." J'kla looked at the face of his friend Z. "He know of God from Anna, and he know of love. He no made like Anna or J'kla but have soul . . . I know it."

She was beginning to really cry. "I hope you're right."

J'kla realized what he had just done. She was so emotional now, anyway, and here they were about to go into the world court to stand with their new friend Elijah to hear the outcome of this bill. They were invited as special guests, and the news would be watching closely; and she would have watery eyes and a red face.

"Children, come on, we don't want to be late." Elijah found them and was hurrying them along. He noticed Anna's face. "Oh my, she's crying again."

"Sorry, my fault," J'kla sheepishly answered.

Elijah pulled out a nice handkerchief and handed it to her. "Wipe your eyes and come."

They entered the courtroom and sat down in the guest seats until the judge called them up. After a few other items were addressed, the media arrived, and the judge motioned for the announcement.

"Representative Elijah, Anna, and J'kla, please step up to the front of this court."

All three stood there before all the representatives, the cameras, and the judge. Only Elijah remained cool and collected; both Anna and J'kla were nervous.

"All rise." The judge stood up and then held up a large piece of nice parchment he had prepared for this day. "By the vote of this court who represents the interests of the various peoples of the World Corps, the Religious Disbandment Act will remain in effect . . ." He paused, knowing the media and the people in the middle of the room weren't expecting this. He built up enough tension and then continued, "However, an amendment was passed, which will be added to the bill. From this day forward, any state that wishes to allow religion within their borders may do so. Other states are not forced to recognize the religions if they do not allow them, and proselytizing inside the borders of a state that does not allow it is not permitted. Also, Amendment B passed as well. The part of the original RDA that criminalized religion has been abolished. It is no longer a high crime to be connected to a faith."

A gentle clapping came from the standing representatives. Anna and J'kla were a little shocked by this, perhaps even dismayed. Elijah still held a smile. He whispered, "Wait, I think you are going to be surprised."

Once the room quieted down and the delegates took their seats, a bell could be heard, and a large flag of Australia lit up on the monitor over the court. The judge banged his gavel once. "Australia has the floor."

Representative Ken stood up. "The people of Australia have authorized me to announce that in light of this outcome, the State of Australia will allow religion within our borders."

The bell rang again, and the flag of Iceland showed up. A younger, red-headed woman from Iceland stood up. "The people of Iceland have authorized me to announce that since this amendment was passed, we will accept religion within our borders."

The bell rang, and the flag of Canada flashed on the monitor. This time, Elijah smiled very big. He had already had a conversation with this man.

The representative from Canada stood up. "The people of Canada have authorized me to announce that with the decision that was passed, the State of Canada will allow religion within our borders." There was a small applause. "Also, the state of Canada would like to extend an offer to the new people group who have come to live on Earth, the B'reann. If you need a home, we will supply you the land and the help you will need."

J'kla's eyes bugged as the cameras all turned on him. He smiled and nodded to the representative. "I ask my people what they want to do. Thank you for offer." He tried to sound very professional right now, but his broken English was still broken.

The judge banged his gavel and waited a second in case another bell rang. None came, and so he continued. "I am sure that in light of this outcome, many of you will want to go back to your nation states and discuss your options. There is one last important announcement from this body." He looked over to the administrator of the judiciary committee. "Administrator Haun has the floor."

A kind-faced, older man stood up and held out a tablet. "By order of the World Corps government, the property of the late Dr. Richard Skye and former Administrator Jessie has been seized. Liquidated assets belonging to said persons amounted to five trillion credits. As of July twenty-second, a lawsuit was placed and decided under the nine justices of the world government in the case of the B'reann vs. Planetary Science Commission. Due to the destruction of property, in the case of their collective homes and injuries sustained, as well as lives lost, it is the decision of the court that damages be repaid through the seized liquidated property. This court now awards Representative J'kla of the B'reann people all said funds to establish new homes and pay for injuries sustained."

More than one gasp could be heard during that speech; no one had known the total value of Skye's and Jessie's wealth. After a moment of shock, the applause became much louder than the standard fair.

J'kla was confused, but Anna was in total shock. She had not heard anything about this. She looked at the smiling man next to her. "Ambassador, did you have anything to do with this?"

"A little. The representative from Australia was the first to suggest this course of action. I merely encouraged it." The sneaky, old man didn't tell her the court wanted to divide the funds between the B'reann and the nation of Jerusalem. But Jerusalem felt they had not suffered enough to warrant taking the money, and the B'reann deserved it more.

The judge banged his gavel once. "This session is now dismissed." With two more bangs, court officially had ended.

About a hundred reporters rushed the center of the room and asked questions of anyone they could get in front of their camera. Many of them wanted to talk to J'kla, as the B'reann had been off-limits to the news people until after the vote. J'kla tried to answer their questions but was a little overwhelmed. Fortunately, Elijah stood with him and helped. Anna held his hand, but the experienced politician guided him through the energetic interviews.

* * *

J'kla sat on the floor with his son and looked at some of the stuff Anna had brought in from her old place. She had a small apartment in the PSC housing district of Pretoria. It was where she had lived while she wasn't flying all over the galaxy as a geologist.

Their little boy, Samuel, was only a month old now and just as curious as his father. Being the first product of a B'reann and a human, he was a little odd-looking. He had the same fur as his father and a tail. But his other features were all human. No claws, no muzzle, no tall ears. Time would tell how other features matured on him. Regardless, his parents loved him and thought he was the cutest baby ever born. The media came to see the birth as her pregnancy had become something of a legend after the whole incident with the PSC conspiracy.

The family was currently living in a temporary house put on the land the Canadians gave to the B'reann. They were given a large section of forest in the far west side of the country in the Rocky Mountains. It worked out pretty well, as it was not too different from the forest they lived in back on New Eden. The days were longer; the animals and vegetation were different; but it felt like home in a lot of good ways.

In the forest, a new tree city was being built. Its construction was guided by some of the best woodworkers of the B'reann. They wanted a home that felt right, and living on the ground was not right. Soon, they would have their web of walkways connecting all the houses and platforms to make up their new city.

Right now, the wise and venerable ruler of the B'reann was taking a long, curious look at a strange device. He held up an eye covering designed to fit around the head. J'kla had never seen anything like this before. "ANNA! What this?"

She came in and smiled at the way he was sniffing her simulator. "That is a virtual reality holosimulator. I use it when I jog on a treadmill."

"Oh . . . what treadmill?"

"It's a thing you use to run in one place."

"Why run in one place? Go nowhere?"

His insatiable curiosity was always charming, though it would get him into awkward situations. "Well, I don't get far, but the simulator helps make it feel like I'm going somewhere. It was a great tool to use when I was in space. I had one on my ship I used to jog with. Go ahead; put it on. See for yourself."

J'kla carefully put the simulator on his head, and she helped him situate it into place over his eyes. Then she flicked it on and watched in humor.

J'kla was now looking at a beach with beautiful blue water, a glowing sun overhead, and a clean path of sand to run on. He threw his arms out and looked around in a panic. "ANNA! ANNA! WHERE YOU GO!"

Anna couldn't stop laughing. Their little boy was staring intently at his father, who flailed around in a dire panic, looking for his wife in the simulated world he was lost in.

"Honey, honey, it's okay." She turned it off and removed it from him. "There, see, it wasn't real."

"That thing strange. I no like it."

"Don't worry, you don't have to." Just then, the computer beeped. "Oh, he's going to be here any time now. I'm going to check Samuel and see if he needs to be changed. You wait here for Elijah."

She took up their baby and went to change his diaper. Fortunately for her, she had J'kla's mother around to help teach her how to be a mother. The basic skills, like changing a diaper, were not taught to people who didn't work in the breeding programs.

Elijah arrived on time with a small group of long-bearded men from Jerusalem. "Shalom, J'kla. You look well."

J'kla smiled and answered back, "Shalom, Elijah."

"You said that very nicely. Are you ready for the event today?"

"No, I nervous. But I always nervous when talking to group. Thankful you there to help."

Elijah snickered. "Oh, I don't know how much help I can be. You talk to your people in your own language. I have no idea what you're saying. Is the church ready yet?"

"Yes. First building of new village done. Everyone happy to have it."

Just then, Anna came back in with the freshly changed baby carried in her arms. Over one shoulder, she had slung a bag filled with all the items necessary for transporting a baby anywhere. "Okay, we are ready to go."

The older Jewish men all turned into a group of grandpas at the sight of the little baby. Each came over to see him; they cooed and patted his furry, little head.

"We'll have time for this at the celebration. Come on." Elijah was hurrying everyone along.

"What about this?" One of the men held out a neatly wrapped package.

"Oh, right. Thank you, Jacob." Elijah took the package and held it up to J'kla. "I brought you back a gift. I thought you might like to wear it, since you are the preacher."

J'kla opened it and pulled out a long scarf with tassels at either end. The cloth was a finely woven wool dyed in purple with a blue lining. On both ends of it were symbols stitched in golden thread. Elijah took it from J'kla and draped it around his neck so it hung on him with both ends resting down the front on top of his vest. The symbols were easier to see now. They were the same messianic symbols Elijah bore on his own uniform he dressed in for court sessions.

J'kla looked at the symbol and asked, "What this?"

"That is an ancient symbol, which signifies the unity between the Hebrew and Gentile people. The fish on the bottom represents the followers of Christ and the Gentiles. The menorah on the top represents the Hebrews. The star that forms from where they connect is the star of David, which represents the heir of David's dynasty, the Messiah Yeshua."

"Yeshua?"

"Oh, sorry. Your Bible calls him Jesus." Elijah felt the cloth. "This was handmade by a group of craftsmen in Jerusalem. You do not have to wear it when you speak, but I thought you would like it."

"I wear it proudly. It remind people I only speak for real King."

"Elijah, the schedule." One of his companions pointed to the clock on the wall.

"Oh, it's time." He led the way out as they headed for the big event today.

The village was still hardly constructed, and everyone was living in these temporary homes until it was. But the church was finished. The people wanted that done, so they could gather to worship inside their very own church. To dedicate it, there was going to be a large baptism event today, which would include everyone, even J'kla. The lake near the village was the site chosen, and the men from Jerusalem came in to help. Elijah would begin by baptizing J'kla, and then the rest of the village would follow. Not everyone was baptized—only those ready in their hearts.

Elijah suggested they should conduct their very first communion in honor of the event and then hold a feast. Truly, it was the beginning of a new era for Christianity, a return which would reignite the Remnant that dwindled, but was never lost.

✶   ✶   ✶

Two men worked at a station in the engineering lab at the university. They had been assigned to decrypt the old recorder box from the destroyed *Terra 5*.

"Look, Dean, this is a hopeless cause. That ship was two hundred years old, and so this box is also two hundred years old. And let's not forget, it went through a huge explosion."

The younger engineer turned the large black box over and pried off a panel to reveal several input slots. "Plug her in any way. If we get even a small iota of data out of this thing, we will make the news." He attached a cable into one of the primary slots.

"Sure, that's why I'm going to school for engineering . . . to get on the news."

"Oh, shut up and find me an old USB255 cable. I think that might help."

The disillusioned engineer leaned back and plopped his feet up on the desk. "A USB255, really. Why don't you ask for a compact disc while you're at it, and let's not forget some punch cards?"

"Fine, I'll find one myself." He got up and rifled through the boxes of various old cables used for this kind of work. He found the archaic cable and connected it to both the box and computer station. "All right, let's see what we find."

"You aren't going to find . . . hey, something's happening." The bored man finally sat up and looked at the screen. On it was a single line of data running across.

"Wait, look at this. It is an old access code request function. Let's see if the decrypter can bypass . . . Yup, I got it." The computer forced the old security clearance request to clear out and allow them to look inside.

The snarky engineer was now glued to the monitor. "Look at all this data usage. Every spare ounce of space in this thing's memory is being used."

"But this doesn't make any sense. All of the recorder data is gone. It has no memory or files from the ship, only this one giant file. This is an extremely complex data stream inside this box. What could it be?"

All of a sudden, the speakers on the console called out in a Z-unit's voice, "Anna, is that you?"

For more information about
Daniel Peyton
and
Remnant
please visit:

www.facebook.com/DanielPeytonAuthor
@DanPeytonAuthor
www.instagram.com/danpeyton_author

For more information about
AMBASSADOR INTERNATIONAL
please visit:

www.ambassador-international.com
@AmbassadorIntl
www.facebook.com/AmbassadorIntl

*If you enjoyed this book, please consider leaving us a review on
Amazon, Goodreads, or our website.*

www.ingramcontent.com/pod-product-compliance
Lightning Source LLC
Chambersburg PA
CBHW061038030726
47504CB00002B/425